Blood Honey

A NOVEL

Poppy Koval

ISBN 978-1-66784-552-4

eBook ISBN 978-1-66784-553-1

June 14

CHAPTER 1:
MIMS

I t was dark inside the car's trunk. The car had been parked for a long time, more than ten minutes, and Mims still couldn't remember the trick for opening a trunk from the inside. She kicked hard every twenty seconds or so, her feet tied together like a mermaid tail.

She was sure there was a trick.

A text message alert went off in her back pocket and then another and then nothing.

Eventually the trunk opened. She tried to kick the man who opened it, but once he threw the thick blanket over her head it was hard to know where he was. She was dragged up and out of the trunk and dropped into a tight, deep space. A lid closed. She was inside some kind of plastic box. Mims's heart beat as fast as the fluttering pages of a flipbook. She found herself wishing for her mother, a thought so odd it snapped her out of panic. This must be someone Teddy hired; he wouldn't kill her. He was a kind person and had a sweet tooth like a child.

The box dragged and then bumped. There was a ramp of some sort and then three steep steps. With each thwack one of her elbows or a vertebra was scraped raw. The bee stings on her shoulder blade and wrist were swollen so tight they felt like they would split open. Then there was stillness. She could tell the man hadn't left wherever the box was because she could hear muffled sounds. She felt woozy, and it wasn't until a few minutes had passed that she realized it was because the floor was rocking. She must be on a boat. Time passed, maybe two minutes or maybe fifteen, and she couldn't focus on anything useful, just that they might be able to identify her body based on her tattoos.

CHAPTER 2:

TEDDY

Teddy Beasley awoke to an email alert buzzing softly against his chest, more like a little electric massager than a cellphone. He sunk deeper into the sofa cushions for a second and then slowly opened his eyes, the neat row of photos on his desk coming into focus first, then the red Frisbee leaning against the back of the bookshelf. He came to realize, gently, that he was in his office at work. The familiar room anticipated his every need, down to the glass of yesterday's water over on his desk and the ultra-soft angora throw draped over his body. He picked up the phone: "Shipment received. The money is in your account." Teddy felt a thunk like a brick between his lungs, stifling his ability to breathe.

He flung both the blanket and the brick aside, wide awake now. It was time to get back to work.

Teddy marched into the hallway, saw the bright tumble of Brittany-Lynne's orange hair rounding the corner, and stepped back into his office before she could see him. After she'd passed, he stepped over the threshold again and down the hall, feeling sticky with dried sweat from the night before. No one could fault him for not wanting to deal with a relationship postmortem conversation right now. He wanted to get through this one day drama-free, move through the choreography of the factory like normal, reset his nerves. Fresh air would help.

The rhythmic clacking of the cherry-pitting machines got louder as he descended the spiral staircase to the factory floor and then quieted again as he exited the building. He took a deep breath and hopped from foot to foot, arms wiggling at his sides. As the tension released from his body he felt ready to start the day as his old happy self. "Let's sell some cherries!" He sounded to himself like a little league coach encouraging uncoordinated children. He followed up with, "You got this!"

A honeybee zipped by and Teddy clenched his teeth. He'd been trying to pretend that there weren't more and more of them flitting about the yard each day, but he could see them congregating over by the wall. "You got this," he said again, more quietly.

New York City had all kinds of wildlife you wouldn't expect: bats, leeches, coyotes once in Central Park. It was certainly possible honeybees had *happened* to start visiting the Brooklyn maraschino cherry factory this spring, when they had never come by before. They kept getting into the spent cherry brine as it was dollied between buildings. Because of the increased production post-renovation, and the hold on completing the new waste filtration system, more and more brine needed wheeling to the disposal drains, so that might explain it.

But what it felt like was that the bees had shown up to needle him, *intentionally*, for all the bad life choices he was making.

He turned back into the building at a different entrance and peeked inside the factory floor for a second time. Even after the renovations the beautiful interior recalled bygone times; the walls were still brick and the floors still smooth concrete. Only the vats and tubs, and the HVAC system above, had the modern look of steel and chrome. He smiled to see people with white coverings on their shoes walking with purpose from place to place—at ease and in control of the machines and the maraschinos.

He took a fortifying, cherry-scented breath, let the door swing closed, and headed off to the weekly management meeting.

Someone had brought chocolate chip cookies. "Wait, are these warm?" he asked.

Teddy had always conflated treats with love, so the brown sugar was a welcome distraction. The operations manager and the CFO stared back at him. Beasley Cherries was a small company, and these three men composed the entire management team. Teddy was the sole owner. "Your loss, I'm eating ten," Teddy said. He stacked two cookies on a napkin and took his place at the table. "Somebody's getting a raise." When he realized Brittany-Lynne must have warmed the cookies he smiled and winced at the same time.

"No one's getting a raise," Matt, the CFO, said. He was wearing his "I'm fun" mint polo shirt, but his muscles were already tense. Matt didn't even know how bad it would be if Teddy hadn't been secretly paying half the overage invoices himself. To top it off there was a party scheduled next month to celebrate the opening of the unfinished, unfurnished building that was to house their new organic division, but Teddy didn't remind them of that.

"You gotta spend money to make money," Jay, the operations manager, retorted in his heavy New Jersey accent. He was built like an old-timey footballer who'd grown thick and jolly with middle age, and Teddy could always count on his optimism.

"We spent all the damn money!" Matt snapped. Jay bristled.

Teddy sat quietly, watching them bicker as he ate his cookies. He bent each cookie in half, observed the chocolate chips pulling apart from their ooey-gooey centers. It was calming for him but also a calculated move to evoke calm by example. It was a trick he'd learned from dealing with his parents.

"Man, I wish I had some milk," Teddy said at last.

Teddy's relaxed demeanor finally infected Matt and Jay and they each took sips of water and stopped talking.

"How much money do we need? Just for finishing the drains in the renovated building and running the electric, gas, and water to the new building?" He really did wish he had some milk, and about five more cookies, and that he was lying in bed with a movie and that none of this was real. A melancholy, fearful hardness was calcifying in his stomach now that there was no more food to distract himself from focusing on it. "And then what would we need assuming we stick it out and don't delay getting the equipment for the organic section?"

He went and got another cookie.

"Twenty-thousand." Jay pulled at the wet armpits of his shirt. He could be counted on to get pink-faced and sweaty when he argued. "For the second scenario, closer to seventy."

"I've already started some loan paperwork." Matt set a stack of papers on the table.

Teddy breathed in sharply, inhaling crumbs. "No," he said between coughs, feeling buffoonish and undignified. "We already have as many loans as we can handle. We'll do the first scenario. I'll relinquish my salary for the next two months to make room. Don't fight me on that, I mean it." If anyone asked, he'd claim to be living off savings; in reality he'd spent everything. The fear in his stomach thrummed again as the text alert from the morning flashed through his memory.

"Works for me." Jay leaned back in his chair. "You remind me a lot of old Irving, you know that? Generous to a fault." Teddy winced at the mention of his grandfather.

"Doesn't work for me." Matt picked up the loan application he'd placed in front of them and re-shoved it across the table for emphasis. "It's gonna be a ghost town for organic cherries. Fucking empty rooms with no equipment! It's the second scenario or nothing."

Matt had a point. The longer the new building sat empty the longer it wasn't generating revenue to start paying for itself. This wasn't a 'cut your losses' situation. They were all in.

"I can get it." As the words came out, Teddy had to put effort into making eye contact.

There was only one person he could ask for the money, and he wasn't sure she even had it. Calling her to New York would be like summoning a capricious, potentially dangerous djinn. He closed his eyes, wanting to drop off to sleep until it was all over.

"We'll have our organic division up and running by the end of summer at the latest," Teddy said. His voice sounded deep, thick, sweet, and somehow far away from his body. He intentionally eased into a serene, cherubic smile. On the inside he was wishing he could go back to the end of the previous summer and do everything differently. The renovations and the new organic division had been his big idea to honor his grandpa Irving and ensure the family business kept up with the times and flowed smoothly into the stream of the future. If he could get a do-over, he wouldn't rock the boat, would not change the course of the boat by even a millimeter. He would not so much as put a new coat of paint on the boat, and the maraschino factory would go clanking into the future at the same pace it had always gone.

CHAPTER 3:

MARLOW

Her first year in Alaska, Marlow Beasley had won the Tok Ladies' Amateur Arm Wrestling Competition. She had been embarrassed at winning, not because she thought it was a silly pastime but because it had had the word "ladies" in it. Since then, her reputation for being strong had endured, even if people had forgotten where that reputation had started.

"Not strong enough," she said quietly. She squinted at the moose, his white breath lingering in swirling circles like cigarette smoke.

It was dark out and the moose was between her and the front door of her cabin but also close enough to her truck that he could charge her before she got the rusty door open. Marlow had lost track of how long they'd been standing this way. She had tried backing up, retracing her steps into the woods and returning later, but the moose was still here, like he was guarding the place. Her nearest neighbor lived seven miles away. Marlow's feet were sunk into the snow and had gone from burning to unpleasantly numb some time before.

As much as she liked to be flashy, Marlow knew how to be smart and how to be patient. Once a decision was made it was made forever; a shrunk sweater could not be un-shrunk. But at some point you couldn't wait for events to align, you needed to make things happen. "Fuck it," she said. She took a crunchy step forward and the moose let out a sharp breath. She took another slow step and then another. The moose swayed his body to the right and then seemed to remember he'd left the kettle on at home and lumbered off to the left and into the trees.

"Asshole!" she called after him. "You couldn't have done that earlier?"

Marlow dropped the kindling she'd been out gathering next to the potbelly stove without slowing on her way to the bathroom. She turned on the hot water and then sat on the edge of the tub and slowly pulled off her boots. Her toes were black, which she wasn't expecting. "Or purple. That could be purple," she said out loud as she lowered her feet into the water. She'd started talking to herself more and more over the last year, but it didn't worry her. She'd been spending a lot of time alone in the cabin, thinking. Mapping out where she was going to distribute the venison (and eventually caribou and salmon) jerky she'd started experimenting with the previous summer: first gas stations then airport then grocery store.

The phone rang in the other room and she sloshed to answer it without drying her feet. Looked like she'd be speaking to another person after all.

"Hello?"

"Hey. It's Teddy," a deep but uncertain voice answered. It seemed like he was going to add "your brother," as if she might have forgotten. "How are you?" She was so surprised to hear from him she forgot her feet were numb and almost fell over when she tried to take a step.

"I'm in excruciating pain, but it's getting better." Marlow flopped on the couch and pulled a faded afghan over her legs. It was the ugly kind that comes from parents, though she'd bought this one herself.

"Don't say it so casually," he said. "Please. Are you okay?"

"You sound like Ma Beasley right now. My feet just got too cold."

"Oh. You love that kind of rugged nature stuff."

"Up to a certain point." There was a long pause.

"I know we haven't talked in a while, and I'm sorry," he said. She wasn't glad to get past the awkward preliminaries and on to important topics. It wouldn't do any good to slog through the reasons for their estrangement now.

"I haven't made an effort either, and I'm sorry," she said. She noticed she was biting her thumb and stopped. But once he'd addressed the issue, Teddy thankfully didn't dwell on their lack of contact. He asked about her dog (Chomper had died) and the weather and if she remembered the movie *Small Soldiers* at all; she'd taken him to see it when he was kid. He'd seen it on TV recently and thought of her.

"I was thinking maybe you could uh, come visit New York," Teddy said next. "Maybe kinda soon." His joke nervous belied real nervous. "It's important but I don't want to talk about it over the phone."

"Oh." For a moment she'd thought he'd just called to chat, that he was initiating a relationship between them. It had been a foolish thought. "Is it about the factory? Because I don't know anything about running the factory."

"Yeah. I mean sort of. I need your help. Things aren't right with some of the waste barrels. It might be a bigger problem than that." His words tumbled out and then slowed again. "Can you please just come?"

Though Marlow was forty-three and Teddy was only twenty-seven, he had inherited the family business when their grandfather died. Over a year ago now. Their parents had died eight months before Grandpa Irving. That Teddy was calling now, when Marlow was trying to launch a business of her own, a different kind of food factory of all things, made her feel defensive. She felt like she'd been caught caring about something she'd publicly said she didn't care about. It didn't help that her jerky project was barely out of the prototype phase.

"Why can't you talk about it over the phone?" When he didn't answer right away she asked, "Is it actually something very bad?"

"Really Marlow, I need your help in person. With the cherry vats, just that." His voice moved fast again, not at all like the measured, slightly amused, mellow intonations she remembered from phone encounters of years past. Even at the funerals he'd been calm and self-possessed.

She didn't know what to make of it. It wasn't like he'd said he felt callous negotiating raises with sob-story employees. He hadn't said the rest of the management team was jockeying for a takeover. He was being secretive about the easiest part of the whole operation—the equipment. You just called the manufacturer or the sales rep!

Had he after all picked up too many bad habits from their mother, for instance believing if you acted pathetic, incompetent, and helpless enough someone would swoop in and save you from even the most minor inconvenience? "Oh, it's just too high, I don't know what I'm going to do!" Her mom squawking in the grocery store, panicked, not ten steps from a stepladder *and* one of those long pincer arms. Like she was talking about making room on a life raft and not reaching for a top-shelf roll of paper towels. Eventually an embarrassed-looking young man had come and got it down for her. Ten-year-old Marlow had been just seconds away from monkey climbing to the top and lobbing the paper towels down at her mother. That would have given her something real to worry about.

"Driving out of Alaska in the winter is like invading Russia in the winter," Marlow teased.

"May isn't winter," Teddy said. Clearly he didn't understand the difference in seasons between New York and Alaska. "Anyway, just fly."

"There's no adventure in flying," Marlow answered. "If I leave tomorrow I'll be there in about a week. It's time for a visit anyway. I'm sure you're doing a great job with the factory though. I'm sure you are." There was no question of her saying no to the visit; it would be like finding out your long lost friend was still alive after a shipwreck and then saying, "Nah, I can't hang out tonight. My favorite show's on TV." A phone call out of the blue was not a sign to ignore. It was an opening to be part of a family again. But she needed the week to prepare mentally.

Marlow paced on tingly feet after they hung up and then remembered the kindling and the stove and busied herself with that. They hadn't said "I love you." It had a weirdly inappropriate feeling to it, the same as hugging did. The image of him as a snuggly five-year-old made sense, swirl of dark hair like a soft-serve ice cream cone, but she had never known her brother as a grown man. She had no frame of reference for how to interact. It almost felt right to say she'd "met him a few times."

She'd run off to play at cowboy in New Mexico when he was only five, leaving him alone in Brooklyn with Mom and Dad. Before she left she'd had one last fight with them—she couldn't quite remember about what. Maybe how Teddy was too old to still be using a sippy cup, even if it was just at bedtime, or maybe they were still pushing him in a stroller. She'd missed him like crazy but it hadn't stopped her from leaving.

After Teddy adapted to life without her as a buffer between him and their nervous-as-deer parents, he never wanted to admit when he didn't understand the joke or couldn't reach the rungs of the jungle gym—he learned early to choose silence over attracting smothering "help." Teddy had probably never failed at anything while their parents were alive, having always picked the guaranteed win and knowing mom and dad would bail him out if things got hard. That was why he was calling in reinforcements for vats.

Eventually the fire in the woodstove caught. She fed it oxygen. "I should have brought you with me on some of my road trips," she said aloud. "You could have scraped your knee for once in your life and learned it wasn't going to kill you."

But something about that explanation didn't feel right. Marlow pulled out her beat-up duffel and laid it open on the floor, a little charge going through her at the sight of it. "Hey, old friend," she said. "We're finally going to get back on the road."

As she made a pile of objects to be folded and compressed inside the duffel, she couldn't avoid thinking it anymore. The most obvious reason for

Teddy's call was the one that made her most uneasy: he wanted to talk in person about what had happened after Grandpa Irving died. He knew he'd never be able to keep her on the phone for it.

It had been a Prince Charles situation all along—no one believed the old man would go while Marlow and Teddy's parents were still young enough to want to take over the maraschino cherry factory full-time. Mom and Dad lived in Westchester and commuted in a few days per week to fulfill their honorary roles. Irving steered the company. No one expected him to have updated his will after their parents died. He was the type to avoid getting lost in emotion by getting lost in work, but it turned out Irving had taken his daughter's wishes into account and had updated his will to reflect what the executor had revealed about her plans for the family business. It wasn't *really* a surprise that they'd skipped over Marlow; thinking back on it now she didn't understand why she'd been blindsided. Maybe it was because her parents had always been such meddlers, and she'd been expecting one last attempt on their part to rope her into the maraschino life. Meddling was, after all, their pathological way of showing that they cared.

"It doesn't matter the motivation behind it, you were bad parents," she said. "And now it's too late to correct it."

There were no do-overs, no second chances. You couldn't un-throw a baseball, un-jump out of second-story window, or un-over-salt the soup. Your brother growing from a baby into a man and you missing it was another thing that couldn't be undone. But as pessimistic as she was, his phone call had sparked a hope she didn't want to fully articulate, as it would be equivalent to speaking the words of a curse out loud just to prove it wasn't real. As she pulled the zipper closed on the old duffel, she couldn't help but wonder what would happen if she showed up in New York and they jumped right into fixing vats, and then added in some spices and adventures for good measure, and kept the rehashing of old times to a minimum. Maybe Marlow and Teddy could start new from zero, blank slate.

CHAPTER 4:
BREAKFAST

Teddy peered through his half–open bedroom door at the woman he'd been dating for three and a half weeks. Her black hair was splayed on his pillow and her eyes were closed, but he knew she was awake and fighting the morning. Teddy pushed the door fully open and padded toward her over the thick carpet.

"Hey, miss," he said.

"Hey, mister," Doe replied groggily. When he lifted the corner of the blanket she flailed a little and then buried herself deeper like a tick.

"Wakey wakey eggs and bakey," he sang as he leaned down close to her.

"It's a trick," she said.

"No, I really am making eggs and bacon," he said as he straightened up. "I'm going to come back and put all the bacon crumbs in the bed in this giant burrito." He tucked in the blanket all around her like a tortilla, humming and saying "uh huh" and grunting a little. She didn't laugh but she didn't struggle either. Teddy had never met anyone who hated mornings as much as Doe did. She was Parisian and at first he thought maybe she was used to waking at eleven and smoking cigarettes for breakfast while peering out the window of a cool, dark Haussmannian building overlooking the Seine. But it turned out she'd been in New York a few years already as a student, and she hated waking up no matter what time of day it was or how much sleep she got. Teddy went back into the kitchen to flip the eggs.

"Really there's bacon?" she called. She emerged from the bedroom wearing his slippers, which were three times larger than her feet. She took big, far apart steps, giving each shoe more clearance than it needed. Her tininess and fussiness made him want to scoop her up and focus only on pleasing her and on how strong she made him feel when he succeeded.

"Give me twooooo minutes," he answered. The smell of coffee drifted through the apartment.

Doe wandered through a living room still cluttered with old man's furniture, which Teddy hadn't moved or changed since Irving's death, not exactly out of pain but because he didn't know what to fill the apartment with instead. She stopped in front of each painting, family photo, and at the writing desk. He couldn't help glancing in at her every few seconds to make sure she wasn't bored or unhappy or slipping back into the bedroom.

Anxiety over Doe's level of contentment ignited a broader anxiety, and soon Teddy's mind was on his financial problems. The apartment was huge—three bedrooms in an Upper East Side doorman building. Two bathrooms and who knows how many square feet. It had been in the family for four generations. He could have sold it, but at what point? The debt for the renovations and construction at the factory had mounted a little at a time and at each step of the way it seemed like such a drastic move to finance it with his home, which was worth significantly more than the debt. Also Teddy didn't consider the apartment truly his, the same way the factory wasn't his. It belonged to his family, already to his children, who weren't born yet. If he lost the apartment out of panic, people would be angry at him generations into the future. They would judge him as incompetent. Now it was too late to sell the place or get a home equity loan—it would take too much time and call too much attention to his finances.

Teddy set two plates on the table with a few halved grapes as an attempt at garnish. Doe made her way into the dining room. Charlotte Gainsbourg was playing softly and he wasn't sure whether that was too on the nose.

"I don't have toast," he said apologetically.

"I don't eat toast," she said.

"Do you like this music?" It was hard to get her to talk sometimes. He was wearing an apron and it was making him feel hot, too similar to the hot he felt when he wasn't living up to expectations.

"I love the music." She smiled and sat down at the dining room table. "I thought you were dead last night, you were so deeply asleep."

"I was up late with work stuff the night before." The non–lie still made his heart beat faster. He brought her a coffee and kissed her forehead and went to turn off the stove.

"Thank you for waking me so nicely." She looked confused. "My mother used to spray me with a spray bottle when I wouldn't get up in the morning, like I was a bad cat. My old boyfriends would have as well, if they'd had the imagination to think of it. No one has ever tucked me in tighter."

Teddy couldn't imagine anyone risking expulsion from her life by squirting her with a spray bottle. The triumph of getting her to open up a little, especially before coffee, was worth every second of kitchen time. "Oh, there's juice, too." He went into the kitchen and returned miming that he was about to spray her with it.

"Well I'm going to be wet anyway." She looked out the window at a sky dark with clouds. "I hate taking the subway in the rain." There was the slightest bit of blame in her voice. His uptown apartment was much farther from work than her Brooklyn apartment. The cherry factory was at the western edge of the Sunset Park section of Brooklyn, backed on one side by the Upper Bay of the Hudson and surrounded on the others by blocks of warehouses and manufacturing, far from subway and bus lines.

"That won't do at all. Let's take a car service; I'll pay for it. I'll just hop out a block before we get there, and you get dropped off out front."

"You care so much about gossip," she said. "There's no paparazzi, you know."

"I know, I just don't want anyone to get all weird or nosy about us. What we're doing is still new, you know?"

Of course the person he most didn't want to find out was his ex, Brittany–Lynne.

Doe picked at her eggs without looking at him. "You can eat lunch alone today if you don't want to be seen with me."

Teddy had to stop himself from reaching across the table to grab her hand. All he wanted was for her to comfort him and make him feel less alone, even though he couldn't tell her about the debt, Brittany–Lynne, or even the unsettled feeling the invading bees gave him. Her touch could momentarily distract him from anything, even what he was doing to make extra money… *Stop thinking about it.*

He focused on her angry little face as she poured the last of the cream into her coffee cup, turning her coffee almost white but ensuring there was no cream left for him. She was adorable.

He could have easily joked with her, prodded, and gotten her to change her mind about lunch. But it was the punishment he deserved, so he didn't. "I'm sorry," was all he said. "We'll tell people soon, I promise."

It drizzled in the morning, but then it stopped, and now the clouds had totally cleared, so Teddy decided he would eat his lunch in the courtyard in the sun. It wasn't as fun as sneaking off to a restaurant with Doe, but at least he would be outside. Marlow should be a third of the way across Canada by now, and that brought a sense of not hope but impending hope.

Just as he was reaching for the door handle to exit the building into the courtyard, the door swung open and Brittany-Lynne appeared framed in a blast of sunlight. They had agreed to stay friends, but the last few weeks he'd spent more time with her than he wanted, which made him feel guilty because of the imbalance of caring between them, so he'd overcompensated by spending even more time—suggesting coffee breaks or a quick drink before meeting up with Doe. His new plan for lessening their hangout time was his running away before she could see him, which wasn't going to work in this case.

It seemed she was going to try to squeeze through at the same time as him, something that would have been thrilling when they were dating or pre-dating, but was now unnerving, especially because he wasn't sure if she was doing it on purpose. He wobbled a little and took a step back so she could get by.

"Hi, Teddy." She smiled pleasantly.

"Hi," he said and smiled back. She started to move away. "Actually, wait, one thing. Thank you for the cookies at the last management meeting, but maybe lay off the baked goods?" He lifted his deli sandwich and pointed at it. "I'm trying to eat healthy and I'm terrible at resisting temptation."

"Sure, Teddy, of course," she said and continued to wherever she was headed. He couldn't tell if she was upset or neutral or if she had taken the word "temptation" as flirting, which it wasn't meant to be. He should have said, "It doesn't seem appropriate for you to still be baking me cookies now that we're broken up," instead of blaming it on his diet. Blunt, potentially hurtful words like that never sprung to mind first, especially not with her. She was sensitive, and if she started crying at work her face was going to turn all red and splotchy for hours, and she would hate that.

But he'd had to say something. Meeting snacks fell firmly into Doe's purview now. Teddy didn't want any suspicion developing over cookies. He allowed himself the briefest vision of the two women in his bed at the same time, not angry but throwing desserts at each other.

It was brisk in the courtyard. He breathed deeply and was glad to be wearing a hoodie with a fleece lining. Teddy walked toward the concrete blocks set at angles in the center of the yard. There were a few puddles along the way from the morning rain, but it wasn't muddy anywhere because of the gravel. Dead bees floated in the puddles, and as he crossed the watery graveyards an ominous feeling built inside of him. Usually there were other people eating lunch at this time, using the concrete blocks as benches, but he supposed they had stayed in the building because of the wet.

He sat on the bench and pulled out his sandwich. During the first bite a bee dive–bombed his head. He ducked as it did. Another careened toward his hair as he was chewing and he dodged it too, but more frantically than the first. Another bee, or maybe the same one, came right up to his meat sandwich and landed. Teddy waved the sandwich back and forth, at medium speed so as not to make the bee too angry, until the insect was displaced. It came right back around and touched down again. Teddy flicked the sandwich harder this time; condiments whipped through the air and a piece of lunchmeat flopped out and landed on the gravel. A third bee joined and together they swooped a cat's cradle around Teddy's head and food. He used his free hand to pull his hood up and cinched the draw-strings tight as he ran back across the courtyard. He stopped. His face was inches from a brick wall. With his eyes closed up in the hood, Teddy had accidentally zigzagged and found himself in front of the garage. *The bees know about the garage.* Worse. *The bees know and they are angry.*

He speed–walked twenty feet to the right, to the entrance to the hall-way where his office was located, with his hand still cinching his hood tight enough that only his mouth and the bottom part of his nose were showing. The grip was comforting. He released it to open the door and then made his way to the kitchen.

He was overreacting. The bees didn't *know* anything; he wasn't even sure that bees had brains. He was being paranoid. Beyond paranoid; he was being crazy. If he got caught and went to prison, it wouldn't be because of the bees.

Teddy had had both hands in a death grip, apparently. The tough hero roll had a fist-shaped dent in it. His heart and breathing slowed to a normal pace as he set the sandwich on the counter, counted to ten, opened a cabinet, counted to ten. He put the mangled lunch on a plate and sat at the table. It was eerily quiet in the kitchen. There was only the hum of the fridge and the hum of the water cooler. No one else was eating even though it was prime lunch hour. He had the urge to go out into the factory and make sure the employees still existed, but he forced himself to stay.

After a deep breath, he took a bite and chewed and was rewarded with the vinegary pop of whole grain mustard. He looked down to take a second bite and saw something tiny and squirmy between the meat and the bread. The pop was reinterpreted as not-mustard. He opened the sandwich and held the bread very close. He was pretty sure there was something moving, but it was the size of a grain of sand and hard to tell. Maybe it was a bee larva. Teddy held the bread far from him, at arm's distance, like middle-aged people do before they break down and buy reading glasses, but still it didn't seem that he could focus on it. The bread wasn't blurry; it was like trying to take a closer look at something in a dream. He went through the layers of sandwich one by one; cheese, meat, meat, cheese, lettuce. Maybe he didn't see anything. Teddy put the deconstructed sandwich in the trash. He was sad that he wouldn't get to eat, the way a child is sad when he's denied sugar-cereal, and his stomach curled in longing protest.

If he stayed in the kitchen he was going to end up clearing out all the drawers and washing everything to make sure there weren't larvae or imaginary weevils or whatever it was infesting the whole kitchen, and he didn't want to indulge his irrational fears any more than he already had. Teddy exited the kitchen and then came back in and tied off the garbage bag, just in case there *was* something crawly inside, and put a fresh bag in the can.

The construction workers weren't around today, and a walkthrough of where the organic wing would be housed seemed like a good way to clear his head.

Rather than cross through the bee zone again, he skirted around the edges of the buildings. The door to the new space glided smoothly open. It smelled like sheetrock inside. There was no power yet, and no light fixtures, so there was nothing to flip on. But through the classic glass factory windows Teddy had insisted on installing high above, light streamed into the looming interior. It was five thousand square feet of potential. The exterior was brick, to match the older buildings, which had been erected in the early 1910s. Teddy walked across the empty space to the back rooms, designated for packaging, storage, brining.

As Teddy walked slowly from room to room he imagined a future without his financial and moral missteps, as if their reality was as slippery as that of the bee larva in his sandwich.

He would personally take part in the interview process of every new employee. He loved job interviews. The conventional area—no, the *classic* area, he was going to start calling it that—the classic maraschino cherry section of the factory had nineteen full-time employees. There would be sixteen new hires for this side. He was excited to choose a mix of people: old and young, stylish, schlubby, ambitious, people with families to support. They'd be paid a decent wage. Beasley Cherries participated in the state's Work for Success program to find employment for former convicts who were ready to build their lives into something new.

Oh god, would he end up a convict?

The Food Suppliers Sourcing Fair in Hong Kong the previous winter had been occasion for him to fly international first class, and he'd felt giddy and important. He was taking the reins of the cherry factory, his grandfather had died just ten months before, and he'd already started work to modernize and build a new wing to open an organic division. Construction had barely started and was already above projected costs, but he hadn't admitted it yet to Matt and Jay. The energy of newness and change and grief that infused those months lent an aura of unreality to everything, almost like he was inside a lucid dream that propelled him through one wonder-inspiring situation or locale after the other. He made decisions but they didn't have the weight of permanence.

Teddy had walked a loop of the entire building. He hadn't even noticed the last few rooms, and it was nearly time for his meeting. He stepped outside.

The sunlight reflecting playfully off the dwindling puddles didn't stop him from retracing his steps along the periphery of the yard instead of crossing it.

When he got to the conference room he was sweating. Jay and Matt were already seated.

"Let's talk about this bee problem," Teddy said. He eyed the snack platter. Store-bought cookies, a pile of walnuts, and a ton of white space. He put some cookies on a paper plate and sat down. "People can't even eat in the yard anymore."

"Yeah I went to take a bite of my bacon, egg, and cheese this morning and it was full of fucking honey!" Jay exclaimed.

"Seriously?" Teddy was excited not to be alone in his bee panic. "I bit into a frickin' larva today!"

Jay started choking and the first thought in Teddy's head was that the bees had got him. Then it became clear that Jay was laughing. "They make the honey in the hives, and they make the larvae in the hives. There ain't no larva in your . . ." He was laughing so hard he could barely speak.

"Yeah, I figured it was probably just mustard." Teddy forced a grin.

"The bees are just out there taking a smoke break. Maybe try putting up a no smoking sign," Jay cackled.

"All right, all right," Matt said. "Let's move on. The bees aren't a big deal, so—"

"They are a big deal," Teddy cut in, calmly but firmly.

"I'll call an exterminator, but unless the hive's located here on the property there's not much for him to exterminate."

Fear re-doused his sweating pits. "I don't want to kill them, necessarily." If their presence was a cosmic punishment, who knew how the torment would escalate if he tried to murder them to cover his tracks. "I called my sister; she's going to come help figure everything out. She thinks outside the box."

Jay made a face Teddy didn't like. It was fleeting but he saw it. "There's really no need for that," Jay said. "It's a pain to cover the barrels, but no one's been stung."

"Yet. We should get a supply of EpiPens and Benadryl just in case."

"EpiPens are $800 each. Do you think maybe you're overreacting to this?" Matt asked.

Of course he was overreacting to it. Teddy had stayed calm and underreacted every step of the way up until now, and look at where that had gotten him.

He took a bite of cookie and it exploded stale crumbs all over the table. "Marlow will be here soon," he said. "She'll probably take care of it within a few hours. You'll see." He brushed the crumbs off the table into his hand and then deposited them onto the little plate.

He wasn't sure what Marlow would do exactly when she arrived, but if one person could ride the wave of pandemonium to victory, it would be her.

Marlow was the free one of the family. She didn't care about cherries and she didn't care about people being mad at her, a special weakness of Teddy's. She could do anything, and she thrived on chaos. When he was seven, their parents spent a week making frantic, not-the-least-bit-amused phone calls over her arrest out in Arizona for trying to ride an ostrich at an ostrich farm a few hundred miles outside of Phoenix. Teddy knew what an ostrich was from the *National Geographic* subscription Marlow got for him when she left town for good. Her antics made her seem like an action hero, a video game character, and a god from the Hercules animated movie all mashed into one. In the end she'd sent him a feather and a dozen ostrich eggs.

She would know what to do, and her judgment wouldn't be clouded by suspicions that the bees were a moral indictment against her . . .

He just wished he had someone to talk to while he was waiting for her to show up.

"Okay, well, I guess we'll hold off until she gets here. Let's talk finances," Matt said. He didn't seem to suspect that Marlow was also the plan for getting more money.

"The contractors say $20,000 to finish up wiring and whatnot is fine." Jay drummed his fingers on the table. "That just leaves the cost of buying equipment and finishing the drains, which would solve the bee problem right there."

"Maybe we should do the drains first," Teddy mumbled.

"How are we going to pay for that?"

"I've got an idea," Jay said. "We don't need a night watchman. No one's coming in here to steal cherries. We lay off Omar—"

"Absolutely not," Teddy cut in. The name seemed to echo around the room; one of his first hires since taking over the factory. His only accomplice. Omar knew about the secret basement below the garage. "No layoffs."

He thought longingly of Brittany–Lynne's cookies. Maybe he owed her an apology. That could be the first step on his road to atonement with the bees; he'd build up to the basement stuff. "I told you, I'm going to get the money. What else?"

CHAPTER 5:
BRITTANY-LYNNE

B rittany-Lynne's great-grandfather had been a mountain man in West
Virginia. There were no daguerreotypes of him in a mining town with
a long beard and dead eyes, but Teddy had seen those photos of other men
and assumed he was the same. Her face made sense in that context—the
slight overbite and the eyes that bulged a little. In certain light her red-
head's skin had a translucent look to it, like butter that's been left out on
the counter—you could press your finger into it and keep pressing until
it pushed clear through to the bone. In other light it was like cream and
beautiful against her brightly colored wardrobe. She was tall and gangly, all
knees like an eight-year-old. Teddy had never allowed himself to think of
her as not-pretty; she just shone in a different way.

They stood inside by a window and she wound cling wrap tight
around the lip of a plastic barrel, sealing the layer that was stretched
taut overtop. The barrel was wide enough that she had to hand the wrap
around to Teddy to do the opposite side and then he'd pass it around again.
This was the process they used to prevent molestation by bees when they
wheeled brining waste across the yard to the building with the filter system and disposal drains. In a busy week several hundred barrels passed
through, and anyone who was free helped out. The incredible inefficiency
and low-tech absurdity of it brought him to the verge of frustrated tears

on a semi–weekly basis. The renovations, intended to solve these sorts of problems, were so maddeningly close to completion and yet financially out of reach.

"Sorry for what I said about the cookies last week," Teddy said. "Who am I kidding with that diet stuff? I gotta keep my cheeseburger layer in case there's a famine this summer." He jabbed a finger at his stomach, which maintained a pork–belly springiness no matter how much he exercised. After a chubby adolescence he'd become "dashing," according to Brittany–Lynne, and the best way he knew how to handle it was with self–deprecating humor.

She smiled that sad, I know it's over smile. "I shouldn't do it, but your sweet tooth is so damned cute."

It seemed she got lost in thought, tracking something just above his head.

"What is it?" he asked, worried she was going to say there was a bee inside.

"I was just admiring your hair in the sunlight. It's so dark and thick it absorbs the entire UV spectrum and doesn't even throw out a highlight." She cast her eyes back down to the task at hand.

"Don't ever change," Teddy said. She glanced back up. "It's comforting to know exactly what to expect from you: extreme flattery and secret desserts."

They both knew from the beginning that they'd have to end it eventually: Brittany–Lynne wanted to move out of the city one day, and she didn't want children; they'd talked about it before they even kissed for the first time. They'd kept going because they liked each other's company. And yet . . . every day they'd been together there'd been a feeling like a two–year–old kicking the back of his seat on an airplane, but it was coming from inside himself. *You know this isn't right for either of us. She is going to be sad when it ends. She's such a nice person and she's going to hate you and you're selfish for dating her knowing she's going to hate you.* He had so dreaded hurting her that he'd been unable to pull the trigger on the breakup for weeks after he'd decided to do it. Teddy had curled up in a fetal position of dread and stomach pain on her bed one night until she guessed what was wrong based on the breadcrumb trail of hints he'd left the preceding days. He was still ashamed thinking about it; other than ghosting, he couldn't think of a more cowardly way to break up.

He handed the wrap back around to her. He couldn't quite muster the courage to ask her what she thought of the bees, which was the reason he'd maneuvered to prep the barrel with her in the first place. He was worried about re-opening the floodgates of her attraction again, but also he wanted someone's perspective he could trust. In the back of his mind, the two-year-old was stirring from sleep. *You just want her to soothe you until your sister gets here, you selfish dick.*

"I can tell you've been sad recently," Brittany-Lynne said eventually. "You may as well tell me why." She was speaking quietly so no one would overhear what was more than a friendly coworker chat, but the quietness itself betrayed intimacy.

"Hey, this barrel's ready to go!" Teddy called. A man started toward them with a dolly. Teddy and Brittany-Lynne followed him out and then split off and walked over to the admin building.

Teddy's step faltered when he noticed an employee walking into the garage.

People needed to go in and out of the garage all the time.

Not only did the trucks leave from there, it functioned as an overflow warehouse.

It was where the cubbies for personal items were mounted.

Teddy wrenched his eyes away from the garage. He held open the door to the admin building for Brittany-Lynne.

"My sister isn't here yet and she hasn't"—he twisted and swatted at his back as he walked—"hasn't been answering my texts. That means she's avoiding me; all I want is a realistic ETA. I feel bad saying that. I know she's doing me a huge favor driving all this way." He whirled again as he talked. "Did a bee follow us in here?"

"I didn't see one," she said. "It's not a favor to come see your little brother. That's love; of course she wants to see you."

He thought for a moment about the difference between doing something out of love and doing it out of obligation *because* you loved someone, wasn't sure if there was a difference, and then said, "Sure, you're right." They were in the stairwell now, their old go–to place for privacy.

"It sucks to have to ask for support from your sister instead of her just offering, but that's life." She smiled at him encouragingly. "Sometimes you have to ask."

They had gone only a few steps up the orange–painted stairwell when Teddy buckled into a seat against the wall. "I've been seeing things," he said. "It's those stupid bees that keep getting into the barrels. I see them out of the corner of my eye: inside the hallways, in my office. But when I look for them they aren't really there. It's like, if you're seeing things but you're sane enough to question if they're real, like you don't just accept that they're real, that means you aren't really crazy, right?"

Teddy wrapped his arms around himself and waited for her to say it was just stress about the factory renovations.

Brittany–Lynne looked down at him, and he had the unsettling feeling that he was a baby in a playpen and she was an all–knowing mother, loving but saddened by the shackles of maternal responsibility. "Maybe you wanted to call Marlow anyway," she said. "But you wouldn't let yourself, so now the bees are an excuse."

He liked her answer better than that he'd called Marlow to borrow money and then she had become, through the mounting anticipation of her eventual arrival, a savior who would also solve all his other problems. Problem number one being the bees getting into the cherry waste, which had initially just been the pretense for asking her to come. "You're a lot brighter than I am," he said.

She had real insights. He himself was adept at faking his way through situations he was unsure of and making decisions without deliberation. It was behavior he'd cultivated in childhood to set his parents' minds at ease. From which flavor of birthday cake to which college to attend, he delivered his answer with the calm assurance of a Zen master and kept his doubts to himself. He'd wanted to change his college major halfway through but didn't dare—any hint of indecision would have set his parents down a panic spiral. So he'd carried on, all the while projecting an easy assurance he didn't feel. Today he called it "their anxiety," making it a problem his parents had, but he couldn't help questioning, especially when he was younger, whether they were always swooping in because of some deficiency in him.

Brittany–Lynne folded her gawky stork legs and sat beside him. "I'm so smart that I'm a glorified secretary at my age," she said. "When your grandfather died the factory only found me a position out of gratitude."

He tried to think of a way to deny what she'd said without it being a lie. She had been Grandpa Irving's caretaker and personal assistant in the year leading up to his death, and it was true that Teddy would always be grateful for her presence during that time. They were transitioning her into a dedicated HR/payroll position, a first for soon–to–be–expanding Beasley Cherries, because it had been awkward to have someone seven years older than he was in such a junior role.

Brittany–Lynne's phone vibrated. Teddy jumped.

"It sounded like a bee," he said. "It's surreal. It's like a tip–off that I'm dreaming, but I'm not dreaming."

"Worst–case scenario they'll leave you alone when winter comes, if we don't get the new drains by then."

He was more concerned about what the bees represented about his mental state than he was about their actual presence, but it didn't matter.

Everything she said was intended to be soothing and kind, and he opened his heart to it and settled in, like accepting a hug.

"I really want you to find a nice man," he said. "You deserve it."

Her breath trembled. He could tell the implication of his comment, that he was not that man, had hurt her.

"And you deserve a nice woman." She squeezed her hands together between her knees. "You think if you're steady enough the depressed, anxious ones will calm down and be happy," she said. "Try dating someone who doesn't *need* you as their anchor. Try dating someone happy for a change instead of someone who needs saving."

She was fidgeting with her fingers and he wanted to tell her that she hadn't been a downer or a burden while they were together, even though just the other day he'd been tiptoeing around her so as not to make her cry over cookies.

"Can you do something for me?" she asked. "Promise you won't keep it a secret if you start dating someone else? You don't have to call me up and tell me, but don't actively lie about it to 'save my feelings.' That will just make it worse, and I know you care too much about hurting people's feelings. I'm still attached to you and I don't want you to make a fool out of me. I'm smart but my heart is slow to . . . It's like the world's most gentle pit bull. Once attached it takes a while to let go. But I'll rein it in if you tell me to stop."

"Okay." He looked down at his feet. He couldn't tell her about Doe *now*.

They picked themselves up and smoothed wrinkled pants. She started up the stairs with him slightly behind.

"Teddy, are you all right?" Brittany-Lynne called. She was far above him now.

"Yeah, just my foot was asleep. But I'm recovered!" He bounded up to meet her as if he were the most care-free man in the world.

CHAPTER 6:
MIMS

New York City was in a lull between landlord scandals, street fairs, and MTA crises, but Mims still needed to find five hundred words before sunrise. She was hungry—literally hungry, not hungry for a Pulitzer—and needed to publish if she wanted to buy groceries next month. It was more likely that something good would come up at the community board than that she'd stumble across a street crime, so here she was at the meeting.

She walked halfway down the aisle of the school auditorium that hosted Community Board 3 and chose a row in which every other seat was filled. It was satisfying the way New Yorkers were so respectful of strangers' personal space, but tonight Mims was feeling lonely. She sat directly next to a stout grandmother instead of skipping a seat and breathed in the older woman's faint camphor smell before opening the schedule.

It was pretty much all liquor license requests, and unfortunately she had filed a "there are a lot of bars in the Lower East Side" story a few weeks before. She would have to come up with something fresh, or at least meatier, if she wanted Aziz to print it.

An elbow pressed aggressively against hers on the shared armrest. Immediately, rage branched through Mims's chest and down her arms into her fingers, as if the grannie's touch had completed a circuit. That she would be challenged into a power-struggle in this space, probably the only gathering of New Yorkers with less going on in their lives than she had . . . She unzipped her small purse, slow, slow, and pulled out a months-old press badge. Fiddling with the edges of the lamination, she let the unwarranted fury settle and fade. She set the badge on her knee, ostensibly clearing space in the purse to more easily dig for a pen. Really it was so the old woman would see it. Mims flipped open a small reporter's notebook, announcing unequivocally her right to be there, welcome or not. She whipped through the sheets of paper until she got to a blank page, like swiping left on a dating app.

The meeting was called to order before she reached the familiar split in the road: feed her indignation by cataloguing past wrongs or descend into shame for being triggered by such a minor affront.

One by one hopeful restaurateurs climbed the steps onto the elementary school talent-show stage and pleaded their case for the privilege to sell booze. Mims looked around the audience as the meeting wore on: elderly man with fanny pack, elderly woman with juice box, middle-aged woman with cane.

Next up was a Mr. Waldron. He approached the stage with a body language different from his predecessors'. He wasn't slope-backed, meek, and deferential. He didn't strike her as a man about to ask permission. Mims leaned forward.

"Good evening," he said, nodding to the community board officers set up at a folding table at the end of the stage. He turned to face the audience; oversized shoes, oversized belt buckle, thinning hair, all-black attire. Leaning into a contrapposto power pose, he gripped the microphone with a bejeweled fist and lifted it from the stand. "I'm George Waldron, and my application for a liquor license has been rejected. It's suggested on the application that you're more likely to find success if you're a member of the community and make some kind of positive impact." What had started out as subtle weight shifts from foot to foot as he took the microphone was becoming a sort of irate waltz. "It's not enough that I donate money and tools to the community garden right across the street from this school. It's not enough because I didn't give money to the *right* local projects, the ones the 'honorable' board members are involved with."

It was a bit far-fetched, but Mims could imagine a world in which the community board members were brazen money-grubbers. Most people when held up to scrutiny turned out to be scrawny, yowling beasts, like a formerly fluffy cat dunked in water.

"I don't have receipts, but I didn't think I'd need them, if we're all a part of a trusting 'community.'" Waldron flicked the mic back into the stand and started to walk away but then leaned back in. "You all suck."

Hers was a special kind of gullibility that came after two weeks of eating nothing but spaghetti with Sriracha and bargain bin olive oil, but still she knew his extortion allegation was bullshit. The board was unmoved and Waldron stomped back to his seat as they straightened papers.

"Now opening the floor to other, unscheduled concerns," one of the officers announced. It was the part of the evening where people complained about dog pee and skateboarders and sidewalk rattraps. Mims put her notebook back in her purse. What a stupid plan this had been, and she'd wasted two hours on the subway getting here. As if the universe owed her a story proportional to the inconvenience she went through to get it.

An older man, even for the community board crowd, shuffled onto the stage before she could make her exit. "Good evening, everyone," he said, slowly. "My name is Charlie Nobelle and I spend a lot of time on rooftops."

She clicked her pen on and off impatiently.

She felt the grannie's eyes on the pen and stopped.

"I'm a beekeeper, you see, and have been for many years now . . ." Decades passed. "And I've been talking to others about this, who are also concerned and aren't sure who to contact." He took a long breath. "You see, my honey has turned red. There's something strange going on here, and if anyone has the resources to help, I really don't know what to do."

There was a kernel of something. She could write about the isolation and loneliness of old people in the city. Lack of senior centers, perpetually broken subway elevators, uneven sidewalks.

Her mood soured again. Sad man with defective insects counted as a promising lead?

She famously disliked bugs, had nothing but contempt for people who claimed to love idyllic upstate farms, which smelled of manure, and was disgusted by baby deer. No one considered that baby deer were infested with Lyme ticks. She didn't leave Michigan to write about bees, or old people. She wanted to write about powerful people, successful people, corrupt people on the verge of being found out. Sad, poor, ineffective community board patrons were never meant to be her New York social milieu. Being here was bathing in failure, and it was seeping into her, deflating her posture. To write this story would be to admit that she no longer had any choices left, even nominal ones, in how she earned money. Waldron's corruption accusation had at least *interested* her. Next stop after the bee non-story would be getting a temp office job and then a part-time job. And then it would all be over: no more journalism career.

She waited around until the end of the meeting, wrestling with whether pride or paychecks were more important. Only bad things were motivated by money. It was a supreme form of dignity to be free of want. That knowledge significantly increased her envy of those whose financial interests and dreams wove effortlessly together. A guy she knew was covering a fashion gala in Atlanta right now. Another was prepping for the Melbourne International Film Festival.

Mims filed into the lobby with the rest of the audience. After a few minutes, the very old beekeeper emerged from the auditorium, his disheveled white wisps of hair making him look like a maniac. Her affected composure stood in stark contrast. It was important that she give the impression of relaxed, off-handed glamour even though—no, especially because—she was flat broke. That's why she wore elegant, wide leg slacks. It was the reason for the delicate chain around her neck, the necklace's pinprick pendant registering only as a subtle refraction of light.

"I need your help," Charlie said to one of the board members. He reached out to put a hand on the woman's arm, but she slipped away. He'd have had better luck if he fixed his hair.

Charlie reached toward another board member. "Excuse me—" No luck. Charlie nodded to himself, as if rebuilding his reserve of energy for the journey home.

Mims stepped in front of him.

"I'm Mims Walsh from the *Free Post*. I'd like to ask you a few questions about your honey, if you have a minute." She offered her hand and he shook it, wild-eyed with a wide smile.

"I read that newspaper. I don't recognize your name."

Mims was surprised anyone would be familiar enough with such a thin local paper to recognize the contributors' names. They handed the paper out for free outside subway stations, a distribution tactic that made it seem like readers were doing the paper a favor by taking one. "I'm freelance, so you have to get lucky to find me. How do you spell your last name, Charlie?"

"Here, take my card." He handed her something that wasn't a card. It was a miniature honey jar, and the contents were electric, cough syrup–red goo. Her breath caught; he'd handed her something radioactive. Charlie's name was prewritten on a sticker centered on the jar, along with his phone number and title, "Beekeeper."

"Maybe you just need to clean your tools or something?" she asked cautiously. Her mind working. Maybe he'd colored the honey himself: lonely old guy wanting attention. But maybe… Mims's lottery mentality was taking over. Like so many who grew up in poverty, success to her was such an impossible dream that hard work seemed too ordinary a means to achieve it. Extraordinary results came from that one lucky break, making it into pro sports or Hollywood for some, finding that one story for her. A single moment propelled you from one plane of existence to another. She was aware of this all–or–nothing defect in her thinking; it had gotten her into trouble before. But what if the red honey was the first clue in a new worldwide bee disease? The last red flag before climate change free fall? People loved reading about the end of the world.

"I've been keeping bees for sixty–four years, and I've never seen this." She looked from one of his watery eyes to the other, checking for sincerity. "It's all my hives, all over the city."

She tamped down the little thrill playing its way past her lungs, see-sawing between cynicism and fantastical thinking. "Could I see the hive this came from tonight?"

Charlie cocked his head to the side like a dog, the wispy hair halo following a second behind. Now she was the crazy, desperate one. Mims checked the clock by the auditorium entrance. It was after 10 p.m. "I meant tomorrow," she said. "What time tomorrow could we meet?"

"Noon tomorrow," he said. "The blue building three doors down from the school." He gave her a frail hug and ambled back into the auditorium.

She dozed on the subway, which for most people would have ended in disaster, but for her it was time travel. She woke up at the end of the line, her stop, and stumbled into her apartment. The lights and noise and life of "the city" were far away from South Ozone Park. While the commute from Manhattan had long since become habit, the feeling of being a kid with an early bedtime, shut out of the party flanking the East River, needled her more and more as the years passed.

In the dark kitchen she added her blazer to the precarious mound of dish towels and outerwear hanging off the back of a chair. She dropped her purse and made her way to the sofa, shoving aside a dog–eared copy of *The*

Sun Also Rises. She blamed rereading it for putting her in such an envious, dissatisfied state of mind. Hemingway's semi-employed journalist characters drank their way through European vacations.

Mims opened her laptop, half closed her eyes at the glare, and vomited out five hundred words in seven minutes. It was a rehash of the "Lower East Side is being taken over by bars" story, but she had to at least *try* to meet her deadline. Aziz would be waking up for his sunrise run in six hours. She gritted her teeth and hit send.

Her empty stomach folded in on itself painfully.

How would she have spent the night if the staff job at *Downtown Voices* had materialized? In a restaurant, maybe, interviewing a producer or magazine mogul, press-badge posturing unnecessary. It had been almost within reach, like a friendly Muppet in an Ambien dream. After five years of pitching and only occasional bylines, she'd somehow landed a full-time position at one of the nation's oldest alternative weekly news and culture papers. It was a Friday. She told all her friends, she told some of her enemies, and she paid for a taxi to the bar where they were going to celebrate. "Wait, did you say *Downtown Voices*?" She had. "They're closing. Like next week." She Googled it and it was true. "Nice investigation work, Mims." Laughter. She never found out whether the person who hired her had been in denial, or if her hire had been part of some sort of failed Hail Mary play to keep the company open, or whether the final decision to close had really been so spur of the moment.

That was four months ago. She'd intended to emerge triumphant somehow, vowing to herself not to appear at social functions again until she had.

Mims stalked into the kitchen and opened all the cabinets in search of forgotten morsels. A few shelves in, her phone buzzed with an email alert from Aziz. "If you submit another gibberish article you're not getting published here again; I don't care if you find out who killed JFK. Fill the column space next week or I'm not holding it for you anymore. Enough is enough." She threw the phone into the living room, where it landed safely on a pile of laundry. More and more it seemed her career was an act, and she wasn't a very good actress. Aziz was her only remaining connection to real journalism. Everything else was tabloid work and paid Amazon reviews.

Her signature red lipstick sat on the counter and she applied it without a mirror. Paint over the doubt and keep going, as always. It made her feel better to be made up. Never let anyone see that you're suffering: that's when they pounce.

She stood straight and attractive at the sink mixing sliced pickles with the dregs of off–brand Cheerios as she formulated a plan for the morning.

CHAPTER 7:
ROOFTOP I

Mims trudged up the roof access stairs of the blue-painted rental building and then paused to brace herself. When she'd woken up that morning the bee story had seemed a lot less promising than it had the previous night, when the only alternative had been Waldron's fake extortion allegation. She flung the door open to reveal a muggy, windless expanse of black tar. The first thing her eyes landed on was a tiny sagging plywood shed, homebuilt and not beautiful. She pushed away, for the tenth time since entering the building, the idea of turning around and leaving.

The only other objects on the roof, at the far end and also appearing tiny, were Charlie the beekeeper, a younger man she feared irrationally was another journalist, and a small stack of blond wooden boxes she knew based on her internet research to be the beehive. Charlie waved her over, his white hair bopping like a feather duster in spite of the still air. She picked her way carefully along the edge of the roof, as if she might fall through if she walked across the center. It was that easy to get sucked in by despair. She watched the two men warily as she approached. They had started without her.

The not-Charlie man was East Asian, tall and lanky with a nice shoulder-to-hip ratio and a thick head of hair. He let the hive cover thud back into place just as Mims stopped a few feet away. Charlie averted his eyes from a bee that got pinched in half where the wood landed. Mims didn't flinch and wasn't sure if she should feel guilty about it.

"Yeah, this honey is red," the younger man said. He held a hive tool to the sunlight and watched the red drop rolling down the edge. A cloud of bees zigzagged around them on their way to and from the hive. He dipped his finger in the red and hesitated a moment.

"I wouldn't," Charlie said. He didn't seem like much of an authority figure with his bushy mustache and his mismatched socks, one whales and the other kittens. The younger man ignored his warning and blotted his finger onto his tongue. He recoiled at the taste.

"So foul," he said.

"Who are you?" Mims asked.

"Kai. Kai Peterson. I'm an inspector for the USDA. I was adopted. That's why the names don't match. Kai is a Hawaiian name."

Charlie sighed loudly at Kai's awkwardness. Mims was enormously relieved: the agent was a legitimizing force that meant she'd still have a chance at a headline no matter what the red turned out to be. "USDA Finds Lonely Old Man's Red Honey Is a Hoax," or whatever. Her presence seemed redundant, as far as actually investigating, but she couldn't blame Charlie for casting a wide net to try to find help.

"What's it taste like?" Mims asked.

"Bitter, with a sweet chemical sting," Charlie said before Kai could answer. "You can come closer, just approach from the back. The guard bees are looking out the front entrance of the hive." The inspector was the only one of the three of them with a beekeeping veil, and it was lying at his feet. He'd taken it off presumably because of the heat reflecting up from the black rooftop. The wet hair matted to his forehead made him look feverish, except he stood with his legs far apart in a confident Superman pose. Mims took a few steps forward, deciding to forgo asking for the veil, which was probably drenched with sweat.

Charlie puffed some smoke around the seams of the hive from a small device that looked like the oil can from *The Wizard of Oz*. "Don't be scared, they're preoccupied with capping the honeycomb today," he said. "Put your hair up if you can. If they get in hair it triggers something in them. They'll think you're a bear and Rapunzel up that hair faster than you can say 'bee sting.'"

"I'm Mims Walsh. With the *Free Post*," she said to the USDA agent as she gathered her hair in a hasty bun.

"I'm off duty now. Inspection's done." Kai replied in a quick, halting way that made it sound like he was interrupting, even though it was his turn to speak. "So if you get stung it has nothing to do with me." He gave a magnanimous but cockeyed wink she interpreted as flirty. Mims kept her face placid, unimpressed. She caught Charlie's glance and saw him nod slightly in approval. That easily, they became a clique.

"You can ask questions though," Kai said, seeing that his joke hadn't landed.

Charlie shook his head.

"How long do you think it will take to do the chemical analysis on the honey?" Mims asked. "Or is that even necessary? Have you seen this kind of thing before?"

"Oh no, no, no," Kai tutted. "This is ultra–weird, testing is necessary. New York State works with one apiculturist. He does the testing for all the various pathologies for the whole of the Northeast—foul brood, colony collapse disorder, etcetera. If he's even equipped to analyze whatever goop this is, it could take a couple of months before he gets to it."

Mims studied Kai's face closely. He didn't sound the–house–is–burning concerned, but he wasn't dismissive either. Her skin was still hot, but she felt a cool flutter through her stomach. She had to admit it was intriguing and a little scary. She didn't care for insects as a genre of professional inquiry, but if she could know the answer to what made the honey red or not know, she would prefer to know. It was the kind of thing you could mention at a party even if you weren't the one investigating it, a nice little topic for one of those NPR podcasts people loved.

"Look at this one!" Every utterance from Charlie felt like the eager tug of a five-year-old at her sleeve. Mims turned.

"Where?" she asked.

"Just here." He slowly lifted his hand to eye level. A honeybee stood on the knuckle of his pointer finger. Its translucent belly shone a garish lipstick red. "That's the honey stomach," he said. "It should be amber." Mims had read about the normal honey-making process that morning. Honeybees drink the sugar-rich droplets of nectar within flowers' centers. But they also store nectar in their second stomach, the honey stomach, to transport it back to the hive, where it's regurgitated and fermented and evaporated down to honey and then stored inside honeycomb to be eaten by the bees over the winter.

"So do you think it's a virus or a bacterial infection that's making it red, or . . ."

"No," Kai cut in. Their ping-ponging interruptions were starting to get to her. "It's definitely something already-red that they're ingesting into their honey stomachs and then bringing back to the hive."

"Mr. Nobelle—"

"Call me Charlie."

"Charlie, what's going to happen to them if we don't get an answer soon?" Mims asked.

"Oh, we're going to have to destroy the affected hives," Kai interjected. "Just in case."

Charlie snorted and the bee flew off. "I'm not afraid of him." He gestured at Kai with his thumb. "I kept bees as a kid; it kept me out of trouble then, and it keeps my mind sharp now. And my body spry!" He said it with what was meant to be a ferocious hop that had Kai and Mims both lurching toward him to make sure he didn't totter and fall. His legs looked frail enough that they'd snap under his own body weight if he tried to jump off anything higher than a curb.

"Yeah, we'll never get past you," Kai said in mock distress. "I'm going to head out." His shirt was soaked with sweat and his face was flushed. "I'll walk down with you," he said to Mims. He handed her his business card, which was soggy.

"I have a few more questions for Charlie," Mims said curtly. A bead of sweat dripped down her temple. "Don't wait." Kai nodded and left, defeated. Charlie smiled. Of the reasons for men to hang around Mims, none were doing it to take advantage of her niceness.

Even though she and Charlie were buddies now, she needed to check off the obvious question. "You're sure it's not something *you're* feeding them?"

"It's not just my bees," he said, more pleading than indignant. "Ask any beekeeper at the farmers markets." Mims felt the cool flutter of fear and excitement again.

"How far will bees fly for food?"

"For 'forage,'" Charlie corrected. "Oh, probably not more than five miles. This spring is unusually hot and dry though, so if they're desperate to find flowers, they might fly farther. There's been an explosion in interest in beekeeping this year, now that it's legal in the city, so there are more bees out there looking. Slim pickings for forage is probably what drove them to turn to the red stuff."

"Maybe I can narrow down a search area for the source based on the locations of other affected hives." The anticipation of work made her feel competent and slightly useful.

"Hey, I'll tell you a secret," Charlie said.

Mims looked up from her notebook. "The queen in this hive, her name's Sheila, and she's named after a woman who wasn't my wife, God rest her soul. Sometimes I imagine that the real Sheila has come back and chats with me through the hive.

"I'm an old man, and I need this. I know places I can hide my girls, other rooftops, if Kai and his buddies want to murder them. But I can't hide them from the red glop. They seem perfectly fine for now, but this substance isn't going to turn out to be good for their health. I guarantee that."

He'd seemed so elated and almost unconcerned for the first part of the visit, maybe because people finally believed him and were coming to hear him out, but now he was somber. "I was serious when I said I need this hive to keep me focused. Keep my marbles from rolling away; otherwise I'll be sitting inside until I get bedsores."

"I'll help you," she said. "I'm going to solve this. I'm very stubborn."

Mims arrived home feeling confident she could get enough details about the bee mystery in the next few days to finish a piece about it by her deadline. Bonus that there could be an additional article if and when the mystery was solved.

An envelope waited for her under the door. Gas and electricity shut-off notice. She scanned down to the amount past due: eighty dollars. It was such a small amount. She'd been living with the lights turned off for weeks, and she hardly used the stove. It occurred to her now that she should have unplugged the fridge, since it was empty anyway. If she didn't pay the bill immediately, there would be fees. Her landlord lived on the floor above and might get spooked if he saw the ConEd man applying what amounted to a car boot for her gas line.

Mims took Kai's business card out of her purse and stuck it to the refrigerator. She grabbed a pen and underlined USDA twice. She was trying to reassure herself that because he was credentialled, this was a legitimate story. After a third underline she was able to halfway believe it. Regardless, it would have to wait. She had a few people she had to call before she could get started on her bees investigation.

CHAPTER 8:

THE NEWSPAPERMAN

Mims's lucky assignment was to get a quote from Sammy Sampson, D-level comedian, about a former costar's recent stint in rehab. He and the addict had starred together in a short-lived sit-com cancelled five years prior, and rumor had it there was still bad blood. Getting the quote was going to be easy, and the job paid well because it was last-minute and involved in-person hassle instead of just writing. Mims knew the assigning editor well enough that he'd give an advance on payment; if he could find two more jobs for her this week her electricity wouldn't be shut off. Once that was out of the way she could get back to the red bees.

Sammy was expected to exit the stage door of his off-off-off Broadway show between 11:45 p.m. and 12:15 a.m. There was no real danger that Sammy wouldn't appear at the anticipated time, that he wouldn't be excited a reporter wanted to talk to him, or that other reporters or fans would be at the stage door competing for his attention.

Mims had left her apartment early to compensate for possible subway malfunctions, so she found herself in the theater district, near Times Square, forty-five minutes ahead of schedule with nothing to do. Towering above the chunky-clogged human river of tourists were the worst offenders among overpriced touristy chain restaurants. The manic, flickering colored light emanating from billboards and digital bus stop posters conjured mind–control videos, and Broadway itself was a Noah's ark of lonely American consumerism, one specimen from each major corporation—M&M's store, Lego store, McDonald's, the shuttered Toys "R" Us . . . She wasn't tempted to ogle the spectacle, and she was proud of that. Her lack of interest suggested good taste bordering on moral superiority.

Jumbled up with her judgment for the corporations and their patrons was a faint uneasiness. If offered the chance, she'd be the spokesperson for Cheerios in an instant. She'd write a jingle for Starbucks, host *The Voice*, make a movie drowned in product placement, and eat a floppy fast food taco with a big fake smile on her face and a $10,000 check in her pocket. She'd sell out so hard and so fast people wouldn't even know she knew she was a shill.

She walked west, away from the lights. If Mims craned her head back now, she would see, perfectly still and in dignified contrast to the bustle below, office buildings. But she wasn't going to crane her head back; she was well aware they were looking down at her. Well–respected and well–known institutions in journalism and publishing were headquartered above the fray, including the *New York Times*, the *New York Post*, *World Gazette*, and *Vanity Fair*. Three blocks farther on, in a neon–free side street, was Miller's Bar. Miller's was the place where journalists hung out and had been hanging out for more than half a century. She'd never been inside.

Fuck 'em, she decided.

Mims walked through the door of Miller's with the swagger of a cowboy entering a saloon. She looked good. She wore a fitted white T–shirt with sleeves that ended in straight lines parallel to the floor. Most T–shirts had carelessly lopsided sleeves that fell with the outer edge much higher than the armpit side and poking out in a sideways mountain peak. She wore cigarette–leg crop slacks. She wore the lipstick. She was also carrying the notebook again, and that felt like a cliché, but no one could see it because it was zipped up inside her purse. Hers was a look that said, "model, but in an editorial spread because she's not tall enough," or also "interior designer," or also "journalist."

The bar ran along the left and was polished wood with a resin inlay. Recessed lights spilled out cones of warmth in what felt like an oversized but narrow reading room minus the books. Only a few people sat at the actual bar, but there was a mass in the back. She recognized a few journalists from their by-line photos.

Mims walked straight for the back but slowed to a crawl as she got closer. She paused at the elbow of a woman with blow-dried hair, just outside one of the pools of light, and listened for an entrance into the conversation. The group was talking about personal matters, not current events. Someone glanced at her and Mims smiled and walked away. She intended to walk only a few feet, to another cluster of people. Instead her feet took her all the way back to the front of the long bar, where she asked for water, because it was free. She could feel her inferiority transmuting into an amped-up cockfight energy, an eagerness to peck some eyes out to prove her worth. She tried to stave it off by breathing deeply but also she was tapping her foot and the two movements cancelled each other out.

"Just water?"

Mims whipped around to find a tallish man grinning down at her. He had sandy blond hair that fell into his eyes, and his oversized teeth had a front gap that gave him a cartoonish farm-boy look. His clothes were all shades of brown, rumpled, and he had one too many buttons undone on his shirt. The outfit reassured her that she was being flirted with by a country mouse tourist who'd wandered in by mistake, not a successful journalist, and so there was no reason to attack. Her heart slowed and then realized it should speed up again, beating out *sex, sex, sex*. She almost laughed at herself for the turnaround. He had kind eyes, definitely not going to peck out his eyes, and she liked that he didn't brush the hair away from them, as if the loitering locks represented a general comfort with himself and his place in the world.

It had been too long since she'd spent the night with someone: she was confusing a hairstyle for a personality trait.

"Yeah, just water," she said. "Technically I'm working."

"You have a great smile," he offered. "I like your tattoo."

"Thanks." She searched for something to compliment in return. She found it comforting that the man's clothes were more worn–out than hers, but that didn't make it a nice thing to say. She liked his big hands . . . too forward, might scare him off. "I like your"—she frowned—"smile too."

"Aww, thanks!" he said in an exaggerated tween girl voice.

These salt–of–the–earth, take me for what I am types reminded her of rural Michigan, where she still visited her mom every year or so. They usually were good in bed or cooked pancakes in the morning or owned well–trained midsized dogs and had the sense not to bring up politics. That familiarity was what she needed right now.

"What does it represent?" he asked. "The tattoo?"

They both looked down at her forearm, where the delicate line work was partially in shadow. She held out her arm so he could see it better.

She hesitated for a moment and then decided to do something uncharacteristic: reveal her true self. Tonight she wasn't going to let her new admirer get all the working–class street cred; she wasn't going to fulfill anyone's "uptown girl" fantasy, even though it was the image she so meticulously cultivated. It was exhausting busting into every new situation trying to figure out which people were all image and no substance and which were all substance and no style and then categorize them all into different hierarchies and try to figure out where she fit in and who might be on to her in her chic chameleon colors. She wanted to demand that someone respect her for who she really was, not for the confident, fierce statue in tailored pants she pretended to be.

"When I was a kid my dad would say the tattoo on his forearm was the state of Alaska and a mushroom," she said. "I never questioned it, even though they looked like terrible representations. My mom mentioned in passing, years later, that it was actually a prison tattoo of the *Playboy* bunny logo, not Alaska, and a frilly letter *P*, not a mushroom. So in his honor I have the state of Alaska and a tiny mushroom."

"That's heavy," the man said. "I'm Sean." He extended his hand and she shook it.

"I'm Mims," she said. "I like how wrinkly your pants are. They're insistently functional."

Sean laughed. "I'm only in town for a few weeks and I only own two pairs of pants."

"Oh? What do you do?"

He paused. "I'm a photographer in conflict regions. Mostly I've been covering diamond mining recently."

Mother. Fucker. Clearly he was undecided whether to feel modest or proud, let alone whether to present himself as one or the other. The sting of her misappraisal of his social status, one of the few things she was good at, and the fearful–mouse–footsteps feeling of being pulled into an unguarded conversation with someone journalist–adjacent after all, put her back into combat mode.

"You're staff somewhere?" she asked.

"The *World Gazette*," he said. Her gaze ran anew over his unkempt hair and loosely laced work boots, this time with an envious appraisal. Did he let himself look this way because he was so at ease with his accomplishments? Or was it as carefully crafted as her look, an exaggerated "I don't care"?

"The *World Gazette* is nice," she said. She took a sip of water. They were bigger than the *Times* and expanding more each year. "Are you from the Midwest?" Did she at least get that part right?

"Ohio!" he shouted. "The state with the most presidents *and* the most astronauts. What do you do? You said you were working tonight?"

"I did say that," she answered. "You could probably write a modern *Down and Out in London and Paris* sort of thing, but maybe no one would care," she said, turning the conversation back to his sloppy clothes, and doing it in the most intellectually snobby way possible. "People are heartless these days."

"What's that?" Sean asked with a complete lack of sheepishness about his ignorance.

"It's a nonfiction book by Orwell, who was a journalist as well as a novelist. It's an exposé where he's traveling around with hobos pretending to be poor, to see what it was like."

"So maybe you don't love my pants that much after all." He winked.

He was so good-natured; she decided to relent by changing the subject but couldn't bring herself to drop her pedantic tone.

"It's funny, it used to be that struggling novelists became journalists to finance their art. These days journalists still publish a lot of books, but it's more because they have built-in connections in the publishing industry, not because it's the job they'd rather have."

"I read part of a book recently that made a similar point!" he said. "I think the author was saying something like . . . the gig economy and also . . . democratization of culture . . . are tricky."

"Yeah, that's probably my friend Gretchen's book."

"Oh, no way! That's *my* friend Gretchen's book. Don't tell her I didn't read it." He laughed raucously and took a swig of his beer. "I wish you'd let me buy you a drink." He leaned against the bar and flagged over the bartender. Pushing Mims's water glass back across the counter, he declared, "Get this lady a fresh drink—water *with a twist of lemon*! And a splash of lime juice too, please! Fancy it up." He slammed two dollars down on the bar.

"Sure thing, boss." The bartender presented the water and walked away.

"I'm surprised I've never seen you around before." Mims sipped the tart water. If he was friends with Gretchen he was an interesting person; Gretchen was the most successful of her social group and didn't have a lot of time for people who weren't clever or remarkable. Hence her own feeling she had to *earn* Gretchen's friendship.

"Well, I'm in and out of town a lot," Sean replied. "I guess we just never crossed paths somehow."

Mims looked at her knockoff Braun watch. "I actually have to go; there's a show letting out and I have to go get a quote. But now that I know you, I'm sure I'll see you around everywhere."

"Are you going to Gretchen's dinner party thing this weekend?"

"I was considering it." She actually hadn't been invited, but she'd been in self-imposed social exile for so long she wasn't surprised. "Maybe I'll see you there." Mims smiled at him and walked out of the bar.

Whether she attended the dinner or not it would be easy to track his movements now that she knew he existed. Not offering her phone number, and not dawdling long enough for him to be able to ask for it, was her one concession to respectability. She was going to fuck him the very next time she saw him. Not only was he hot, something about sex with a successful man made her feel like she was equally qualified to be successful. As if the universe matched up sex partners by the caliber of their worth as human beings. Most people did end up partnered with someone of the same attractiveness level and socioeconomic status. Mims stepped outside feeling powerful and mostly recovered from her encounter in the back of the bar.

The alley Sammy Sampson was supposed to traverse had splashes of burrito all down the length of it, and refried beans were ground into the pavement like streaks of tracked-out dog shit. Instead of going up to the stage door, Mims staked out one end of the alley, gambling that she'd picked the side he was going to use for egress, and breathed through her mouth. After a few minutes the door swung open and a man emerged. Without looking in her direction, he headed toward the opposite side of the alley from where she was stationed.

"Sammy Sampson!" she shouted. He turned.

"I'm a journalist," she said. "Can I get a quote really quick?"

"Yeah sure," he said, but he continued along his way. Mims picked her way through the alley, marinating in the smell of rotting food. With each step her description of him became less generous. A man of medium build with copper hair became a slight man with thinning hair became a man insensitive to the state of his own fame with a pronounced bald spot and no chance at a Netflix special.

"Yo, Sammy, stop playing hard to get," she said, too harsh, and she twisted her ankle as she said it. Her foot slipped but she didn't fall, and she wasn't hurt, but it was too late and she couldn't feel it anyway because all she felt was crackling–dry fury. He was toying with her because she'd been too familiar when she called out to him; she hadn't shown deference and pretended to be 10 percent starstruck. Mims finally emerged from the alley onto wide and cheerful Eighth Avenue. Sammy had turned and was waiting for her, prolonging the moment, with a big smile on his face.

Lots of people were better than she was, but Sammy Sampson was not one of them. "Do you have any insights, as a fellow ex–famous person, into what lies ahead for your old friend Chuck Shine, career–wise?"

It didn't even take him a second of shock or confusion before he registered the meaning of her words. He was all too ready to hear disrespect and understand it. "Fuck you, cunt," he said and walked away.

Jesus, she was so mean. She needed this job, she needed this money. It paid cash, immediately, and she'd still have to hustle the rest of the week to scrape together funds for toilet paper and MetroCards. *Salvage it*, she thought.

"Can I get a fuck you for Chuck?" she called after him.

He lifted his middle finger in the air as he walked. "Fuck you, Chuck! Drunk prick."

Okay, close enough. Hopefully the magazine would take the quote.

Mims could hear her own breathing. As she was writing down Sampson's exact words, she was already spinning the story of their encounter into something funny she could reel off at the party she might not go to. Midway through zipping the notebook into her purse the blood drained from her fingers and she was unable to tug the zipper all the way closed. It wasn't a funny encounter at all. Sammy Sampson had gone through trial by fire in the entertainment industry and was shown not to be good enough to come out famous, so instead he came out swinging, and the same was happening to her in journalism. She couldn't handle seeing her failure mirrored in Sampson's.

Her angry outbursts had been building for years and had cost her more and more clients, and that was a large part of why she was so desperate for work that she had to slip–slide her way through Shit–Burrito Alley. Mims walked to the subway, lost in unkind self–analysis.

CHAPTER 9:
ROOFTOP II

By the time Mims hung up the phone she had a list of registered honey-bee hives with addresses throughout the five boroughs. Kai had been eager to help but difficult to get off the phone. She'd had to compose an email begging tabloid work while simultaneously mumbling "mm–hmms" into the receiver.

In the afternoon she stepped off the bus into the Brooklyn Navy Yard, shielding her eyes from the sun with her hand. The Navy Yard hadn't actually serviced boats in many years. It was currently an industrial park with the stated mission of assisting small manufacturing tenants to ease their employees into the middle class; the not–for–profit developer also had an eye for sustainability. Mims picked her way through a maze of brick buildings with signs for sprinkler fabrication, textile design, sweater man-ufacturing . . . Her destination came into view: a rooftop apiary. Up an ele-vator ride and a set of stairs was her first beekeeper appointment of the day.

Anna turned out to be young and tousled, an earth–goddess type. She extended a hand ringed by dirt and friendship bracelets. She couldn't be much older than eighteen.

"I've been repotting some plants," Anna said apologetically. In spite of the effort she put into hiding a flare of anger, Mims must have made a face. If she wasn't meeting serious people, she should be looking for gigs that were guaranteed to pay. Time spent on the bizarro honey investigation was all speculative.

"Would you mind opening up one of the hives?" Mims forced a smile. "I'd love to see the honey for myself."

"Of course."

Mims trailed after her, to where the turquoise-and-white-painted hives were clustered.

"When did you first notice the change?" Mims asked.

"Oh, only a few weeks ago, maybe a month. They weren't very active before that because it was cold."

"Any other behavioral or health changes?"

"Not that I can tell."

Anna gestured for Mims to stay put, about ten feet from the hives. She walked the rest of the way alone, slung a hive tool from her belt, and pried open the top of one of the boxes without the benefit of smoke. She wasn't wearing a veil or protective clothing, and her bare arms and legs were dark tan even though it was spring. Mims had dismissed Anna as some kind of rich-familied, yoga-Woodstock showboat, but it was genuinely impressive how at ease she was around stinging creatures. Anna brought back a wooden frame, about six by eighteen inches and very thin, with honeycomb suspended between the edges. Only a few bees clung to it. The comb itself was dull yellow, but the honey was shockingly bright, especially with the sun shining through it.

Mims scanned the skyline, as if she'd see a geyser of red shooting off in the distance like an oil derrick. There was nothing, just a half-finished luxury high-rise, a crane, and a faint septic system smell.

"Do the bees drink the water from the canal?" Mims asked, connecting the smell to its source.

"I suspect not," Anna replied.

The Gowanus Canal was polluted, but it wasn't red. "Maybe the water turns red when it rains? Runoff from the industrial park?"

"They use permeable asphalt so that rainwater can soak into the ground where it lands instead of flowing into the sewers." A bee landed on one of Anna's knuckles as she spoke, and she rotated her hand and arm so that the bee was continually upright as it explored, as if her hand were an M.C. Escher drawing. Anna cooed at the bee as it passed her wrist and then she made a soft trilling sound. "And they grow water–loving plants on the ground and the rooftops. They soak up as much as they can. We serve mother Gaia as well as we're able."

Mims bit her lower lip until the urge to summon Captain Planet had passed.

"That's right, mamma. You're so pretty," Anna said. To the bee. It flew off and she returned her attention to Mims. "Besides, it's been unusually dry—not much runoff into the canal."

"But not unusually dry enough to make them drink the canal?"

"Bees wouldn't be coming from all over the city to drink that. They'd probably just die. There's cadmium in there, and lead. And there are no color changes even after a huge storm when the sewers overflow."

It was delusional thinking that she'd hit the jackpot and solved the mystery at the first stop. "Thank you for your time."

"Do you know what I think it is?" Anna clasped Mims's wrist.

She sensed it was going to be something along the lines of Mother Earth's revenge.

"I think they're eating the rust off the old ships. They're probably missing some essential nutrient and they've turned to eating iron, the way starving people sometimes eat clay earth."

Mims nodded. "Interesting," she said. Mims didn't know much about bees, but she knew they didn't eat rusty boats.

She tried unsuccessfully to fit Anna into her complex mental hierarchy of New York professionals and misfits. Mims couldn't quite grasp how someone could be competent and crystal-healing simultaneously. On the way down the steps to the street Mims made a note to write an article at some point about the Gowanus pollution and the curious rich-person apartment buildings going up in the middle of it.

Then she was back on the bus. She'd brought *A Sport and a Pastime*, but it was a hot day and the bus made her motion sick, so she couldn't read it. It was a long trip into Queens for her next stop to meet a beekeeper named Pete, so Mims spent a lot of it studying the ugly blue pattern of the fabric seats. There was a crusty spot next to her that had clearly at some point been sticky, but now it was just brown with filth. Outside the window Brooklyn neighborhoods sped by, and she tried to distill the essence of each to a one-word descriptor. Warehouses. Children. Brownstones. Cyclists.

As she stepped off the bus in Queens, she got an email alert on her phone. It was a job offer to write film reviews for eight dollars each, screeners or tickets provided free. She responded yes without even researching the company. That was one day of unlimited subway rides per article.

Queens Aerial Gardens loomed above her as she hit send. It was one of the largest rooftop farms in the world, nine stories up and over an acre in area. Their thousands of pounds of soil, lifted by crane a decade earlier, offered up over sixty thousand pounds of organic produce per year. She went inside and rode the elevator to the top.

The online description hadn't prepared her for the reality of it. Mims passed through a world she had barely known existed, through pea trellises and rows of lettuce, drawn to the edge of the roof by the skyline. She moved with urgency, as if she was swimming toward the surface of a lake, racing to burst through its surface before her chest was crushed by the water. If it wasn't for the view of Manhattan anchoring her, she might have forgotten she wasn't on the ground. It was as if this flat roof were the real earth and if you tipped over the edge there was hell below. Scorching hot, concrete hell. It was difficult to process. She loved the city and hated rural life, didn't she?

Mims was apparently alone in her confused unease—photographers, tourists, and volunteers walked about unfazed.

All those times she couldn't find a story it turned out she'd had a hippie-shaped blind spot. If there was a beekeeper niche and a plant keeper niche and a Gowanus niche, what else was out there? She associated her rural Michigan hometown with hardship and a sort of nothingness—no jobs, no education, no sophistication, no parental wisdom, no gluten-free restaurants, no skinny jeans, no *stories* worth telling except about opioids. Whereas the city she associated with complexity and success and everything you could fill yourself up with. It hadn't occurred to her to seek out rural topics in the city. But of course there would be New Yorkers who romanticized rural living, or even genuinely missed it, and they were as likely to read newspapers as anyone else. She'd probably stepped over a Peabody Award on her way to cover a bar opening without ever noticing. Mims turned back from the skyline, mentally prepared this time to behold the lush garden and to allow the faintest nostalgia for the woods of her childhood.

She knew Pete immediately when he stepped onto the roof—he was wearing the full getup of white pants, boxy white top, yellow dishwashing gloves, and veil. Of the three beekeepers she had seen in action, he most looked the part. It made her suspicious he might be compensating for lack of skill. Mims made her way back through the green and brown strips to meet him.

"You must be Mims," Pete said. "Welcome! We're always glad to get reporters, but this is the first time it hasn't been for publicity." His big Bradley Cooper eyes shone through the mesh of veil, his cheerfulness apparently unaffected by the red mystery. "A real story!" he said.

"I . . . yes, nice to meet you, Pete." *A real story.* She relaxed a little. "Which way do we go?" She donned the extra veil and gloves he handed her, but the rest of her body remained exposed.

Pete led the way to the hives, puffed the edges with smoke to calm the bees, and revealed the rows of frames hanging inside.

"Let's peel one open," Pete said. "Hold this a sec." He handed Mims one of the frames of honeycomb and bent over to reassemble the hive before she could refuse and hand it back. Although she was holding the frame at arm's length like a live bomb, she could smell it, and she was sure the bees could smell it. It was sweet and flowery. The comb, held by the topmost edges of the wooden frame, which she held with the barest tips of her fingers, was heavy, like pregnant dog heavy, drooping with potential. She couldn't look away from it.

"Away from the hive though," Pete said, cheerful still. He gestured with his shoulder back toward the main part of the garden. Mims made her way backward toward a tool table near the elevator bank, afraid that if she spun around or walked with the frame out in front of her the air resistance would cause it to break apart. Pete joined her a second later, taking the frame and setting it on the table. He used a long knife to peel away the thin layer of wax capping. He lifted the comb vertical and liquid the color of old blood ran out, brown not red.

"It seems thinner than honey," Mims said, curious. She removed the veil and gloves and smoothed her shirt back into a perfect front tuck, back in control of herself if not her surroundings.

"It is. Something in its chemical makeup doesn't allow it to thicken like honey would. Later this week we're going to put up feeders with sugar water at the opposite edge of the roof. We're hoping that the bees will just frequent that for a while and lay off of the red stuff. Though it's not healthy long term to eat sugar water instead of nectar, and what the bees make out of it the USDA doesn't technically consider honey."

"Why is it unhealthy?"

"Commercial apiaries do it all the time, but sugar water, or high fructose corn syrup, that's what most of them use, doesn't have the same pH as nectar. It's like if a human ate processed food instead of whole foods—it seems to affect their immune system and make them more susceptible to mites."

"Do they *prefer* sugar water over nectar?"

"That I don't know," Pete said.

"Is it worth keeping them if they don't make honey?"

Pete gave her a disappointed–teacher frown. "We keep the bees to pollinate the garden and also just to help out the global honeybee population. Beekeepers wouldn't be harvesting honey in spring anyway, unless it was to steal whatever excess the bees had made last fall and not eaten over the winter. With the new stuff being red, it's safest to just not take any of it."

"Oh."

"I pray this strange–colored honey isn't something serious. Bees pollinate so many food crops, even in these industrialized times. Most people don't realize that. Millions of bees are shipped to California every year by flatbed truck just to pollinate the almond trees."

Mims had to admit that Pete was just as well–informed as Anna and Charlie. She was ashamed of how ingrained the habit of ranking the people she'd met had become. "I guess the world is lucky to have beekeepers as knowledgeable as you," she said.

"It's a learning curve." He shook his head. "My first year here we accidentally froze the bees to death. Three hives worth. We all have successes and failures, you just have to keep moving and doing better."

"Indeed." His words felt like a personalized admonition for her flirtation with giving up journalism for tabloid writing.

The brown liquid had run out of the frame onto the roof and bees were landing at the edge of the sticky pools to sop it back up. It reminded her of dogs re-eating their own vomit.

What did it mean that this honey was brown? Mims had set out on this journey expecting the honey would be either red, like Charlie's in the Lower East Side and Anna's at the Navy Yard, or not–red, as a binary. Charlie had said bees might fly up to five miles for forage but usually stuck to two. The Queens Aerial Gardens apiary was apparently nearing the northern edge of where the red had reached; that would explain why the honey here was more pale and brownish.

"One last question. What do *you* think is causing the honey to turn red?"

"Bodega flowers, maybe."

"How do you figure that?" Mims asked.

"Those flowers aren't really those colors. It's all dye."

"Thank you, Pete." Mims continued on her circuit of the city. She didn't know enough about plants to know how crazy the bodega suggestion was, but it took only a few stops at corner stores to discover that the bouquets displayed out front were sitting in normal–colored water. Stealthily she stuck her finger in the centers of some of the flowers and swirled it around, but the pollen came out yellow, not red.

She went farther north, to a residential hive on a Bronx rooftop, and the honey was completely standard–issue amber. She made her way back down through Queens and Brooklyn and then passed into Manhattan around Fourteenth Street.

She arrived home just after dark, having eaten nothing but a street pretzel all day, and sat down to plot out the locations on a map. She only had twelve data points, not enough to narrow the area sufficiently to show an epicenter. The next day she began the quest again, balking for the second time in two days at the price of an unlimited daily MetroCard. Her feet started to hurt after the first hour.

Her last stop was the green market in Union Square. The sunlight was fading and people were starting to close up shop. She went to the local honey guys, three booths from different apiaries, and all of them were selling candles and wax products but no honey. The previous year's harvest had sold out already. She asked about the red and the locations of their hives and got the names and contact info for friends of friends with unregistered hives. When she'd walked into the farmers market it had had an aura of glowing enlightenment to it, like she was about to have a breakthrough she had earned through two hard days of searching, but she walked out no more certain than when she'd gone in. There were several hundred hives in the city and she'd visited only twenty.

Just outside the green market, near the Gandhi statue, a guy juggled tiny white balls. She didn't stop to watch because she didn't want to pay him. As she walked closer to the subway entrance to go home, past the men sitting at chessboards, one of them called, "Hey, beautiful, you're so sexy, come play me." She turned around and walked the three feet back and kicked his board into the air.

"Go play with yourself, asshole."

Even before she'd opened her mouth, while the black–and–white board was still spiraling through the air, and the pieces seemed suspended in slow motion, she regretted doing it. It wasn't that she was sorry for the destruction, the man deserved what he got, but she had lost control of her temper. As she speed–walked to the subway entrance and down the stairs, a guy with a skateboard lifted his cell phone and started recording her. She was grateful not to hear his commentary.

Mims got back to her apartment exhausted and perplexed, and once again chided herself for slipping into optimism when she knew better. She wasn't any closer to finding the source of the red honey except to say that it was well south of the Bronx. She plotted her new info over the map of New York hoping to see a pattern emerge that was more specific than what she was holding in her head. It wasn't. The source was somewhere below Central Park in Manhattan and Astoria in Queens. She had been unable to locate any hives south of Borough Park, and that honey was still pretty red, so it was hard to say how much farther south the source might go. She was missing data points, but it didn't seem more hive visits and more unlimited MetroCards were going to add much clarity to the map.

She cleared off a corner of her kitchen table and tapped away at the article. It was lackluster and although she left it open–ended, allowing room for a follow–up piece, she was at a dead end and didn't see how to get any farther. The honey in the city was red and people didn't know why or whether it was dangerous. The energy she'd felt being out of her element, and the magnanimous, enlightened feeling of giving "rural" topics a chance, fell away. Kai could still come through with the lab results in the coming weeks, and that would be good for another paycheck, but she didn't just want a check, she wanted to figure it out. *A real story*, as Pete had said, if only to the community of beekeepers who'd been so welcoming and grateful the last two days.

Scowling, she sent the article to Aziz and then skimmed her unread emails.

There was an invite from an acquaintance for a book reading, politics–themed. She deleted it without responding. From Bennie, her supposed best friend whom she hadn't seen in three months: "We're getting a house in Montauk for July—you want in?"

"Who's going to be there?" Mims replied. A stuck–up *no* was better than an "I can't afford it" *no*.

She was watching the last of her youth flow by, not able to jump in and play.

The next email was from *Tween Celebrity Blog*. "Your assignment, should you choose to accept it, is to publish a triweekly gossip piece. Thirty–five dollars per article." She accepted immediately.

Five Weeks Before

CHAPTER 10

THE BASEMENT

It was three thirty in the morning when Teddy hit the off switch and watched the labeling machinery whir to a stop. He checked the equipment four times to make sure it was really shut down. He was afraid he'd missed something and the metal would clang to life in daylight hours, alerting everyone in the maraschino cherry factory above to the secret room below. He walked to the crudely wired light switch by the stairs. The panel extended almost two inches from the wall and he rested his hand on the metal box as he took a last look around. The labeling machine gleamed silver and the room smelled faintly of ink. He felt like Rumpelstiltskin—in the last seven hours he'd spun twenty thousand golden jars of honey from China through the machine, and they'd come out labeled "Made in Vermont" and then shot into neat rows in cardboard boxes.

Teddy groaned when he realized he hadn't shredded the old labels, but he was so tired he forgot again immediately and flipped off the lights with only a vague feeling that he was missing something. He walked up the rough lumber steps and emerged into the truck bay of the garage. He slid the secret panel, which was on rolling casters that peeked out barely a centimeter from their groove in the floor, back into place. He thought he could still smell the ink, and that it was warmer by the door from the machinery below. The air seemed to still buzz from the vibrating metal. It all seemed so obvious and damning.

His pecs clenched involuntarily when the door to the admin part of the building opened and a flashlight shone through.

"Teddy?" a tight, scared voice asked.

"Yeah, it's me," he said. His own voice was hoarse. The industrial section of Sunset Park was far from the bustle of residential streets, so middle-of-the-night people sounds were amplified and frightening, regardless of the fact that the intruders were himself and Omar, the young security guard he'd roped into helping transport the relabeled honey.

"The truck's ready," Omar said. "Sorry I didn't text you back—my phone died. I didn't realize you'd be working on your side project tonight."

"I didn't either. What was supposed to be one shipment got split up into several, and the supplier was vague about exactly how many. This one should be the last one." This was untrue. There was only ever supposed to be one shipment, period. There was going to be one more, please let it be just one more, but he didn't want Omar to spend time anticipating it if he didn't have to. Teddy worried Omar thought he was purposely taking advantage of his immigration status to pressure him into driving the truck, which was riskier for him than it would have been for someone else. Teddy simply hadn't known any other truck drivers to ask. The ones who ran distribution and picked up shipments for Beasley Cherries were gruff older men who wouldn't laugh at jokes; he couldn't broach the subject of tariff evasion with them. Omar showed up each night for his security shift with a crossword puzzle folded in his pocket, and it was always filled in fun colored inks, like purple or orange. As a way of making conversation he'd ask for input on the puzzle even when he already knew the answers.

Omar was a shining beacon of approachability. Plus he worked at the factory overnight anyway, and he had a commercial license that he used to pick up extra shifts running between the factory and the docks when the regular drivers were busy.

"They say the only things you can't cheat are death and taxes," Omar said. "All you have to do now is cheat death."

"It's not even *my* taxes. Sorry to keep dragging you into it."

Omar nodded but he stopped short of saying "it's okay" or "don't worry about it." Instead he said, "Yeah, I noticed construction had started back up again."

It stung that Omar alluded to Teddy's culpability in this mess when it was just as easy, and more fair, to blame the guy who kept sending over additional, un-agreed-to, and unwelcome honey shipments to label.

Tariffs kept honey from China from flooding the US market at prices too low for domestic producers to compete. The honey supplier had smuggled these jars into the United States under the guise of high fructose corn syrup, which carried no tariffs. In exchange for applying Vermont honey labels, Teddy had been paid enough to cover a big chunk of the ballooning overages on the factory upgrades.

"I was so sure I'd sunk my grandfather's business . . ." Teddy felt a painful tingle high up in his nose, but he sniffed it away before it turned into wet eyes. He'd been running the factory for less than two years and he'd already almost destroyed a hundred-year legacy. "I'm way too tired right now," he said, shaking his head. "I'll go turn the lights back on. Thanks for coming out."

Omar and Teddy ran the boxes up the stairs for the next four hours. Teddy grumbled, he hoped comically, about how the men who'd dug out an entire underground room and installed the shoddy overhead lighting could have put in an elevator. Eventually the truck was full.

"It's the same transfer point as before," Teddy said. "The other driver will be waiting."

Omar nodded silently. Soon the honey would be out for distribution by someone who had no idea it hadn't rumbled into town from the Green Mountain State.

"Well, good night," Teddy said. "Oh, actually, here. Figured you might want one." He picked up a jar of honey he'd set near the wall and tossed it to Omar. By the way Omar looked at it Teddy could tell he didn't want it.

He'd tried it already, just to make sure it was safe before sending it off into the world. The supplier had assured him they'd ultra-filtered the honey—if anyone ever questioned the provenance of the jars, there would be no telltale Chinese pollen for the USDA to discover. It would ring alarm bells that it was pollen-free, but aside from that it was perfectly normal.

"You think the ultrafiltration takes out banned pesticides, Mr. Beasley?" Omar asked. It was the first time he'd called Teddy "Mr. Beasley" since his job interview.

"It's just regular honey, Omar," he said, collapsing a bit inside.

Omar put the honey in his pocket, where it bulged awkwardly and insistently, and drove out into morning.

Teddy walked into the main building.

In the restroom he splashed his torso with cold water, not willing to wait for the pipes to heat up. He dried himself with two rough criss-cross swipes of a paper towel, put his shirt back on, and stumbled to the couch in his office, where he was asleep instantly, all signs of guilt erased by exhaustion.

In the morning the day repeated itself, dreamlike, as it had after the previous three shipments. The couch, the blanket, the photos on his desk, and the buzzing notification.

"Shipment received. The money is in your account."

The only thing more nerve-wracking than sending out the honey with Omar in the mornings was seeing the ill-gotten money in his account the next day, like an accusation of amenable consent. From the twenty thousand jars he'd just labeled, he'd been wired a generous 12 percent of shelf price. Almost $10,000.

"Not sure if you received my last emails," Teddy wrote. "We did not agree to these shipments. Do NOT initiate any new shipments." Send.

As the email program on his phone refreshed, a second email came through.

"Shipment arriving Saturday afternoon. Same vessel as shipment two."

Teddy squeezed his eyes shut so hard that the splotchy shapes in the darkness began to converge into painful white, but when he opened his eyes the email was still there.

CHAPTER 11:
DINNER PARTY

Mims shut her laptop on her latest celebrity diet article and walked into the kitchen to find carrot ends and flabby chicken skin in her sink, just as she'd left it that morning. She paused for a moment then continued on without cleaning it up, to the kitchen table where the jar of red honey was sitting. She dragged the table over to the wall with the overhead shelving. Standing on top of the table, she reached behind some plastic crates until her hand found a bottle of cheap, dust-covered wine to bring to Gretchen's party. She'd have to return to society eventually, triumphant or not. From her high-up vantage point, looking down at her sparse but carefully chosen furniture, her apartment didn't seem a glamorous mess so much as just a mess. Clothing lay draped over every surface like wilted soldiers on a too-hot Romantic-era battlefield; she pictured *Raft of the Medusa* but on land.

She jumped down and gathered draft paper from the couch and living room floor and put it in the recycling before changing into her expensive shoes—scuffed, but expensive nonetheless.

An hour and a half subway ride later, Mims arrived outside Gretchen's brownstone. There was a help-wanted sign in the window of the coffee shop next door, and it felt like an accusation of immaturity, pridefulness, denial. There was work available if she'd give up her delusions of being a writer. She gripped the wine bottle tighter and went upstairs in search of the newspaperman and free food.

The crowd was as she'd expected: tattoo sleeves under rolled oxford sleeves and men too young to be drinking scotch sweating into their beards and pressing up their black-rimmed glasses. It was as if she hadn't disappeared for a winter of humiliated wound licking and career pushing; nothing had changed in their lives either. Gretchen had lined up tables of mismatched height for the twenty dinner guests, and a nightstand was serving as one of the seats. Probably because Gretchen hadn't been expecting her until she'd texted that morning.

Someone touched her elbow.

"Hey," Sean said. "I hoped I'd see you here." He was wearing the same pants as the night they met. "Did you get that quote you needed? Anyone I'd know?"

"I did, thanks for asking. And I doubt you would—he's not that famous." She tried to say it in a blasé enough way that it would be ambiguous whether he was actually super famous and she was just being a snob about it.

"Mims!" a short girl exclaimed, too loud, from just a few feet away. Her hair, teeth, tortoiseshell glasses, eyes, and cheekbones all reflected the light as she eased into orbit around Mims and Sean.

"Bennie!" Mims enthused back. Bennie, a Barnard alum, had recently started a travel and food podcast; she was already sponsored and would be internet-famous imminently, and she fully deserved it. Bennie was so enthusiastic about every aspect of life, sublime and foul alike, that Mims could spend time with her almost without feeling judged. She was the person Mims had been most tempted to text from inside her hibernation pit of failure. "This is Sean," Mims said. Sean held out his hand and Bennie placed hers inside of his, rather absentmindedly, and then removed it without shaking. She was too focused on Mims and excited for gossip.

"Did you meet Jessica's roommate?" Bennie asked.

"The fitness model? Yeah. She's the kind of person who pets service dogs," Mims intoned. They were standing by a window and Bennie pulled it open a few inches and lit a cigarette with the end bobbing just outside. Another girl gave her an angry look and moved away from the smoke that drifted inside.

"She looks like a realtor . . . in Texarkana. Those eyebrows." Bennie took a drag from the cigarette.

Sean seemed uncomfortable. "It's a game," Mims explained. "Whoever can make the least insulting comment into the most biting put-down is the winner."

"You look like someone who keeps a bottle of hand sanitizer clipped to his bag," Bennie said, looking him up and down.

Mims laughed. "And you," Mims said, "look like one of those girls who puts her face too close to her friends' faces in photos." Bennie rolled her eyes. "And I'm so glad to see Sarah getting over her eating disorder," Mims continued, nodding toward the newly plump "other woman" Bennie's ex had cheated with. Bennie smirked and Mims realized Sean didn't know the backstory, and perhaps it was an over-the-line comment regardless. His face was a mix of contempt, disgust, and fear.

"The insults game is not for kindhearted men," she said. "I'm sorry you had to see that." She smiled and then bit her lip to stop the smile from getting away from mysterious and into big-toothy territory. He smiled back and she bumped his shoulder gently with hers.

"So what kind of person are you?" Sean asked.

"I'm the kind of person who pushes the close button in elevators." She peered up at him over the rim of her drink.

Gretchen bowled through the middle of their threesome, grabbed Bennie's cigarette, and stubbed it out on the radiator and closed the window. "American Spirit Lights are for pregnant women. You know you don't smoke, Bennie." Gretchen twirled back into the kitchen.

"She's such a good host," Mims said with true admiration.

"She has another book deal," Bennie said.

"I heard."

Mims looked out the window at her reflection with only a dim awareness of the drone and laugh of Bennie and Sean's voices beside her. She'd attended a cheap state school in Michigan on scholarship over nicer out-of-state schools she'd paid forty to eighty dollars each to apply to out of pride but which hadn't offered much financial aid. The harassing collection agency phone calls her mom received a few times a day were what tipped the decision. Freshman year came and Mims commuted an hour each way while living at home. She wrote most of her papers in pen at a desk made of stacked milk crates and a plank of particleboard taken from a busted dresser, and then she copied them over onto a computer at the school library. She couldn't stay at campus late to type the papers directly because the buses stopped running. Due to her only-child status her family wasn't worse off than other, big families in her town. Her family had cable off and on; they went to restaurants on birthdays; and until age fifteen she'd spent most weekend summer days swimming blissfully in frigid local lakes. It was only in comparison to her New York friends that her childhood had been rewritten as harrowing and dramatic.

Midway through her senior year, putting the name of her school on resumes before sending them off, Mims began to reevaluate her choices. Deep Valley was barely a step up from community college. The spring following graduation Mims moved to New York City, or rather the outskirts of the city, expecting to just slip into success, like a woman in an evening gown entering the stream of a party, glittering and carried along by hellos and little kisses on the cheek. In her mind she had earned success already by leaving Michigan when everyone had expected her big leap to the middle class to involve getting a job at the local office park.

The story she'd been telling herself in the six years since arriving in New York was that she wasn't as far along in her career as she should be because she hadn't met the right people—she was naïve not to go to the right college, she hadn't been able to network and make connections, and afterward she hadn't been able to afford to take an unpaid internship. It was a bitter tale she'd been telling herself up until this very moment. Looking around the party, it was hard to miss that as she and her peers tipped over into their late twenties, people around her were becoming successful all the time. She *was* surrounded by the right crowd. The only long-term result of her debt-free lifestyle was that if she ever went missing no one would come looking for her. The reason she hadn't made it in New York lay elsewhere.

"So Mims, what have you been up to all this time?" Bennie asked. "I haven't seen you since winter." There it was. The first of many times she would have to answer this question tonight. *Being lonely; pitching into the void; fortifying menstrual pads with paper towels, origami-style, in public restrooms, to make them last longer; reading Fitzgerald; sleeping twelve hours a night. All in service of holding on to the truth of the statement, "I am a professional writer."*

"Writing articles here and there."

"About what?"

"Corruption, almost. Liquor license stuff. I like the local interest pieces, like . . . caring about people. Bringing individual stories to light." She glanced at Sean. It seemed like the kind of answer he'd want to hear.

"What are you working on now?" he asked. Four minutes too late she thought of a good insult for him. He looked like someone who memorized *X-Files* dialogue.

A text alert sounded from somewhere in Sean's pants region. Mims didn't let her eyes linger too long, following the arc of his hand back up. By the time her gaze reached his face it was doing something she hadn't seen yet—looking sad. "Sorry, guys," he said. "It's just my ex. We recently ended a long distance thing. She's still processing, you know? I want to be respectful but also it's like . . . a lot of processing at this point."

Mims couldn't help but speculate that his comments were meant to telegraph emotional unavailability, but the thought was interrupted by her own phone pinging in her back pocket. She pulled it out to check the text. "Bro!" Sean said. "Do you have an ex too?" His face was back in eagerly-joking mode.

Her text was from Aziz. "The bee article works. What have you got for next week? What I said last time still holds: I'm not going to set space aside for you anymore if you don't use it."

"Please don't call me 'bro,'" Mims said icily. "'Bro' was what men called their male friends or the gruff female friends they weren't attracted to but might fuck drunk during a dry spell. Sean's sparkle dimmed a little, but then he met her eyes and said, "You're right, I won't."

"Ugh, get a room." Bennie set her empty glass on a bookshelf. "So did you used to play sports or something, *bro*?"

It was silly how much contempt they all had for "sports people." A baseball hat meant a guy was unthinking, tribal, and would destroy your living room aesthetic with a giant television.

"I played football in high school," Sean said sheepishly. "Back before I knew I was artsy." He laughed after he said it, like making fun of himself neutralized his lumbering teenage attempts at selfhood, and the belittling word "artsy" deflected potential accusations of having become pretentious. His face blossomed pink like the frosting on a cartoon donut. Mims supposed he was so uncomfortable about his former self because of how it would look if a picture of college–Sean, screaming, beer–chubby, post–keg stand, ever surfaced on the internet. Side by side with his serious work headshots and best grieving face.

It was intriguing though. His current persona was "comfortable with himself" guy—the wrinkled clothes, disheveled hair, casual self-deprecating jokes. It seemed genuine enough—did the self-acceptance just not extend back into his past?

"So just to clarify, do you believe that the lessons learned on the field are applicable to life at large?" Bennie asked. "That's the definition of 'jock,' by the way, so careful how you answer."

"Ah, leave him alone," Mims said.

Sean and Bennie both turned toward her, their expectant faces beaming like full moons. Bennie's was wobbling a little, drunk. "Fine then. Tell us what you're working on, currently, specifically."

"I'm . . ." She should have let Bennie go after Sean.

"My aunt is looking for a personal assistant, like a part–time thing, a few hours a week, if you know anyone—" There was caution in Bennie's eyes, and a kind of shifty searching.

"I'm doing an article about bees in the city for one of the smaller papers. Something is turning their honey red."

"Is that important?" Sean's eyes were bright and he seemed to be genuinely asking, not belittling the topic.

"Potentially. It might be nothing or it might be dangerous." More likely one than the other. "There's this man, a beekeeper named Charlie, who was very shaken up about it."

The music cut out abruptly, to Mims's great relief. She had few further details on the red honey and no ability to answer follow–up questions. "Dinner's ready!" Gretchen announced. Mims took Sean's hand and led him to the table.

Glasses raised to toast. "To Gretchen, congratulations so much on the motherfucking book!" one of the generic bearded men said. A promo editor at a streaming service.

"Thank you," Gretchen replied, luminous and happy. She sat and conversation resumed, but it hadn't reached full volume yet when Bennie called out to Mims from the far end of the table, "And watch for Mims's article coming out, you nonbelievers. She's gonna save the honeybees." Bennie did a sloppy, unacknowledged toast into the air and then drank. Several faces dotted around the table turned toward Mims, and two of them were gossips. *Nonbelievers.* So they did know she was the journalist equivalent of an ambulance chaser.

"It'll be a few weeks, probably," Mims said faux-proudly, but not loud.

"Since when do you care about bugs?" someone asked, but they were far enough away there was no pressure to answer.

"Make sure you don't shut the publisher down this time," Garth, a sound engineer, shouted joyously. He had a fiancée and a starter home in Jersey City, financed by his parents. There was guffawing all around. It was the kind of humiliating attack her fits of rage at the smallest slight were meant to preemptively ward off, but now that the moment had finally arrived she had no riposte at the ready. Her face felt frozen.

But only for a second.

"In a few years I'll be accepting my Loeb and you'll be settled into a numbing suburban existence and cheating on your blown-out, nursing wife." Garth sputtered and left the table, but no one else had the guts to acknowledge what she'd said.

A tray of devils on horseback made a circuit around the table. No one looked at her and she didn't look at anyone, not even Bennie.

As Mims took one of the browned rolls of bacon, its jaunty toothpick aloft like a conquering flag, she had the distinct sense that her skinny hands were raccoon paws, stealing little snacks and unearned friendships alike. She didn't dwell on the thought—her mouth was like a kiddie pool being flooded from below by two garden-hose-force saliva glands. Mims had trained herself not to be ravenous in public and waited until multiple people had finished their appetizers before she lifted hers to her lips. She closed her eyes and breathed in, but in a furtive, shallow way, so that no one would notice her lingering in the smell of the Medjool date and blue cheese cocooned within the salty-crisp bacon. In that abbreviated moment of sensuality she was surprised to find that the bacon was radiating heat, and she could feel it farther and then closer to the skin of her face, then her lips, as she brought it into her mouth, like a tiny bacon sun.

Mims excused herself between roast and dessert and went into the bathroom to borrow Gretchen's nail clippers. She'd accidentally dropped her own into the toilet the month before and hadn't retrieved them, and while she'd been filing her fingernails weekly, her toenails had gotten long and jagged.

How could she ever pretend she was too good for a nowhere piece about insects? She should be grateful to be publishing in a newspaper at all.

With each angry click of the blades she counted off the woodsy activities she'd spent her childhood avoiding, starting from age six, at great cost to her social standing among the other kids, out of an innate sense that she was the kind of girl who should have been born in a big town, next to an old library (a library like you might find in a castle, not the way libraries really looked). She was meant to be cultured and metropolitan. Lightning bugs; spider-infested club houses; digging holes; BB gun squirrel chases; assembling two-dollar model cars from the grocery store to use for target practice in the lumpy field at the end of the road; picking produce at the area farms for a few unscheduled hours at a per-pound rate alongside the laborers from Mexico to get money for candy; deer (cold) and duck (wet, cold) hunting; the clearing in the woods where the boys set off illegal fireworks; camping, always in cotton street clothes. To say nothing of her refusal to help pull roadkill clear of the lane or Pine-Sol away the scent trail of ants campaigning their way through the kitchen. And in the end she'd landed here, with red bees.

When she got back to the table there was a small pot brownie at her place setting.

"I'm actually going to take mine to go," Sean said as she sat. "I'm still super jet-lagged. But it was really great running into you again. I hope I can see you again soon." The hair was tumbled on his forehead again and he still didn't seem bothered by it. She pushed her own hair behind her ear to compensate. She suspected he was leaving because he didn't want to be seen with her after what she'd said to Garth. "Can I get your number?" he asked.

She stared down at the brownie for a long three seconds before accepting that the idea of how she thought she'd move through this social space tonight was so at odds with how she'd actually navigated it. She was not going to leave as a conquering hero, to be fucked into peaceful, dreamless slumber. But the *next* time they met she'd make it happen. She reached for his phone. "I'll enter it."

When Mims got home she tried to convince herself that her threshold of what topics were beneath her was arbitrarily set, but she could see the boundary clearly and knew that it wasn't. She'd already debased herself in so many ways. By taking tabloid work, for example. But those jobs were tangential to something that did interest her: entertainment and celebrities. It was like working in catering when you really wanted to be a chef, as opposed to working in printer sales when you really wanted to be a chef. The community board story, the possibility of it anyway, had *interested* her. Politics, crime, travel *interested* her.

She would keep trudging forward on the bee story for Charlie's sake, if Kai got back to her. Aziz could print it or not, if the information came in after the one week deadline had passed. After that, she was going to follow where the money led her. If that meant sinking fully into the swamp of celebrity gossip, so be it. She wouldn't have anything to answer for at the next dinner party if she showed up well-fed and luminous with success. Having one foot in journalism and one in paid writing wasn't working. She had to choose.

"Will you marry me?" Sean asked before downing a shot of garlic-infused vodka.

"So that means you agree it would be nice to retire to France one day?"

It was the second time he'd asked her to marry him tonight, their first date, and as a flirting tactic it made her uncomfortable. Her initial attraction was in large part due to his wide-eyed earnestness, and she fully expected to become that dark-edged fling he still jacked off to in his retirement years, but surely he wasn't joke-admitting that he liked her *that* much. They'd barely broken the surface of Lake Small Talk. Or was he *pretending* to like her more than he did to get her into bed, completely missing the obvious telegraph of her overnight bag-sized purse? Even if that was the case, she wanted more substantial, sincere, and specific compliments. She was annoyed also that his proposals were a bit thrilling, and she told herself that was just her ego acting up. She was not at risk of becoming a romantic. Especially not for a man who lived on another continent and with whom she had a professional mismatch the likes of which hadn't been seen since Jennifer Garner and Scott Foley . . .

"Fields of lavender, fresh tomatoes in the French countryside," Sean was saying. "Who wouldn't want some peace and tranquility? You should drink yours or I'm going to be the only one reeking of garlic."

She'd been thinking Paris, not Provence. Mims took a sip and set the glass back on the table. "I can't drink this."

The waitress came over and asked in Russian how they were enjoying their drinks. At the far end of the bar a woman in enormous earrings settled in at the piano. The Russian Prince restaurant lived up to its name. None of the Russian patrons, all middle-aged, seemed to notice that the gold veins in the marble tabletops were fake, nor did they seem to notice the dust on the kitschy chandeliers. She wondered if she and Sean were interfering with the others' ability to enjoy the illusion of opulence and importance. They were both dressed casually and perhaps laughed a bit too enthusiastically at each other's nervous jokes, the way strangers about to leap too soon into intimacy do. The Russians had as much right to pretend they were fancy with their piano bar as she did with her tailored clothing, and she wished she'd worn a dress for them. She hadn't worn one for Sean because she didn't want to look like she was trying.

"The drinks are wonderful, *cpaceeba*," Sean assured the waitress. He turned to Mims. "Midtown isn't all bad. Where do you see stuff like this in Williamsburg? And my hotel looks like some kind of eighties coke den. The carpet is animal print. It's great."

"I would have to judge that for myself," she said, inching her leg closer to his under the table.

"Let's get out of here?" he asked.

As they walked together under the red neon of Broadway, Mims bumped her shoulder into Sean's and he bumped hers back. Occasionally they passed a clump of tipsy, insomniac tourists, but it was late and mostly they were alone. Midtown was as Midtown as ever—dead and vibrant simultaneously.

"When do you leave?" Mims asked.

"Two Tuesdays from now. I'm going back to Yemen."

She glanced sideways up at his face, but his eyes were turned to the ground. It was disquieting to think of this sweet jock of a man jostling his way through collapsed streets with a camera around his neck.

"I like that you're brave," she said. "I like that you asked me on a date with a phone call instead of a text and didn't try to play it off as 'hanging out.'"

Sean smiled down at her and then kissed her lightly. "I can't wait to fuck you," he whispered as he pulled away. So that answered that—they'd have an uncomplicated affair not ending in marriage, just as she'd originally intended. At least she wouldn't have to feel guilty later breaking his heart.

The alcohol hit him in the elevator. By the time they got into bed it was clear his clothes weren't coming off. They lay facing each other in the deep pillows with their knees touching, whispering about whatever Jungian beasts ranged into their minds. He'd liked *Blues Clues* best, she'd preferred

Dora. She saved sea glass instead of shells from her infrequent trips to the beach; she relished the crushing feeling cold water brought when you dived in. He always asked for ice in his water, even in developing countries. That thought led to a flooded riverbank, his first assignment overseas.

"I was fine until three," Sean said, his eyes tearing, "and then I was fine again until the body count got to nineteen. I don't know why that number."

His eyes dried again, as he described seeing a father and son reunited after an insurgency, riding shotgun with an ambulance driver, watching women emerge from a voting booth for the first time.

Back to breakfast cereals, circulation socks on transcontinental flights, first books they read that had sex scenes, then Charlie's red bees, their stomachs as neon as Times Square outside Sean's hotel window. She almost but then didn't tell him how diminished she'd felt when she'd taken the job. She knew it didn't make sense and couldn't fully untangle why her self-worth would be proportional to the glamour and social status of her subjects. "Charlie's like a piece of Ikea furniture," Mims said instead. "He's sturdy where he is, but he can't move. He'll fall apart if he tries to start over upstate. Do you ever think of our parents being that frail?"

"My parents met in Edinburgh on July 15, 1994," Sean said. Mims blinked in surprise.

"Wait, let's stop there a moment," she said.

"No, listen," he slurred.

"Your parents met *after*—"

"Listen!" he said with the urgency of a kindergartener with a story to tell. He scooted his pillow a little closer to hers.

"—after I was born, " Mims finished.

"And they were married on July 20, 1994 in Cleveland," he said. "They're still together." He closed his eyes and his breathing slowed.

She ran her fingers through Sean's tangled hair. She was twenty-seven and he was younger than she was by almost a year and had accomplished infinitely more with his career, a career that seemed to be powered by a genuine drive to help people. Perhaps all his good fortune sprung from that initial parental union of love and certitude. She couldn't tell how much of her attraction was uncomplicated lust and how much was a desire to experience his successes vicariously. He fell asleep with her still smoothing his hair.

She woke him a few hours later with a kiss and a hand against his thigh. He obliged her and was more tender than she expected; afterward she lay calculating how many more times they could have sex before he left the country. Mims was almost asleep when a bright light flashed on from the other side of the bed.

"Are you really checking your phone right now?" It wasn't yet six in the morning.

"You know what it's like. We're firefighters. We have to know what's going on in the world."

"We're not really like firefighters. Unless a firefighter's job is to watch the flames and scream really loud hoping someone will come and put the fire out. So basically we're more like reporters reporting on a fire in the hopes that firefighters will show up."

Sean looked crestfallen, his shoulders actually stooping.

"Still a valuable service," she added. She was always insulting people without meaning to. Or maybe she *was* always meaning to insult people, but it was because she had a quick temper and a fragile ego, not because she truly wanted to hurt them.

"I'm super awake," he said. "Jet lag. I'm going to go into the office and get some work done."

"Do you want to wait an hour and get breakfast first?"

"Let's hang this weekend," he said without turning to face her as he loped toward the door. "Sorry to talk your ear off last night. There's yogurt in the mini–fridge." He wasn't fully in his clothes yet.

"Wait, I'll walk out too!" Mims said, scrambling out of bed. She didn't want to part without smoothing things over. "There's this patisserie right down the street. It's so early there won't be a line. You have to try it while you're in New York."

There had been a buzz since celebrity chef Gerard Babineaux opened his new place in the fall, debuting his signature pastry, *le baiser de l'abeille*. Customers lined up before dawn each day, waiting to order the baklava-like layers of dough. Each *baiser* was intended to be consumed in exactly five bites, and according to *Grub Street*, each layer of miraculously dry and flaky pastry floated like a brittle tectonic plate over a razor-thin film of honey. He charged twenty-four dollars each and there was a limit of one per customer. Mims had wanted to go in the fall, when it was new and only the au courant had been, but she hadn't been able to afford it.

As a gesture of goodwill it seemed grand enough.

"I guess yeah, if it's on the way," Sean said. He stood with his hand on the door handle as she slipped into her shoes and twisted her hair into a messy topknot.

Her spirits brightened as they approached the line, which was only five people deep. There was one tourist in puffy white running shoes and an asymmetrical Midwestern haircut, but there was also a skinny couple in all black speaking Dutch and two women who looked like they could be local foodies or bloggers, midriffs and white teeth bared in the predawn light as they took selfies. Ten more people arrived in the first minute of their waiting, and as the sign switched to "ouvert" and the door to the bakery unlocked and opened, her chest bubbled over with excitement. "You're about to see what my kind of honey is all about."

Sean was standing far from her and looking at his phone. Something had gone really wrong already between them and she wasn't sure if it was recoverable. She tried to mirror his apparent interest level by increasing the distance between them as they stepped inside.

The walls were painted matte gray, the shine saved for the gold running along the edges of the pastry cases. The glass was so spotless and non–reflective it seemed you could just reach inside and grab one of the colorful desserts, lined up in neat rows like identical runway models one after the other after the other. The woman behind the register wore her hair in dramatic, oversized braids. A man with deep–set eyes and an embroidered name tag that read Gerard welcomed the crowd with a dramatic bullfighter sweep of his arm. They both wore trim, fashionista–only jumpsuits. Mims was thrilled to catch a glimpse of Gerard Babineaux himself.

An elaborate sign next to the *baiser* display claimed that the desserts were made with only local New York City honey. "Bullshit," she blurted out. She couldn't help showing off. "I would bet money they're not."

Gerard's gaze followed them as they journeyed toward the front of the line, as if they were potential shoplifters. Sean was looking at the pastry case in a bored sort of way and didn't seem to notice.

"How can I help you?" the woman asked.

"These look really sweet," Sean said, gesturing at everything.

"We'll split it." A relief, since it would be cheaper than buying one for each of them. Half an apology pastry was plenty; she hadn't been *that* mean about the firefighters. "One *baiser de l'abeille*, please," Mims said. The pastry chef was still looking at them, hovering behind the register. The woman behind the counter handed Mims a folded black square of a box with little handles on the top. Mims dug through her purse for her wallet with one hand. The press badge flopped out onto the counter.

"I'll get it," Sean said. He extended his credit card. Mims hoped he didn't realize what the badge was—she was carrying it around like an amulet, or worse, a soothing security blanket.

"You're press?" Gerard's eyes were black pools surrounded by white.

"Him too," she said automatically, and pointed to Sean with the box. His credentials legitimized hers.

Gerard beckoned them toward the rear of the bakery, behind the counter, and turned without waiting to see if they'd follow.

Mims pushed through the folding countertop, eager to be invited into the realm of elite journalistic intrigue, but when she turned to hold the countertop flap open for Sean his face was flushed with embarrassment. "This is going to be something stupid," he mouthed.

They walked past stainless steel racks of trays. Gerard's office was small and had no door; she could see back through the shelves and rows of cooling pastries to the front of the store and the line of people. Gerard sat at a tiny desk, Mims across from him, and Sean leaned against the doorjamb. She tried to tamp down her excitement into a blasé cool. She set the pastry box on the floor.

"I would like to head off your investigation into the *baiser*. Can I say things off the record and they won't be printed?" Gerard asked, imperious.

"Yeah, sure," Sean said.

"Okay, this is: Off. The. Record." The chef said it like a magical incantation. Mims winced. Sean had been right to be skeptical. Gerard thought they were doing a hit piece on his local honey claim.

"I resent having to justify the price of the *baiser*," Gerard began. "I've done so in part by pointing out, in various interviews, the cost of New York City honey, the flavor of which has no equal. On the record, that bit, actually. Off the record: this spring there's been a dearth of farmers market honey. Or that can be on too. Off: I began experimenting with store-bought stuff. My assistant came back with a new brand, very cheap, and while ordinarily I would have poured it out, I was overwhelmed with a desire to play the mad scientist, to push my culinary genius to its limit, as it were."

Sean looked at his phone. Gerard didn't seem to notice. He was animated, leaning over the small desk.

"I spiked the yellow slop with an infusion of peat moss and coffee grounds to capture the *je ne sais quoi* essence of the city. The smell was a perfect match. But the honey was too thin, too cloying, missing the granular texture that is sensed more than felt, and it soaked through the *baiser* dough. I was a little apprehensive at first but emboldened when the plebeians in line didn't notice. I relented after a few days and added a bit of cornstarch to the honey mixture to firm it up. How can I serve soggy, limp–dick *baiser* even if no one can tell the difference but me?" Gerard tented his fingers at either edge of his desk. "So how do you explain why the honey behaved so strangely to begin with? This part is on the record: The honey . . . is fake. It's not honey at all."

"Rough," Sean said.

"Excuse me?" Gerard asked.

Mims pushed the specially folded box under her chair with her foot, like that would hide that she was one of the plebeians. She knew it was better not to get excited about anything, pastries, sex, and rendezvous with famous people all included, until the outcome was clear.

Gerard offered her his business card and she took it. "I'll trust you'll contact me when you find something, before it's printed," Gerard said. "The brand of honey is Vermont's Wonderful."

Gerard was trying to distract from his own deceitful honey practices by claiming there were bigger fish to fry.

"So in exchange for this hot tip, you're expecting Mims not to write an article calling out your non–local honey?" Sean asked. He was in a lighter mood now, smirking down at her. For the first time since he'd sobered up, she felt they were in cahoots again. "If it turns out to be a big case maybe we'll need a team on it."

"This is bigger than me." Gerard stood with a shooing motion, clearly not sensing that they didn't believe him.

Mims caught the chef's sleeve as they re-emerged into the main area of the bakery. "Wait, hold on. I can't eat this," she said, gesturing down at her pastry box. She looked to the racks of pastries and pointed. "Are these éclairs real?"

"But of course," Gerard replied. "Made with the finest organic cream."

Mims used tongs to grab two and drop them into the box atop the defunct *baiser*. After a short hesitation she took a third and then reclosed the lid.

Sean and Mims pushed through the crowd and back onto the sidewalk. In the end she did like having insider knowledge, even if the insider knowledge was that the chef was a weirdo. She turned to Sean with the beginnings of a smile just as he started to speak.

"Wow, so it was your kind of honey after all."

She felt her face go cold and the rest of her hollow. *Your kind of honey* meant low-quality, fake? Or he meant because Gerard had turned out to be a character, like Charlie, and her stories involved only outsider types? Or it was because demanding free éclairs was trashy . . . For once angry words didn't spring from her mouth fully formed like war-waging Athena. It was like the fuck-yous and you're a cliches and your pants are uglies and you lucked into your positions got clogged, all trying to escape at once.

"Well, I gotta get to the office," he said, looking at his phone, distant again after their shared moment in the back of the pastry shop. He smiled though and waved, as if he'd done nothing wrong.

As she fingered the top of the pastry box, Mims considered the refined drape of her black clothing and the thin gold chain lying feather-light and shiny against her neck and how Sean couldn't possibly have the x-ray ability to see the rottenness of the insides of things, no matter how much time he'd spent with tragedy and killers. If he hadn't been told, he wouldn't have known about the store-bought honey inside the *baiser* any more than she would have. And he couldn't see inside of her. Maybe by "your kind of honey" he'd only meant that Gerard's choice to ditch local honey was prompted by the same red she was already investigating. She took a bite of éclair, chocolate and lightly sweetened cream melting on her tongue. Not everything was hiding trash inside. She looked in the direction Sean had walked, but he was already out of sight.

Exposing Gerard was a salable topic. However, since her scuffle with Sammy Sampson she'd been rethinking the glee she got from unmasking fakers.

A few hours after arriving home Mims decided to be mature and text Sean.

"Hey, things felt weird this morning."

"Sorry, just jet lag. Dealing with some stuff with my ex. I'll text you after work tonight."

CHAPTER 12:

SUGAR IS SUGAR

Teddy watched as Omar backed the truck out of the garage. It was Saturday and no one was at the factory. When the truck was clear of the overhang Omar got out and then came around and lifted the gate to check that it was empty, as was the usual protocol before going to pick up a shipment. This would be the fifth honey run in the last two months. Four more than Teddy had agreed to, and the interval between them was getting shorter. Omar and Teddy stood silently looking into the empty truck bed.

"Well, I guess it's time to pick up the 'last shipment,'" Omar said finally. He slammed the gate down and Teddy jumped and then stiffened, trying to hide that he'd been startled.

Omar swatted absently at the bees that flew past his head in the dull heat. He inadvertently hit one and it bounced softly away then ricocheted against Teddy's thumb.

"Fuck!" Teddy shrieked. Pain radiated out from his knuckle.

"Oh, sorry man," Omar said. "It definitely meant to get me, not you."

Teddy started to pull the stinger out of his thumb with the nubby, nail-chewed fingers of his other hand.

"Stop!"

Teddy looked up.

"You'll squeeze more venom out of it," Omar said. "Scrape it out with your fingernail."

"I don't have fingernails." The knuckle on his thumb swelled red.

"It looks like a baboon's ass."

Teddy lifted his hand again, ready to tweeze with his fingers.

"Give it to me," Omar commanded; he grabbed Teddy's hand and scraped the stinger out. Teddy was grateful for the moment of caring, grateful also that there was one other person in the world who shared the burden of knowing about the illegal honey.

"You know crows recognize human faces and bring presents to the ones that feed them?" Teddy asked. "These bees know what we're doing." He was only half joking, testing the waters with his theory.

"The jars are sealed," Omar said. "They can't smell the honey."

"They can see what's in them," Teddy retorted. "If they can see the colors of flowers they can see the color of honey."

"Listen, man, you're losing it. I don't want to do this anymore. You drive the truck, I'm going home." Teddy was stunned that Omar would quit so abruptly over his comment, but in a way it was a relief to hear he was "losing it"; at least that meant the bees weren't *really* after him. Omar and Brittany-Lynne had both confirmed that they were just regular bees.

"They won't let me into the marine terminal without a driver ID," Teddy said.

"They don't look closely. We look enough alike, and they recognize the truck." Teddy was Jewish but looked Arabic enough to be stopped at airports, in spite of his Americanized last name. In the context of New York

City, his trim beard and penchant for flannel shirts made him look like a racially ambiguous hipster lumberjack. Omar had dark skin and no beard, but they had a similar build, aside from Omar being shorter. Their faces were completely different.

"That's not allowed," Teddy said.

"What, *now* you're concerned about doing something illegal?"

Teddy gave him his most forlorn, dignified look.

"Don't act like this situation has *befallen* you and you didn't agree to it, man. I've got Amazon packages coming today that I gotta wait for. I'm going home. This is nothing but bad vibes."

"Give me the key." Teddy extended his swollen hand, hoping Omar would take pity on him and relent. Instead he gave him the key and his marine terminal ID. This was never going to work. Teddy reached forward with his other hand and grabbed the crossword from Omar's shirt pocket. "I'll give this back on Monday."

Teddy jumped into the cab of the truck and displayed the crossword prominently on the dashboard and then turned it at a slight angle so it looked less posed. He wished Omar wore a signature hat that he could have borrowed. Teddy took a deep breath, feeling the hot plastic seat burning the backs of his arms, seeing the dust motes, listening to traffic in the distance. He'd heard grounding yourself in sensory perception could stave off panic attacks. He'd heard it from the internet while researching "going crazy hallucinating bees." With a sharp exhale he stuck his head out the window. Omar was already halfway to the fence. "I'm sorry, Omar," he called after him. "You won't hear another word about it. I got this."

The Red Hook Marine Terminal was just over two miles from Beasley Cherries; it sprawled over eighty acres but was meticulously signposted. Teddy drove as slowly as someone on weed so he could be sure to avoid making wrong turns and appearing lost.

Two men were waiting for him in the loading bay. One had a pot-belly and a scowl and the other had the Long Island look that cops have, but he wasn't dressed like a cop. "He's not a cop," Teddy told himself.

He jumped down from the truck and the potbelly man gestured "get over here" with his head. He handed Teddy a pink slip of paper.

"What's this?" Teddy asked without looking at it.

"It's a customs slip," the man said.

Sometimes Teddy tried to talk in dreams and found himself unable to fully articulate his lips, paralyzed by sleep. This was like that except the effort of trying didn't wake him up. Customs didn't check every bottle or even every shipment that came through the docks; they did spot checks. It was bad luck that the honey had been chosen out of all the thousands of goods. His hand throbbed. The bee sting was bad luck too.

The word "luck" had gone from meaning atheistic coincidence to a solid, real thing, like what evil eye amulets guarded against. "Oh. What's it say?" he ventriloquized softly through his teeth.

"Just that it was inspected. There's an on–dock customs exam station here. They do a quick chemical analysis to confirm it is what it says it is. It takes no time at all. You want to see it?"

Teddy looked down at the paper with unfocused eyes. "I didn't bring my reading glasses," he lied. "What does it say?"

"Nothing." The man was confused. "It just says they examined it." There was a crash behind him and Teddy turned to find a forklift backing up to his truck. It started loading the pallets of honey. Teddy looked down at the slip again. His arms were cold and he was pretty sure if a sword sliced him he wouldn't bleed; all the blood was pooling in his fight–or–flight muscles. It didn't make sense. The exam station should have found that the jars labeled high fructose corn syrup were actually something else. They were honey pretending to be high fructose corn syrup.

"Hey, are you allergic? Maybe you need a doctor?" Potbelly man gestured to Teddy's hand.

"No, it's just swollen. I'm good. Thanks for this," Teddy said, waving the paper. He walked back to the truck needing to pee.

Teddy had a lot of time to think over the next few hours as he carried boxes down the stairs into the basement labeling room. He wished Omar were there to keep him company, even if he didn't want to help with the boxes.

He sat down on the back of the truck and pulled the customs inspection form out of his pocket to read it again.

He thought back to the Food Suppliers Sourcing Fair in Hong Kong the previous winter, not long after he'd taken over the company. Teddy was at the fair to introduce himself face-to-face to old Beasley contacts as well as to seek out new partnerships. He remembered impressions more than specifics. The men behind the corn syrup supplier his family had been using for years turned out to be high-energy, heavy drinkers in bold-colored ties.

"My brother's beekeeping operation had a bumper crop," Wang Jie had said. That's how it started. They'd wanted to make the most of this one-time good fortune. The atmosphere of the brightly lit restaurant next to the convention center, raucous with the joy of men making deals, permeated their brainstorming session. The Chinese businessmen paid each other in cash as a matter of course, and Teddy marveled as suitcases full of it were passed from hand to hand across tables. The place had the energy of a casino where everyone was winning.

"We'll ship the honey to you labeled as corn syrup for the cherries. There's nothing to tip off customs except that it's in small glass jars instead of bulk containers, but the small size will make relabeling easier for you," Jie had said.

They'd all laughed deciding between calling it "Vermont" honey or "Maine" honey as Teddy explained the subtle differences between the states.

"We're the true free-market capitalists!" a middle-aged man with a diamond-studded watch had declared. "The import tariff on honey from China is unfair, meant to discourage competition."

A round of shots was delivered to the table and they all toasted; Teddy remembered to do as Matt had told him and hold his glass lower than the older men's, as a show of respect.

"But by the time you build the room for the relabeling equipment and pay me for my part, will it really be worth the trouble?" Teddy had asked.

"Even a little extra money is worth it," Jie had responded. "My brother has been struggling for so long; with this boost he could expand his operation and have a strong company to pass on to his son." It was an impulse Teddy understood—modernization and expansion in order to create a stable legacy into the future. The missed tariff revenue would be nothing to the United States government, a drop in the bucket. And one honey shipment was hardly going to undermine American beekeepers' prices. But to Jie's brother it would mean everything.

Jie had been so casual about the whole thing and so at ease, it had seemed as illegal as overstaying a parking meter, or as the knockoff handbag he'd bought for Brittany-Lynne that morning, more mischievous than sinister.

After the fact, it turned out the beekeeper wasn't Jie's brother, it was a cousin. Friend of a friend's cousin. It was a guy named Lin that Jie had never met, he'd just been paid to make an introduction. Jie took no responsibility, but by then it was too late. When the unexpected costs at the cherry factory continued to mount, Teddy realized he'd painted himself into a corner by accepting even the first payment and transferring it into the cherry factory's accounts. There was no way to apply for loans or ask for help without someone getting suspicious.

It really was high fructose corn syrup, not honey at all. He'd been scammed, and the end consumer had been double scammed. The cost of corn syrup from China was a fraction of the cost of honey from China, which was a fraction of the cost of honey from Vermont. The loop of denial followed by betrayal and then sorrow and then fear hadn't slowed any since the first time he'd read the customs form. Teddy folded it into a perfect square and put it back in his pocket and then loosened his fear–stiffened legs with more trips up and down the stairs.

He walked up to the Sunset Park library just before closing, not wanting to have the query "punishment for evading import taxes versus punishment for selling high fructose corn syrup as honey" pop up in his browser history at home. He realized on the steps that a library, being full of government computers and possibly monitored, was a terrible place to perform the search. He should also leave the neighborhood, he berated himself. He took the subway to Midtown and bought a cheap tourist hoodie, pulled it down past his eyebrows, and went into an internet café.

An email alert blinked on his phone as he was reading about "adulterated food products." "There is another shipment arriving in two weeks. Please confirm. Details to follow." Teddy deleted it with a slight flutter in his heart; he wasn't going to accept any more shipments. What was Lin going to do about it, come over from China and make him?

He composed an email to his sister asking for an update on her arrival. He decided it sounded too needy, erased it, and sent a text that said "ETA?" instead. He looked back to the rental screen and was distracted by a caption below the food article. "Stampeding Elephants Stop Rampage to Comfort Crying Child." He hid his swollen hand in the front pocket of the hoodie and leaned in to read. Some animals really could read human emotions, and perhaps that included remorse . . .

CHAPTER 13:
MARLOW'S ROAD TRIP

Marlow passed the sign so fast she didn't have time to read it. She was on a two-lane highway beneath a canopy of redwoods with no traffic coming, so she glided to a stop and made a U-turn. It was the right choice—Astoria, Oregon, was the direction she wanted. She knew from the Oregonian she'd met at a rest stop outside Whitehorse, Canada, that the little houses would be a cluster of pastel against the dark sea and that the continuous truss bridge across from Washington was the longest in North America.

Just after three thirty she arrived into town and parked her truck in a dirt lot halfway between a gas station and a bar. She went into the gas station first. The lanky clerk who rang her up looked maybe nineteen, but she couldn't tell. Everyone under twenty-five was an undifferentiated mass of youth. The clerk's eyes were so clear and blue, so beautiful, they seemed swapped with those of a fairytale princess.

"Where you headed?" he asked. He'd seen her Alaska plates.

"I'd really like to take the Pacific Coast Highway south," she said. "To the bottom of California."

"I hitchhiked it last summer," he said. "You're going to love it."

"Yeah. I'm supposed to be headed east though. We'll see. Maybe I'll drive half of it and then turn."

The clerk smiled placidly, tan and unlined. She walked out with her bag of car snacks. Marlow tossed the bag into the front seat through the open window and went into the bar. It was a shame to be in a dark, windowless place when there was so much beauty outside, but the beauty was intoxicating. She'd been in it all day and in love with it and couldn't focus out there. She pulled out a map and unfolded it at the empty bar. She ordered a Dark & Stormy. Staring at the map didn't make the lines move the way she wanted—the Pacific Coast Highway definitely would not take her any closer to New York.

She hadn't counted on her wanderlust reemerging with such ferocity. She missed learning strangers' life stories, sharing a connected moment, then moving along to the next town or state or country.

Marlow was still leaning over the map, white hair billowing around her like a prized angora bunny, dark, bushy eyebrows frowning down at the highways, an hour later. The line on the map wouldn't move. In one direction lay adventure and in the other lay a dreary factory and a pile of unpleasant conversations. She'd already been driving for ten days and was barely farther east than when she started. The door to the street opened behind her, letting in a blast of sunshine, and then swooshed shut just as quickly.

"Hey!" the boy from the gas station said. He was young enough that seeing the same outsider twice in one day was unexpected and exciting.

"Hi," she said back. "My name's Marlow."

"I'm Cordy." He must be older than nineteen then, to walk into a bar so casually.

They chatted about the sea and how salt corrodes metal, how blood tastes like metal, and how Astoria should have a parade if the population ever broke ten thousand. Tok's population was something like twelve hundred.

"I want to see how the locals live," Marlow said.

"I'm a local," he said. "Come see how I live."

Worship, tame, cower. Most men reacted to her in one of those three ways; even the young ones still did. A lifetime in the sun and now five years in the cold and wind had weathered her face. Her hair had gone prematurely gray. She felt wild and part of the north. And still Cordy would fall into the worship category if she gave it long enough. Because of her "energy." It was preferable to those who were terrified or the ones who tried to fix her, but still off-putting.

They stepped out into the sunlight. If not for the existence of Teddy and New York, at this very moment she would be at peak happiness. Possibilities and choices and new tastes, breezes, caresses, bird trills stretched out before her like infinite trees in a forest, beckoning her deeper. Oysters! The truss bridge! Instead of exploring the misty goody bag of the Pacific Northwest, she was supposed to drive to Brooklyn and teach her adult brother to Google "how to power-wash cherry vats," or whatever it was he needed help with.

Marlow gave Cordy a ride home; along the way he pointed out the Astoria Column and the derelict Queen Anne–style Captain George Flavel House. When they got to Cordy's she came in for the tour. He showed, without realizing he was showing her, the Christmas lights over the entrance to the kitchen, the video game console, the refrigerator containing only taco ingredients and condiments. She ran her hand along the smooth, unpolished banister from the upstairs bedroom to the plywood living room floor buried beneath off-white wall-to-wall carpet. She held a clean bath towel to her nose and it had the same unclean mildew smell all boys' towels had.

"What are you doing?" he asked.

She smiled back. "Nothing."

The tour ended on the rough checkered couch in the living room.

"I love that there's a beer bottle in your bathroom trashcan."

"Sometimes I'm fancy," he said. "I like to drink beer in the shower."

"I wouldn't call that 'fancy.'"

"I imagine I'm drinking it under a hot waterfall."

She clapped her hands, delighted, and let out a big belly laugh.

"Now I'm embarrassed," Cordy said. He hid his head under the blanket that had been half balled, half draped over the back of the couch.

"Don't be," she said.

She was distracted. Instead of being fully immersed in the weirdness of his drinking under a hot beer falls, or being flattered that a woman her age was in his home at all, she was feeling guilty and suspecting her subconscious had an ulterior motive for her quick fascination with Astoria, Oregon, and its inhabitants.

"Do you like the house?" he asked.

"I do," she said.

"You could stay here tonight." He pulled the blanket down off his face, which was almost not-red, but Marlow was too busy having a reluctant epiphany to really give much consideration to Cordy's offer.

She was struggling with getting closer to New York, not with leaving the splendor of Oregon behind.

Her so-large-and-painful desire to reunite with her brother had been subsumed by fears of entrapment. The same aversion to factory-entanglement that had led her to leave her home state at twenty-two had resurfaced, and it snarled fiercely whenever she tried to get close and examine it. Marlow was worried about having to parent her brother. She wasn't a nurse-a-wounded-baby-bird-back-to-health person so much as a leave-the-human-baby-to-toughen-up-on-the-mountain kind of person.

On the one hand she didn't think Teddy would call her asking for help unless he had real problems. On the other if he had real problems she didn't want to get sucked into them. And problem or no problem he was going to want to *talk*. Money talk. Dead parents talk. Two million dollar Manhattan apartment vs. four hundred square feet cabin talk.

"Marlow?" Cordy asked, pulling her back to the dorm–style interior décor of his living room.

She made her decision about which direction to drive and retroactively judged it had been made before she'd even stepped into the bar; she'd just been coming to terms with it this whole time. It was important that she think of herself as brave, in both an emotional and physical sense.

Marlow stood abruptly. "Sorry, can't do it. It's going to be all motels and continental breakfasts from here on. I need to make up some time."

"Oh," he said.

She flipped on her headlights and headed east down the highway. "Sorry, Teddy," she said aloud. "I'm coming now."

CHAPTER 14:
THE CHEF

Mims hit send on her third movie review of the day and went to the stove to reheat her water. She'd been using the same scraggly teabag all morning. It had been over a week since her beehive outings, and she hadn't done much since then but watch movies and read about celebrities. She'd stopped checking in with Kai about the USDA lab results.

She took a sip of weak tea as she scrolled through *People* online and then various social media apps looking for inspiration for her next article. Maybe something about celebrity pets would be good. She hadn't seen anything on that topic for a while. Right off the bat Miley Cyrus's "maltipoo" looked promising. Maybe if she ever attended another party she could go in strong flinging maltipoos and celebrity breakdowns and no one would think to ask about boring old bees. Money was rolling in, at least in the context of how much income she usually had, and with a few weeks of saving up she'd be able to accept a brunch invitation from Bennie.

After a few hours of labradoodles, aluskies, wolamutes, and shepradors, it was time for lunch. Mims made her version of avocado toast—toast with an ungenerous film of butter that didn't quite reach the crusts and then a dusting of hot pepper flakes. Avocados were for rich people. The toast looked pretty on the plate nonetheless, and Mims's next blog topic became clear: competitive cooking and baking shows. Maybe the differences in tone between American and British versions would be a good starting point. The American ones had a lot of yelling and the British ones were supportive.

An hour into her research, the name of a guest judge for a celebrity baking show in New York caught her eye: Gerard Babineaux, the chef she and Sean had met after their date. She felt like she'd just drunk a shot of espresso. Maybe she wasn't ready to let the tides of mediocre tabloid journalism take her just yet . . . According to the website, Gerard was a supertaster. A supertaster was someone who could tell by taste and smell what ingredients were in a dish, down to the brand of breadcrumbs. Down to the precise factory the breadcrumbs had come from. Through a combination of genetics and training he had a hyper-sensitive palate, and she had the perfect test for him.

A moment later she got a text alert—from Sean.

"Hey," it read. This was the first time he'd contacted her since he said he'd be in touch "tonight," which was about a week ago. She knew exactly what the text meant—the thing that had scared him away after their date wasn't that she'd insulted his firefighters metaphor. Sean wanted her to know he wanted just-sex, and that she'd done something (mysterious, unspecified) that made it seem like she wanted more. Rather than verbalize any of this, he was expecting her to figure it out. She was offended, but there was no way for her to tell him explicitly that she wasn't a lovesick fifteen-year-old without it sounding like a "status discussion," which was something only people who wanted intimacy did. Any attempt to clear her name would become a "the lady doth protest too much" situation. She hadn't even checked to see if he was on social media, for fuck's sake, how had this happened? He was the one who'd proposed marriage.

"Hey, stranger. What are you up to?" she wrote back. There wasn't much choice but to go along with it if she wanted to hook up. Their last encounter had not sated the tendrils of desire making their gentle, electric way through the lower half of her body, silently reaching for light. Why not feed the one kind of hunger she was capable of satisfying?

"Day drinking and thinking about you. I'm at an award ceremony thing and I lost. It's going to go for a couple more hours, but do you want to meet up after? I'm leaving the States tomorrow." That was very ahead of schedule.

"Sure, where?"

He sent the name of a bar in Brooklyn. Mims checked the clock. She had just enough time to get ready and arrive in two hours. She could contact Gerard first thing in the morning.

Rushing around to get ready helped her blow off the thought that she was blowing off work for a boy.

When Mims arrived at the bar Sean was already there with his friends, presumably coworkers, but they seemed to be wrapping up. One guy was looking for his jacket and someone kept saying, "Where's Carly, where's Carly? Cheap bastard, she only left three dollars tip."

"Jesus, I'll pay it," Sean said as Mims approached. He smeared a five-dollar bill onto the table.

"Hey, babe," she said. *Power move*, she congratulated herself.

"Mims! You made it! Let's get out of here." He grinned and swayed toward her.

"After you," she said and gestured for him to take the lead. She couldn't help smirking at the looks she got from the other women as he reached back for her hand on the way out the door.

Once outside it was less fun. "Where are we going?" she asked. Sean weaved his way down the sidewalk, his focus having shifted to the brownstones lining the street. "Don't you stay in Midtown?"

"I got sick of the hotel, so I'm doing this Airbnb tonight. One night, that's all they'll pay for. Come on, it's really cool."

A few blocks from the bar he stopped in front of a building with a chocolate-brown façade. "This!" He took a few steps toward the entrance and then said, "No, wait!" and walked to the next brownstone over. "This one." He leaned heavily on her going up the stoop, and inside the building he stopped halfway up the first flight of stairs.

"A minute," he slurred quietly. Mims caught herself letting out a loud mom-sigh and ran her hand up and down his back instead, maybe a little too roughly.

"We'll get you some water inside," she whispered.

"I have a *Playboy* story too," he said, not whispering. He was referring to the tattoo on her arm and the story she'd told him about her dad. Sean bent over, bracing himself on the railing.

"So tell it," Mims said.

"When we were like seven. Oh shit I ruined the ending already by saying it was about *Playboy*."

Mims laughed. "It'll be nice, like a bookend. Tell it so we can get out of this stairwell."

"When we were like seven these kids and I would go to the edge of the suburban development where we lived and if you pushed through all these bushes and through some trees, you entered this other world. Or it felt more like leaving a world than entering a world, if that makes sense. It was the highway. We would wait by the side of the road for hours at a time waiting for semis to go by, and we'd pump our arms to make them honk, and when they did we would cheer and jump around." Sean straightened up and made the pulling gesture with his arm and then leaned over again.

Mims inserted her childhood self into the scene as she was listening, spying on the boys from the tree line as everything went down. It happened naturally, so similar to the way she was always stationed just out of eyeline in her real childhood memories, watching the others play.

"Once while we were trying to get a semi to honk, the driver threw a porno mag at us. We all huddled around it like it was an oracle, flipping through the glossy pictures."

"You didn't know what an oracle was when you were seven," Mims cut in.

"It was the first time I'd ever seen a girl's naughty bits all on display. We'd take turns with it every couple nights. Five boys sharing the same porn mag." Sean straightened up again and rubbed his eyes. "Onward!" he said. He clomped up the stairs.

Mims climbed quietly beside him. It was a cute story. She looked at his face trying to read what it signified, but his expression was inscrutable and it could mean anything. Was her tattoo some kind of metaphor to him about the kind of woman she was and what use she should serve in his life? Was his story told in intimacy or drunkenness? She shook her head clear—she was seeing significance in places it didn't belong.

At last they made it to the top landing. Sean was surprisingly adept at inserting the key in the lock and opening the front door. "Ta-dah!" he said as he presented the place.

The apartment was covered in overlapping, patterned throw rugs, the embodiment of cozy. It was also clean, and the word Mims couldn't shake was "whole." Couch, ottoman, fireplace, paintings, coasters, books, candles, but not too many or too large of anything.

"It's a real home," Sean said. "I get to sneak in here at night like a little gremlin and pretend I'm a people."

"It must be hard being based so far away and traveling so much, but you'll have a stable place one day." Mims ran her fingers along the edge of the key holder fastened to the wall near the front door. "You could have it now if you really wanted it." Even as she dismissed his longing she went into the kitchen and opened a cabinet. There were stacks of matching dishes inside. "That's nice," she said. They had the full set of classic Pyrex mixing bowls too.

When she turned around Sean wasn't listening, or even in the room. She used her investigative journalism skills to surmise that the dark, open doorway next to the couch led to the bedroom, and she stripped off layers of clothing as she crossed the living room to join him.

Once on the bed they tumbled and twisted and Sean kissed her passionately and not too wet and his body seemed to have an autopilot setting where it knew what to do even when wasted, the way Mims knew how to get home on the subway even blackout drunk.

She unbuttoned his pants and unfastened his belt and then Sean shuffled and kicked to get his pants off, comedic on purpose, but then it turned out he still had his big work boots on, in the bed, and the pants got stuck.

"Let me help with that," Mims said and they got his pants off.

She repeated, "Let me help with that" with his next problem, but there was no helping it.

After he fell asleep she started masturbating but then was angry that she'd waited until he was asleep. Let him be emasculated by it. She kicked him so he would wake up, but he didn't. She was too angry to come then and lay with her arms crossed over her chest until she fell asleep that way, like an angry Dracula. In the morning she slipped out before his alarm went off even though she could see through the sheets that his dick was working fine now. She'd show him who cared less.

Mims rode the subway home with bleary eyes. She told herself she was attracted to his vulnerability, which she told herself most people probably didn't even pick up on. He was loud and joking and crass and unselfconscious, except in those twilight, tipsy moments when he wasn't. He was lonely and wanted a home. But a deeper part of her knew his "vulnerability" wasn't just the usual boy–who–feels–emotions trapped inside a man–who–was–told–not–to–cry body. Vulnerability in this case was a whitewashing word for PTSD and burgeoning alcoholism, and those weren't cute, fixer–upper qualities. He was on a path not easily corrected, and it wasn't a path she should follow him along, even at a distance.

The lighting was even and nothing cast a shadow. Peaches by smell, kiwis by hardness. Always check that the eggs aren't cracked. Mims stood in front of the refrigerator section turning each egg. She leaned in to let a cart pass behind her. Her parents had taught her how to choose produce in that unobtrusive way you teach by example, and she didn't know until later it was a form of love. She'd met kids in college who didn't even know how to avoid mealy apples, and it was one small way she got to feel superior. The paycheck she'd cashed on the way to the grocery store hadn't elated her for more than the few seconds it took to pocket the bills. It all went to rent and utilities; her brunch fund was still zero. Mims was somber walking through the aisles. It shouldn't be this hard.

She found herself staring down the sappy amber honey jars in a cowboy faceoff. The raw honey was eleven dollars. With a heavy sigh she eventually put it in the basket. She put the four–dollar honey next to it, the brand the chef had said was corn syrup. He'd requested she bring a jar of each for a taste test during their interview. She needed to humor him so she could ask her question.

The next morning she dressed slowly, willing calm and positivity. She opened the silverware drawer for a spoon to stir her tea and a cockroach scuttled away. "Fuck it, you win," she said and took the silverware out of the drawer and threw it in handfuls into the sink. She scanned her apartment. There was a stark contrast between it and the picture–perfect home she'd slunk out of. Her "I'm too glamorous to be bothered to pick up" clutter combined with interminable poverty made her feel she'd invited the cock-roach. She'd been using the same towel for a couple of months now. The piles of scarves and ropes of long beads did nothing to obscure the shab-biness of the furniture underneath. While Mims owned only a few nice pieces of clothing that she wore regularly, her apartment was nevertheless sagging beneath the weight of cheap and cheaply made shirts and slacks and belts and socks she called *accent pieces* and wore once or twice before relegating them to the backs of chairs.

And what weight was *she* sagging under? Not just the preemptive loneliness of being away from her friends before they could reject her and the ever-itching need for physical intimacy, but the most coarse, animalistic need of all: that of continuous hunger, heavy and scraping like gizzard stones in her stomach. Some days it even drowned out the war of accusations and excuses—that she was exactly where she deserved to be in life, the world having seen through all the black clothes and the pearl earrings to the ignorant white-trash woman underneath, never having been fooled in the first place. She was tempted to vow to straighten up, but the supposed virtue of "clean-scrubbed, dignified" poor people with threadbare aprons and stiff upper lips offended her. She left her mug in the sink with the silverware when she went out.

The Upper East Side apartment building where the chef lived was one of the old ones with cornices and gargoyles, and the elevator man rode with her up to the correct floor.

Gerard opened the door in off-white linen pants and a linen jacket. Mims was pleased to see his hall closet doors didn't close correctly due to too many coats of gloopy white paint, just like everyone else's in New York. She didn't feel mean about it; it connected her to him in a small way in spite of his pants and his wealth. He led her to a large modern industrial table by the windows and gestured for her to sit.

He ran a nervous hand through his blown-back, puffy hair.

It was thinning.

He was tan and bony.

As she took him in, the crazed details of their first meeting resurfaced and she started to regret coming. She'd done that desperate thing again where she gambled on an unreliable source for the 10,000-to-one chance something fruitful would sprout from the interaction.

"Your paper's called the *Free Daily*? What is that?" he asked.

"*Free Post*. It has a circulation of about three hundred thousand," she said. "It's a local paper."

"This is a story worthy of the *World Gazette*." His lip curled in disgust.

Anger prickled at the inside of her skin and then receded before it could puncture through. She'd spent her whole store of adrenaline on the cockroach and there was nothing left for the pastry chef. Mims rose to go, not sure if she was sabotaging herself or saving the last vestiges of her dignity.

"Wait," he said. "I trust the integrity of your publication; I only ask for an assurance of anonymity. If anyone traces the fake honey back to my desserts it will mean financial ruin."

Mims hovered with her butt out of the chair. She'd wanted to keep an article about Gerard Babineaux overcharging for *baiser* in her back pocket. Committing to keep his secret felt as wrong as exposing him for a paycheck did.

"Think about it," he cautioned. "This is important. You could make a lot of money selling corn syrup for honey prices, even at the lowest end of the market. Corn syrup is forty cents per pound, bulk, and dropping. This brand is everywhere, all over the city, who knows the scale of the operation. Unlikely just New York, New Jersey. Think, think. The entire country may have been hit simultaneously."

She sat, nodded, and wrote "cook = kook" in her notebook. If he was so outraged about the supposedly fake honey, why was he still using it? "I'll look into it," she said. "Infiltrated by whom?"

"That's what you're going to find out," Gerard said.

"Forgive me, but I'm not entirely convinced there's really a problem," Mims replied. He was a verified supertaster; it was possible *something* was strange about the off-brand honey. Either a James Bond villain–style distribution network was churning out fake honey bottles for the benefit of a crime lord millionaire, *or* the chef was lying so that Mims would go off on a wild goose chase instead of telling people he was using store-bought honey in his fancy desserts.

"Promise me you'll protect my anonymity in exchange for this information."

She thought of Charlie suddenly, and decided helping him was worth letting go of the chance at an exposé of the pastry chef. Who cared if his rich clientele overpaid for pastries? "I promise," she said.

"Let's do the test!" Gerard walked briskly from the room. He returned before she could decide if she was supposed to follow him. "Tie this around my eyes," he said. He flapped a scarf open to demonstrate that it wasn't full of holes and then folded it in an accordion pattern.

"All right, let's do this," she said. She tied it snuggly behind his head and put a dab of honey each on two spoons, one organic and the other supposedly corn syrup. To Mims they looked and smelled exactly the same.

She expected him to mull the samples around in his mouth for a moment, like a wine tasting. Instead there was only a quick lizard flick of the tongue, then another on the second spoon. "The first is the cheap honey," he said. He took off the blindfold. He was correct.

"Let's do it again," Mims said. He'd had a fifty–fifty chance of getting it right.

He chose correctly five more times. "You have your proof!" he said and flung the blindfold forcefully away. It didn't cooperate and fluttered gently to his feet.

Mims put more honey on two clean spoons. Just because he could tell the difference between the two bottles didn't necessarily mean that one of them wasn't honey, she cautioned herself. And suppose he genuinely did believe one was corn syrup—supertasting and mental instability weren't mutually exclusive. If Gerard was a conspiracy theorist with delusions of grandeur, instead of just being a liar, how delusional would she have to be to get drawn in? The idea that she, Mims Walsh, world's shittiest reporter, would stumble onto an important honey smuggling story by way of pastry chef . . .

She closed her eyes and visualized flowers versus corn, but they both tasted the same to her. "Try breathing up the back of your throat as you do it," he said. Still they tasted the same. "Here, maybe this will help," he said and scampered off again. She was struck by the difference in his demeanor when he was paying attention—theatrical and controlled, versus when he was excited—like a lurching Quasimodo in a 5k. Gerard returned with a bottle of pure corn syrup. She was wary of ingesting anything pulled from the recesses of his apartment, but she dripped the clear liquid onto a spoon, sniffed it, and then licked it clean anyway.

"Euch! Neither of them taste like this," she said. It was sweet and slick. So slick she pictured seals diving through water, she pictured lube in sex shops.

"I'm not sure you're committed to this story." Gerard looked down his Roman nose at her in obvious disdain.

"I'm tasting the best I can," she protested. "I'll try to track down where this questionable honey came from. But I need something from you as well." Mims pulled the small red jar out of her bag. "There are ethical implications to my asking you to taste this," she said.

"What is it?"

"That's what I need to find out. It's supposed to be honey. It came from a rooftop hive here in the city. It's the reason you couldn't find local honey at the farmers markets this spring." The jar glowed, bright and unnatural.

"I have no respect for danger!" he said. He dipped his pinky finger in it, unwashed, extended his tongue, and smeared the red goo in a line across it.

"Jesus."

"This is corn syrup too," he said simply. He seemed disappointed. "What we tasted from the store was cut with flavoring agents to make it passable to consumers like you. This is cut with red food coloring. Industrial food grade."

"But it came from a hive."

"I don't care," he said.

She didn't believe him outright, but a slow smile tugged at her lips. If he was right, Kai could confirm for her. And if Gerard turned out to be correct maybe she'd look into his counterfeit honey empire; you only had to win the lottery once to recast the habit of playing from embarrassing to brilliant.

CHAPTER 15:
DYE

Mims set out with a printout of her map of affected beehives. It was time to find the source of the red dye. She knew already that the source was probably somewhere in Brooklyn, but unfortunately the chef's revelation hadn't narrowed down the search as much as she would have liked. He'd gotten a phone call and ushered her out right after the conclusion of the taste test. Some research revealed that red dye 40 was in jams and jellies, barbecue sauce, fruit snacks, cereals, salad dressing, pizza, candy, yogurt, potato chips, toaster pastries, beef jerky, hot dogs, cheese balls, gum, lasagna, cold medicines, cough drops, mouthwash, and butter-flavored popcorn. That the liquid was mostly corn syrup didn't help at all: corn syrup was in basically everything.

Her first stop after the industrial kitchens and bakeries in Gowanus was an open-air food festival in Williamsburg that ran every weekend from ten to four. It was crowded with people but no bees. It was a stupid idea; surely someone would have reported a festival overrun with bees. She went to a farmers market in Boerum Hill. Not many bees and not much dye. She looked at the free samples of jam—bee-free.

"Do these ever attract bees?" she asked.

"Once in a while, but not really."

"Definitely not enough to fill up multiple beehives?"

"I think I would have noticed that."

She went to a few pharmacies and tried to meet up with a dumpster-diving advocate, but it didn't seem likely there was a pile of red liquid–gels lying in the trash out back of a pharmacy somewhere, so she dropped it. She went to where the most flowers were, just in case—the parks. McCarren, East River State Park, Commodore Barry, Prospect. Nothing suspicious was going on in the parks. She went up to the picnickers and grills and hovered around the edges of birthday parties—nothing. She had a flash of inspiration and did an internet search for sports drinks companies, but there weren't any headquartered in Brooklyn. As the day was winding down she stepped into a bar in Cobble Hill that hosted whole hog roasts every weekend. There was BBQ sauce but not bees, and she was starving. A heavy sense of déjà vu settled over her—this search wasn't going to be any more successful than her initial triangulation of the hives had been. She took a longing look at the pig and then headed home.

Mims had put rice on the stove and sat down to skim through the half–written celebrity wardrobe critique on her laptop when her phone vibrated a text message alert.

"Hey, I don't know how you feel about the drop–by, but I think I'm in your neighborhood."

It was Sean. Mims appreciated that he had a "Living Like Weasels," Annie Dillard sort of approach to sex; he apparently had no memory or care about being rebuffed in the past, and certainly no plans for the future. Pussy was all present–tense for him. She surveyed her apartment. She cleared a path to her bed; she removed piles of clothes from the bed and put them on one side of the couch. Unappeased, she gathered the rest of the dirty clothes from the apartment and put them on the couch as well. Then she texted him her address.

A few minutes later he buzzed and she let him in. His shaggy hair was clipped back from his face with a barrette; it looked playful and feminine, which softened the broadness of his chest and the stark utility of his clothes. Mims wondered if the contrast was intentional. He looked good.

"What are you doing all the way out here?" she asked.

"My trip got cancelled. There was a huge line at the taxi stand at JFK so I took an unlicensed cab and the guy was trying to fuck me over." He had a small piece of luggage with him. "He thought I didn't know my way into the city from the airport. I told him to just let me out."

"In the middle of nowhere," Mims said and laughed. "As a world traveler you're supposed to know not to go with those guys."

Sean grinned and rubbed at his neck nervously and then set down his luggage.

"I brought beer from the bodega." He offered a six–pack. Sean's eyes didn't roam the floors or tables; he gave no indication that he recognized her apartment as untidy.

"You can sit." She moved some mail off the other kitchen chair. "I just made dinner if you're hungry. Rice and vegetables."

"I'm okay," Sean said.

She was glad. She doused her meal in hot sauce hoping he wouldn't notice that the "vegetables" were onions and cubed carrot. She ate quickly.

"So . . . we don't have to hook up," he said. "You're really interesting and I want to keep you in my life as a friend."

"That's worse," she said. "I want to hook up." Mims went to the sink to put her bowl in it. She moved slowly, shuffling through thoughts and trying to piece them together into a coherent picture of why she'd allowed him in. She never gave up on anything, that's probably why. She'd check the same empty box of crackers every day for a week before finally throwing it away.

When she turned around again Sean was reading the article on her laptop. Her favorite kind of celebrity stories were the ones that revealed something terrible about someone supposedly great.

"'Aging fashionistas take heed: crepe paper knees mean you're not allowed to wear shorts.' That's harsh."

"I don't really feel that way. It's just part of the persona for the website."

"These low-grade celebrities read their mentions, you know? From this guy's perspective and the perspective of his friends you'll be some bully on the internet. And he won't be wrong."

"Not all of us can get by writing articles that save lives and crash dictatorships. I have to supplement my newspaper writing if I want to pay rent." She snapped the laptop shut.

"At some point the line between acting like an asshole and being an asshole breaks down and they become the same thing," Sean said. He seemed stern but not angry, and her indignation that he would dare to look so placid and patronizing opened in her chest a rage of such force it could crush diamonds. Somehow she had the presence of mind to know yelling would mean he'd won. She leaned as casually as possible with shaking legs against the kitchen counter and spoke like someone who had only stubbed a toe.

"So when you said you wanted to be my friend you meant you wanted to have the freedom to come to my apartment unannounced in the middle of the night to talk at me but also not give me your dick. Nice. You can go." She pointed toward the door.

"Hey, I'm sorry." The judgment had gone from his voice. "I know I shouldn't come into your home and tell you how to live your life. I'm an asshole too, the condescending kind, which is especially bad. We're both assholes."

Clearly he didn't get that he, a man who in the *most generous interpretation* had *unintentionally* given off mixed signals about how much he liked her due to the extreme dearth of communication skills that resulted from living thousands of miles from the women he was trying to court and screw, was the last person allowed to accuse her of being an oblivious cocksucking son of a bitch. *Of course* she knew he was right about the article, she wasn't a psychopath. Being vocal about injustice was Sean's *raison d'être*, so it wasn't surprising that he'd called her out, but he didn't understand the compromises to be made when you were broke. If there had been a shipwreck she would have cannibalized poor Sammy Sampson before they'd even built a tree shelter. Imagine if Sean had seen that. But she wanted to change. It was easy to not be a cannibal if there was other food around; it was harder to hold on to your values when there wasn't.

Sean had made no move to leave her apartment. They really did want the same thing from each other but it wasn't sex. Every time they met he got to play at being a couple, with the marriage proposals and the hand-holding and the furnished apartment. The problem was that he wouldn't allow her to pretend at all. It was healing to fantasize about being in a loving relationship, almost like having the real thing but with none of the risk of engulfment or rejection or failure that came with it. Her friends were going to start getting married soon. And if someone got pregnant she was supposed to say congratulations, not offer condolences. She imagined how Sean felt when he flew back to the United States once or twice a year and saw his friends each time more competent and calm and stable. Was it like flipping through a photo album and realizing with each jump of the page that these scenes had already happened and were in the past and you'd missed it all? Not only that, but you somehow hadn't aged with everyone else and were still a child.

She looked down at him. He was still seated and she was still leaning against the counter. "I'm being defensive because I care about your opinion," she admitted.

"I care about your opinion too."

He went into the bathroom.

"How is your bathroom so clean?" he called. She heard his laugh echo off the bathtub and tiles. "The toilet doesn't have even one errant pubic hair."

"It's an old habit. When you have an alcoholic mother, growing up you keep the toilet clean," she said. She winced at the word "alcoholic"; she didn't usually call it that.

He didn't answer.

"In case of vomit," Mims clarified. She could hear his stream thundering into the porcelain bowl and was momentarily distracted from all thoughts but cleaning up the splash–back on her floor. "It's compulsive," she said.

Sean didn't answer, of course, of course. The revelations about their sad sameness had all been inside her own head; nothing had changed in his. He still wasn't going to give her a turn pretending.

"I miss college," she called into the void. "When all it took to fall in love was both of you knowing who David Bowie was."

"I heard you about your mom," he said as he emerged from the bathroom. "I wasn't ignoring you. I just didn't want to answer while I was peeing."

They went into the bedroom and lay facing each other on the bed. Mims told him about her mom. The day her dad went to jail was the first time Mims noticed her family wasn't normal and good, wasn't of a separate kind from the trailer park kids' families. After that the evidence was everywhere. The day her father was supposed to come back, Mims tied her hair into pigtails as best she could; it had been six months. She was eight and sat waiting on the couch watching cartoons. She could hear her mom in the kitchen arguing with her boyfriend. "Mom, is Daddy going to be mad about Mr. Armstrong?" she wanted to ask, but the kitchen was too far away and she wasn't supposed to yell in the house. When the front door opened, she hopped up and ran into his arms. "Daddy!" she yelled. "Baby!" he called as he scooped her up. That was the last word he spoke to her for another six months. Her mother, drunk of course, had forgotten he was coming home that day. Mr. Armstrong was not supposed to be present for the reunion. Her dad left, Mims felt guilty for not reminding her mother, and her mother seemed to have come to the same conclusion about who was at fault and left Mims with her aunt.

"My aunt was perfectly nice," Mims said. "I didn't even have to change schools. Eventually my dad stopped being angry and my parents got back together. I went back to living with them and no one ever mentioned it again."

"I stayed with my aunt the summer I was twelve because she had a beach house," Sean said. "I cried myself to sleep the first five nights." He smiled, encouraging and sheepish. "I really admire how far you've come."

"Thank you," Mims said.

A realization unfolded in front of her. She had never felt taken care of, and it was too late now because she was an adult and no one takes care of adults, so she was angry, not this moment but also always. The anger poisoned everything. She saw herself stomping through life hissing, "Fine, I'll do it myself! I'll do it all myself!" like an overworked parent coming home to find the chores not done. She laughed at that. "Sean, I just realized that I never do chores because I did them all as a kid. I think we have a limited number of floor-sweepings and dish-washings in us, and I used all mine up before I left puberty."

"I wasn't going to say anything." He gave an exaggerated turn of the head toward her cornucopia of a closet. "I don't actually know if I'm messy or not. I don't own enough stuff or stay in one place long enough to find out. How much clutter can you make with two pairs of pants and four days' worth of takeout containers?"

Sean and Mims lay with their heads in the crooks of their elbows. "Come closer," he said.

Mims glanced at his lips and then back to his eyes. "No, you come over here," she said. He leaned forward and kissed her gently and then slid his body toward hers.

It was their first alcohol–free encounter, and sober his words were more tentative, his voice almost shaking when he said, "Tell me what you want," but his hands were more certain.

Mims woke up in the middle of the night to find him gone. She was sad looking up at the light of a rumbling truck pass across her ceiling. "Fool me twice," she said quietly and then got up to make sure the door had locked behind him. She jumped in surprise at the sight of him in the living room sleeping propped up on the couch. The pile of dirty clothes was mostly crushed underneath him, but he had a dress draped over his chest like a blanket.

"What are you doing?" she said. "Hey, come to bed."

He stirred groggily. "I get jet lag," he said. "Couldn't sleep. I didn't want to wake you up."

"Come back," she said.

"Also I don't like cuddling when I sleep, and I snore, and I didn't want you to feel rejected."

She suffocated him with a throw pillow. "The things you do are the opposite of the things you should do."

He slid out from beneath the cushion and grabbed her wrist playfully and then let go. "I could say the same to you. You say you just want to fuck and you're only mad because I'm disrespectful, but I think you like me."

"I don't know you well enough to know if I like you," she said, surprised at the panic weaving lightning–quick but quiet through her rib cage. Why was it an insult to accuse someone of having feelings? And what was there to be careful about, whether she liked him or didn't? It was impossible for a dreaded *obligation* to develop with him living on another continent. Maybe that was the very reason she allowed herself to pursue him in the first place.

"Okay." He smiled weakly but his eyebrows pulled down in the middle.

"I'm not trying to trap you. I know you don't live here."

In the morning Mims poured milk over the leftover rice and ate it like oatmeal. She offered some to Sean and he took it but sat stationary.

"There's honey," she said and nodded to the expensive bottle she'd brought to the chef to taste–test.

"Sure," he said, "why not," and reached for it.

"If I'm in Midtown again when you're there, do you think I could come up for a tour of the *World Gazette* building?" Mims asked. "Apparently the way the light interplays with the architecture is so beautiful someone made a photo blog about it."

"That might be hard—"

"Forget it," she snapped. "We got off on the wrong foot and there's no way to right it at this point. You're just going to see every interaction as fawning affection and neediness."

"Listen," he said. He placed his hand on top of hers. "We dig each other and we're going to stay friends. I have to get going. I can tell things are hard for you right now, but don't give up. A big part of being an investigative journalist is building up a trove of seemingly useless information and contacts that you can then pull from and connect the dots when needed. Just keep your eyes open."

"See ya," she said. He waited for a moment and then left without saying anything else. She didn't want his advice on how to be a journalist, and she wasn't going to let either of them pretend anymore that they were lovers.

CHAPTER 16:
BARGAINING

Teddy sat on the edge of his bed with his knees far apart, much wider than he would have allowed himself on the subway, in consideration of the space needs of other passengers. He wore his soft flannel pajamas. He was alone, but the last time Doe was over she'd repositioned a mirror into the bedroom so she could see herself full-length after she got dressed. He was looking into the mirror now. He slid the pajamas bottoms off and then sat down again, in just his boxer briefs. He looked fine. Teddy's grandfather used to sit on the edge of his bed in his boxers to talk to him, and his balls were so long they always dangled out. Teddy wasn't sure if that was going to happen to him. He missed his grandfather.

Teddy had been sitting across from his grandfather when they got the call about his parents. Not here in the apartment they shared together, but at a restaurant, with all their balls in.

"That waitress was looking at me," Irving said, before the call. "If she gives me her number, you have to stay away from the apartment tonight."

Teddy was only half listening. His eighty-three-year-old grandfather joked about dating a lot—nurses, waitresses, cashiers. Teddy was more interested in the food at the next table—the *shakshouka* the woman was eating looked good, but whatever the man was eating looked even better.

"If you lean any farther over those people's table you're going to get beard hairs in their coffee," Irving cackled.

The couple smiled but didn't engage and Teddy waited a beat too long to feel comfortable asking the man what he'd ordered.

Then Irving's cell phone rang and Teddy's rang a few seconds after and he was in a wind tunnel hearing about his parents' car crash, but when he looked across to Irving he was aware enough to know his grandfather was receiving the same news. Teddy's whole body became jittery and not numb exactly but cold, probably the sensation of floating away in space, untethered to anyone or anything that could pull you back in and take you home.

His parents were both dead. His mom had been driving. Although Teddy hadn't been there, he had something like a memory of the crash that his brain spliced together from real moments driving with his parents.

"You didn't put the toilet seat down again this morning. You should be sitting if you can't aim," his mom had said. Windshield wipers, slate sky. Westchester motion blur outside the windows.

"I aim fine, and if I don't I clean it up with a wad of toilet paper. I dab the rim; there's no mess." His dad replied in a pitch that didn't earn back any of the masculinity so casually snatched from him.

"So that's where all the toilet paper goes! You're not the one who has to order it. This is exactly why we need to remodel the bathroom; I've been waiting on it for years. You never take my dreams seriously."

And then in order to make sure she got her way his mother had started crying. She pounded the steering wheel with the heels of her hands a few times, fingers spread for emphasis, bauble rings large like arthritic knuckles. And then she took her eyes off the road to glare at his father and then they crashed and her chest was crushed and his neck snapped and it was all over.

Teddy didn't remember what happened at the restaurant after that or how they left.

It was after the accident that Irving had started grooming Teddy for factory ownership. Irving's health started to decline around the same time, as if the knowledge he was imparting to Teddy was his own vitality that he was passing along. But of course the withering of his body had been triggered by his daughter's death. Previously Irving and Teddy had more of a college roommate relationship. Teddy had moved in after returning from school in Philly to take an unpaid internship at a sports podcasting company, and he'd been taking his time deciding where to go after it ended. They drank coffee together in the dining room over newspapers; Teddy went grocery shopping and introduced Irving to Netflix. When the two of them weren't hanging out, Teddy came and went as he pleased. After the car accident, Irving hired Brittany–Lynne to come by a few days a week to help with the increasing load of pills, paperwork, laundry . . . Teddy would have been happy to do it, but he could tell Irving didn't want Teddy to see up close what was happening to him.

He and Brittany–Lynne had started dating a month after they met.

Teddy got off the bed and went into the bathroom to pee, grabbing his cell phone off the nightstand along the way. There was a new email from Lin. He'd been receiving one check–in per day for the last three days, since he'd failed to respond to Lin's email about the upcoming shipment. He'd also not confirmed receipt of the "honey" still sitting in the factory basement. He'd been hoping Lin would take the hint and give up. "You will pick up the next shipment of honey. And you will respond to this message. Your response will be appropriately groveling now or else it will be exceedingly penitent later." The previous email, from the night before, had simply read: "So you will toast but you won't drink?" That one was creepy because it was weird, but the escalation today sent a momentary tremble through his breath. There was still no response from Marlow; supposedly she'd left Alaska weeks ago. He'd come to feel surprisingly neutral about her silence and absence, as if "Marlow on the way" was the usual and permanent state of things and the crisis at the factory wasn't unfolding so much as it was stasis.

Teddy turned off email notifications on his phone but then opened and refreshed the app every few minutes the whole subway ride to the factory. The fear of getting in trouble for selling fake honey had blotted out concerns about the factory's finances, but now he was letting himself get swept away by fear of a loading icon. Nothing, nothing, two emails from Lin, three. Little spikes of adrenaline played a carnival strongman game with his heart. By Cortlandt Street Teddy was overwhelmed and deleted the emails as they came in, unread, with a swipe of his finger.

He started the workday by detouring through the factory floor on the way to his office; his legs were still sore from stashing the haul of not–honey over the weekend, and he felt like walking to help get the stiffness out and settle his nerves. He found comfort in things you could count on at consistent intervals, like sunrises, sleep, meals, hot showers, tradition, and routine. The cherry factory, with its set schedule and continuity with the past, had lost its mechanical feel years ago and seemed as warm and familiar as pies every Thanksgiving, as organic as the cycles of the cherry trees themselves.

Teddy's favorite machine was the one that looked like a giant's sluice box. Hundreds of thousands of bright red cherries floated in the long, open–air tub, and at the far end a steep conveyor belt with little steps on it lifted the cherries a few hundred at a time to the next stage of their journey. Repetition, serenity, predictability, calm. He stood watching for a couple of minutes and then continued on his own route through the factory. Glancing out a window, he caught sight of someone transporting barrels of brine across the yard, unwrapped, at the exact moment juice sloshed onto the ground, right outside the door.

"We have a process for this," Teddy said to no one in particular.

"I'll get it," Jon said. He was one of the guys who stirred the vats so the cherries didn't form a clog.

"No, I'll do it. I can do it faster than anyone."

Outside he uncoiled the hose and directed the stream, on the most powerful setting, at the spill. At first it seemed the red spot was just getting larger as he added water to it, not washing away. A swirl of panic was accompanied by its opposite, a fantasy of dead honeybees floating in puddles, like they had the day they'd ruined his sandwich. His grip tightened on the hose but then it softened. The cherry spill diluted to pale red and then to pink and then washed clean enough that he didn't think the bees would come. He rolled up the hose and put it away, but just as he was about to go inside a thought stopped him. Teddy looked over his shoulder toward the center of the yard, where the bees usually congregated.

He walked toward the spot with a feeling of trepidation, like he should have made an appointment. Teddy grabbed the cell phone out of his back pocket as he approached. "Hey, fella," he called softly to one of the passing bees, but it didn't stop. There were a few on the pavement, so he hiked up his pants and squatted down to be at their level. "Little captain, I want to show you something," he said. He smiled the lopsided grin he knew girls liked and pulled up the two emails from Lin that had arrived, and he hadn't opened, since he'd shown up at work. "Check this out. I'm not doing it anymore. You can disperse now." One of the bees buzzed away without seeming to notice him and another bee did a slow fly-by but didn't seem interested. "I'm sorry for what I did. Here, look, I mean it," he said. Teddy navigated on the phone to the "manage accounts" setting.

If he deleted the account he'd set up specifically for communicating with Lin, he'd be unable to reinstate it and they would be permanently out of touch. With an extra-stiff and determined finger he hit "confirm." He took in a deep breath and the air seemed to be 100 percent oxygen, leaving him giddy. A bee landed on the edge of the phone and walked across the screen and then took off again. Teddy nodded in satisfaction. Of course it was easier to talk through his options with the bees than it was to actually confront the person threatening him and disrupting his life, but at least he'd made a firm decision. It was only after he'd deleted his email account that he realized his out-of-proportion avoidance of reading the emails was because he hadn't entirely trusted himself not to cave and agree to some sort of compromise with Lin.

"Well, glad that's settled," he said and laughed, partially at himself for talking to bees and partially out of relief. As he stood back up, the bees on the ground took off, and he brushed at the dirt on his pants. Explaining the situation to them wasn't any more silly than talking to a cat or dog or a photo of a deceased loved one, which people did all the time. Even though he knew the bees didn't know about the honey in a concrete, scientific sense, he couldn't shake the superstitious feeling that someone, God, the universe, the essential-source-of-bees-themselves, had sent them to prevent him from blowing off his guilt. He didn't *fully* believe it, of course. Ten percent, tops.

"Teddy, is everything okay?" Brittany-Lynne stood a few feet away. He put the phone back in his pocket. "I was coming over to ask if you wanted to get dinner tonight."

"Everything's fine. Just asking the little misters to chill out and report back to base that it's time to move on."

"They're females," Brittany-Lynne said.

"All of them?"

"Yes. The worker bees are all female, and the queen is female. The boys just lounge around the hive and eat. Until the fall, when the others kick them out and let them freeze to death. My uncle used to keep bees."

So bees had it in for men even if they weren't honey launderers. He wasn't sure if that made him feel better or worse.

"Teddy, Jalen has been looking for you everywhere," Doe said from behind him. "You have a phone call from the equipment salesman and it's urgent. We need to get a cordless phone for the front desk so Jalen can come find you when you're not in your office."

As he turned to face her his back broke out in sweat. There was rarely a reason for Doe and Brittany-Lynne to be in the same place at the same time since Brittany-Lynne had finished training Doe as her replacement. Thankfully they hadn't connected on a personal level, so they rarely even chatted.

"I'm heading into my office now," Teddy said. "Sorry, it's urgent!" he called to Brittany-Lynne as he headed off, leaving the two women alone, but only for a moment. He squinted at their reflection in the glass of the door into the building and saw Doe was walking back toward the entrance closest to the front desk. Brittany-Lynne stood alone.

Of course he wanted Brittany-Lynne to be happy and also not lonely, but he was tired of those things being his responsibility. She was like a piece of old luggage he was tired of hauling around and didn't want to admit it because it would hurt the luggage's feelings.

That afternoon Teddy sent an email to Jay and Matt with an idea for cutting costs: they could switch a couple of people from full-time to part-time. They agreed immediately. Just like that, Brittany-Lynne and Doe wouldn't have overlapping schedules anymore.

CHAPTER 17:
ATTEMPTED MURDER

Teddy held the door open and Doe walked through it, into a SoHo art gallery packed with paintings, understated LED sculptures, and fashionable buyers and browsers. He hadn't told her where they were going ahead of time. Doe wanted to start her own jewelry line one day, so Teddy had taken a guess about what that sort of lifestyle would entail.

She was wearing a red dress that was more elegant than tight, but one of the shoulder straps kept falling down. Each time it did Teddy stopped what he was doing or saying to watch her small hand slide the strap up her arm and back into place.

She caught him looking and scowled.

"I've never met anyone so angry at being beautiful," Teddy said. He pushed the strap into place for her.

"Tell me the truth. Do you only like me because I'm small and French and 'exotic-looking' because my grandmother is Vietnamese?" There was something disorienting about a woman speaking so candidly about her own attractiveness. That that awareness was paired with an accusation of racism and attraction to embarrassingly old-school gender cliches was uncomfortable.

"I like you because you express your emotions and don't let being liked by others get in the way of truthfulness." Her eyes opened wide like mouths, hungry, and he could tell she was pleased with his answer. "Would you like a glass of wine?"

"Red," Doe said. She walked up to one of the paintings hung on the near wall. It was blue and bumpy with white streaks along the bottom. Teddy went and got the wine.

"This gallery is run by my mom's college roommate," he said when he returned. "What do you think? Is a New York art opening all you hoped it would be?" He kissed her lightly on the cheek.

"I want to belong here," Doe said. "Among these people. Do you think this date will make me forgive you for taking away my hours at work? How will I afford this painting?" she asked and pointed. Usually her French accent was very slight, but the effort of making "painting" into a question left it coming out like "panting."

Teddy grinned and nuzzled his beard into her neck, tickling her, and then danced his fingertips along her ribs. "This painting is $60,000," he laughed.

Doe laughed too and grabbed at his arms. "I was so close to affording it!"

He stopped tickling her and she stood on her tiptoes and still couldn't reach his lips, so he bent down.

"You'll be able to afford these paintings one day," Teddy said. "You're ruthless. You're going to have more money than I do soon."

Doe toasted his glass and then fit her elbow into his and they moved on together to look at the other art.

The next morning Doe and Teddy rode the subway to work together and didn't stagger their entrances. "It doesn't matter," Doe said. "Maybe we ran into each other on the sidewalk. It's normal to arrive at the same time." Teddy mostly agreed.

He spent the first part of the morning going over financial projections and returning vendor phone calls. The monthly all-company status meeting was set to happen at 11:00 a.m. in the kitchen. People were always prompt to the team-building get-together because they served donuts and flavored coffees and espresso drinks. Usually Teddy was the spokesman to share company-wide news and introduce new hires, and then everyone would hang around and joke for a few minutes. For today's meeting Teddy had told Matt that he was going to be late and that they should start without him, but to save him a donut.

At 11:03 Teddy slunk down into the basement and grabbed one of the jars of high fructose corn syrup. He slipped past the kitchen, where he could hear rousing voices but nothing distinct, and onto the main factory floor, past the conveyor belt that sorted cherries and past the one that pitted them. He started to dash up a ladder to the top of one of the brining vats, but the metal clanking of his feet was too loud, so he stopped and did a ninja jump back down. His gaze darted from station to station before settling on a target. He went over to the rinsing station and untwisted the top of the jar and held it aloft. And then he paused. He was certain the contents were high fructose corn syrup—the lab at the loading dock had proved it. It wasn't dangerous. How else was he going to get rid of all the jars sitting in the basement? Even if he poured one extra jar into a vat each day it would still take him eighty years to go through it all. There would be a bump in filtration and waste management costs, but he was counting on it blending in to the added volume of business they would be doing thanks to the renovations.

He lowered his arm and looked around again. There was a plastic barrel of spent brine sitting by the exit waiting for the top to be wrapped in plastic and sent across the yard to the waste filter system. He poured the jar contents inside. On his way back to the administration part of the building he buried the empty jar under some other rubbish in the bottom of a recycling bin. Then he went into the meeting.

"There he is!" Jay called. Doe handed him a plate with two donuts on it.

Teddy looked around at all the expectant faces and felt pride and protectiveness all at once.

"I don't have anything to say except good job, everyone. It's a factory—it's always the same; nothing changes, that's the whole point. What did you expect?"

People laughed. "Now eat these donuts and let's get back to work."

"The machines can't go without people manning them," Matt said. "However fast you can eat a donut without choking, do that."

Teddy laughed. "Guys, take your time."

Omar stood by the kitchen counter. Today was the day he made delivery runs to city bars and restaurants. Teddy caught his eye and smiled. In return Omar's mouth flatted into a downturned, lipless line and he nodded his head.

At 11:30 Teddy went out to say goodbye to the construction crew for the last time. They'd made the extended deadline somehow. Teddy had half expected the construction to go on indefinitely, like Marlow's trip and the "honey" shipments.

"Hey, you going to invite us back for the ribbon cutting?" the foreman asked. He was a tall man with big forearms, and the accoutrements of his tool belt shone in the sun. Whatever hardships the guy might have in his life, they were normal and with a proscribed path to navigate out.

"It may be a while," Teddy said.

"I thought the opening was going to be a couple weeks from now when you have the big party?"

The party was happening, but the opening was not. They had put non–refundable deposits on the party stuff months before, and it was promised to the employees; he didn't want to disappoint them or freak them out. Bumping Doe and Brittany–Lynne to part–time had already started rumors of financial trouble. "Yeah, we'll see," Teddy said in a tone of voice he hoped conveyed that the foreman and his crew weren't invited.

The foreman frowned, but he refrained from apologizing for going so far over budget and schedule.

They did one last walkthrough of the new building to make sure nothing was left behind. Teddy stooped down and picked up a tape measure by the wall in one of the rooms. He noticed some trash and empty paint cans in one of the others but didn't say anything. He'd clear out the last of the odds and ends himself. He just wanted the workmen gone.

Teddy walked the foreman to the front gate. "Well, thanks for everything," Teddy said. "What about this dumpster?"

It was sitting outside the factory gate just a few feet from the Beasley Cherries sign. A few pieces of taller debris peeked out the top, but it was mostly empty.

"You have to call someone to pick that up."

Teddy took a deep breath, and then he felt a small hand on his elbow. "Teddy," Doe said. "Come quickly."

Teddy patted the foreman on the arm. "Well, see ya. Duty calls." He followed Doe back into the factory. A few people were standing around a steel bench.

"Look," she said and pointed to a half–gallon jar of cherries, fully labeled and sealed and ready to go.

"It's nothing," someone said.

"They were going to throw it out without telling you, but I know you worry about the bees," Doe said.

Teddy walked up to the bench and grabbed the jar of cherries in both hands. There was a bee pressed up against the inside of the glass, dead, like a formaldehyde baby. He stood looking at it for a long moment, and then he said, "Check the others," and walked out.

He crossed the courtyard standing tall and unafraid and didn't swat at the bees as he walked. If they wouldn't accept his apology, if they wanted escalation, so be it. In the center of the yard he untwisted the jar lid and poured the contents on the ground. The cherries and then the dead bee plopped out, like the guts of an animal. The splash–back got on his sneakers. He continued on across the courtyard into the waste management building and threw the jar, too forcefully, into the recycling bin. It bounced back out and spun around on the floor, leaving a crime scene blood spatter. He kept walking.

The barrel of waste brine to which he'd added the high fructose corn syrup that morning had been wrapped and carted into this building, and now it was sitting on a dolly waiting to be fed into the filtration system. Teddy went into a closet and grabbed a small white box of powder and then returned and got the barrel and wheeled it out to the yard. When he got back to the puddle of slop, there were about ten bees on it and a fly. An image was fastened in his mind of heat drying out their little bodies as they became husks, hollow and crunchy. He had held up his end of the bargain by ending the illegal shipments. It wasn't enough—they wanted to ruin him and would not be dissuaded from their fixation on punishing him.

He set the box on the ground and scooted the barrel off the dolly and began unwrapping the cling wrap from the top. "This is what you came here for, right? This is what you wanted? Drink up, fuckers."

"You look like a movie villain unwrapping facial bandages."

Teddy felt as if a giant rubber band had snapped him in the back. He turned to find Jalen, the front desk guy, watching him. He held some paperwork in one hand and a cordless phone in the other. Jalen was baby-faced–young and had recently returned from a refreshing Miami vacation. That in combination with his bright floral-print T-shirt and the brand-new pink-frosted tips on his mini–twist hair could not have been in starker contrast to the brooding unwholesomeness Teddy felt within himself.

"What are you doing?" Jalen asked.

They both looked down at the white box at the same time. It said rat poison.

"Maybe I'll go back and um . . . research this for a second to make sure it's safe and legal," Teddy said.

"I might," Jalen replied. "I'm going to put these on your desk. It looks like your hands are full." But then he stood there until Teddy had mostly finished rewrapping the top of the barrel.

"My sister will be here soon. I'm sure she'll take care of it," Teddy mumbled. "Can you get someone to clean this up, please?"

He left the dolly and walked back to his office and sat on the couch with his head in his hands for a long time.

Three Weeks Before

CHAPTER 18:
SUNSET PARK

Mims rubbed the linen scarf between her fingers and then let it drop. She didn't need another scarf. As she walked around the rest of the shop a physical tension grew in her chest until it pulled her back around to the display case. It was rare to find such a high-quality scarf for the price, and didn't she deserve to own something that wasn't basically trash from a sweatshop? This piece was so expensive because of the craftsmanship that went into it. It was dyed so delicately the flaxen threads moved like water, or like hair in a commercial for conditioner. She wrapped the scarf loosely around her neck and looked in the mirror.

Ostensibly she had come to Sunset Park to look for red food products before her afternoon deadline with Aziz, but really she came to walk and clear her head. The search for the source of the red honey was becoming a metaphor for her career overall. It was sad seeing herself go farther and farther down a road toward nothing, trudging forward and not giving up when she knew she should. Just like with Sean. Today she'd seen an industrial kitchen that made small batches of red sodas; she'd also peeked in at a tiny space that made raw sauerkraut out of ruby cabbages. Mostly she was just walking. One thing she hadn't come to Sunset Park to do was spend money. The relief she felt at the register was remarkable and she couldn't help but think it was the hit of dopamine an alcoholic gets taking a sip of wine. Shopping addiction could maybe be a topic for the blog she was writing for, but at the same time she didn't really want to know if that's what the feeling was. Because of her mother's drinking habits Mims had gone through her entire life avoiding learning anything concrete about the biology or psychology of addiction. It was a superstition of hers that if you said its name aloud it might appear, as Bloody Mary might.

Mims left the shop wearing the scarf, declining to take a bag, as if to hide the evidence that she had made a purchase. She was standing deflated and penniless on the sidewalk when a bee nearly grazed her nose as it zoomed by. It was the first one she'd seen this whole time, aside from when she'd been steps away from rooftop hives.

She turned and casually followed the bee for a step before deciding fuck dignity and all the rest of it and breaking into a sprint. She ran in the direction the bee had gone and was sure it had turned right at the corner and then turned again and kept running straight for several wide, industrial blocks even though the bee had left her far behind. She knew it was absurd to chase a bee, but she was angry and didn't know how to turn it off.

She stumbled to rest midblock and bent over coughing. Mims was in the sun and in all black except for the pale yellow scarf, which she unwound with sweat dripping down her neck. The block seemed deserted in the way all the extra-wide industrial blocks did. It was time to go home. No more shopping and no more men; it was time to admit defeat and clean her apartment and settle into a life of lowbrow celebrity gossip. And yet her eyes roamed the brick buildings and fences as she caught her breath.

As soon as she felt she'd be able to speak, she pressed "call" on her phone. Her fingers trembled as she did. If this was the end, she needed to be clear with herself that she'd tried everything.

"Gerard Babineaux," he answered.

"Mims Walsh," she said. "Sorry to bother you, I just need a moment. Was there any other flavor in that red honey you could identify? Anything faint or that you weren't 100 percent sure of? Someone else who tasted it said it was bitter, like chemicals. What might—"

"No, just as I said before, the corn syrup and the dye. And well of course the fruit."

"Fruit? You didn't say fruit!"

"You can practically smell it, even you could taste it—"

"I DIDN'T TASTE IT AT ALL, IT COULD BE TOXIC FOR ALL I—" Gerard hung up before she could finish. She called back frantically. He didn't answer. "Which fruit?" she pleaded with the ringtones. "Which fruit?" He'd rushed her out the door seconds after the taste test at his apartment concluded, suddenly uninterested in her when his phone rang. She wondered now if he'd fully understood at the time that she was asking what the red honey was so she could physically locate the source. It was possible he'd understood but just didn't care.

Mims walked up and down the blocks, up, over, up, over. The warehouses and other brick buildings all looked the same. Mostly they didn't have signs out front, but where they did she squinted up at them. Auto parts. Distillery. Refrigeration. And then Beasley Cherries. She stumbled forward a couple of steps, transfixed by the sign, and as she did a slow gate opened in front of her and a truck drove out. Framed in the gap of the gate entrance was a gravel yard; a giant cardboard box; a dark, well-dressed man ascending a ladder to the top of the box; the man freezing. There were bees flitting about the yard. Mims walked through the gate.

The man descended the ladder as she approached, keeping nervous but steady eye contact with her. He was around her age with beautiful black hair and a beard. "Can I help you?" he asked. His voice was low and soothing. It made him seem safe—a man who never yelled.

"Yes, please," she said. "I'm Mims Walsh from the *Free Post*, and I'm looking for red bees."

CHAPTER 19:

TEDDY IS DISCOVERED

Teddy was silent. He stared at Mims Walsh from the *Free Post*. Her eyes were wide and her breath was coming quickly, like she'd just stepped inside an enchanted forest and was taking it all in. She looked more like the women in SoHo than what he imagined a scrappy young journalist to be—subtle details he couldn't pin down in hair, layered jewelry, and straight shoulders added up to expensive and demanding. With the color combo of her black clothes and pale yellow summer scarf he couldn't help thinking the bees had sent her. He was relieved to be caught, and he felt relaxed for the first time in weeks. At least the tension of dread was over. He descended the ladder and shook her hand.

"I'm Teddy Beasley, and this is Beasley Cherries." It was so surreal he didn't know what else to say. *Are you a bee hunter? Are these your bees? Are you here to destroy my life? The bees have won.*

"There's a beekeeper named Charlie who's going to be very excited that I found out where his bees have been going." Her smile was bright and jubilant, not vengeful or accusatory in the least. "The bees have been getting into your red dye, right?"

Teddy walked her into the main building, giving a well-practiced history of the factory along the way. Beasley Cherries was opened by his great-grandfather Otto Beasley in 1914, right at the height of the East Coast cherry boom. Maraschino cherries had only arrived in the United States in the 1890s and hadn't seen much demand until cocktails and soda shops became all the rage. The original Beasley imported brined cherries from Italy as the raw material for his maraschinos. Teddy's grandfather, Irving, was born in 1931—the same year Ernest Wiegand at Oregon State University perfected the modern-day preservation process by adding calcium salts to the brine. This solved the problem of domestic cherries being mushy. "Huge problem," Mims said and nodded solemnly. A tariff was introduced on Italian cherries soon after. Teddy stumbled on the word tariff. Otto beat out the other East Coast factories in switching to Oregon fruits first, and today Beasley Cherries had no serious domestic competitors outside of the West Coast. And they did most of their brining in-house. Teddy was proud of his cherry pedigree; his dad had taken his mom's last name when they married, so they could all be Beasleys. He pointed out photos of his forebears, and himself and Marlow as children, that lined the hallway of offices.

"Good morning, Teddy," Doe said as they brushed past each other.

"Good morning, miss," he said. She blushed.

He winked at her in the reflection of the door to his office before ushering the reporter inside. Mims sat in one of the cushy leather Cogswell chairs and Teddy went around and sat behind his big wooden desk. The couch corner, where he slept after all-night honey shifts, glared accusingly.

"You said you started noticing the bees about two months ago?" Mims asked.

"Yeah, yes. I didn't think about what they were doing once they left here. The honey is actually *red*? Do you want some coffee? Tea?"

"Neon red. Everyone is going to be so relieved. And no coffee, thank you." She looked immediately regretful. "Actually, yes. Could I have a coffee, please? I suppose you offer coffee to all the journalists who come by?"

Teddy pressed a button on his desk phone. "Jalen, can you bring in a coffee, please?" He had never seen someone look so giddy about being offered coffee. "Do you think people will be mad when they find out?" Teddy asked. "About the bees? We've been trying everything. The tanks where we brine the cherries range from five to ten thousand gallons each, and we transport the spent brine afterward—across the yard from one building to the other, where the disposal drains are. We've been using cling wrap while we try to come up with a better idea, but somehow they get under it. Sometimes they chew through it. And the barrels are only in the yard for a few minutes at a time. We're going to have a more efficient operation soon, with the disposal closer to where it's needed, but we've stalled on funding for the moment."

He didn't want to offer too many financial details, but it seemed like a good way to get sympathy. Teddy hated the idea of all those poor beekeepers being angry he'd ruined their harvests. He never would have imagined the stream of bees cycling through the yard would be enough to affect so many hives, but on the other hand he also couldn't fathom how many trips to different flowers bees needed to make to collect enough nectar to make normal honey. It was mind boggling that so many little voyages could add up to something so big.

Jalen brought in the coffee and a miniature tray with sugar and milk.

"I'm glad you didn't try killing the bees," Mims mused as she took it from him. Jalen gave Teddy a look on his way out. "That beekeeper I mentioned, he's wonderful. I'm sure he'll have ideas on how to keep the bees out."

"I appreciate that," Teddy said. He had a sudden urge to confess about the fake honey in his basement. He wanted to give his own theory as to why the bees were tormenting him. As much as he wanted to claim the bees were malevolent, they were just drawing attention to his illegal behavior and the poor management decisions that precipitated it. It was a punishment he deserved for being both incompetent and underhanded.

Teddy's eyes roved again over Mims's scarf. Maybe driving him to confess was part of their plan.

He bolted upright, shocked awake. These were crazy thoughts; the bees were just regular insects. Maybe sure in a poetic sense the bees represented something, but in non-metaphoric, actual-real Brooklyn they were not sentient or magical. He just needed to hold it together until Marlow showed up and helped him figure a way out.

Teddy pulled out the emergency Twizzlers Pull 'n' Peels he kept in the top drawer of his desk for stressful situations. He offered one to Mims, she shook her head no, and he started the soothing process of separating the strands and coiling them into his mouth.

"Who would have thought bees were so attracted to corn syrup?" she asked. "Like little fat kids."

Was she implying the bees were attracted to the corn syrup *in the honey bottles*? Was she on board with the poetic interpretation? Did she already know all of it?

"Sometimes the bees know better than we do what we're feeding them," he said carefully. "I would never feed a bee corn syrup unless I thought it was honey. The bees can't be mad about that if they're the ones who know it's corn syrup and we don't even know."

Mims tilted her head to the side. He had to pull himself together. He didn't truly want to get caught, regardless of what the bees "wanted."

"What I mean to say is a lot of people, human people, are up in arms these days about high fructose corn syrup and food dyes and foods that are perceived as 'not natural.' I stand behind our product; Beasley maraschino cherries are wholesome and safe. I have no qualms about them. But I also respect our customers and want to give them what they ask for. That's why we're starting an all-new organic cherries wing. No high fructose corn syrup, artificial preservatives, colors, anything. We're even going to use cane sugar instead of sugar from GMO beets. And there's going to be an 'old world' line that's actually preserved in alcohol, like the original European maraschinos." He handed her a brochure.

"Would you mind if I came back with a camera in a couple of hours?" Mims asked. She started writing in her notebook.

He hesitated. "Do you really need photos? If so, I could send a photo. We have some nice ones we use for promotional materials."

Her pen slowed. "It's a big article. It will need a current photo. What's your reservation?"

"Just . . . that it's a huge waste of time for you to leave and come all the way back," Teddy said. Unlikely as it was that she'd been tipped off about the tariff evasion or that she'd happen upon the entrance to the basement, he wanted her gone. The relief he'd felt when she introduced herself in the courtyard had been fully obliterated awhile back. "I have an SLR some-where. It's not the fanciest camera, but I bet you could get something good." He started opening drawers.

Mims hadn't started writing again. "You're not breaking any laws with the way you're transporting and disposing of the cherry waste? Supposedly manufacturing in the city these days is all solar panels and artisanal pickles, but the history of the Gowanus Canal shows that people will save money by dumping if they can get away with it."

"Of course we're not doing that." Teddy was expert at scanning faces for any little sign of disapproval. It was second nature. He'd been focused on other people's reactions for so long he'd inadvertently stopped pay-ing attention to what *he* felt; his wants had receded so far into the back-ground he couldn't even call them up or identify them anymore. All he felt, and it was an overwhelming feeling that took up the whole canvas of his life, was a compulsion to track displeasure and steer his way clear of it like a ship through a field of icebergs. He could see that he'd made Mims Walsh suspicious.

"I'm going to research it," she said.

"I hope you do." He folded his arms across his chest but was still breathing slowly. There must be another reason he could give for not wanting her snooping around . . .

"The party!" Teddy blurted out. "There's going to be a party next Wednesday to celebrate the opening of the organic wing, and some guys are going to be here in an hour or so to take measurements and drop off parts for the stage. If you come back later the photos are going to be all cluttered with men and stuff."

"Can I come to the party?"

He was making everything worse. "I would prefer to just take care of this situation without publicity, that's my reservation," Teddy said, pleading.

"Why?" she asked. He hated her "hard–hitting journalism" voice.

"I don't like the attention and I don't want to bother anyone. I love animals." Maybe all he needed to do was remain calm and affable and she would think she was overreacting. It was his usual tactic and it usually worked. He remembered the camera was in the filing cabinet, set it on his desk in front of Mims, and leaned back in his chair. "Because of one magazine writer's typo *years ago*, a lot of the public still thinks maraschino cherries contain formaldehyde. He meant to write 'benzaldehyde,' a flavoring oil. Our benzaldehyde is extracted from cherry pits. You can see why I'm wary of journalists and the unintended havoc they can wreak." He gestured toward her.

"We're a small company," he continued. "The buildings here are large, but there are only seventeen full–time employees. We don't need bad press for ourselves or our industry. It wasn't our fault the bees came here, and we haven't done anything wrong. I hope you understand that."

"I'll make you a deal," she said. "In exchange for exclusive access to you and to your factory, I'll write it as a charming, feel–good article."

He was silent.

"It will be good publicity for your new product."

"Okay," he said. "But I don't want to be in the photo, just the factory."

"Okay. And I want to come to the party."

"Okay, fine."

The onslaught seemed to be over. "I'll walk you out." He handed her the camera. "When you're done, go to the front desk and Jalen will transfer the photos for you and email them. You can leave the camera with him."

"Thank you," Mims said. Her voice was non-combative for the first time since she'd received her coffee. "It's really so kind of you to let me use your camera. You won't regret helping me out."

Teddy breathed a sigh of relief. "I'm glad I won you over," he said. This was either the end of the bees causing him trouble, or the beginning.

CHAPTER 20:
HOMECOMING

A man was crying and a woman gave him a thin sweatshirt and he blew his nose in it and then she took his hand and he followed her away. Marlow was staring at them from behind a tree, and she was dying to know their story. She'd always thought of the Upper East Side as a neighborhood of white gloves, service entrances, and elderly ladies with plastic surgery, not crassness and crying. Things had changed since she'd moved away.

She'd been standing outside her grandfather's building for an hour and a half waiting for the doorman she knew to come on shift. She wanted him to let her up without an announcement.

Finally he came around the corner of the building. "Sanjeep!" He was shorter and his hair was gone, but otherwise he looked the same as when she was a child.

"Miss Beasley," he said. "Welcome back." She walked with him into the building.

Marlow asked if he knew anything about the crying couple outside and he responded with a vague wave of his hand. He'd told her once in a rare show of anger that her questions were invasive, and that she wanted to consume the people around her. Marlow had liked that. Instead of answering about the couple, he said "Mr. Beasley is looking really good." That was a relief; Teddy couldn't need her that urgently if he was looking good. "The famous Beasley vigor!" Marlow replied.

Unimpressed as Sanjeep was with Marlow's antics, he let her through with a nod and a smile, so she considered that a victory.

As the elevator doors closed she was flooded with memories of visiting Grandpa's place with her mother when she was little. One hundred percent of the time, her mom pushed her way into elevators without letting people off first, shuffling Marlow in ahead of her with a grip on each shoulder. It was because she was scared the elevator doors would close on them; fear trumped politeness. All children are embarrassed of their parents, but with her mom it shot straight past embarrassment to a feeling akin to floating solo in the middle of the ocean. So far alone as to be unable to fathom contact. She didn't understand her own mother, couldn't reach her.

Even the act of being hugged by her mom, which imparted a feeling of sturdy strength when it came from her grandfather, instead passed along a sort of nervousness, like a vibration passing from one strip of thin metal to another. Before she was old enough to have the words for it, Marlow had known on a deep, body level that she would have to take care of herself.

She turned the doorknob to Teddy's apartment, their grandfather's apartment, and found it unlocked.

Teddy was standing next to the dining table with a phone to his ear.

"Beard!" she said when she saw him. "What's this, it's so thick and manly!"

He laughed.

"Doe, I'll call you back," he said. "My sister just got here."

She ran up to him for a hug and then stopped. An embrace suddenly seemed presumptuous, though she hugged near–strangers without a thought.

"How did you get it so luxurious?" she asked. Marlow inspected the beard closely, her face inches away, hoping clownish antics would cover her discomfort.

"With conditioner," he admitted with slow caution.

She rewarded his honesty by not making fun of him. Marlow stood tall and narrowed her eyes. "Let's do this," she said, and they both laughed and clasped each other in a bear hug.

"That could have gone worse," Teddy said as they pulled apart. "How was the drive?"

She told him about the trip but left out the fun parts and the detours. She could sense it would upset him to hear why it took her longer than her initial ETA to get there. It had been almost a month since his phone call. Her truck was parked in a garage nearby and they'd both made the same assumption that she'd be staying in one of the spare bedrooms.

"It was clever of you to make it a mystery about the vats," Marlow said. "Wanting to know the details drew me inexorably closer to New York each day." She pantomimed the slow progress of her truck with one hand.

"It felt pretty exorable to me," Teddy said under his breath, but in a tone of voice like he was joking.

"So what's the problem with the factory?" she asked.

His expression darkened a moment and then faded back into a pleasant, cow–like dumbness. He'd always been too amiable, avoiding conflict at all costs. They walked together into the living room and he gestured toward the sofa. Marlow sat.

"Bees were getting into the spent brine as we transported it across the yard. First they would just come for the spilled puddles, then they started getting into the barrels themselves. Now hundreds of them show up every day."

"Lids?" she suggested.

"We've been using Saran Wrap and they get under it."

"They won't get under a lid," she said. "Is this really what you wouldn't talk about over the phone?" It was a surprisingly interesting problem, exciting even, but it was missing the part that would make it worth being secretive.

"It doesn't matter now anyway," he said evenly. He didn't seem upset, but the way he flopped on the couch was a little *too* casual.

"Why doesn't it matter now?" she asked.

"A reporter came by the factory this afternoon," Teddy said from his lounged-out position. "Apparently the bees belong to a bunch of different hives, ones people are keeping on rooftops; they aren't wild." He got back up to take a glass from the coffee table into the kitchen and then stopped to straighten some papers on his way back. "Their honey is red now and everyone was looking for the source. The reporter put me in touch with a beekeeper. He's going to come by Monday and walk the factory, give some tips. He said draping the barrels in fabric sheets soaked in vinegar might work."

"I'm *definitely* coming for the tour." Marlow pictured an elaborate Rube Goldberg setup for dispersing the bees, and she wanted to help build it.

"He's coming at seven in the morning, so you'll miss it. Another option is to build rolling wooden lockers. Or place feeders with sugar water on the roof to distract them."

"I'll 'miss it'? So I'm too late is what you're saying, and you're upset with me."

"Not at all. I'm not angry, I'm just annoyed."

"It's okay to be angry. Tell me I'm a dick, I know it's true."

"I'm not going to call you names," he said.

"It will help."

"Can you just stop for a minute?"

"I'm being serious!"

Marlow stomped toward the bar in the corner of the living room and poured herself a whiskey. She couldn't recall even one time where he'd ever been honest about his feelings if they were angry or aggressive, no matter how obvious it was that he should be.

She walked slowly around the apartment with her back to Teddy, appraising the curtains and the old–man furniture. "These tumblers are ugly, like something you'd get at a garage sale," she said. She twirled the glass in the orange light of a slag desk lamp. "You should have young–man glasses, Teddy."

"Now you're angry at *me*? What did I do?"

"I came all the way down here to listen to you and now you won't talk. You didn't call me down here just for bees."

"Why would I want to depend on you for anything at this point? You clearly don't care about me that much or you would have been excited to get here on time."

Marlow had to stop herself from superimposing her mother onto Teddy. Guilt and bleary, self–pitying tears were the number one weapon in mom's manipulative arsenal. No amount of kowtowing was ever enough to please her or cheer her up, but people never stopped trying. Maybe her mom thought if she could control the world, people included, she'd finally feel safe.

Teddy was not her mom.

"I care very much about you," she said. "I wouldn't have come for bees. I came for *you*. Don't be stupid."

Teddy stood with his hands in his hoodie pocket. Bearded five–year–old.

"We sound like bickering children." Marlow softened her tone and set the whiskey aside. "Let's start over. Let me take you to dinner."

Teddy nodded and went to the front entrance, gathering wallet, keys. "I should pay for dinner," he said.

"So we're just going to get it all out in the open right away then?" she roared.

Teddy dropped his shoe. "I just meant . . ."

She knew what he meant. He thought he should pay because he was the one with the factory and the apartment and she had gotten almost nothing. Teddy swatted at his head. "What is this?" she asked, irritated, imitating his gesture.

"Marlow," he said. His face looked like maybe it was about to crumble, but she couldn't tell under the beard. "I thought there was a bee, but of course there's no bee in here. It's just habit now to swat whenever I feel anxious. I did call you about the bees, in a sense. I'm worried about myself. I can't stop thinking about them. I'm worried that they bother me so much."

He really had called her to the city in a big-sister capacity. With him standing there so vulnerable, she didn't feel at all like she'd expected and been avoiding. Teddy *was* anxious but also Marlow *wasn't* trapped by it. She wanted to help.

"Get your shoes," she said gently. After Teddy slipped them on, he stepped into the kitchen and tossed a lobster claw oven mitt under the sink. He looked self-conscious. It was sad to think she was making her own brother feel small and emasculated. They were the last two Beasleys; she wanted him to feel as big and as ready to meet adventure as she did.

"I'm sorry I said that about the money," he said when they were on the street. "I should have realized you would be sensitive about the inheritance."

"I'm not upset about you getting the factory. I'm not cut out for office life and everyone knew it. I said I didn't want it and our parents followed through."

"Do you have anything left?" he asked tentatively. "From the money?" She'd gotten a small lump sum; Teddy had gotten everything else. She'd gone back to Alaska straight from the will reading without telling him she was leaving.

"I invested in something that won't go away when the stock market inevitably tanks," Marlow said.

"Real estate?"

"Self-improvement."

Teddy's "active listening" smile was pretty transparent; she could tell he was trying to figure out if she was joking.

"I'm building a jerky company in Alaska," she explained. "I have a smokehouse, took some business classes. I have my *own* food factory now." The idea was to make her own fortune, and prove she could follow through on something, away from prying eyes . . . in case it didn't go well. But she'd just told Teddy, so that was out.

"Congratulations," he said softly. He didn't ask how much volume she did or how much money her jerky factory made. The answer was none, yet, but he didn't know that. She hadn't expected him to be impressed with her little venture, but he seemed downright gloomy. Marlow was irked that he wasn't more excited, didn't have more faith in her, so she didn't reassure him that she still had money in her childhood trust fund and could make it stretch for years with her backwoods lifestyle.

At the restaurant Teddy ordered the cheapest thing. She ordered four appetizers and two entrees. It was a nice restaurant, but it was still New York, and a cockroach skittered up the wall near the window while they were waiting for dessert. Marlow whipped her arm out, reflexes as fast as ever, and crushed it with a loud thud on the heel of her hand. Everyone in the restaurant turned as she wiped it in her napkin. She was satisfied and calm, in her element with the judgment and awe of onlookers, when the manager came over and offered to comp their meal.

So far New York was going pretty well. Teddy seemed uneasy, but they were basically strangers, so that was to be expected. He'd opened up about his stress levels, and once they were working side by side building an obstacle course for bees, fun and sibling bonding were sure to follow.

CHAPTER 21:
KAI

"**H**ello, this is Kai Peterson," he announced.

"Hello, this is Mims from the *Free Post*."

"Yes! I was just going to call you. I got the results back from the sample you sent over. Let's set up a time to meet and discuss."

"I'm actually hoping to submit the article today if everything checks out. Could we talk on the phone for a few minutes?"

"Let's meet for coffee."

"Oh, is it bad news? Did the samples not match up?"

"I didn't say that. Can you meet me at Saturdays in two hours? Bring your notebook."

"Sure." Mims hung up with a childish trill of excitement. Saturdays was in SoHo and Kai's office was in the Bronx. Maybe he'd chosen the location to be polite, because it was halfway between his office and her apartment, but maybe he'd chosen a place so far from his work because they were about to have a Deep Throat–style secret meeting where she learned about global honey conspiracies. Which reminded her, she owed it to the chef to ask Kai about the supermarket honey, though she probably wouldn't call Gerard again even if she chose to look into it further. Mims never apologized to people after blowing up at them because it felt like something an abusive husband would do, like bringing flowers after breaking his wife's nose. She wasn't allowed to apologize until she was sorry enough to change her behavior, which had basically never happened.

Two hours later Mims sat on a bench outside Saturdays. It was a surf shop staffed by male models, mostly blonds, and there was no menu board. You had to be cool enough to know they served coffee and to ask for it.

Frenetic movement caught her eye. Kai was speed–walking toward her, his jacket billowing at his sides, but when he saw her he slowed to a more dignified gait.

"Hey, thanks for meeting," Kai said, his fast breathing belying the casual pose he struck when he reached her.

"Hello, Kai," she said with a smirk. "You always seem so pumped about life. The USDA must be a fun place to work."

They went inside and Kai ordered an iced coffee, and was handed one, premade, from beneath the wooden counter. "I've never been here before," he said. "But it looks really cool. My coworker recommended it."

"Can you make mochas here?" Mims asked the barista. There was no obvious espresso equipment. She wasn't sure how much the drink would cost, but she had five dollars in her pocket. If Kai didn't offer to pay, she'd be eating into her subway fund.

"We're out of syrup, but yeah, I can do that." The surfer took a chocolate bar from the display next to the register and started crushing it into pieces.

"Did the maraschino cherry runoff match what was in the red honey from Charlie's rooftop hives?" Mims asked.

"You cut right to it. It did! Mystery solved."

"It's why I came here," she said, annoyed that he hadn't just told her over the phone. It was impossible to hold in a smile though—she really had solved it, and the article went well beyond what Aziz had asked for. It was a lot easier to feel magnanimous when things were going well, which maybe said something unflattering about her strength of character. "You got the answer a lot faster than I expected. You said you would have them rush it, but one–day turnaround?"

"Oh, it's actually really easy to get people to test your samples fast if you ask the right way."

"When we were on Charlie's roof you made it sound like getting in at the lab was like trying to cut the line at an emergency room."

The surfer handed her the mocha and she reached for her five, slowly.

"I got this," Kai said and counted out exact change.

"Thank you."

"Oh, almost forgot," Kai said. He pulled a one out of his pocket and extended it to the surfer, she assumed as a tip. "This has something sticky on it. Can you give me a clean one?" The young man exchanged it and Kai put the fresh dollar back in his pocket.

Kai seemed more oblivious than willfully dismissive toward the prominent tip jar on the counter, but both were equally inexcusable to Mims. She dropped her five in the jar with a scowl.

"There are seats out back," Kai said cheerfully, oblivious still.

"What else did you want to tell me about the lab results?" Mims asked. She decided there would be no discussion of honey crime syndicates; he was about to waste a bunch of her time on a fake date when she could be finishing the article. She wasn't about to prolong the interaction. Mims crossed her arms in front of her chest. "Did you lie about the timeline for testing Charlie's honey so that your work would look more harrowing and important?"

"I have a printout," he said and extended it toward her. "It's got the lab name and everything if you want to mention it in the article."

Mims didn't reach for it.

"Yes," he admitted. "I wanted to look cool in your story." She uncrossed her arms and took the paper. "But it really is a lot faster to compare two samples to see if they match than it is to try to figure out one thing just based on molecules, and they weren't going to cut the line for that. They work really hard, I swear. The lab is *very* understaffed. If I'd asked them to speed up the process earlier they might have said no."

Kai went on about inspection protocol and then vacation policy at the USDA and then the brand of cupcakes they got for office birthdays and how he always drank the coffee from the office coffee makers, but it was way more exciting to leave the office. Like he was a real New Yorker and not just living in New York! Mims was bored. Kai pulled a nose hair out of his nostril and wiped it on his pants. She dutifully averted her eyes, pondering how it was more rude on the rudeness hierarchy for her to call him out on nose hair pulling than it was for him to do it.

"This has been great, but I should go submit my article now," Mims said. "I want to catch my editor while he's still in the office."

"All right, thanks for meeting!" Kai said, unfazed. She was impressed with his confidence in his own likability.

"This isn't a date," she said.

"That's fine!" he said.

She turned to go and then turned back, curiosity overtaking grumpiness. "Hey, is there such a thing as a honey crime syndicate?"

"You betcha! Illegal honey is a $3 billion a year industry."

She was stunned.

"What does that mean, exactly?" she asked.

"For imported honey, people lie about the country of origin to avoid tariffs or to avoid being screened for banned pesticides."

"Do people ever sell corn syrup as honey?"

"That's kind of old-school. It got so common that customs labs knew exactly how to test for it, so most people switched to rice syrup or other sweeteners."

"But I thought honey prices were at an all-time low," Mims said. It was something Pete had told her. "Why would you make a fake version of a product that doesn't sell for much?"

"Here, sit back down," Kai said. He patted the seat she'd just vacated. Mims shook her head no.

"It's cheap *because* of all the fake honey," Kai explained. "The bee population is a fraction of what it was a few years ago because of colony collapse disorder, but demand for honey is at an all-time high because of the natural foods trend. Suppliers are finding creative ways to fill the gap between supply and demand. And if you think that's bad, you should hear about the maple syrup cartels coming out of Canada. Let's hang out again and I'll tell you all about it."

"Sure, maybe." She'd follow up with Kai via email. Maybe she could convince him to test out the chef's "fake" honey or put her in touch with one of the customs labs he mentioned. It still seemed a little too good to be true that a story like that would fall in her lap. Mims walked a few blocks and sat at an empty chessboard table in the park to finish her article; at the last minute she decided to mention Kai by name and referred to him as "tall." That was as much of a thank you as he was going to get. She emailed the article to Aziz and started the walk to the newspaper office to discuss in person. Putting in some face time, she hoped, would get her in rotation for assignments.

"Mims, get over here!" Aziz shouted as soon as the elevator doors opened.

"You like it?"

"I wanted to get you a congratulations drink, but there's nothing in the office. You want a seltzer? Here, have a seltzer."

Mims smiled, proud and speechless.

"Come into my office! Really, this is great investigation work. I want to get you on more serious pieces . . ."

That night Mims emerged back into society, meeting up with Bennie and a few other friends at a bar in East Bushwick. She let them buy her rounds without considering it charity. "I'm a goddamned writer!" she toasted herself.

CHAPTER 22:
MARLOW VISITS THE FACTORY

Marlow stepped out of her truck in front of Beasley Cherries at 6:45 a.m. She'd pretended to be asleep as Teddy fumbled around in the kitchen, and as soon as he was out the door she sprung out of the guest room and down the service elevator. She was waiting out front of the factory with a mug of coffee when he came through the gate.

"So where's this Charlie guy?" She took a sip.

Teddy smiled and shook his head.

An old Subaru pulled through the gate a few minutes later and an old man stepped out of it.

"Hello," he said. "I'm here to have a chat with your bees." There were already a few gliding into the gravel yard. Marlow loved Charlie, instantly, for the way his cottony wisps of hair bobbed after him as he strode forward. After a round of introductions Teddy went inside and Marlow helped unload the car without him.

"You know they kick out the male bees in winter—all they do is laze about all summer," Charlie said. He eyed the door Teddy had gone through.

"He works hard." She wanted to defend her brother; it made her sad not to know him well enough to have an explanation for his leaving. "So tell me about these syrup guzzlers."

160

"Come take a look." Charlie knelt down next to a scraggly flower that had pushed its way through the gravel. Two bees were just taking off. "Worker bees have different jobs throughout their lives, and forager is the last stop—starting at about day twenty-two. Usually a bee dies of 'old age' while out of the hive, mid-task, within a few weeks of her first flight. They fall from the air laden with pollen or full of nectar. Can you imagine being so committed to your work?"

"No," said Marlow. "Committed to play, maybe."

After he finished telling her about the bees' Latin name and their social structures and their guts, including one stomach for eating and one for nectar transport, she was sorry to see them go. "They're so tiny to have so many discrete parts," she said.

Marlow poured the last of her too-sweet coffee on the ground and then stuck her hand out above the pool, hoping for one of the bees to alight in a Disney princess scenario, but none of them played along.

"So if the option is between labor-intensive screened lockers for the barrels as we push them across the yard or distracting the bees with freely available goodies on the roof, I choose to feed them," Marlow said. She climbed with Charlie up to the roof, carrying supplies and a tool chest, and helped him assemble trough-like feeders.

"Someone will have to come from time to time to make sure they're full," Charlie said. He splashed sugar water from a gallon jug into one of them.

"I'm sure it won't be a problem." Marlow sat back on her heels. "We should do a rooftop garden! We could plant flowers up here that bees like. Do you have a list of which ones do well on rooftops?"

"Oh definitely!"

Back on the ground they schemed as they hammered mesh into wooden frames Charlie had brought as temporary covers for the barrels. He handed her printouts for plans for vinegar spritzing stations to post at the door where the barrels were wheeled into the courtyard. When the barrels tripped a pressure sensor on the floor they would spray a fine mist like the water that freshens vegetables in grocery stores. The smell on the barrel would last long enough to deter the bees until the barrels made it to the building with the disposal drain.

"Did you invent this?" Marlow asked.

Charlie laughed. "It's a tweak of someone else's invention. I wish I had. I've learned a lot of tricks over the years. When I was more nimble, I used to specialize in catching swarms that were out looking for a new home. That's much more low tech. You want to know the most common method for capturing a swarm?"

"You know I do, Charlie."

"If you have eight, ten thousand bees all clumped together on a tree limb, waiting while the scouts are looking for a new place to live . . ." He trailed off dramatically, hushed.

"Well?!"

"You put a big cardboard box underneath, file–box size, and you knock them into it with a broom. Or you just shake the branch if you can reach." Charlie cackled. "They fall down in a clump. Put a lid on and just drive them to where you have a hive box waiting. Then you use a bee brush to push their little butts into their new home."

Around midday Charlie left. When Marlow hugged him she felt his shoulders buckle like chicken bones. She went inside the building and found Teddy in his office.

"Do you have architectural plans for the buildings?"

"No, what for?" Teddy asked. Sweat broke out on his forehead, right below that luxurious hair of his.

"That question makes you nervous?" Her brother stressed about unexpected topics. She wondered if it would seem flippant to suggest Lexapro. "You must have them somewhere, but it doesn't matter. I'll draw a diagram of the roof. Do you have a really long measuring tape? I'm going to go visit Charlie and we're going to figure out how much weight it can bear. I'm making us a rooftop garden. Doesn't that fit in perfectly with the new organic wing? All sustainable and shit."

"How much is that going to cost?" Teddy asked.

"Doesn't he remind you of grandpa?" Marlow sat on the sofa and swung her legs over the arm. She picked up a magazine and started flipping through the pages, too fast to read.

"Not at all. They're both old, but other than that they have nothing in common. If Irving had met that guy at a poker game, he would have left with the deed to his house."

"Maybe. We're going to have some screens custom-made for the tops of the barrels, simple ones, easier than plastic wrap. We made temporary versions today, but they don't fit snugly enough. And we're going to put in a vinegar spritzing station by the door. The bees will be a lot more lazy about trying to get through because of the food on the roof, so they shouldn't be an issue anymore."

"So the bees aren't actually gone, just relocated a few feet away, and we're planting a garden to attract more of them." He turned off his computer monitor and stood up. "I'm going to go for a walk."

"Why are you upset?"

"I'm not upset!" he said, but his eyes were very wide, as if he was scared.

"You had me come all the way down here from Alaska to handle these bees, so I did," she yelled after him. "What about lunch?"

"I'll be back after I do a walk-through of the new wing."

After he disappeared around the corner of the hallway, Marlow sat at his desk and turned the computer monitor back on. It was suspicious that he'd turned it off, and it was odd he'd been so exasperated by the inarguably fantastic, multifaceted, and super-fun solution she and Charlie had come up with to the bee problem. Forget Lexapro, she should probably force him to do some aversion therapy or something if they bothered him that much.

Marlow took three energy–focusing yoga breaths when she saw the password screen. "Maraschino," she typed. No. She tried "Irving." No. She tried "Irving" with a number one for the "I" and it worked. In a folder labeled "financials" she found budgets and account balances. The construction on the organic wing went so far over budget it threatened the rest of the company; the renovations for the original structure had come in slightly over budget. Profits the previous year had been lower than expected, due to market fluctuations, not mismanagement, as far as she could tell.

A few saved newspaper and food industry articles suggested Teddy was considering diversifying beyond cherries. She was impressed and a little surprised at his ambition. He had put up an enormous amount of personal money to keep the factory going. "Don't pierce the corporate veil, Teddy," she mumbled aloud. It also appeared he'd downplayed the extent of the debt on the reports he shared with the rest of management. Also concerning, some invoices had been paid with money that didn't have an obvious source. Skimming through his projections, everything would even out in the next couple of years assuming commodities didn't go up and people didn't suddenly stop drinking tropical cocktails. Marlow drummed her fingers on the edge of the desk. Contractors were like that friend who, when running late, always said they were ten minutes away, even if they hadn't left the house yet. But Teddy was too young to have known that.

Marlow leaned back in Teddy's chair. "I knew you didn't drag me down here because of bees," she said. It wasn't lost on her that he was too absorbed in his own problems to want to talk about the past; that she'd left without saying goodbye after the funerals hadn't been on his mind at all when he called her. The inheritance and her disappearance turned out to be her hang–up, not his, and she felt weird about that. But if he'd brought her to New York to ask for money, why hadn't he asked yet?

The day's nervous energy had started as a manic reaction to the bees, and now it was adrenaline from the impending confrontation with Teddy. She decided to stroll the old buildings until he got back from the new buildings.

Marlow walked onto the main factory floor. The sounds she expected, but the smells she had forgotten. She closed her eyes and breathed deeply. Without resentment she donned the customary hairnet, booties to cover her shoes, and gloves in case she wanted to touch anything. Everyone who stepped more than a couple of feet inside the cavernous room was expected to wear them. Somehow the ritual reminded her of putting on a life preserver when taking off for the open sea. She made her way to the back so she could climb the stairs up to the catwalk and take in the big picture, as she used to do with Irving when she was little. Cherry cleaning, cherry sorting, cherry pitting, cherry brining, the fruits getting progressively brighter, cheerier, and less natural–looking as they made their way through the stations.

And then outside this room there was Teddy and debt and the bees. She'd never expected the factory could contain so many surprises.

CHAPTER 23:
A SMALL BUSINESS OWNER

L in walked through the Customs and Border Patrol doors and assessed the customer service queue. Passports were checked before anyone left the ships, so these were all men with problems and without the intelligence to solve said problems on their own. He skirted around them and approached the counter. "I'm captain of *Xiamen Peak*. Where would I find the bus off the marine terminal?"

"Sir," the clerk said. "You'll have to wait in the line."

Before the clerk had finished speaking, Lin turned his back and walked away.

"Where do I find the bus off the marine terminal?" Lin asked the last man in the queue. The man looked at him with confused deference, a reaction he'd come to expect from Americans upon hearing the vaguely British clip to his Xiamen accent. The clerk had been an anomaly.

"Go two buildings down and then you'll see a red sign," the man said.

It took almost ten minutes for the shuttle to cross the terminal, with its endless canyons of shipping containers stacked four high, and pull up to the transfer point for the city bus into Manhattan. From the highway twelve cargo ships were visible in the harbor, each held low in the water by thousands of enormous multicolored boxes. These were older ships; newer ones held tens of thousands and shuttled only between Asia and Europe, too large to fit into New World ports or through the Panama Canal.

Cranes were already starting work on *Xiamen Peak*, whose load was mainly T-shirts. None of his fleet held more than five hundred containers each, but Teddy Beasley was going to finance an upgrade.

An hour after boarding the transfer bus, Lin alighted in Midtown and began the walk to Brooklyn, eager to move of his own volition after thirty-four days at sea. His pace didn't slow until he entered an industrial zone of windowless warehouses.

A block from Beasley Cherries, Lin put on a baseball hat and pulled the brim low over his eyes. He approached the gate and buzzed and some-one let him in without even asking who he was. White gravel crunched under his boots as he crossed the yard.

A man came out of one of the buildings and lit a cigarette.

"Where is Teddy Beasley?" Lin asked him.

"In his office, probably. In the other building."

"Could you ask him to come out, please?"

"Sure," the man said. He hesitated but stamped out the cigarette and went to do as he was asked. Lin swatted at a bee that zoomed past his shoulder.

A few minutes later a young man in a green hoodie and tight jeans, much taller than Lin was, came outside. His pant cuffs were rolled up to reveal colorful socks. Beasley's appearance was in line with what he had expected: young and soft, but big. Lin could tell the exact moment Beasley realized who he was because he stopped in mid stride.

Lin gestured for him to come closer.

"Our partnership is very important to me," he said as Beasley approached.

"Maybe we should talk somewhere more private," Beasley suggested.

"I was about to say the same thing."

Beasley led him to an alley between the buildings. The sounds of the machines inside came faintly through the brick.

"We're all full up on cherry supplies," Beasley said in a caricature-ignorant voice. "We won't be needing any more corn syrup for a while; I'm sure your brother, or was it cousin, will understand that we found a cheaper supplier." His performance seemed to be a mix of comedy and wishful thinking. Beasley was the kind of man who had never been in a fight, never killed an animal for food or in defense, never been in danger.

"Corn syrup," Lin said quietly. He shot forward and swung his fist but stopped short of contact. Beasley scrambled back and tripped into the wall. Lin laughed. He lowered his fist. "Funny," he said. "You pretend about corn syrup and I pretend too." He continued to chuckle as if they were friends remembering an old joke. "I'm talking about the honey rolling your way, over the high seas."

Beasley straightened back up. "Listen—"

Precisely when the fear had passed from Beasley's eyes, Lin hit him. The oversized man–baby slammed back hard, and the impact with the wall stopped him from falling.

"You're going to keep pretending you haven't seen the emails?" Lin asked. By the time he returned to China, Teddy Beasley would be accepting shipments bimonthly, indefinitely. First there was the matter of the shipment which had been picked up at the docks but hadn't met their distribution truck at the allotted time.

Beasley bent over at the waist, looking down at the ground and dripping blood from his mouth. "Your emails got really angry really fast. How would I even respond to something like that?" he asked without looking up.

"So your silence was a demand for a return to civil communication? It was manipulation and not cowardice?"

"I don't belong in the middle of this," Beasley said. "It's a mistake . . ."

"I don't see how. Your actions have led directly to this moment."

"Then I choose something else." He looked like he was struggling to make his face brave, which was pretty amusing. Beasley ought to be grateful Lin was about to make him rich. "We've only been working together a few months. Let's call this a trial run, and it didn't work out. You got some distribution out of it and now we're good. I'll even return the last payment."

"No," Lin replied. "The next honey shipment is arriving on schedule, this Saturday. Be there at the Red Hook terminal to receive it. And the previous load that never arrived at the rendezvous point—have it ready. You will hand off that honey at 3:00 p.m., two days from now. I'll send a truck for it."

"It's not honey," Beasley said.

"It's viscous yellow sugar," Lin responded without losing a beat. "That's honey."

"Is there anything I can do to—"

"You say you don't want this, but I know that you do. Your greatest desire is for life to be easy and comfortable, and to men like you that includes having no difficult choices as to what you do, limited responsibility, limited awareness of how your actions impact others. I've done that for you. So you can go home and sleep peacefully tonight knowing we've had an honest interaction here—you've asked the universe for something, dirty money without the moral burden of taking the initiative, and I've provided it. Your future riches are not your 'fault.' This is one of the few interactions of integrity you'll probably ever have."

Lin left the alley and walked back to the entrance gate. "Buzz me out!" he called with a wave of his arm, not turning around, and someone did.

CHAPTER 24:
MILD DISCOMFORT

Teddy sat in the dark on the floor amid the relabeling equipment. The cement floor was uneven and dusty, rough against his legs. It was after 7:00 p.m. and he wasn't sure why he was still sitting down here, sore from carrying boxes but with so many more to go, but it was maybe to force himself to acknowledge that the room was real. He pressed his tongue, so gently, against his front bottom tooth and it felt loose. With that his blood pressure dropped. At least the more flowery execrations from Lin's emails made sense now that he'd met him in person.

He had gotten into a situation so far outside his everyday experience that he had no clue how to get back out. "I wish we made croutons instead of maraschino cherries," he said to the wall. "I could have left a Hansel–and–Gretel breadcrumb trail and backtracked. Wait, then I'd have rats instead of bees . . ." He sighed and bowed his head. There it was again, a wish to escape or go back rather than an urge to move forward and confront. Lin's words gnawed at him. He'd spent his entire life trying to prove that he was a man who could stand on his own, but when things got hard for the first time, he'd wanted to call out to his parents for rescue, but they were dead, so he'd called in Marlow to save him instead.

When he was ten, two years after he'd almost drowned in a riptide at their family's summer place in the Hamptons and become terrified of the water, he had approached the ocean again for the first time. Marlow hadn't noticed he was following her down to the water's edge; he didn't want to make a big deal of it. But he'd trusted his big sister wouldn't let anything bad happen to him. He felt stupid thinking of it now. His sister was a real person, not the childlike conception he'd had of her as larger than life. The moment Marlow arrived in New York it had become obvious she excelled only at silly things, not meaningful ones. She skimmed reality, touching down for the interesting bits and the drama. Ten-to-one chances the jerky factory was a countertop dehydrator and a load of horseshit, and there'd be no consequences for her when it failed. It was easy to glide through the world without anxiety if you never took anything seriously.

A gate slammed down somewhere above. Teddy ran up the stairs, through the garage, and into the front corridor that led through the offices. Brittany-Lynne was walking toward the building; the workday had ended at five. Teddy peeked his head out.

"You scared me. I thought someone was breaking in again," he said.

"I forgot my sweater in the garage," she said. "Your poor face."

He held the door open for her. "It'll be better in a week."

He walked into his office and she followed. The story he'd told everyone was that a mentally unstable homeless man had been wandering around the factory yard and when Teddy confronted him he got hit. He felt bad; he knew it was wrong to stigmatize mental illness and the unhoused. Brittany-Lynne was the one who'd innocently opened the gate for Lin. Twice. Teddy flopped on the sofa and Brittany-Lynne sat at his feet. "It looks kind of sexy," she said hopefully. Her eyes rested on his lips.

"We shouldn't," he said. Doe would be waiting for him later. They hadn't been seeing each other long, but monogamy had been implied since the beginning.

"Is it hard to eat?" Brittany-Lynne asked.

"No, I just need to be careful how wide I open my mouth. I brushed against the bruise when I was pulling off my sweatshirt and it stung all the way down to my chin. There must be a nerve there."

Brittany-Lynne touched the corner of her lips, the same spot that was scabbed on Teddy's. "It really makes you appreciate nuance and delicacy, things that can be done with mouths," she said.

She leaned toward him and rested a hand on his leg.

"We really shouldn't," he said.

"Shouldn't what?"

Teddy laughed. She wasn't acting like herself.

"But why not?" she said. "You are going to die one day. And you can die having had the experience of me sucking your cock in your office or not." From the way she pronounced "cock" Teddy was pretty sure she had never said the word out loud before, and he was enthralled by it.

A buzzing in his brain prevented him from thinking clearly or moving quickly.

It was like he was a genie, and now that she'd summoned him he was compelled to become whatever she asked of him. He let her unfasten his pants.

Later she sat next to him, both of them leaning their heads back on the cushions and looking up at the ceiling. He felt sort of clammy.

"We can't do that again," he said.

"I know," she said. "I felt bad about you getting hurt."

"Hey, my sister might come by again when the bee guy is back and I don't want her messing with my stuff. Can you show me how to change the password on my desktop?" He leaned forward and wiggled the mouse to wake up the computer. "I'll go get your sweater," he said.

He walked calmly to the garage entrance and, once out of sight, rushed to the secret door to the secret basement and pulled it closed. He grabbed Brittany-Lynne's sweater from a corner cubby. He'd allowed it to happen because . . . he wanted . . . to be held, maybe. To experience care and desire instead of violence or criticism. Because it was exciting. It was the opposite of emasculating. He wished he could take it back.

"Just type in the password you want here," she said when he returned. She angled the computer monitor toward him so he could see.

"Here's your sweater." The sexual tension had drained away and there wasn't even awkwardness in its place. They were just coworkers.

Brittany-Lynne took the sweater and smiled on her way out the door. "See you tomorrow. Don't stay here too late."

It was pre-dusk when Teddy went outside, and the sky was bright, dishwater gray. He marched to the center of the yard, but there was no one there to confront. Only one bee, and it was leaving. He stalked the edges of the yard, unsuccessfully.

I know where to find them.

He went into the building and when he re-emerged on the roof it was raining, but the drops were small and far apart. Three jugs of sugar water with little feeder tips sticking off the bottoms were set up near the base of the low wall that marked the edge of the roof, and there were a few bees shuttling sugar back to their far-off homes in spite of the increasing darkness and the threat of heavier rain.

"Why are you doing this to me?" he shouted. It hurt his lip. "And now Brittany-Lynne!?"

The bees seemed neither more nor less angry than they had previously.

Teddy paced up and down the roof in between the feeders and the door to the stairs.

"It's your fault! It wouldn't have happened if you weren't here stressing me out all the time."

The bees were indifferent. Like talking to a cat or a dog or God or himself or his dead parents.

"I didn't even ask for this job!" he yelled.

After what was probably a long time, Teddy's voice was hoarse from yelling questions, accusations, and defenses. His T-shirt was wet and a feeling of calm came over him.

"All right, fine, you can stay," he said. "Just stay up here on the roof. Don't be a shitty roommate."

Teddy went back to the labeling room and trudged more boxes into the back of the truck until the last of the jars had spun through the relabeling machine. The machine labeled faster than he could carry, so he locked the back of the truck knowing he'd be spending another late night to finish loading them in. The boxes were going to be trucked out the same day as the ribbon-cutting party.

Teddy arrived home feeling dejected. His feet were heavy, his heart was heavy.

"I'm here already!" Doe's delicate voice trilled from the bedroom as he stepped inside his apartment. "You should lock your door and also tell the doorman not to let strange women up."

"Is my sister here?"

"No! We still haven't met. I don't think she's real."

His sister had failed to protect him from the reporter. His sister had failed to protect him from Lin. His sister had failed to protect him from the bees. He should never have called her. If he couldn't do it on his own, he deserved to sink. Teddy dropped his bag on a kitchen chair and walked to the bedroom, where Doe's frame was dwarfed by pillows and comforters and extra pillows she had taken from the sofa.

"That's true about the doorman, especially after what happened with that guy getting into the factory. But it's such a relief to have you here waiting for me. I'm sorry I'm so late." He was so sorry.

Doe threw her arms open. "Come sit with me?"

He changed into soft sweatpants. "What's with all the pillows?"

"We're going to watch a movie!"

He snuggled in beside her in the pillow nest. Teddy turned on the TV, but the screen was a blank menu. He flipped through settings on the remote even though he knew what the problem was.

"It looks like the cable is out again," he said.

Doe was silent. She considered it a character failing that his internet was always going out and they couldn't watch shows. A competent man would have forced the cable company to do a better job.

"Hey, miss. You can't be mad at me, I got beat up today." Teddy bopped her gently with a pillow. "I'll read you a *New Yorker* article instead."

"Whatever you want," Doe said evenly. "I'm going to shower." She left the bed. The comfortingly familiar but uncomfortably critical voice of his mother played in his ears as he lay hugging a pillow and waiting for her to come back.

CHAPTER 25:
HONEY LAUNDERING

Marlow came down from the factory roof pleased with her work. She'd made neat rows of stones marking where the edges of wooden decking should go, and she'd made a sketch of where planters of flowers could sit versus tall grasses for a windbreak versus chairs. She still needed to figure out some kind of shade structure. The green oasis would help Teddy relax. Living in the artificial wonderland of the city wasn't good for people on a neurological level. Humans needed to roam and they needed plants. She hadn't talked to him about his financial problems because he'd gotten popped in the mouth. She'd save it until he was cheered up.

Marlow peeked through the glass door of Teddy's office, but he wasn't there. She wanted to take him for drinks or to a guerilla art installation that had sprung up a few blocks away. The walls and the floor and the furnishings in a flatly lit room were all painted the same shade of blue. It was disconcertingly easy to bump into tables without noticing them. Teddy was too hung up on the stress part of being a boss and not taking full advantage of the part where he could leave in the middle of the day to do fun stuff without anyone complaining about it.

She was taking her mandate to come down to NYC and fix his life very seriously, even if he didn't appreciate it yet.

On her way to go look for him outside, she heard crying from the garage. Marlow's hand hovered near the door for a moment. "Sure, what's a little more drama?"

There was a goose-faced woman sitting on the floor, leaning against the wall with a plastic net over her hair and her knees folded into her chest. She ripped the net off when Marlow walked in. Marlow had trained herself not to react when plates broke in restaurants or glasses dropped in bars; similar to Teddy, she refused to appear rattled. The woman glared up at Marlow with bright eyes and Marlow held her gaze and then shrugged.

"Let me see your hands," Marlow said.

The woman looked confused but held them up, still in plastic gloves.

"Okay, good. Just making sure there wasn't an industrial accident. You've still got all your fingers."

"No accident," she said. Her eyes drifted up to Marlow's frizzy gray hair and then back down. Marlow could see she knew who she was. "I'm fired. Yesterday I buzzed in a man without asking his name and he turned out to be a crazy guy. The one who attacked Teddy."

"You shouldn't have done that," Marlow said. Protective anger flared in her, like the first wispy winds of a hurricane.

"Teddy said there was nothing he could do. It was the board's decision. There are only three people in management. He had a choice, he just didn't take it because he's a coward, and then he didn't even take responsibility for letting it happen, because he's a coward. He didn't even have the guts to pull the trigger himself. Matt did it."

Marlow walked around to face the woman and squatted down in front of her. She looked her in the eyes.

"What he did was wrong," the woman repeated. Although Marlow was an advocate of non-hierarchical employment arrangements, the casual way this straggly ex-employee spoke of Teddy bothered her. She wanted people to respect him. It bothered her also because the woman's words were plausibly insightful.

"Some people are so unwilling to experience physical discomfort," Marlow said. "We went camping once and he insisted, as a ten–year–old, on having a blow–up mattress. Emotional discomfort is a form of physical discomfort, if you think about it. Teddy's unwillingness to be uncomfortable for a minute to tell you you're fired makes him a coward, sure, but getting fired is what you deserved. You're incompetent." Marlow smiled into the woman's face.

The woman leaned against the wall to scramble, not–gracefully, to her feet. The wall bowed slightly, a sight so disorientingly odd that time seemed to slow. Marlow could almost hear it bend back into shape. Her eyes darted to the ground and saw casters at the base of the wall, fitted into a groove in the floor. They were near–invisible.

The woman, who was much taller, glared down at her. It wasn't a feeling she was used to, being tall herself, but Marlow had mostly lost interest in her and wanted the exchange over with so she could check out the wall.

"Your whole family is selfish," the woman said.

Marlow looked up at her. "You expect me to not defend my brother? You have bad judgment."

"Undeniably." She took a deep breath, her floppy lips quivering.

"So what are you going to do about it?" Marlow asked.

"I'm going to apply to social work school," she said. "I shouldn't be here anyway. I don't care about junk food, and I want to be in an environment that rewards merit, not nepotism. Plus if I'm going to be somebody's therapist, I want to get paid for it."

Marlow didn't know what she meant by that last bit. The woman went to the cubbies and grabbed her purse and cardigan. She dropped the plastic gloves on the floor and then pressed the button that fully opened all the bay doors at once. She made her grand exit into the sun with Marlow witnessing dutifully until she reached the gate to the street, and then Marlow pressed the "close" button and also locked the door that attached the garage to the building interior.

She dropped to her hands and knees in front of the "wall" and turned on her phone flashlight to get a better look at how she might open it.

"I wouldn't do something like that," Teddy said, out of breath.

"But did you though?" Marlow asked, also out of breath.

"I . . . It wasn't my idea! *I* didn't do it."

"You were always the good one!"

Teddy had walked straight out of the gate as soon as she'd seen him. She'd been too excited and had yelled, "We need to have a chat, Mr. Basementpants" from across the courtyard. She'd given herself away and he'd had too much of a head start getting out of the factory. At one point he'd started jogging and she'd trotted after him, but now they were in a more populated neighborhood. He finally stopped speed–walking ahead and away from her, and she caught up with him in front of a donut store by a subway entrance. A rush of commuters and coffee seekers flowed around them and then dissipated.

"I'm going to be late for a meeting with the electrician. Stop follow-ing me."

"Teddy, look at me," Marlow said.

He turned his head from where he was studying the details of the hand–painted anthropomorphic donut on the store window. Teddy's bot-tom lip was no longer swollen, but it was bruised and a scab ran all the way through to where the regular skin was. That skin was slightly yellow.

"Why is that labeling machine in a secret room in the basement? Is it stolen? You've got to help me out here."

"It's for smuggling," Teddy said reluctantly.

Annoyance turned to pleasure. "I've always wanted to be a smuggler. What are we smuggling?"

"Stop it," he said.

"All right, no jokes," she said, fighting unsuccessfully to turn off her smile. Was Teddy Beasley a coward or a *secret swashbuckler*? Maybe she hadn't been giving him enough credit and they were more alike than she'd thought. Crime wasn't a route she would have taken to get the factory out of debt, but it took balls.

"I was relabeling jars of honey from China as being from Vermont."

Marlow nodded her head in admiration. A pedestrian pushed between them to reach the donut shop. "Let's keep walking," she said and grabbed Teddy by the elbow. "Just honey?"

"Legally it's better for you if you don't know the details," he said.

She screwed up her face at him and dive-bombed his hair with the palm of her hand, mussing it into frustrated, skinny peaks. "Bullshit."

"Telling the truth is a luxury right now," he said. "I found out it's not really honey," he blurted out immediately after. "It's high fructose corn syrup." He seemed to relax then; she could see the flood of stress chemicals flushing his system. He smoothed his hair back down.

"So you bailed on them or what?" Marlow asked. She pointed at his bruised face.

A flush dappled Teddy's neck and cheeks and he looked away, but he didn't speak.

"You've already been caught, just tell all of it," Marlow said, exasperated. The novelty of her brother the smuggler was already dimming; evading customs was brave but unethical. Evading Marlow's questions was impermissible. "I keep giving you chances to take the dignified way out and confess and you keep not taking them! Grow a pair, admit what you did, build some character."

"Fine, yeah, I bailed. It was only supposed to be a one–time arrangement, but he keeps sending more shipments. I thought, *Well, what is he going to do, come all the way over from China?* But that's exactly what happened. I was ashamed to be a thief; I don't also want to tell you I was a sucker. There's another shipment arriving soon, two Saturdays from now."

"Who are these guys, like gangsters or like dickhead amateurs?"

"Businessmen, I think. Amateurs at tariff evasion."

"How sure are you?"

"Like 90 percent."

"All right. Here's what we're going to do. The money's spent already?"

"Yeah."

This explained the mystery cash infusions listed on Teddy's computer.

"Close the bank account so they can't wire any more. If this guy had 'people' he would have sent them instead of coming himself. We're not going to go pick up the next shipment. He's going to get mad, he's going to make threats, we hide out in a hotel for a while and add some security at the factory, he admits defeat and gives up. They aren't going to waste resources on a lost cause." Marlow was cocky about her solution, but she trusted her understanding of human nature. The sums of money were too small in the grand scheme of things to expect this guy had any experience cutting off fingers. Exciting as the situation was, she was glad Teddy had come around on his own to wanting to get out.

"Do you think there's a way to make it look like the money came from you? Like a loan or a gift?" Teddy asked.

"We don't want to fuck with anything banking–related. Just close the account and let it lie. You know what we do need?"

"What?" They had circled the block by now and were back at the donut store and subway entrance.

"A big magnet. To destroy your computer. I'll walk past it in your office, like I didn't know it would happen, and—"

"No fucking way," Teddy said. Then he softened his tone. "Thank you," he said. "I was blowing things up in my mind, but you're right. It's simple, really. We just wait it out."

She ruffled his hair again, with affection this time. She'd worried after his phone call that he had an itchy trigger finger when it came to asking for help, but it turned out his problems stemmed from not asking for help early enough after things started to go wrong. All he needed was more life experience. "We got this, Teddy. I love you, I'll love you no matter what you do, and I'm going to fix this. I have to tell you though, you're at a turning point in your life. Twenty-seven is when you decide who you will be— either you calcify into the immature version of yourself you have been, or you make a last-ditch effort to expand into your potential. 'The chick that would be born must first destroy a world,' or whatever. I know about the debt at the factory. This is not the way to handle a crisis."

Teddy sighed heavily and looked at his feet. "This was my one act of . . ." He searched for the words. "Manic, spontaneous, rebellious adventure, and it turned out horribly. I'm not like you. You're Han Solo and I'm like . . . Luke Skywalker's aunt."

"I didn't say be a knockoff version of me, I said be the best version of you." Like a really handsome safety inspector or something.

"I can still make that meeting," Teddy said. "And then I need to check in with the caterer. I guess we carry on and act normal until after this weekend."

"Yup." Marlow watched him descend into the station then started searching on her phone for sublets, barbed wire, and bodyguards.

CHAPTER 26:
ANOTHER PARTY

The courtyard of Beasley Cherries was illuminated mainly by string-lights hung in a wave pattern along the fence, a few feet above head level. Blue and red lights onstage cast music–venue shadows across gravel and people, and the windows of food trucks and lamps at the freebie booths added pools of yellow to the mix.

"This is nice," Mims said to a young woman at one of the booths. "It's like a cross between a food festival and a holiday party."

The woman shrugged. "Would you like to try our new Local–Loco–Cocoa–L Power Smoothie? It's coconut and cacao with a hint of fruit. Starting next month it will be made exclusively with Beasley Cherries." The woman handed her a sample in the kind of white plastic cup dentists used.

"What's it taste like?" Mims asked. She sniffed the cup. Ordinarily she wouldn't be interested in small talk, but she was seeing the world from the brink of a new perspective, that of a normal adult professional. Small details filled her with wonder, and she wanted to share the experience with someone. Not being in the midst of a fight–or–flight response to money woes and social status challenges was almost like an *Alice in Wonderland* trip.

The woman thought a moment. "It tastes like vanity," she said. "It's bitter." She was wearing yoga clothes and had a mandala charm around her neck.

"Okay," Mims said and laughed. She drank it and it was bitter. "I'm sorry you're having a rough night."

"We all need to pay rent," the woman said with a genuine-seeming, if tired, smile. Mims had submitted her invoice for the crepe paper knees article that morning and was still feeling conflicted about it.

She walked down the line of booths, shoving free samples of super-food energy bars and tiny bottles of Brooklyn-made bitters in her purse. Not all of the vendors had a direct relationship to Beasley Cherries, but she got a sense of the scruffy-bougie "maker" community Teddy wanted his new product to be a part of. An MC interrupted the music to announce raffle numbers for free Shirley Temples. Mims scanned the courtyard to make sure there were no other journalists, as was the agreement. The crowd was bigger than she expected. There were what appeared be to bouncers stationed throughout, not just at the entrance to the party. Mims had been at enough bar openings and event venues to know that meant thrash pits or famous guests, potentially terrorist threats. For a night like this it was overkill. She took a few photos of them with her phone.

Mims spotted Teddy and a woman standing by the stage, leaning toward each other and laughing. She guessed from their similar noses that they were related. The thickness of the woman's hair, like Teddy's, was a statement of health and vigor, but on her the volume was unseemly. A woman her age usually had smaller, tame hair, not a wiry, white, windblown beach look. It was excessive. And yet their two heads bobbing together in conversation were perfect, like salt and pepper.

Watching them Mims smiled but then wished she weren't an only child and scowled instead.

She walked over. "I like the vibe," she said. "There's the start of a nice little community here. If you build a story around that it could be part of your brand strategy."

"Thanks. We're really glad you could make it," Teddy said warmly.

"Really? I got the sense that I bullied you into letting me come. You care a lot about making people happy." Teddy stared but the woman standing with him nodded her assent. "And I *am* happy, so I appreciate it. Who are all these people?" Mims squinted into the shadow where Teddy was standing. She couldn't tell if there was something wrong with his face—a faint bruise under his lip.

"This is my sister, Marlow." She shook Marlow's hand. "Those guys are dye suppliers," Teddy said and pointed. "We buy equipment from those tall guys." He pointed to two other men. "Those are distributors there; those women use our cherries at their bar. That woman designed all of our new packaging and the new logo. Those guys with the mustaches live in the converted warehouses two blocks over. That group by the little tent— those are foodie magazine people." He didn't point out any of the men who looked like bouncers.

"Who's that guy?" Mims asked, gesturing toward one of them.

"Not sure, who do you mean? Raoul? He works for us."

He'd said it casually enough, but his face for a split second had looked like that of a kid caught with his hand in the cookie jar. And it seemed odd to pretend he wasn't sure she'd been asking about the six-foot-four guy with a crew cut. Her suspicion of all things seemingly wonderful stirred from sleep, along with her love-hate relationship with happy, successful people. Mims couldn't help looking for other cracks in the façade to pry at.

"What's up with that huge dumpster out front?" Mims asked. She had tried to get some photos outside when she arrived but there had been no way to frame the building without the dumpster getting in the shot.

"Is this for the story?" Teddy asked.

"No, it's just ugly and you're having a party."

Teddy nodded but didn't answer. Mims scanned his face. *Was* something strange going on with him, or was clamming up his normal reaction to aggressive women?

"It's left over from the construction," Marlow said. "We've just been too preoccupied to deal with it."

"I see. Well, it was nice to meet you. I'm going to wander around a bit and take a few more photos. I'll find you to say goodbye."

She scanned the party again, resenting that Teddy had so many friends and associates while she was so lonely. It was unclear to her whether that resentment was what was really driving her suspicions toward him. Regardless, she set off into the crowd determined to ask Raoul and his cohort what they were doing there.

"Okay, let's carry on with introductions," Marlow said. She couldn't believe Teddy had invited a reporter to the party, but at least she hadn't seemed to notice Teddy's busted lip. "I want to leave feeling like a good sister, totally caught up on office policies and politics. Also point out which people may suspect that you infused the factory with cash from your own pockets."

As they were lifting their drinks from the edge of the stage, the stooped woman from the garage approached; she stood straighter now and wore a flower print dress.

"Brittany–Lynne! I'm so glad you made it," Teddy said. "This is my sister, Marlow."

"We've met. How's grad school, Brit? Can I call you Brit?" Marlow was glad for a chance to follow up on what, at the time, had been the most dramatic encounter of her trip. She hoped Brit's "therapist" quip didn't mean Teddy had told her about the company's financial stress. They must have been close if Teddy had still invited her to the party, and it would explain why she was so indignant about getting fired.

"Yes, I like 'Brit' a lot. We got off on the wrong foot." Brit came in for a hug and Marlow hugged her back. She hugged Teddy too. Marlow was glad to see there were no hard feelings. "And I've narrowed down options for where I'd like to apply, it's sweet of you to ask. Leaving Beasley Cherries was actually just the kick in the pants I needed to get my life on track. How are you enjoying New York?"

"Getting used to the crowds again has been a trip," Marlow replied. "Although I suspect people don't pay much attention to what you're doing, no matter how many of them are on the sidewalk. No one even looks at me." Marlow bobbled her head and felt her fringe of wiry witch's hair sway and then settle. She'd woven flowers into it for the party and no one had commented on it.

"No," Brittany-Lynne said, "mostly they don't." She seemed crest-fallen since only a few moments before. "Being overlooked is still better than actively avoided," she said.

Marlow didn't like when people fished for sympathy, especially with vague statements that begged for follow-up questions. She also didn't want her second conversation with Brit to be as explosive as her first, so rather than call her out she tried to affect a gentle, guidance counselor tone. "I'm not sure what you mean by that, but you seem upset. Is it maybe . . . boy problems? Or man problems, I guess?"

"Yes." Brittany-Lynne nodded. "I don't know myself whether to classify him as a boy or a man."

"There are easy ways to know if he's a man," Marlow said, excited to lighten the mood with vulgarity.

"How?" Brittany-Lynne asked.

Marlow grinned. "If he'll fuck you while you're on your period, he's a man. If not, he's not."

Brittany–Lynne's face turned red. "Your brother is not a man then."

Marlow felt her own face burning. "Fuck! I didn't know you were talking about Teddy. It takes a lot to make me blush." Teddy had slipped off somewhere. Brit had turned sad because he was avoiding her.

Brittany–Lynne laughed. "I know it's awkward for me to tell you this," she drawled, "but recently I can't help talking about it. He insisted I come tonight supposedly as an apology, but when I approach him to chat, he disappears into a different conversation across the way."

"I don't know what to tell you," Marlow said. "Teddy has been under a lot of stress recently. I'm sure he still values your friendship. He's a good kid. Man, or whatever. He's a good 'guy.'"

Brittany–Lynne smiled. "Let's talk about something else," she said.

"Where's your accent from?"

As Brittany–Lynne answered, Marlow spotted Teddy in the distance talking to a slight woman with a tousled black bob. The woman's body language swayed between aloof and clingy, her small fingers on Teddy's arm. Marlow pegged her as one of those crisp, jealous women who experience sadness as anger.

"Hey, miss." Teddy kissed Doe's hair. He straightened back up and put more distance between them, in case any coworkers were watching. It was the dance they'd been doing in public since they met.

Starting her second day of work, they'd embarked on a string of casual, cautious new–friend hangouts. They stopped at a vintage store after work, went to the bodega for emergency snacks during work, and walked to a wine bar on Van Brunt at sunset. Getting his new friend to smile felt like he was a lab rat working on little puzzles: a joke here, a cute story about his grandfather there. When Doe's smile came her eyes would light up and widen like she was surprised about it but game. One night after too many glasses of wine he stole a look at her reflection in one of the shop windows on the way to the subway. He thought she wouldn't notice, but their eyes met. She seemed slightly displeased seeing the longing in his face, and he couldn't tell if it was because he'd ruined their friendship with his desire or if it was something else. The following night he took her to a bistro for their first official date. Their behavior in front of coworkers had remained the same the whole time.

"You look especially French tonight," he said. She was wearing all black and her hair was a little messy. In spite of everything else going on, when he was around Doe she focused his attention and left him feeling warm. Standing beside her, he was just a regular guy, maybe even a masculine guy, drawn as any man would be to the enthralling light of a beautiful girl. "I like that red lipstick."

"You just want my lips to look like cherries too," she said.

"That reminds me, I brought you a drink." He presented her with the rum and cola he'd been hiding behind his back. It had as many cherries as ice cubes.

She smiled, a once rare gift that she was finally giving more easily. "You are so silly." She speared a cherry and brought it to her mouth.

They could go to a lake house somewhere for the rest of the summer—hide out until the honey situation blew over. When Marlow had confronted him, it felt like a tiny window opened that redemption might fly through: the truth was out in the world. He'd relaxed into weakened legs and was happy to hand the responsibility over to someone else, just as Lin had said.

An image of Lin scaling the factory fence and contaminating the cherries chased the lake house away. Teddy would have to stay in the city and keep an eye on everything, even with Marlow in charge.

"Maybe this fall we could go somewhere," he said, admitting to Doe and himself at the same time that he could see a future for them beyond the summer. "Do you like cabins? With electricity, of course. Not too rugged."

"Well aren't you two the cutest?" Marlow had approached without him noticing, and it seemed like she'd done it on purpose. Since the revelation of the secret room she seemed to really enjoy taking on the persona of a smuggler who slinks in the shadows.

"This is my friend Doe," he said. Doe frowned. "This is my sister, Marlow."

"That's quite a drink you've got there. Big fan of the factory? We could probably get you some kind of bulk discount."

"I get free cherries already." Doe looked off at the crowd, uninterested. It was because he'd said "friend."

"She works at the factory," Teddy said sheepishly. "We're dating, but we're trying to be private about it."

"Really? That's . . . *surprising*," Marlow said.

Marlow seemed angry now too, and he wasn't sure why. If it was because they worked together, it was exactly the kind of judgment he was trying to avoid by keeping their relationship a secret in the first place.

"Excuse me a minute," Marlow said. "They're about to make the announcement about the party end time. One sec." She slipped back into the crowd.

Teddy smiled at Doe. "Well that's my sister. She's real."

The music faded out and the MC came on. "Hey, everybody, just a quick heads up that R train subway service is ending early tonight, so you'll either want to take a car service home—go to the Junior's Limos booth to get a business card!—or skedaddle for the train before eleven. Or you know, Lyft. Prince Charming's already found his Cinderella though, so there's no reason for anyone to run off!" The MC pointed toward Teddy and a floodlight thunked on with the brightness equivalent of ringing ears.

Teddy's pinky finger was entwined with Doe's and everyone was looking. "Hey, congrats you two. Love is beautiful."

Teddy looked from the MC to where Marlow was standing beside the stage. She shot him two thumbs up and a malicious grin and then the light turned off and he couldn't see anything for a few seconds.

Doe leaned into him and grabbed his arm more tightly. "I'm glad we're telling people," she said. Marlow, with no responsibilities and nothing but freedom, of course would be careless about others' privacy and hypocritical about when it was time to commit. She was the type of person who'd throw a kid into the deep end of the pool to force him to learn to swim.

And what if she'd put Doe in danger, if Lin somehow had overheard the announcement?

"I still feel like taking things slow is . . ."

Brittany–Lynne approached, as if in slow motion, except that he could see her whole body was shaking, and that was in real time.

"How long?" she asked.

"Not that long."

"So at that happy hour when you didn't want to share a taxi, you were already together?"

"Around then," he said, squirming.

"That was a month ago, not recently."

"Teddy, why is Walrus at the party?" Doe asked. Teddy could see her red pout from the corner of his eye. *Walrus*? Doe had pieced together the implication of what Brittany–Lynne was asking, and it was a bad sign that her first reaction was name–calling.

He was silent. Brittany–Lynne was thinking, her eyes going into the past. His heart hurt. He had wronged her. Why hadn't he felt this clarity, this empathy and desire to do the right thing, before, when she had asked him to be truthful? He hadn't wanted her to be sad, but also... also he'd liked the flirting and the secret cookies. It made him feel good about himself.

Doe was tugging on his arm, but he couldn't turn his face away from Brittany-Lynne. If he did he would never be able to look anyone in the eye again.

"And Jalen's birthday party? You were already together then," Brittany-Lynne said. It wasn't a question. They'd gone bowling as a company after work; Doe and Brittany-Lynne had ended up on the same team while he was distracted ordering food for everyone. He hadn't been able to stop it. She was getting closer to those overlap weeks, when he and Doe were just hanging out, tentative. Pretending, with catlike disinterest, to find themselves in each other's presence night after night by chance. Their first actual date had been April 11. The delineation was so clear and obvious in his mind, but now it seemed indefensible, a technicality.

"Yes," he said.

"'Not that long,'" Brittany-Lynne said with a sneer. "We broke up on April 10. Did you cheat on me with her?"

"No!" he said. It was a thought he'd only prodded at gently, like stitches, not something he could explore too deeply.

"Oh, you have the right to be offended?"

"I just wanted everyone to be happy," Teddy said. "So I didn't want to tell you; I knew you'd be upset."

"Do you want everyone to be happy? Or do you want everyone to like you? Because those are two different things." Brittany-Lynne's eyes filled with tears then, but she turned before they could fall. She stomped to the front gate and away.

"Teddy," Doe said. He turned toward her, his hands hanging limp at his sides. Her face wasn't questioning at all, not looking for reassurance; she'd already made up her mind about what sort of man he was. "I asked you when we started dating if you'd been with anyone else from the factory," she said.

"I know," he said. He felt tears roll down his cheeks.

"You don't get to cry! I get to cry!" she said, but her great brown eyes were clear. "You are a piece of shit." She said it as calmly as when she'd read him the weather in the mornings. Doe turned and wound her way through the crowd and out the gate only a minute after Brittany–Lynne.

Marlow stood a polite distance away. When she saw Doe's tiny body disappear into the mass of guests, she approached Teddy. He'd just dabbed at his eyes with a tissue and seemed composed.

"Did you do that on purpose? Tell me the truth," he said.

"I always tell the truth, Teddy," she hissed. "It's something you should try sometime."

"My relationship is ruined; my friendship is ruined." He still appeared calm. He sighed and took a sip of the drink Doe had left behind.

"I did it on purpose, but I did it for your benefit. Sometimes you need to blow it up and start over." Maybe Teddy couldn't see it right now, but deception was no basis for a friendship or romance. There would have been a stain on both of those relationships forever. And more importantly, Doe and Brit had a right to know.

"It's not your place to"—he brought his voice back to a low volume—"to blow it up!" It didn't matter; no one was paying attention to them. "You haven't changed at all from the person who ran away and left me with this mess. You have this idea that you're fearless, frivolous, and carefree but you're irresponsible, judgmental, and you leave a path of destruction wherever you go."

Marlow wasn't going to let him change the subject. "You shouldn't do things you're ashamed of, Teddy. No one can have power over you if you don't have secrets. Are you honest in any part of your life? The honey, the debt, the women. Are there other things I need to know about?"

"You don't know any of it! I told Brittany-Lynne I didn't want to hook up anymore and she didn't listen. She should have listened when I said no."

"So you're not even sorry then?" Marlow felt a rare but unmistakable bolt of panic. Could it be that her sweet baby brother had no moral compass? She had tried since her arrival in New York to act as though they were picking up a thread of intimacy left dormant but strong all these years, but now she had to admit she was facing a stranger. He had the same penchant for soft blue cloth, same eyebrow shape as the little boy she knew as a young woman, but ultimately she did not know him. She had conflated his love of family and duty with being good.

Normally under knotty circumstances she would charge ahead, but Marlow took two quick steps back, as if Teddy had become scalding water, then turned and took long, swift strides toward the exit.

"You hurt them!" he called after her. She could hear by the sound of his voice that he was following. "You hurt them worse by telling them; everyone was happy and it was going to turn out fine. You're going back to Alaska?" Behind the anger there was a note of hysteria at the prospect that she was going home. "Good, go back to fantasy land."

Marlow stopped but didn't turn toward him.

"So you don't even feel guilty?" she asked.

"Of course I feel guilty!"

Teddy came around to stand in front of her. He looked forlorn but his posture was straight.

"Well, guess what," Marlow said. "Just because you feel guilty about something doesn't make you less culpable. If you go around simultaneously doing shitty things and feeling bad about them, it doesn't make you less of a bad person. Your impact on others remains the same, regardless of your level of self-hatred." She wasn't sure it was a concept one could impart with words, or at all. It was something you had to feel. "I have to go, Teddy," she said and started walking again.

"Well, good, you'll be safe," Teddy said. "You're so great at disappearing, Lin will never find you. I can't run away."

Outside the gate to Beasley Cherries the air seemed cooler and Marlow could breathe. She remembered as a very young child overhearing her grandfather discussing wages. The workers were threatening to unionize, but of course there were too few of them. It was a small factory. "Whatever the market will bear; they aren't family" was his attitude, and he wanted to replace everyone—if there were people willing to work for the wages he was willing to pay, he was morally in the clear. Her parents had eventually convinced him that happier workers were better workers, but the contradiction between his core attitude toward his employees and the snuggly presentation he had with his grandchildren and friends had never left her.

Teddy had justified "hooking up" with Brit by saying she was a party to it too. It was a theme Marlow had encountered and railed against many times in her wanderings—whether it was price-gouging a roommate who "must have known and not cared about" the market value of the room, or card-skimming a stranger "too dumb" to check the ATM, or downloading movies on a neighbor's unprotected Wi-Fi, it was the same blame-the-victim mentality. The onus was on the trampled party to stand up for himself if he didn't like the treatment, regardless of the imbalance of power or information between the two people. If the aggressor got away with his behavior, he convinced himself he'd done nothing morally wrong.

Her disgust with the mental backflips involved in making the family business maximally profitable was a part of why she'd run away from the Beasley clan the first time. She had been scared if she hadn't, it would have corrupted her, as it apparently had her hapless baby brother.

Two Weeks Before

CHAPTER 27:

ANOTHER BOAT

L in kept a small boat at a marina in Flatbush under the name Tommy
Han. There were 150 slips at the marina, all full but none of them well
maintained. The boat next to his was partially sunk and appeared to have
been that way for a long time, a positive indicator for privacy. Nearly every
time a ship laden with goods came into the Red Hook Marine Terminal, an
officer or crewman would want to stay for a few weeks on the twenty–foot
cuddy cabin and catch a ride back with the next ship. Lin took careful note
of the men for whom he had done favors.

The green numbers on the digital clock ticked up. Five minutes
elapsed with Lin locked in plank pose; at minute five he held his breath.
The numbers blurred and he collapsed onto the floor sometime between
minutes six and seven. The idea of someday being blown overboard in
a storm, unlikely as that was, concerned him enough that he wanted to
be able to perform all the normal conditioning exercises without oxygen.
He also liked to dominate in the casual feats of strength that sometimes

cropped up on the ship when the crew got restless—push-up contests, wall-sit contests.

He lowered himself onto the bench that took up most of the rest of the boat's living space. The foam cushion was disintegrating with age; it crumbled beneath his thighs as he flipped through the pages of a manufacturing catalogue. When his heart rate was back to normal he put on his *Vietnamese for Beginners* lesson. Vietnam had been put on the US watch-list for countries that falsified honey country of origin for the benefit of Chinese beekeepers; he intended to find people there who could give tips on growing his Brooklyn operation.

After the lesson ended, he called his cousin, Weihong, in China.

"You might need to get back here sooner. I've been looking at airfare," Weihong said. "If you go on the ship it's going to take six weeks, and I need you here for the corn harvest negotiations."

Lin's negotiating skills were superior, but to say Weihong "needed" him involved in his corn syrup business was flattery. He wanted him there because it would be faster, easier, less work for Weihong.

"I would prefer not to leave a paper trail. I'll return by ship."

"There's another thing too. When you come back by airplane, can you bring New York City bagels?"

"I'm not flying, and the flight is long. What's the point in bagels that are more than twenty-four hours old?"

"You can shrink-wrap them. They have machines that wrap them in plastic and suck all the air out. You can send the machine back on the boat."

"I'm not doing that," Lin said.

"You're so scary all the time. 'I'm not doing that.' Maybe you think talking in a formal way makes you more intimidating to your crew, but it doesn't work on me. Anyway, you can still be a tough guy and fly on a plane with bagels. I want plain and cinnamon raisin."

"I'm here in a moldy boat following a disciplined schedule, and you're getting so soft you can't even negotiate commodity prices on your own anymore." The closer they got to true wealth and success, the more Lin felt he was on his own taking the last few steps. His cousin was already celebrating.

Lin cared more about the process than the outcome—his lifestyle after they had the cash reserves to be taken seriously by the banks, receive loans, and pay bribes, would remain the same. The money would be merely an outward signifier out what had always been true: he understood the psychological workings of men and was above them. He could behave as he wanted and no one would stop him.

"You should get used to me being soft." Weihong's delighted laugh was almost a giggle. "I'm going to get soft on bagels. . . Did you make contact with Beasley?"

"Everything is back to how it should be. Anything else?"

He was glad he'd never shared with Weihong his belief that Beasley would ask to become his protégé.

"There's also this dessert I want you to get for me and shrink–wrap; it's called the *Le baiser de l'abeille.*"

Lin hung up on Weihong before he could explain. His cousin didn't respect him because they had known each other since they were children and were therefore overly familiar. At the same time, Weihong was his last friend. His other family members and childhood friends no longer contacted him even for weddings or birth announcements. His ascension from poverty to success had made clear to them that he was inherently worthy and talented, and they weren't. But a larger share of the rift came because he couldn't help speaking to them in condescending tones even when he saw them approaching the limits of their patience with him.

He texted: "Maybe bagels."

Lin returned to his workout—pull-ups in the low doorway. Before beginning he hung from extended arms, knees bent, for a full minute waiting for his back to straighten. As he'd come into puberty he'd unconsciously hunched his shoulders to keep himself as far from view as possible, and somehow his spine had retained that slight S shape several decades later. His posture no longer matched his confidence level. He was considering getting a mechanical posture gadget he'd seen advertised online—you stuck it between your shoulder blades and it buzzed at you if you slouched for too long. His only hesitation was if Weihong found out, he'd use it as evidence that he was being changed by money too.

A few vertebrae popped. He lifted himself up to the ceiling and began his backward count. Fifty, forty-nine, forty-eight . . .

CHAPTER 28:
SUCCESS

Mims sat in a plastic chair outside Aziz's office. The night before, she'd left the party without saying goodbye to Teddy. His employees had universally described him as sweet and relaxed, sometimes playful, and that hadn't meshed with her experience of him as jumpy and evasive. The men who looked like bouncers had nothing to say at all; each claimed to be a guest from the neighborhood. One definitely had an earpiece, and two of them she could have sworn had radios clipped to their belts, but it had been too dark to tell for sure. If Teddy had been suckered into paying some security firm too much for party patrol, why didn't he just admit it? Lying about it, if he had been lying about it, was the suspicious part. Mims had been unable to find Teddy or his sister again, and the question mark of his skittishness had plagued her as she'd written the article.

Aziz's head emerged from behind his office door. "Come inside," he said.

It was overheated in the office. She sat in a chair that reminded her of dusty car interiors and childhood carsickness.

"You saw the article," she said. "But as I mentioned in my email, I'm hesitant to publish it just yet and wanted to discuss it in person. I feel like there might be something more going on."

Aziz's eyes twinkled with suppressed laughter. "You're really milking this story. The article is great and I'm going to run it as is."

"Then give me a chance to do another follow-up—"

"A local interest piece about rooftop honeybees and an organic cherry factory opening isn't the best showcase for your investigative journalism chops. Don't become a one-trick pony with this bees thing."

Mims opened her mouth to protest but stopped. That probably meant a no for the chef's honey too.

"Rather than run this one success into the ground, go write me a story about that city council member residency scandal. Chauncey lives in Cold Spring, and we all know it. If he wants to vote on city affairs he needs to ride the subway like the rest of us."

It was a real assignment, a dignified assignment. An assignment not launched by paranoia—hers or a random pastry chef's. He was giving her a shot and she was going to take it. Beasley could wait.

"Thank you, sir," she said.

As soon as she was back on the street, she called Bennie.

"Guess who's going to use company money to buy a Metro-North ticket upstate?"

"Oh my God! What's the story?"

"Guy who doesn't live in the city being on city council. You know, *politics*."

"Do you think you'll get invited to correspondents' dinners from now on?"

"Probably." It was another hot day and Mims was wearing charcoal gray, but it didn't matter. The city had never seemed more hospitable. "Do you want to meet up for a drink?"

"Yeah, a bunch of us are meeting at Lavender Lake later. Come out! We'll turn it into a congratulatory sendoff."

"You can bring champagne to break over the bow of the commuter train," Mims said, knowing she couldn't celebrate too hard or she'd give away just how much of a big deal it was for her to get a decent assignment.

She would walk to the bar. TriBeCa to Carroll Gardens, Brooklyn, would take about an hour, but she'd save subway fare and arrive around the same time as the friends who couldn't head over until the workday was done. Her legs were springy with energy, and for once it was pride and happiness, not anger, that compelled her to stride and strut down the streets of New York.

The next day Mims emerged from her apartment early and feeling important. She'd had only two glasses of wine the night before and then gone home early, accomplishment and prosperity still pulsing from her eyes, nothing dulled by alcohol. This morning she wore her real-gold bangles and her messy bun was perfectly tousled and devil-may-care. She passed a newspaper stand and grinned. "I'm coming for you," she said.

Further on, about thirty feet from the subway entrance, there was a youngish man handing out copies of *Newspapers*, the other free newspaper in town and the *Free Post*'s main morning commute competitor. Mims stood next to a trashcan doing "research"—she flipped quickly through the pages, casually scanning headlines and absorbing factoids. The third-page top headline was "Beasley Cherries Dupes City Bees." Her joie de vivre ran like a firework in reverse, sucking back into a tight ball of self-doubt and knotted muscle. A crowd emerged from the subway and bumped around her and she let them, not moving out of the way.

The headline came the same day as her own feel-good follow-up article about Beasley Cherries' new organic wing and how Charlie himself was helping deter the bees from pillaging the waste barrels. The *Newspapers* piece was short and it posited illegal dumping—along with city bee overpopulation, an unusually dry spring, and accidental cherry juice spillage— as a possible reason for the bees' colonization of the factory. No sources were cited. The author must have seen her original article and decided to do a knockoff version. Was it just conjecture, or in his drive to one-up her had the *Newspapers* author found some clues she hadn't? Was she the terrible journalist or was he? If it was true that the bees had shown up because Beasley Cherries was improperly disposing of sickly sweet, sticky waste, the article she'd published this morning made her look like a fool.

Her text message alert tinkled. She looked down anticipating a Commissioner Gordon moment with Aziz. Instead: "Hey"

It was Sean.

"Really, motherfucker? I got real problems. Busy. Don't text me," she wrote. She barely registered that the response was the least contrived thing she'd ever sent to him, so focused was she on speed-walking back toward her apartment. Then she broke into a run. Her frustration wasn't spent as she reached the stairs, but by the landing it was focused. She grabbed her audio recorder from her apartment in case her phone died, as it probably would, and trotted back out of the building. Beasley had some explaining to do.

Outside Beasley Cherries Mims pressed the intercom button and waited. The system was brand-new, upgraded since just two nights before, and a camera orb distorted her face from above. "All Guests Must Be Announced," a sign read. After some back and forth she was buzzed in, but at the front desk Jalen informed her that Teddy wasn't around.

"Is there anyone here qualified to speak to this?" she asked, pointing to the *Newspapers* article.

"It's absolutely not true," Jalen said. "But you'll have to speak with Teddy. Would you like to make an appointment?"

"Yeah, or have him call my cell when he gets in."

"You know," Jalen said in a conspiratorial voice, "you should speak with Teddy's factory exes. *Both* of them." He shrugged his shoulders in an "I don't like to gossip" gesture. "Maybe one of them spoke to the other reporter."

He wrote down their names and contact information on a piece of paper.

It turned out Teddy was a sneaky little snot in at least one area of his life.

She went back outside. The dumpster was still sitting in the street, so she hoisted herself up to take a look inside. She wasn't sure what she was looking for, surely not open tanks of bee–attracting waste right here at the curb. It was only construction debris and empty paint cans. There were a few cracked jars of honey tossed in there as well, the same brand Gerard the chef hated so much. Mims laughed at the coincidence, although it felt a bit like a slap in the face from the universe. They must have been bought for the party. Or to go with the tea they served to all the journalists who came by. She was genuinely curious now what the deal was with Vermont's Wonderful. It did seem to be everywhere. Who knew rich people liked serving cheap–ass honey so much.

She snapped some photos and jumped back down to the sidewalk. Mims checked the time. At this point there was only one more Metro-North train heading to Cold Spring for the day.

The receptionist had seen the *Newspapers* article, so Teddy had probably seen it too. If he was scrambling to tighten a cover–up, it was happening right now. She couldn't leave the city.

CHAPTER 29:
SEVERANCE

Teddy stood outside Doe's apartment building, a run-down brick walk-up in Gowanus, trying to build the courage to lift his finger to the buzzer. He wasn't quite through with his dramatic self-reckoning when the door opened from within and a man in running shorts stepped out. The man held the door open for Teddy. "Oh uh, thanks," Teddy mumbled as he slipped inside. So much for taking the time to steel himself. He walked up the three flights to Doe's floor and knocked.

Shuffling.

Silence.

The door flew open.

"Why do you scare me like this, on top of everything else? For people who don't have a doorman like you, an unannounced visitor in the middle of the day is an exterminator or a *murderer*. A *murderer*, Teddy." Her lips were purple; he'd never seen her drunk before.

"Someone was going out and held the front door for me before I could buzz, and I didn't want to just . . . I'm sorry. I should have buzzed," Teddy said.

He was wearing his threadbare blue hoodie because it looked as pathetic and sorry as he felt, but she had told him repeatedly she found it too casual. He wished he'd dressed differently.

Doe turned her back on him and walked into the living room. He followed. She perched on the edge of her love seat, the apartment was too small for a sofa, and retrieved an overfull glass of red wine from the end table.

"I won't take you back," she said. "So don't bother trying. I can't be seen with a man who would make love to a woman who looks like a deformed animal." She looked regretful as the last few words were leaving her mouth. "Now that I've called her ugly you can hate me," she said more quietly. "You can feel superior because I'm so petty and then you can feel less guilty for what you've done." Teddy took a step farther into the living room, but there was no place to sit except the love seat next to her. He stayed standing. "I assumed you didn't have experience with other women at all, you're so bad in bed," she added, faux-contemplative.

He brushed the insult aside. He couldn't know if she meant it or not, and regardless he had to take whatever it was she said to him. He owed her that. He just wished she weren't so mean about Brittany-Lynne's appearance. It was like he was wronging her again by not objecting.

"It's not her fault," Teddy said. "She didn't know."

"You didn't even come here to win me back, did you? I was right to be wary. To you I'm just the tiny French girl with the accent and the Asian lips, nice to look at but not to get attached to. So many fetishes packed into one. When Brittany-Lynne came over at the party you didn't even answer my question about what was going on. Like I wasn't even a person."

Teddy sighed softly, like his last breath was leaving him. "I'm sorry I hurt you," he said. "I wanted to talk to you. You weren't at work yesterday and didn't call in, and I couldn't reach you, so . . ."

"I quit!" she said.

"Don't quit."

"Because you're worried I will sue you?" She looked bright and triumphant. Teddy didn't know if she was the kind of woman who would sue him; he'd been too busy basking in her tininess, her exotic beauty, and her French accent. He had wanted to know her more deeply, he just hadn't pushed against her defenses with any urgency. He'd thought they'd have time.

She threw her phone at him. It thudded against his chest and he fumbled and then caught it. "Read it!" she said. "That's what I'm sending to everyone." Wine sloshed on her arm. "Look what you did!"

Teddy handed her a paper towel for her arm and then he wiped the floor as he began reading aloud.

The email started with a description of their conversation about whether he'd dated anyone else from the factory, his lie that he hadn't, and then devolved into a string of personal attacks. Shamefully, it felt good to hear all the things about himself someone else noticed, even if it was the bad stuff; it meant at least he wasn't out in the world exclusively to notice others and to take care of them without ever being seen himself. When he reached the end, Teddy looked up from the phone.

"Thank you for not telling them about my nipples being too close together," he said. "That was generous of you." He smiled weakly.

"That's not why! It's because I want them to judge you for your personality, not for your body." The edges of her mouth tugged into a smile in spite of herself. "Don't joke, Teddy," she said, regaining momentum. "You told me when we started dating that the most important thing was for me to be my real self. And I was! I was vulnerable for you, showing you my real self, which is bitchy and cold." Teddy opened his mouth to protest but she waved at him to be silent. "I've been told that, I know. And you would say, 'No, no, if I just wrap you up in my arms, you'll be warm . . .'" Her anger was overtaken by sadness and she trailed off. He wanted to give her a hug but didn't let himself. He'd known all along her aloof irritability was a test and a protective wall. It hadn't bothered him; he'd seen it as a challenge.

But her reaction now was why he hadn't told her about Brittany–Lynne when they started dating. He didn't want to make a big deal of it, or for there to be drama, or to have to tell Brittany–Lynne. He hadn't wanted a tiny, ended thing with Brittany–Lynne to grow out of control and mar the delicate beginning of his time with Doe, whom he'd been drawn to instantly, crushingly, from the moment she'd walked into his office for the first time asking for help reaching the coffee filters. His mouth had lied before the rest of him could stop it, and then he'd just let the lie sit there until it was too late to take it back.

Ironically, Doe was finally raw, unguarded, intimate now that they were over. It was a reason beyond resolutely taking his punishment for him not to interrupt or defend himself: he didn't want her to stop talking.

"You told that story!" she said, gesturing at him with the wine. "About how your ex didn't tell you for nine months that she was bi and how hurtful that was that she didn't trust you. This was a way bigger lie than that. You said everything would be ok and accepted and loved as long as I was truthful about who I was. You did all the things to me that you asked me not to do to you. You hid yourself from me. And you *stole* from me. You took affection I would not have given if, if . . ."

"I take responsibility," he said. He had come through the door sad; he hadn't realized it was possible to feel dramatically sadder.

"Why did you do it?"

"I don't know," he said. His eyes stung.

"'I don't know,'" she scoffed.

"I brought you something to read too." He handed her an unsealed envelope. It was a contract. "Don't quit," Teddy said. "I've talked with the board. We'll fire you, not because you were at fault, and give you a year's severance. In exchange you don't sue and you don't do anything to try to disrupt the business or its reputation."

Doe's hands started shaking as she flipped through the pages. There was a check paper clipped to the last page. With a year's income all at once she could start her jewelry business. Teddy had paid attention; she had many half–finished pieces. Finally there would be time to take photos, and with finished work she'd be able to convince her roommate to make a web-site for her.

Between this and the new security system, all the honey money was spent and then some.

"I just have to sign?"

"Yes."

"And it won't look like I did something wrong when I look for other jobs?"

"No."

She went into her bedroom and came back with a pen. She set the papers on the kitchen counter to sign and then extended the papers to Teddy. "I don't want to ever see you again," she said.

"I know," he replied, quiet. "Thank you," he said, and then "I did care about you." He put the envelope in the pocket of his hoodie and left.

CHAPTER 30:
SLEUTHING

Mims buzzed apartment 4RE of the last building on the tree–lined Gowanus street. The Brooklyn neighborhood smelled a little like low tide, but she couldn't see the canal.

"Who is it?" a sultry voice hissed.

Mims identified herself as a journalist. "I have some questions about Beasley Cherries," she said.

She was buzzed in. The pretty girl with dark hair Mims remembered from her first visit to the factory opened the door. Her lips were stained purple. Doe gestured for her to come inside.

"I don't think I heard you correctly," she said, her voice less sexy but still as angry as over the intercom. "There's nothing newsworthy about Teddy being a cheater."

"No, I heard about that," Mims said, "and I'm sorry. But that's not why I'm here. I wrote the article about the bees. I'm wondering if you have any additional information about why they showed up when they did."

"Ah, no," Doe said.

"Was Teddy acting strangely about it? Like more so than you would expect?"

"No, he was acting very normal," Doe said.

That's not what Brittany-Lynne had said when Mims visited her. She'd said Teddy had gone full-blown Edgar Allan Poe about the bees' interest in the factory. What reason would Doe have to protect Beasley or his company after what happened at the party? Mims was still miffed that she'd missed the blowout, but she was getting a voyeuristic thrill out of seeing each of the women up close today.

"I won't take up too much more of your time," Mims said. She rubbed at her nose. "I'm so sorry, could I get a tissue? My allergies are really bothering me today."

"Yes, of course," Doe said. She left into the back of the apartment and Mims looked around the kitchen as quickly as possible. Ripped photos of Teddy in the trashcan. Wine cork by the sink. Mims was embarrassed. What was she even expecting to find, detailed plans of the dumping schedule for a back-room drain? Would that explain the maybe-bouncers? They wanted to keep party guests away from illegal disposal areas? Sitting under some keys on an end table by the front door was a bank receipt for a deposit of $42,000.

"Oh shit." Was investigative journalism really so easy? Teddy had bribed Doe to keep her quiet. Mims snapped a photo.

When Doe returned, she accepted the tissue and left. Outside on the street she felt like she was missing something physical, like she had left an umbrella in a restaurant three stops back and was both lighter but also incomplete. She couldn't believe it when she realized what it was: her generalized always-anger had seemingly vanished. She wasn't raging and frustrated at Teddy's lies, Doe's covering for him, or even *Newspapers* taking over her story. The anger had coalesced into a tiny point of focus: What was unfair yet changeable, and how was she going to change it? Mims didn't have a lot of connections to rely on in this city, but somehow she was going to find someone who could help her get inside that factory and determine whether negligence or malfeasance had enticed the bees to come in.

Don Pedro was pretty empty even though it was in the heart of Williamsburg. It was Saturday night, early, and the bartender was in the back helping tape up the corner of a speaker. The patrons were underemployed and over-styled to the point that their clothes looked like costumes. A jazzercise instructor and an old–timey butcher sipped beers at the bar, sucking foam from their mustaches.

Mims and Sean sat in an alcove where the brick was papered over with drink tickets and photocopied flyers of past events. Sean peeled a drink ticket from the wall.

"Sean," Mims said.

"What, you don't like that?"

"No, it's stealing." Like many poor people, she was constantly para-noid about being accused of shoplifting. "The bartender is going to see that and be upset. You think he's going to say 'Silly drunk people! Those lovable rascals, they got one over on me'?"

"I couldn't give less of a shit about whether or not some beer lackey is bummed when he sees someone stole a drink ticket. *Which he won't be.* Plus it's like wallpapering with money. You have to expect someone is going to take it."

"'Beer lackey'? Fuck you, classist dick."

One of Sean's friends from journalism school had gone missing in Syria. It was possible he was fine; it was also possible he would turn up in an execution video. They were avoiding talking about it. It was why Mims had agreed to see him, but she couldn't fully reconcile comforting him with forgiving him for not liking her.

"You have bad self–esteem," she said.

"Are you serious? I think so highly of myself."

"If that were true you wouldn't need to prove to yourself how awe-some you are by showing how the normal way of doing things doesn't apply to you."

She tried to grab the drink ticket out of his hand, but he shoved his fist into his pocket. "Come and get it." He had a challenging smirk on his face. His lips looked soft and his eyes looked drunk.

"You realize we never actually have fun together or have our guard down when we hang out? We just fight; we barely know each other, we certainly aren't invested enough to fight."

"But it feels so comfortable, doesn't it?" he asked.

"It feels familiar, if that's what you mean. I'll get this round."

Mims went to the bar and sat on a stool to await the bartender's return. She swiveled to face Sean and made an "I have my eye on you" gesture toward him and then the drink-ticketed wall. He looked sheepish, rolled his eyes, then made a show of chewing a piece of gum, sticking it on the back of the stolen ticket, and pressing it back into place on the wall. It was disorienting to interact with this version of Sean, the one that didn't have the energy or inclination to put on the happy-go-lucky bashful former jock persona. She liked the raw honesty of it, but she wished she could make his pain go away.

Mims grabbed their drinks and headed back. She toyed with possibilities for later, but try as she might to convince herself that Sean's baggy underwear was sexy because his disdain for fashion was a sign of an interesting life elsewhere, she couldn't do it. He looked silly in the baggy underwear. He was an ugly duckling filling in and he wasn't nearly done making the rounds, getting confirmation from all the young lady-swans that he was desirable now. She wasn't going to take him home with her this time. She handed him a beer.

"So what do I do about this thing at the cherry factory?" Mims had been unable to get in touch with the other author and was still uncertain whether his suggestion of illegal dumping had been a recklessly casual claim or whether the other paper knew something she didn't. Brittany-Lynne and Doe's answers pointed in the direction of Teddy's guilt.

"This is just one more example that goes to show the importance of reporting the news without editorializing," Sean said. "They should be kicked out of the Society of Professional Journalists . . . if they're a member."

"But what if there *is* truth to it . . ." Mims stopped. She was certain Teddy was hiding something. She'd learned that legally disposing of excess cherry liquid and other spent ingredients could run into the tens of thousands of dollars per year. It was wrong to exaggerate how much evidence she had, but what about the moral obligation to find the truth about Beasley? "Sean, it turns out there is a source at the factory, an anonymous source, who says there's been illegal dumping of the cherry runoff. *Newspapers* doesn't know about it and isn't going to pursue it. I need you to help put me in touch with people who can get a warrant. No one is going to take me seriously if I show up claiming wrongdoing without naming my source, but you must have friends of friends who know you're reliable and could put you in touch with someone."

An image of dopey, thick-haired Teddy intruded into her mind's eye. He had been so kind and accommodating. Like an overgrown teddy bear but also a little sexy. *But he's betrayed the public trust*, she told herself, even though she didn't know precisely in what way yet. His betrayal justified her own.

"I don't know if I can do that," Sean said. "And really how big a deal is it anyway? The bees have been dealt with, and the owner probably got scared and stopped the dumping the second you showed up. Aren't you supposed to be focusing on this city council story now?"

"Please," she said. "If you'd been there you would have seen for yourself how suspicious the whole thing is. Please do me this one favor. If he didn't get rid of the evidence before, he's certainly doing it now. There's no time left."

Sean looked to the door, where more patrons were filing in, all young and all smiling.

"You're sure this source is reliable?" he asked. "You're not going to make me look like a fuck–up?"

"I certainly hope not," Mims replied.

"Fine," he said. He held up his glass and they toasted. "Let's get you a search warrant."

CHAPTER 31:
LIKE A FACTORY, BUT ORGANIC

Teddy sat on his couch at home, staring at his laptop screen until it turned black. He wiggled his finger on the trackpad and the screen brightened again, then he went back to staring, this time at the window across the room. It was Monday afternoon, but he hadn't gone to work. It wasn't because he was embarrassed. His usual drive to be at the factory just in case something bad happened, anything from discovery to invasion, had been submerged beneath images of Doe in a cocktail dress, Doe in the bath, Doe's lips swollen and red eating pineapple. He missed her.

His sadness wasn't all-encompassing enough to stave off boredom though. Usually he would text Brittany-Lynne at a time like this and she'd send him funny gifs. He rested his face in his hands for a few seconds, sorrow and defeat momentarily robbing him of the energy required to keep his head upright. Everything bad that was happening at the factory was his fault; every decision he'd made since taking charge took the company and each person who worked there one step closer to ruin.

He walked to the window. The street was too narrow compared to the height of the building for him to see the ground below, and he couldn't really see the sky either. He wanted out.

Back at the couch, the laptop was waiting for him. He woke up the screen again and it showed him the contact page for a honey distributor he'd been researching. It would cost too much to buy real honey and sell it as Lin's honey. He wouldn't have to deal with confronting Lin or have the guilt of selling a potentially contaminated product, but it was prohibitively expensive and logistically insane. The refrain he kept coming back to and dismissing was that he could give up and do what Lin wanted: take the money and relabel the "honey."

Now would be a good time to have a wise grandfather, or an older sister, to ask for advice. He hadn't spoken to Marlow since the party and assumed she was a good part of the way back through Canada by now. Teddy pulled on a sweatshirt and headed for Brooklyn.

He trudged up to the roof with his hands in his pockets. Just as he swung the door open a gust of wind caught it and yanked it nearly off the hinges. He scrambled to grab hold of the door and realized as it clicked shut again that for those few seconds he'd been focused on the task at hand and not caught up thinking about his ever-expanding number of crises. It wasn't comforting to think that only mini disasters could take his mind off meta disasters.

Taking in the expanse of top-of-the-factory, he was thrown for a second, and the impossible thought crossed his mind that he was on the wrong rooftop. Large planters of grass sat on the roof, along with a lawn chair. Marlow must have put them up there sometime before the party, though he couldn't imagine how. The planters looked like they weighed a hundred pounds each. The sugar water feeders had been moved to the opposite side of the building, and where the feeders had been there now stood a stack of golden boxes. Teddy recognized the boxes as a beehive. His reaction at seeing the hive wasn't surprise, it was *of course she would.*

"Hi," Teddy said. "Sorry for bothering you. I've come to ask for guidance on something."

The bees didn't say anything, but he felt the wind again, and it was like the bees' voices were inside it, like the white noise of a rotating fan turned up to the volume of a waterfall.

"My sister went home," he yelled over the whirlwind. The wind died down. "I should have brought you tribute or something," he said, looking around the roof again. "A housewarming present," he corrected. "Tribute" sounded too dramatic and formal. Too crazy. "Marlow's always making me look bad—I didn't bring a lawn chair or anything."

Teddy went downstairs and rummaged through the kitchen cabinets looking for bee snacks. He didn't find any, not even a jar of honey in with the tea supplies, but on the way out he grabbed the little vase of flowers off the lunch table. He took it with him to his office and pulled out his secret stash of cookies. Teddy mashed the cookies in the bottom of a mug and then mixed in some water from the vase—it was chunky but probably the water was sugary enough that the bees could drink it. He took both the mug and the flowers up to the roof.

"Here," he said and placed the items at the base of one of the grass planters. He gestured toward the offering and then inched a little closer to the hive. He wanted to talk to the queen herself. The hive was capped off with a flat metal top with a lip that overhung the boxes by about two inches. Teddy took off his hoodie and wrapped it around his hand and forearm; with a quick, powerful flick he flipped the roof off the hive and jumped back, flinging the hoodie to the ground.

A flurry of bees escaped the hive, but then most flew back in again as Teddy watched, waiting for the commotion to subside. Bees crawled over and between the wooden slats that hung inside the hive like folders inside a filing cabinet. He approached again, bees swirling. "Your highness?" he asked.

He pried up the edges of one of the frames, slowly and carefully, and pulled it out from between the others and into the open air. It reminded him of the board game Operation, where you had to pull out a plastic "organ" from a hole in an illustrated patient without the metal tweezers touching the sides of the hole and setting off a buzzer. Teddy's heart beat faster and faster as he held the frame aloft. It was covered in bees and little hexagons, some of which were capped with wax and some not. The dozens of bees all looked the same to him; he couldn't tell which one was the queen and wasn't sure what he was looking for. He flipped the frame to inspect the other side. Right in the middle was a bee with a super-long butt. The bee was bigger than the others and seemed preoccupied with the comb, oblivious to no longer being in the dark sanctuary of the hive. That must be her.

"Bee-Queen, what should I do?" he asked. "I need advice." The queen continued her circuit of the comb and the other bees continued their duties seemingly without being directed, crawling over and between each other, focused and unperturbed. The wonderous little hexagons that made up the honeycomb somehow fit together so precisely. A beehive was the perfect combination of unpredictable life and predictable structure. The little bees were like living pieces of a machine, chugging together in concert, to form the larger honey factory. He should never have been afraid of them; if anything he should have seen their interest in the cherry factory as auspicious. What had they done but try to guide him away from crime and back to himself?

Bees were crawling over his fingers now and they tickled and their feet felt like they were made of little shards of ice. "How do I get out of this?" he asked. He closed his eyes to better hear the answer, but as soon as visual distractions were out of the way all he could feel were the bee feet. One of them was approaching the edge of his sleeve. He was scared he was going to drop the frame, especially if he got stung. He inserted the frame back into the hive, careful not to knock it into the sides. He picked up the hive cover and placed it back. As it thudded back into place, he knew that the bees were on his side. They'd given him an answer, not the queen alone, but all of them together. A beehive could run itself if the queen bee got sick or died; the remaining members of the hive would just make a new one. All

Teddy needed to do to save the factory was get out of the way and let the factory run itself without his interference.

Teddy showed up to the bank's main branch in the financial district in Manhattan wearing his suit. It was the same suit he'd worn to his family's funerals and to the ill-fated meeting in Hong Kong.

The revolving door was heavier than expected, so he emerged into the lobby off-balance. The gravitas of what he was about to undertake was undercut by a dog-treat dispenser. An LED screen sported animated dollar bills and piggy banks.

"Follow me, please," a young man said. He led Teddy past a double row of cubicles to the enclosed offices where important people sat.

"Hello, Mr. Beasley, what can I do for you?" an older gentleman asked. He had a white beard, a vest underneath his suit jacket, and tiny round glasses, so Teddy felt better about the lack of marble columns out front.

"Hi." Teddy shook the bank manager's hand. "Hello, I mean. I'd like to know what the process would be and the timeline to turn my company into a co-op. I'd like to transfer factory ownership over to the workers."

"A valuation will need to be scheduled and performed. The employees would have the option to contest the valuation. Once a price is decided, appropriate papers are drawn up, presumably by your lawyers, that specify which members have access to the bank accounts, lines of credit, what-have-you. A restructuring of that sort would take a day or two to initiate and up to three weeks to finalize, from the date the valuation is accepted."

"Hey, I'm ready to sign now. I wouldn't be selling to the employees, I'd be handing it over to them. So we could skip the valuation."

"That would have very serious tax repercussions, Mr. Beasley," the manager said gravely. "I suggest you confer with your lawyer first."

Teddy had imagined it would be as easy as signing over a deed to a car, but maybe signing over the deed to a car was complicated too. He'd never done it before.

"Mr. Beasley?" the manager asked. "Are you all right?"

"Yeah, I'm good, thanks," Teddy said. His co-op plan wasn't going to be stymied by a little paperwork. It just wouldn't be as easy to pick up and leave as he'd wanted. It contrasted sharply with Marlow's freedom. He could tell from the way the manager was looking at him that he'd been silent too long. "You seem really concerned about the lawyer part. We have a guy on retainer, I'll call him up," Teddy said.

"I'll walk you out, Mr. Beasley," the manager said.

As Teddy retreaded his steps through the rows of cubicles, a doubt found its way into his head and started buzzing around. Where was this feeling of urgency to unload the factory coming from? Was he really doing this for the good of the company, the good of the employees, or was he just running away? Same old Teddy, avoiding confrontation under the guise of generosity. He pushed extra-fast through the revolving door, prepared for it this time, and left the doubt trapped inside the bank. He was doing the right thing. That he would be free for the first time in his life would just be an added bonus. It didn't even matter that he didn't know if a queen bee could survive on its own the same way a hive could survive without a queen bee.

Outside the bank Teddy took off his suit jacket as he walked. He folded it and placed it on top of a trashcan and kept walking. He unbuttoned his shirt and draped it over the side of the trashcan at the next corner. In his undershirt and slacks he made a beeline for a discount clothing store with ten-dollar gym shorts in the window. He would never wear the bad luck suit again.

CHAPTER 32:
A BUST

Mims was so excited she thought she would hyperventilate. She was wearing a lanyard that said "Press" and Joe the cameraman was standing beside her. He had a real SLR and shot almost everything that ended up on the front page of the *Free Post*. Three policemen and two women from the Brooklyn District Attorney's office were looking at a clipboard. They had an administrative search warrant: a team of twelve agents from the city Department of Environmental Protection and ten from the state Department of Environmental Conservation were waiting in and around three vans across the street. Someone at the DEP had apparently had questions about the quantity of open sludge at the cherry factory since reading her initial bee article on the subway one morning, and New York State was always eager and alert when it came to collecting fines. The judge had given no pushback when the warrant was requested. No one had said press was welcome today exactly, but Sean's contact had told her what time the raid was happening and everyone seemed to be ignoring her, so her plan was to be as unobtrusive as possible until someone asked her to leave.

"Joe," she whispered. "Get a shot of that." She pointed to a patch of bee–speckled dandelion growing up from a crack in the sidewalk. The sign for Beasley Cherries loomed in the background.

"Okay, let's go," one of the policemen said.

They rushed the front gate, much slower perhaps than DEA or SWAT agents would have done, and Mims scampered behind them.

The warrant was presented to Jalen at the front desk. He looked horrified when he recognized Mims standing in the back. "Mr. Beasley isn't in yet," he said.

"When he gets here, he can come find us," one of the lawyers said. Mims didn't want to miss the look on his face when he realized he'd been caught.

The most likely area of the production stream to check for improper disposal of cherry waste was the dye process, since the bees and their honey had turned red. Cherries were boiled in red dye for several minutes, then rinsed in boiling water with citric acid added, then rinsed again to remove the excess citric acid. The citric acid was to minimize dye bleeding into fruitcakes, ice cream, fruit salads. Improper storage or disposal of the rinse water could have led to the bee infestation.

The inspectors fanned out and Mims followed a group onto the main factory floor. Just as they entered, what looked like hundreds of pounds of bright red cherries plopped and thundered into a clear holding tank. She was awed by the scale of it.

"Hey, you can't come in here! What about hygiene?" a man shouted, gesturing at their uncovered heads. The workers had hairnets and little white slippers over their shoes.

"Shut it down," the officer said.

The agent slated to lead the inspection of the sewer grates was exiting through a door at the far side of the room, so Mims slipped away from the chaos of shouting workers and whirring machinery to follow him. She snapped a photo with her phone over her shoulder as she left.

In a back area behind the buildings there was a large drain. Two of the agents got to work turning the screws. With a loud screech the grate was pulled up and a man jumped in to take samples. Glancing around the light gray pavement Mims didn't see any staining that would indicate cherry spillage. There were no hoses for cleanup.

The man in the hole handed up some swabs in plastic containers then went back down, leaning farther into the darkness.

"This will be handy!" he called up. Mims leaned over the hole in anticipation.

The man's hand emerged clutching a handful of trash. Among the refuse was the frayed head of a push broom. "This will have acted like a trap," he said. Another agent held open a plastic bag and he dropped it inside. The "raid" wasn't quite as interesting as Mims had taken for granted it would be. She passed Joe on her way back into the building. "Make sure you get a shot of the bag," she said.

She walked from room to room to see agents scrubbing and collecting diligently. As the minutes passed, the doubts Mims had been suppressing began clawing their way in.

"How's the raid going?" Sean texted. She shoved the phone in her pocket and walked quickly to the accounting office. A cluster of agents flipped through files and binders.

"Here's the recycling plan," a factory employee in a polo shirt said. He handed the file to one of the agents, who then made a photocopy. "We have printouts back to 1993; earlier than that they're archived off site. Do you want all of these?" The recordkeeping was meticulous. Mims flipped through a file called "trucking logs." The employee gave her the side eye and took the folder out of her hand.

"What gets trucked?" she asked. The man's eyes rested on her press badge for a long time before he answered.

"Sweet cherries are brined to firm 'em up and to leach the color out—so we can obtain uniform color when we dye them. The pH of the leftover brine is very low, and that acidity creates air and water pollution if improperly disposed of—it sucks the oxygen out of rivers the same way fertilizer runoff from farms does." His voice was authoritative and soothing like Neil deGrasse Tyson's but with a thick Brooklyn accent. "We *do not* dump untreated water into the NYC sewers to flow out to sea. We reduce the SO2 concentration of our brine and rinse water using lime and manual filtration. Then we ship the water to a disposal facility in New Jersey where it's buried in deep wells." He slapped the folder in his hand. "And we have the records to prove it."

"Oh . . ." Mims said, mostly to the floor. The DEC agents photocopied around her. She peeked in one of the other folders on the desk. It listed truck arrival and departure times and volume of liquid; there was another folder with invoices from the disposal company; there was another with maintenance reports on the equipment used to manually filter the water before it was shipped off.

It was still possible there had been dumping of untreated liquids into the sewers in addition to what was listed here, but it was starting to seem unlikely. The bees really had come and pilfered the cherry juice one tiny mouthful at a time, from unguarded barrels of brine being carted across the yard, like eroding winds that seemed insignificant day-to-day but that formed canyons over time. "And you looked at that dumpster out front already?" she asked one of the agents, trying hard to mask her despair.

"Yes, it's just construction debris."

"Uh, hi guys."

Teddy stood in the doorway. He was wearing baggy gym shorts and an uncharacteristically cheap-looking hoodie but seemed the least like a cornered animal that she had ever seen him. "I'm Teddy Beasley, the owner. I guess I got here kind of late for the raid. Jalen said you're finishing up."

"Maybe think of it more like an audit than a raid?" Mims said.

"Don't try to downplay my factory losing a half day's production like it's some kind of routine inspection."

Mims found it hard to keep eye contact with him. "I guess the bees are kind of attention whores," she said. "Bringing so many people here." Teddy took a step into the room, dignified and commanding, and Mims shrunk away from him in shame.

"I invited you to my party not just because you're a reporter and you made me, but because you seemed cool," he said, then turned to the polo-shirted man. "Matt, if anyone needs anything, I'll be in my office. Get these men some cookies. Jalen can bring around bottled waters."

Mims felt the reminder buzz of her text message alert in her pocket.

She had been wrong. Not just wrong; she was bad: bad at her job and a liar and a bad judge of character. She had assumed the worst of Doe and of Teddy because she assumed everyone was hiding something, but maybe they weren't, maybe only she was. There was no way to return to just scraping by now that she'd been too confident, too ambitious, and bought into the idea that *she* had discovered a great hidden truth that somehow everyone else had missed. It was narcissistic delusion. Her phone buzzed again; there was no need to answer, everyone would know soon enough.

Marlow sat on a bed in a Crown Heights sublet she'd gotten off Craigslist. She'd paid in cash and wasn't asked to show identification, so the partially furnished, slope-floored basement apartment was hers for the next twenty-six days. And she'd been able to get her head right. In a way she felt responsible for Teddy's shortcomings because of her failure to step in and be a teacher when he was younger. In her resistance to becoming their meddling parents she had swung too far the other way, but she resolved never to abandon him again.

The doorbell rang and she buzzed without confirming the caller's identity first. "Oops," she said. She had assumed she'd be more of a natural at intrigue. After initially being disappointed to find that bodyguards wanted to know if you were doing something illegal before taking the job, she'd been excited to challenge herself by taking care of her own "advanced personal safety needs." When she looked through the peephole it was her delivery lobster. Marlow put on a baseball hat and pulled it over her eyes and then opened the door.

Back at the bed, she laid napkins down carefully, reminiscent of the way her mother had shown her to cover toilet seats, even in their own home, and then spread out the lobster feast. The whole room quickly filled with the smell. Just as she was getting to the point of wiping up butter spatter and carrion, the cheap black smartphone sitting next to the delivery bag lit up.

"Hello?" a heavy, tentative voice asked.

"Bro!" she replied.

"Marlow?"

"I'm so glad this worked. I had a bike messenger drop the phone with Sanjeep, but I wasn't sure it would get to you."

"What is this?"

"It's a burner phone, Teddy. Just to be safe, in case you've misjudged our smuggler friends. I'm going to text you the address of the place where we're staying until this blows over. Don't come straight here, and make sure no one is following you. Take the subway and change cars a few times. I had an idea. We disassemble the labeling machine, get it out of there. Put it in that stupid dumpster and schedule a pickup. Then cave in the room somehow. No room, no labeling. Anyway, we'll discuss everything else when you get here."

"So you want me to pretend the party didn't happen?"

"We can talk about it when you get here. There are only five days left until Lin tries to force his next shipment on us, and there's a lot we need to work out."

"I'm not coming."

"Fine, we'll talk about it now." There was silence. "I'm waiting," she said.

"You don't care about family."

She had never been at ease in the presence of her family, but she had loved them in a generalized sort of way. "Because I don't want children, because I'm old and single, because I left yeah, yeah. I've heard all of this before. Guilty. I regret leaving you. Sincerely."

"That's a nice laundry list," he said. "That reporter got the police to come raid the factory today, and I was there all alone. You weren't there when she showed up the first time, and you weren't there when Lin attacked me. That's three times something terrible has happened and you weren't there, and that's the whole reason I called you down here. Brittany–Lynne was like real family to me, and Doe I could have started an actual family with, and you drove them away."

"Both of them were so obviously . . ." Damaged. Sad. Energy–sucks. Like weighted anchors. While Marlow was set on leaving family troubles in the past, Teddy seemed intent on recreating the dynamics from their childhood with his girlfriends over and over until he could figure out how to bring about a different outcome. "You can fuck a smile onto the face of every depressed woman in New York, but you still won't be able to save her. Our mother is dead."

"Why do you have to talk that way? Not everything has to be crass and mean and . . . Freudian."

"Our dad couldn't cheer up our mom and she ruined our lives with her anxiety–driven control freak bullshit. On some level, you think you could have done better than he did. The world is a disgusting place, Teddy, and I'm all about radical honesty. We're rotting bacteria sacks. Get over here before I eat all the lobster." She'd already eaten all the lobster. She'd order more.

"You talk over me. Like . . . with your emotions. Everything you want is more important than what I want."

"Teddy, that's not true," she said. "I know I can be a flake, but I always cared about you! Remember how I got you that *Nat Geo* subscription when I moved away?"

Teddy answered in a calm monotone. "I was five and you said you'd call every day with updates on your adventures and then after four days you stopped and sent a subscription to *National Geographic* instead and I didn't hear from you again for two years."

"You were supposed to think of me and feel close every time you read one." The magazine subscription had been one of her top three proofs to herself that maybe there was enough positive history between them to salvage a relationship.

"That was supposed to be a stand-in for a person?" Teddy asked. "It was too much of a burden to keep in touch, so you substituted this other thing. Like a fake paper cutout version of yourself. And what you pulled at the party, *that* was controlling, Marlow. Like you don't trust me to lead my own life correctly. You're like Mom."

"I'm trying my best," she said. She felt ridiculous then, sitting on the bed surrounded by lobster carcasses. Her new phone was smudged with butter and slipping out of her hand. She was a child as much as he was.

He *had* been doing an undeniably shitty job of leading his own life. Honey laundering, losing fistfights, disappointing women, getting caught. She didn't know how to guide the way without just taking over. How do you lead by example how to extract yourself from a smuggling operation? His words cut through her nonetheless. He was right—it wasn't her place to make moral choices about his dating life for him. She was the one acting like their mother, not him.

"Teddy?" she asked.

"I know," he replied. "Send me the address."

"Don't bother coming back here or submitting to any of our editors," Aziz said.

"I can't believe you called me all the way into the city to yell at me in person." Mims leaned back in the plastic chair as much as was possible and crossed her legs. She'd already sat through ten minutes of berating, long enough to regain her bearings and act blasé about it. Somehow Aziz had found out about the cherry factory bust; a successful raid would have distracted from the fact that she hadn't gone to Cold Spring for the other story.

She realized that since Aziz had just become no–longer–her–boss, she wasn't obligated to listen to him. She stood up to go. "You're acting very unprofessional," she said.

"You're going to be really disappointed when you realize that this whole industry is about happy hours and watching somebody's cat when they're out of town and blowjobs and who your friends are and access and nepotism. It's a small community, and you fucked up. Talent isn't enough, which you may not even have, it's who you know, and right now all I know is you aren't working for me ever again."

"Clearly you don't know many people, or you wouldn't be working here," Mims said, gesturing at the dingy room. She walked out with her best runway strut, but she was at a loss as to where she was going.

As the elevator descended it was as if she were dropping below the clouds obscuring a mountaintop, and her anger got thinner and easier to see through with each floor. Her lie to Sean had killed her career, but her lost temper with Aziz had cremated it. No resuscitation possible.

She wasn't sure how to even begin to put things right by Sean or the Beasleys. Saying "I'm sorry" wasn't enough unless she could make reparations. Mims decided to stop by Beasley Cherries on the way home. She wasn't sure she'd have the guts to go in, but she was going to force herself to look at the building, look at herself, look at her actions. Maybe it was envy that had motivated her vendetta against Teddy. His family had given him so much and she had tried to destroy it.

CHAPTER 33:
CHERRY JUICE

T eddy pulled on his work gloves.

"Hey, who am I?" Marlow asked. She leaned behind the relabeler and then jumped out. "Cherry juice!"

Teddy laughed. They hadn't talked again about the party since his arrival at the "safe house," as she insisted on calling the Crown Heights rental. He could tell her jokes were an attempt to make amends. "You're Mims Walsh."

"What about now? CHERRY JUICE!"

"That inspection could have gone very differently," he said. It was 6:30 p.m. on Tuesday, the day after the raid. The last employee had gone home an hour and a half ago, but Teddy felt exposed knowing it was still light out, not just light but sunny and wholesome and bright, just a few dozen feet above their heads.

"That chick is intense," Marlow said. "If you were able to stop freaking out about the bees being a sign, she should be able to."

Teddy's feelings toward the bees had changed from alarm and persecution to grudging respect and then peace, but he wasn't going to frighten Marlow by explaining it to her. His lawyer hadn't taken his co-op idea seriously, especially after he mentioned that the social structure of the hive was his inspiration. The lawyer had insisted he think about it for a week and then come back.

Marlow lifted a wrench over her head and swung hard. It nicked the edge of the bolt she was aiming for and the bolt spun loose. She unscrewed it and wriggled free the metal plate it had been holding in place.

"When you reverse the order of the Chinese characters that spell out 'honey,' it says 'bee' instead. Isn't that cool?" Marlow asked.

"Let's stop talking about bees, please." Teddy walked over with a section of conveyer belt and placed it in the utility cart with Marlow's pieces. He looked around the underground room. "This is taking forever. Less than half of it is disassembled." They'd started early in the morning, taken a break during the workday, and had to finish by the end of tomorrow at the latest. Marlow's plan was for the equipment to be disappeared so there wasn't even a question of relabeling the next shipment.

"Should we hire some day laborers to help?" Marlow suggested.

"No. I hope you're joking."

"They wouldn't tell anyone," she said. "I'll take this load up."

"Maybe we should wait until dark? What if there are investigators out there watching the place?"

"There aren't. And also there's nothing suspicious about hauling scrap metal out to a dumpster. We can pretend it's from the new wing. We have to be bold and stay the course at this point. There's a certain flare to doing bad things in the open. Just like it's style that lets you off the hook for being a heartbreaker. You don't have it, but watch and learn."

"I don't want to learn." He didn't want her to joke about Doe and Brittany–Lynne, or even mention them at all, but he thought saying so would stoke the flames of her disappointment. He didn't have the words to express, nor did she have the attention span to listen to, how much loneliness and heartbreak he was feeling.

After a few minutes she came back with the empty utility cart. "Help me with this big piece," he said, and she did.

Mims arrived at Beasley Cherries just as the sun was starting to set. The factory was closed, but maybe that was for the best—Teddy Beasley didn't owe it to her to give audience to her apology. An apology wasn't going to change his mind about her, nor should it. An apology wouldn't give him back his day of lost production or undo the embarrassment of having government agents running around the place.

She stood across the street and watched the brick turn gold. The entrance gate glowed. The peaceful scene was marred only by that stupid dumpster that still hadn't been moved. The party had been almost a week ago. She wanted to capture the moment anyway, so she pulled her phone from her purse but then dropped it.

"Fuck!" She kneeled on the ground and lifted the phone gingerly. The screen was cracked.

Mims was half positioned behind a truck tire when Marlow came out of a side door next to the main gate. She was pushing a cart. Marlow looked down the road to the left and then to the right and then scanned the tops of the buildings across the way, far above Mims's head. Mims felt awkward then, as if she'd be caught, when she hadn't intended to be hiding. Simultaneously she was struck by how odd it was that Marlow was searching. Adrenaline surged through her limbs. "No," she told herself firmly. Marlow was probably just acting paranoid because of the raid, but she wasn't actually doing anything wrong. The sister of the owner of a multimillion-dollar company was definitely allowed to take out the company's trash.

When the cart was flush with the dumpster, Marlow did a weight-lifting squat and lifted it above her head, to the rim of the dumpster, and tipped. Metal clanged out. The cart clattered back to the sidewalk, then Marlow pulled it back to the side door and went inside. Mims started to stand but the door reopened and Teddy came out with two enormous clear garbage bags filled with shredded paper. He hefted them into the dumpster, then he stepped to the curb and leaned out, looking down the block as Marlow had done. Mims shrunk behind the tire. She could see his feet, and they weren't moving. Her thighs cramped and she wondered how long she should wait before trying to pull off a casual emergence from behind the truck. The feet were joined by a second pair, Marlow's. Finally the siblings walked down the block to the left. Mims peeked out; they were looking over their shoulders as they walked. When they disappeared around the corner she stood and bolted for the dumpster.

She hoisted herself up and was leaning down to reach one of the plastic bags when she heard voices approaching. She scrambled inside the dumpster as quietly as possible.

"Maybe tacos?" Teddy was saying. They had circled the block. "Should we just drive?"

"Nah, I don't want to try to park my truck by the taco place. Too crowded."

The voices passed her by and disappeared again. Mims ripped a hole in the plastic bag and pulled out a fistful of shredded paper. She could tell in spite of the thin ribbons what it was—labels for the off-brand honey. She was having a hard time grasping the coincidence of the labels with the bee infestation. She looked around for other clues. The metal Marlow had dumped didn't help explain anything: it was just bent pieces of scrap and a bunch of screws. Could it be that Teddy was responsible for the cheap "honey" flooding the supermarkets? Because she'd initially blown off the whole idea of fake honey, she hadn't scrutinized Gerard's premise that the operation distributing Vermont's Wonderful was colossal and extensive. But of course in fitting with the times and Brooklyn's "buy small, buy local" zeitgeist it could be a small, local version of corruption. But how did the red honey fit in? Was Teddy stealing the city bees to make them manufacture it? Was he turning the city honey red to free up market share for his cheap honey? He wasn't a comic book super villain; none of those explanations made sense. Did the honey labels have to do with the opening of the organic division? She shoved the label confetti in her purse and snapped photos of the dumpster contents as best she could with her broken phone. The voices approached again.

"Okay, that's twice, there's no one on this block, can we go now? We have to eat and get back."

"Yeah," Teddy said warily. "It seems fine. I'll be glad when Thursday has come and gone. What time is the truck coming to take the dumpster away?" The voices receded and Mims couldn't hear the answer. Today was Tuesday.

She stayed in the dumpster for a long time, thinking. The good thing about having been exposed as a dodgy journalist was that she was freed of the frenetic drive to project the image of being a reputable one. She was left with two courses of action: improve her inner substance, so that she *became* a competent journalist, or admit finally that it was impossible and give up. Mims took a fistful of shredded honey label in each hand and crunched them so that they made sounds like fall leaves. These labels were real enough, but did she want accomplishment and recognition so badly that she was becoming delusional about the labels' importance?

The sun fully set and Mims found herself still leaning against the side of the dumpster with pointy metal bits poking into her thighs. If she decided to trust herself, it meant risking not just what was left of her professional reputation and dignity, but a second fruitless betrayal of a kind–seeming young man and his weirdo sister.

"Could we talk in person tonight? It's urgent," Mims wrote. There was no way her theory about Teddy would sound sane via text. Sean's status updated to "read," but he didn't respond. She hadn't spoken to him since the raid, and her silence may as well have been an admission that she'd lied to get his help. She hadn't been ready to face him. If he would hear her out and help her one more time, maybe she could undo some of the damage her lie had caused. "I want to talk to you about what happened at the cherry factory." Send. "And apologize." Send. A green circle appeared next to his status. That meant he'd blocked her.

"Gretchen! Can you believe it's already been a month since your party?" Mims texted.

She paced on the sidewalk outside of the subway closest to Beasley Cherries. Whenever a person or car came into view she stepped into the doorway of a nearby bodega until she was sure it wasn't Teddy and Marlow. After three minutes of waiting she sent another text. "Do you know where Sean is? He's mad at me right now, long story, but I need to talk to him. It's urgent."

The response was instantaneous. "Busy," it said. There was an accompanying location ping. The quandary now was whether "busy" meant exasperated or just busy. The little map showing Gretchen's location was either meant to be an explanation of what she was busy doing, or it was an invitation to come join. Mims knew one definitely wrong answer was to text again asking for clarification. She got on the subway and headed to Forty–Fourth Street in Manhattan, to the fabled Algonquin Hotel. Mims had been saving her first visit to the hotel's Round Table restaurant for a celebration of her first publication in a national newspaper, the way some women saved Paris for their honeymoons. It was a tourist spot, and she'd heard the food was just okay, but in the 1920s Dorothy Parker had issued tear-inducing pronouncements of wit and savagery from within, surrounded by playwrights and Pulitzer winners.

Mims walked through the hotel lobby into the dark wood-paneled restaurant. Gretchen wasn't seated at any of the tables, which was a relief. She didn't want to interrupt a dinner between Gretchen and her agent or a publicist. A waiter told her where she could find the Blue Bar, so she went to check there. Coming all the way to Midtown from Brooklyn to ask where she could find Sean was a humiliation somewhere between finding a coffee stain on her shirt and discovering she'd been mispronouncing "mirror" as "meer" her whole life.

But now that she'd committed to believing in herself and her investigation, any amount of embarrassment was worth it to prove she was right about Beasley.

The right side of the room glowed blue from lights placed above and within the bar, and a Smurf version of one of Gretchen's friends set down an empty martini glass. Then she saw Jessica, Sarah, lots of people she knew. She felt like she was walking through a wildlife video, anticipating the moment the animals would notice her and attack.

Sean. Sean was near the back wall surrounded by friends, at the far end of a tunnel of clinking glasses and coy smiles and bravado. A fay woman stood a few feet in front of him, partially obscuring Mims's view with her mounds of bouncy brown curls. As Mims walked toward him she glimpsed herself in the mirror behind the bar. She'd been sitting in trash for an hour and was missing an earring, and the blue light made her look like a corpse. Under the guise of brushing her hair behind her ear she slipped the orphan earring out and into her pocket.

Her heart beat faster as she got close enough to hear his voice, which was at its most raucous and engaging. "If you compliment any girl's shoes she'll be like 'They're comfortable!' And if you compliment her dress, she's like, 'It has pockets!'" Mims would never say either of those things in response to a compliment. She hadn't been asking for a relationship, she'd just wanted him to fall for her a little and to have a memorable summer capped off by a teary, life-affirming goodbye. She wished she had her anger back instead of the black sadness that seemed to be collapsing her bones from the inside.

Someone grabbed her elbow and yanked her toward an alcove.

"What are you doing here?" Gretchen hissed. She was in a cocktail dress.

"You invited me," Mims said. "Who is that?" She nodded her head toward the delicate hand landing on Sean's forearm.

"Sean's new girlfriend, Molly." Mims had heard of an ethereal Molly Alaoui, though they'd never met; she existed at the outermost, most successful fringes of Mims's social circle. Molly photographed refugee camps for a living and her mother was an ambassador.

"We *just* fucked like a week and a half ago, no condoms," Mims said. "Of course he's got a girlfriend now." Ivy League grad school, serious work for serious causes in dangerous places, she came from a nice family. She didn't wear frivolous red lipstick.

Gretchen crossed her arms in front of her chest as if to ward off the threat of status-lowering drama. "You met Sean like a month ago. Were you even dating? What do you care?"

They had in fact been on only the one date. Mims hadn't even wanted to *date him* date him, but the idea that he'd met someone so dazzling that he wanted to date *her* . . . "May the best woman win, I guess. I didn't know it was a competition though, and I wouldn't have wanted to get stuck lugging around the prize. He's always drunk."

"Mims, listen to me." Gretchen hooked her fingers into the flesh of Mims's upper arm until she looked her right in the eyes. Gretchen had probably been using mom tactics on people since third grade, she was so practiced at it. "I've heard you've been struggling with work recently, and I can see you're going through a hard time, but work is not a reflection of your worth and neither is this. Molly is not better than you and Sean is also not better than you. Although he's also not 'always drunk,' I don't know where you got that idea. We are all amazing, alive human beings. We are also all vile, as you should know, with that game you and Bennie play. Let it go." But if they weren't better than she was, how did it cross Gretchen's mind to deny it? How much had Sean told her?

"But did he have to bring her *here*?" She knew as she said it that she'd committed one too many transgressions of etiquette. Gretchen was a consummate host, and she breathed politesse. Mims had crashed two parties in five weeks, among graver sins (including gossip, stalking, and accomplice to indoor smoking). They'd been closer a few years ago, but they'd never hung out one on one. As Sean's friend, she was not the appropriate person for Mims to look to for sympathy. Complaining about him to Gretchen was bad manners.

"Do you even know what 'here' is? It's Molly's birthday party. There's nothing unique about liking Dorothy Parker, and some of us work in this neighborhood. We all read books, Mims." Gretchen couldn't know Mims read so much because she spent four hours a day on the subway. If she didn't spend that time living other people's lives through the page, it would just be wasted. "Maybe Sean did like you, then he got to know you and realized you weren't compatible after all. Maybe he doesn't like that you're a bitch, maybe he doesn't like your temper tantrums, maybe he just doesn't like your blowjobs. It doesn't actually matter what he doesn't like about you, it's done, move on. Have some dignity for fuck's sake. Sean's a good guy. He hasn't done anything wrong here, so please don't make this a side-choosing *thing* in the friend group."

"You're hurting my arm," Mims said weakly. She'd never seen Gretchen lose it before. A lonely, shelter–animal part of her had to admit that Sean's behavior hadn't really been confusing. Hot–and–cold never means "he likes you," it means something bad. She'd been wrapped up in her own ego, constructing stories about how she was a lusty, emotionless siren and he was her prey.

Gretchen sighed and released her. "I can't believe you came all the way out here for this."

"No, even better," Mims said. She lifted her chin slightly. "I came to ask him a preposterous work favor." Surely Sean knew someone who could grant her access a second time to Beasley Cherries, either through a second warrant or some other means. This time she knew what she was looking for.

She pushed past Gretchen and covered the last few feet to where Sean was standing. When he saw her he tried to back away, but he was already too near the wall. "Why did you come here?" he asked.

"Can we—" The pinched look on his face said he wasn't going to give her a private audience. She resisted the urge to whisper; there was no use trying to hide from those standing nearby what she had to say. "I'm so sorry I lied to you about having a source at the factory. I know that makes me look like a crazy person, and I know it hurt your credibility and reputation. It was a huge betrayal, and I was wrong." Mims took a deep breath; she realized at the top that she was like a frazzled kid about to blow out birthday candles. In contrast Molly stood quietly, poised. Mims let the breath tumble out anyway: "But there really is something strange going on at Beasley Cherries, and I think it has to do with the honey Gerard Babineaux wanted us to investigate."

"Who?" His whole body puffed up with indignation when he remembered the name. "That nutty pastry chef? Are you out of your mind? Have you been talking with that guy?" Just as quickly his look turned to one of pity and concern. He thought she was crazy.

Mims pushed on. "I assumed that the off–brand honey was an enormous operation, if it was real at all, just because that's what Gerard assumed and I didn't take it seriously enough to think about it. But it's tiny and local. I'm pretty sure Teddy Beasley is the one distributing the fake honey. I know it's a strange coincidence, but I just need help one more time getting into the factory..."

"You *do* need help, but not the kind you're asking for. Please leave."

Gretchen's manicured fingers grasped her elbow again and Mims let herself be led away. A waiter crossed their path carrying a tray of bar snacks and she eyed it hungrily as he passed. They came to a stop by the entrance, just at the point it seemed like Gretchen was going to toss her out the door.

She was seized by a sudden urge to confess who she really was. If she was going to be expelled from the garden either way, she may as well try. Maybe she had been wrong this whole time to assume she'd be ostracized if her friends knew her true financial situation and career prospects, as she'd been wrong about so many other things. What if they lovingly accepted her for the irascible failure she was and would have all along?

"I'm not just going through a downturn," Mims admitted. "The last major thing I published was that *Bust* article three years ago. The club publicity pieces I write are unpaid, and I don't qualify for food stamps because of the spotty nature of freelance." Not that she would ever apply for food stamps, but she wanted to head off the suggestion before Gretchen could come up with it. Whatever attempt at helpfulness she responded with, it was going to sting.

But there was no surprise on Gretchen's face, maybe just disgust. "Then get a job. What are you talking about? Be a waitress or a caterer or a temp or leave the city. Why are you living that way?" She closed her eyes for a long moment and seemed to be breathing in composure, stiffening and straightening the longer she inhaled. Her eyes opened. "I shouldn't have said waitress, I'm sorry. There are other things you could do like marketing or event planning; you just need to decide now before you get too old to change careers."

At least Mims had an answer about whether Gretchen would have contempt for her if she took a job in a coffee shop. A waiter approached. "Ma'am, your table is almost ready. Do we need to fit in an extra chair?" Gretchen flinched at the word "ma'am."

"No," Mims and Gretchen said at the same time. The way Gretchen rushed the word made it seem like she was worried Mims would say yes.

"I'm sorry, Gretchen," Mims said. "I'll consider your advice. Have a good night."

Mims walked out of the restaurant and found herself once again in the streets of gaudy, screaming Midtown. She was alone, but she deserved it, and it was only an official version of how she'd been feeling all along anyway.

There was one last thing she could try. It was time to speak with someone as invested in honey fraud as she was.

CHAPTER 34:
AFFOGATO

Kai approached from down the block but Mims couldn't bring herself to walk toward him. He was wearing sunglasses through which she could easily see his eyes, but he didn't seem to be aware of that fact. He was staring at everyone as he passed, at women, at dogs, at ice cream cones, at men holding their phones like walkie-talkies as they chatted. His pants didn't reach his ankles and they flapped as he walked. She waved, more abruptly than she'd intended, as he slowed to a stop in front of her.

"Nice to see you again," he said. His eyes flitted from her breasts to her face.

"Did you want to get an ice cream instead of coffee?" Mims asked. "You seemed really intent on those ice creams."

"What? No." Then he laughed. "You're really good at reading body language."

"No, heads up, your sunglasses aren't reflective and you're ogling everything like a creeper."

He seemed a bit crestfallen and pushed the sunglasses up into his hair.

"Let's get you an *affogato*," she said. "Come on." She led him into the café.

She ordered a drip coffee and went to the back to claim a table, leaving Kai to order his *affogato* alone.

"You know," he said as he approached the table, "if you weren't so insecure about your own coolness you wouldn't have an issue hanging out with less cool friends."

Her first instinct was to declare she wasn't his friend, but she took a deep breath instead. It was such a similar accusation to what she'd said to Sean at Don Pedro. We hate the flaws in others that we most don't want to acknowledge in ourselves . . .

"I respect your directness," she said. She needed Kai's help; no fighting for once. "Growing up, my family's furniture was made of milk crates. My clothes didn't fit. I never had friends over. Childhood emotional experiences stick with you. Being cool means a lot to me. But you're right, I should have waited while you ordered your coffee. I'm sorry."

"'Childhood emotional experiences'. . . try being an Asian kid adopted by white parents. On top of that I turned out so freaking tall."

Mims reinterpreted his gawky forthrightness. *Accept me! Accept the ugliest, rawest version of me so I know the acceptance is real!* he was saying. His refusal to make a more socially acceptable or trendy version of himself in order to garner love was a sort of test to see who genuinely liked the genuine him enough to stay. It was the opposite of her pretending–to–be–worthy approach, but it had the same end goal. She wasn't sure of exactly how self–aware he was about his behavior; she'd only recently begun parsing her own. It seemed risky to just straight–up explain her theory. But if the outcome he wanted was friendship and acceptance, maybe the first step was honesty and a few pointers on how to not scare people off before they could get to know him.

"You just come off as a little desperate," she said. "You could be cool. Try doing all the same things you'd do anyway but slower. Like put on your coat, but slower. Take off your sunglasses, but slower." She'd meant it in a helpful, conspiratorial way, but his face fell. If she was going to convince him to assist her, she needed to try harder not to come off as a dick.

She had explained over the phone what Gerard's accusation was and that he was qualified to make it because he was a supertaster and how she had found the shredded labels at Beasley Cherries. Before calling Kai she had called the grocery store where she'd bought the honey for the taste test and gotten the name of a distributor with no website and a phone number that rang and rang. Kai had been intrigued, but ultimately the evidence wasn't that strong and the lab was too busy to test her samples, and they especially couldn't do it within the next few days. If he could offer any help at all, he was going to do it based on simpatico, and simpatico wasn't her strong suit. She felt a bond with him over their shared insecurities, but perhaps there was no way to navigate that mine field without continuing to hurt his feelings.

It was hard to think how to channel the most chatty and open but also not-mean version of herself, doubly so after how opening up to Gretchen had turned out. She felt like her skin was thin rice paper and her bloody muscles and ragged heart were all right there beating dangerously close to the surface. Telling him about the milk crates had felt like stumbling out of a desert to trade her firstborn child in exchange for life-giving water.

She reminded herself that his reaction had been to commiserate, not reject her.

"You know," she said in a cheerful, conversational tone, "I met a woman recently whose openness was shocking to me, but what she said stayed with me. It was one of the two women Teddy Beasley was dating, the ugly one."

"Come on."

"I mean it as a descriptor, not an insult. He was dating two people at the same time and his own sister called him out at a party. More evidence of what kind of person he is. So this woman said we fall in love with archetypes, not real people. So we should never take it personally when someone doesn't love us back. We just don't fit whatever fucked-up image got imprinted on them when they were little."

"I'm listening." The server brought over Mims's coffee, which she wished were a more expensive latte, and Kai's *affogato*. He poured the espresso over the ice cream and took slurping sips.

"It was so sad," she said. "They were obviously never going to make it as a couple—they were mismatched in every way. But Brittany-Lynne wanted Teddy to tell her that she was funnier than the other woman. Or that she was smarter, or more interesting, more fun in bed, had nicer-smelling hair. *Anything*. The other woman could be better at everything else, she just wanted him to say one thing about her that made her special to him, that he preferred. And it had to come from *him*, this guy who honestly I doubt is as smart as she is, and is way younger, because when she was little she'd failed to get validation from the sweet boy-next-door. That's what was imprinted on her as the only kind of boyfriend who would do. But bad luck for Brittany-Lynne, Teddy's focused on getting validation from the aloof French chick. He wants to be the knight in shining armor who can show up at a moody woman's doorstep and be single-handedly responsible for her transforming into a cheerful ray of sunshine."

"Maybe he should date you." Kai laughed at his own quip.

Although friendship-level, intimacy-and-trust-building, interesting conversation had been what she was going for, she felt like she was coming close to drenching him in emotional vomit. The archetype theory was a comforting explanation for why Sean hadn't chosen her; it wasn't that she wasn't good enough, it was just that she wasn't the right fit. It wasn't until he'd rejected her that she'd felt a spark of deeper interest in him. It was fucked up and she couldn't help wanting to talk it out with anyone who would listen, the same as Brittany-Lynne. She sipped the not-latte and waited but Kai didn't say anything else. "He hadn't even been in touch to apologize, let alone give her a compliment, and they'd been so close, sharing the experience of going through his grandfather's death."

Kai took another sip of his espresso and looked thoughtfully off into space for a long moment before reestablishing eye contact.

"Maybe people tell you this stuff because you're a reporter—like you can pass objective judgment and tell them they're right. Or maybe they want *your* validation, since you're so judgy."

"So judgy!" she agreed. "And I'm catty too. That's why I gravitate toward gossip rags. This guy I'd been hooking up with, he can't share an intimate moment more than once every few weeks without running terrified to another continent." There it was. She couldn't stop herself. "Last night I found out he has a girlfriend now. Better than me in every way but one. Forehead: huge. Biggest forehead I've ever seen."

Kai snorted his ice cream soup and coughed and laughed. "I thought this was going to be an insightful story about childhood trauma, not a shit-talk fest. You care so much about appearances."

"You care about what other people think too," Mims said flatly. "You lied to me about how long the honey lab work would take and how difficult it was so you would look more impressive in the article I wrote."

He peered at her over the rim of his bowl. "I wanted to impress you. You're cool. If I can get you to hang out with me, that means I'm cool too, right?"

She was at another crossroads, but the choice was easy this time. She wasn't going to mislead and flirt her way into getting what she wanted. "I'm going to be honest. You're a funny guy and I would like to be your friend. Like for real, I'd hang out. You have thoughts on self–image and validation that I'd be interested in hearing. But I'm not attracted to you. I want to be upfront about that before asking you for favors. You know why I asked you to coffee."

"You need another search warrant and can't get one."

"Correct."

"I know some people at the DEP but there's no way they're going to go seeking another warrant after what happened last time. There's no way I'd ask them to, and there's no way a judge would approve it."

"Yeah . . . but you understand why I had to try."

"I'll make you a deal," Kai said. "I have two cop friends. We're supposed to hang out tonight, and I'm sure I can win a bet whereby the losers have to stop by and keep an eye on the cherry factory for a little while after work tomorrow to see if anything suspicious is going on. But there *needs* to be something suspicious going on. You say this guy could be part of a honey–laundering chain, but I'm not convinced—shredded honey labels are suspicious, but I need more than that. You don't have a lot of credibility right now."

"Yes! Thank you, yes. I'll go get better photos, or hopefully video—I'll text it to you. And if I deliver, your friends meet me there tomorrow night?" She wished it could have been tonight, but she'd take what she could get.

"Deal."

"What's the bet going to be?" she asked.

Excitement beamed out through his face. "I've been working on my hot sauce tolerance. We're going to a place that has ghost pepper–infused vodka."

Mims lifted her coffee cup and clinked it against his bowl. "To infused vodkas."

CHAPTER 35:
ATONEMENT

The metal was perched between the edges of the dumpster and Marlow was standing on top of it like it was a trampoline.

Teddy was fed up with her high spirits. "That's not safe," he called up to her. "Cut it out."

The metal bent and then popped back as she hopped. Bent. Popped. Bent.

Teddy heard something confusing and quiet but swift, like the sound of running. He turned just in time to see Lin closing in on him with his teeth in a grimace. Lin dropped into a baseball slide, his legs tangling with Teddy's and bowling him over. He tried to scramble up but Lin kept him pinned with his legs. He looked instinctively to his sister.

Marlow grabbed a cylindrical piece of scrap and wedged it under her armpit before easing her way down from the dumpster. Just as she brought the metal pole down Lin jumped up. It clinked against the pavement where he'd been sitting.

"That's my equipment you're swinging around at me," Lin said, calm again, as if he hadn't been mad and on the ground a few seconds before. Teddy couldn't help blaming Marlow for being so brazen about her jumping and the thunk–pop sound it made, as if the noise was what had alerted Lin to come to Sunset Park, even though he knew it wasn't.

"You can have it back if you want." Marlow looked around and then lowered the metal slightly, so it appeared less weapon–like. The neighborhood was sparsely populated, but there was still a chance someone would walk by. "We're done with it."

"You're going to need it."

"You're a criminal and a liar. You took Teddy by surprise with your scheming, but we know what's up now and we're out."

"Your lawyer?" Lin asked Teddy, gesturing toward Marlow. "Bodyguard?"

"Don't answer that," Marlow said.

"Regardless," Lin said, "she needs to understand that I never take anyone by surprise. Everything I do is a logical progression of what went before. You chose to be where you are by the decisions you have made up until now. I don't jump out at strangers at the cash machine wielding a knife, demanding pin numbers. You agreed to this deal in the beginning, and you were warned of the consequences that have now arrived."

"We'll buy you out," Teddy said. His whole body was shaking, and it felt like if he tried to stop it, his ribs would separate from each other and he would pull himself apart. "For the cost of this shipment."

"Teddy," Marlow said in a low voice.

"I don't care—I'll go bankrupt if I have to, I'm not doing this anymore."

Lin gestured for him to continue. Teddy suspected he just wanted to see him grovel, but if there was any chance at all he could buy his way out of this mess, he would take it.

"If you jump out at tourists using an ATM in Rio, you could argue that they were asking for it by the nature of their being comparatively rich and also careless. If you jumped out at a hedge fund bro at his local bank branch in a Boston suburb somewhere, you could just say it's a consequence of his having hijacked the world's economic system to generate the extreme wealth inequality that's led to your contempt and also your need and his status as financial target."

"Don't explain my system to me," Lin said through clenched teeth, though he was still speaking toward Teddy, not acknowledging her. Fear was creeping down Teddy's arms. He didn't like that she was provoking him.

"Oh, forgive my slang," she said. "'Hedge fund bro' means—"

Lin yelled something short in what sounded like Mandarin, finally turning toward her. He pulled a ten-inch boning knife from the long cargo pocket on his thigh, and when Marlow smirked instead of turning scared, the veins on Lin's neck engorged with rage. "I'm going to press this skinny blade so far into a fleshy part of you that it will come out the other side."

Teddy wanted his sister to be safe somehow. Why couldn't she take anything seriously? Lin took a step toward her.

"I'm going to shoot you," she said.

Lin's eyes roved quickly over her body, and so did Teddy's. Marlow was wearing jeans and a loose-fitting V-neck. Obviously she didn't have a gun on her. "Then it looks like I have no other choice than to cut you," Lin replied.

"Everyone calm down," Teddy pleaded, his arms outstretched in a gesture of appeasement. "We'll talk about this. You don't have to do anything—there's no gun. There are no firearms allowed anywhere in New York."

"There's a rifle in my truck," Marlow said and took a step toward it.

Lin lunged at her and she swung and hit his hand with the metal bar. He didn't drop the knife.

Teddy took off running toward Marlow's truck, which was parked across the street. He knew the driver's side window was rolled down because it had been annoying him for days and Marlow had refused to roll it up. *Decisive, decisive, decisive* was going through his head like a mantra, no thoughts, just the word. *Decisive.*

He reached inside the window and yanked the door open. He felt around under the front seat—nothing. The passenger front seat, nothing.

He could hear a scuffle behind him but there was no time to look. There was a mini bench seat in the back. His hand slid along the carpet underneath and encountered crumpled food wrapper, penny, grit, metal. He pulled the gun from beneath the seat and ran back toward where Marlow and Lin were still swinging at each other. They both had thin spatters of blood across their shirts, but he couldn't tell where it had come from. Lin would never believe Teddy knew how to fire a gun, or that he was capable of pulling the trigger. He felt impotent.

Lin swiped at his sister again with the knife and she danced back and swung the metal bar, missing him but also dodging the blade. Lin's hunched body seemed permanently poised to strike.

"Here!" Teddy called when he was a few feet away. Marlow and Lin both turned slightly to face him. He was holding the gun in two hands, like a cane in a dancing routine. He didn't know how to get it to her.

"Shoot it," she said.

Lin eased his weight onto his back leg. Teddy wasn't sure which of them he was going to lunge at.

Marlow yelled, "Flip the metal along the top and pull the trigger not at him just fucking fire!"

The shot went at an angle over the fence toward the factory and blasted some brick off the façade. Red powder and chunks rained down in the distance and the sound of the shot was deafening and echoed for a long time. Firing the gun made him feel more afraid, not less.

"Cops are coming get the fuck out of here," Marlow said to Lin, triumphant. "Every person who heard that is calling right now."

"The police won't still be here in the morning. And if they are, I tell them what's going on, from a distance of course, and you get arrested. A crew is going to show up at sunrise to put this equipment back together."

"We're going to be discovered either way," Teddy said. He could feel his pulse in his face and in the web of flesh between his thumb and pointer fingers. Mims could be planning another raid for all he knew; countless government agencies could have Beasley Cherries on their radar. An employee might decide to stop by after hours to pick up a left cell phone. "You need to understand that these honey shipments can't continue."

It was grounding, stating this concrete fact, after the shakiness of the gun and his fear for Marlow. His pulse was still fast, fast, and in his skin.

A siren rose in the distance and was quickly approaching. "Don't get caught," Lin said smugly as he ran off.

When he was out of sight Marlow threw the piece of metal on the ground. "Give me that," she said. Teddy handed her the gun and she headed for the gate. "If they get here before I'm back tell them you heard what might have been a shot, you're not sure, maybe a car backfiring. It was nearby but you're not sure what direction because of the echo."

Teddy nodded obediently.

"And if they ask about the blood on the ground," she called over her shoulder, "tell them it's cherry spillage."

Teddy looked up at the dumpster. There was no way they'd be able to wait out the police and then disassemble everything and get rid of the dumpster all by morning, and Lin might still be watching them. The hauling company wouldn't even be able to move up the pickup time on such short notice. He considered trying to move the equipment into the back of one of their trucks to cart it away. Impossible. There just wasn't enough time. A police car rounded the corner, its lights like electric gumdrops.

The long walk from the subway to Beasley Cherries was starting to become familiar. Mims recognized the street names and some of the buildings. A block over from the factory several police cars were parked quietly but with their lights flashing.

"What's going on here?" she asked.

"Do you work around here?" one of the officers replied.

"No, but I'm a journalist. I've been working a story in the neighborhood."

"A few people called in that they thought they heard shots fired. No one saw anything. Probably just a car backfiring."

"Do cars still do that?" Mims asked.

"Sure."

"Did you ask at the cherry factory?"

"Not specifically."

"Can we go over there? There's something strange happening at that place."

"We aren't going anywhere," the other cop said. "Are you that loopy reporter who called in the raid? Do you have any idea how much money that wasted?"

"Thanks for your time," Mims said. She walked far enough away that she could frame the car and the officers with her phone and started taking video. Just as she hit record, they turned the lights off. "The light was just on," she said aloud. She sent the video to Kai. It was difficult to navigate to his name because of her cracked screen. Her shoddy battery was already down to thirty percent. "Shots reported near the factory," she wrote. "Possible shots," she corrected.

"Not good enough," Kai responded. "Is that even the factory? It looks like a boring empty car on a boring empty block of warehouses."

"It's nearby," she typed back.

Mims walked over to Beasley Cherries. Everything looked the same as the last time she was there except the dumpster was more full. She took more photos but didn't send them. The sidewalk and road were wet, as if they had been hosed off. She kicked the dumpster. What if they'd spilled illegal honey, hosed it off, *and she'd missed it?* She pressed her face up against the gate but didn't see anyone inside. A bee flitted by, peacefully, and veered up toward the roof. She tracked it with her eye and noticed a chunk of brick missing a few feet from the top of the building. She couldn't say for sure whether it was a new crater, and the wall was too far away to make out whether there was debris on the ground below. Mims held up her phone, but there wasn't enough resolution to see the notch in the brick. She took some more shots of the wet cement by the gate.

Mims walked back to the police car, but it was gone by the time she got there. She went back to the factory and waited, she wasn't sure for what. It was boring sitting on the curb. After an hour she walked to the gate, looked up at the security camera, looked away, and tried to climb. The bars were slippery and she couldn't grip them. She walked the periphery of the fence—there was no way in. She walked back to the front and waited longer. It was hours past closing time, but she had a vague idea that if someone had worked late, she'd be able to somehow, stealthily, slip past him as he left. Her stomach gurgled like the antique garbage disposal in her mom's kitchen sink back in Michigan. Her eyes were dry. The pain running through the balls of her feet made her think of the deal Hans Christian Andersen's little mermaid had made for a chance at starting a new life far away from home. Mims was sure the second she walked away something would happen.

At two in the morning she gave up and headed home. At the subway her MetroCard was declined. "Insufficient fare." The money in her checking account was untouchable until after her rent check cleared, just to be safe. The pile of change set aside at home for subway refills didn't help her now. *I deserve to suffer.* She started the eleven–mile walk of atonement back to her apartment.

As the sky was brightening, she arrived at her block. Mims looked above the buildings and trees hoping for a transcendent moment, but sunrises were fast and colorless compared to sunsets. It got light and nothing happened. A man in a tracksuit exited a neighboring building and his tiny dog went to the dead center of the sidewalk and squatted. Mims pulled out her keys. Inside she fell asleep fully dressed, still hungry.

CHAPTER 36:
MORNING

As the sun was getting up, eight silent men unloaded from a van in front of Beasley Cherries. They were mostly older for day laborers; all of them were East Asian. The van drove away.

Marlow grumbled as she watched them. There was a chill in the air and she wasn't wearing a jacket. The men started pulling debris from the dumpster. The lead man stopped in front of the closed gate. He kept staring forward, not acknowledging anyone or anything. Eventually Marlow punched in a code and the gate opened. As soon as there was clearance the men stepped through, dragging pieces of metal behind them.

"I guess we're doing this," Marlow said, angry. They hadn't bothered staying at the safe house the night before—it somehow still smelled like lobster, and Teddy's apartment was more comfortable—but she believed Lin's threat that he would report them if they didn't comply. Marlow walked ahead of the lead man and opened one of the bays of the garage. Once inside she slid open the secret panel.

She walked back out to where Teddy was still standing by the dumpster. "Should one of us go inside to keep an eye on things?" he asked.

"No, Teddy," she said.

"There's no way they're going to be done unloading before employees start to show up for work. Should I send an email saying the factory is closed for the day? I could say a water pipe burst."

The men were sprinting now, with very heavy pieces of metal. Their breathing was surprisingly soft.

"No."

"I guess you're right. Jay and probably Matt too would insist on coming by if I said a pipe burst. But even if these guys do get everything inside in time, it will make noise assembling it," he said.

"Okay, here's the good news, Teddy," Marlow said. "Lin has clearly realized that he's not going to be able to control us. This is the last shipment he's going to send through. The bad news: I've concluded this is Lin's train of thought because he obviously doesn't give a fuck about us getting caught after this batch of honey. People at the factory are *for sure* going to realize something stupid is going on. But by the time anything concrete comes of it, the honey is going to be relabeled and gone, and we're stuck holding the bag."

"Oh," Teddy said glumly. "That makes sense."

"Best-case scenario we can get rid of all the equipment again before the police come investigate, but if we do that as fast as we need to, people are definitely going to see the door to the dug-out room. What explanation could we possibly have for a secret room under the factory, even if it's empty?"

"It's not illegal to have a—"

One of the workmen accidentally bumped into Marlow's butt with a piece of conveyor belt. "Watch what the fuck you're doing," she said.

"It's not his fault," Teddy said.

"Are you serious right now?"

"It's not illegal to have a secret basement. Maybe we won't get in trouble."

"I'm going to get a coffee. Do you want anything?"

"Please don't leave me here alone," he said.

"Fine." She softened. "Come on, come with me. I have a feeling these guys will be all right without us. We'll be back long before any employees arrive."

They walked in silence for ten minutes until they got to the closest place for a coffee—a bodega that was just opening its gate.

"Wait five minutes for the coffee," the bodega man said.

"That's fine," Marlow replied.

Teddy walked aimlessly through the aisles, running his fingers along the tops of candies and Slim Jims as if they were shrubbery or flowers.

"We should have tried harder to reason with him," Teddy called.

It was a bad sign that he wasn't trying to be secretive anymore, that he was resigned. Not that the bodega guy would know what they were talking about. Still, it might come up in court . . .

"No, Teddy," Marlow said, approaching him so she could speak quietly. "We tried plenty hard to reason with him. It will get you into trouble assuming that an abusive man will ever admit that he's a bad guy, if only you explain it to him well enough how his behavior if affecting you. Best-case scenario he'll act hurt or surprised and then you'll get confused and think, *Huh, maybe the truth is somewhere in the middle and he didn't realize what he was doing.* But the truth is not in the middle: Lin is a bad man, a dangerous man, he knows exactly what he's doing, and he doesn't feel sorry for us. There is no reasoning with a man like that."

Teddy's shoulders were stooped as if a few vertebrae had been removed overnight. "What are we going to do?"

"I don't know yet. If you have any ideas, don't hold back."

He nodded and walked toward the register with a pack of chocolate mints, still looking dazed. Just a few weeks ago she'd been avoiding New York because she was afraid the factory would be boring and Teddy would be needy, but now all she wanted was to help him navigate through his last few hours as a honey smuggler and then hopefully back to normalcy.

"I'm glad you never outgrew your sweet tooth," she said. "It's cute."

"It's an emotional coping mechanism." He laid the candies on the counter. There was no emotion in his voice. "It's an addiction. And a way of remaining a child." He gestured to the man behind the counter. "Two coffees, please."

Mims woke to the sound of a text alert. "Tick Tock" the message said; she'd been asleep for two hours. She washed her face but didn't change clothes. Gathering her MetroCard change, she hurried to the subway while chewing gum to mask unbrushed teeth. It was later than she'd hoped— she would be lucky to arrive in time to blend into the flow of employees entering the factory gates. Her all–black ensemble and kitten heels could be masked by white slippers and an apron once inside.

Lin watched Beasley Cherries from a rental car far down the block and across an intersection. Getting a car in case he needed to make a quick getaway was a logical step flowing from the gun incident the night before. It was an obvious solution to a potential problem, nothing to be concerned about. Even so, he was going to grind Beasley down all the harder for having herded him into taking an action he would not otherwise have taken. The rental agreement meant proof of his movements in New York.

He lifted his binoculars every few minutes. The workmen were progressing quickly; he hadn't caught sight of Teddy or the woman yet. He'd prefer to be closer, but every time he thought of Teddy's insane bodyguard, fear chemicals shot through his chest. He had no doubt she would risk jail to shoot him. Lin tested his physical response every few hours, visualizing the woman holding the gun or lunging toward his face with her fingers out-stretched. The physical response never got weaker. Lin didn't fully believe in emotions for this reason—they were nothing more than squirts of hor-mone cocktail. At the same time, he had no interest in letting adrenaline cloud his judgment or make his muscles tight while he was on lookout.

He started the *Learn Vietnamese* tape. He was going to have to change his whole business model.

The beauty of Beasley Cherries as a base had been its simplicity. There was no lease, no overhead, little build-out and initial investment, no gov-ernment bribes, no long list of co-conspirators, no paper trail. A straight, nonnegotiable percentage was wired to Beasley's account after each ship-ment. His mistake had been making the percentage too generous, meant to ensure continuing interest on Beasley's part. A lower amount would have been better, made Beasley less afraid. Men like him were scared of bold-ness, of too-great success. They were comfortable only in mediocrity.

A thin woman in all black, black sunglasses, black pearls, marched toward Beasley Cherries from across the way, kitty-corner to where he sat. Lin knew her. He'd read Mims Walsh's articles about the factory that morn-ing. Beasley must have summoned her.

Once she was halfway down the block, Lin started the car and rolled slowly down the street. She turned around sooner than he'd hoped. New York women were jumpy and suspicious. He sped up to pull along beside her, which scared her more. She took a step back from the sidewalk but didn't bolt.

He got out and rushed around the bonnet of the car toward her. "Hey, what—" she said before turning to run. He caught her by the torso and they both went down, but he was able to spring back up first and pull her by the ankle toward the passenger side door. Her heel grazed his knuckles.

The reporter turned onto her belly on the ground and grasped, pathetically, at some weedy flowers. They pulled straight through her fingers and she yelped. Bees menaced her head before flying away and he almost laughed. She'd been stung.

Lin yanked her up into a chokehold and wrapped electrical tape around her mouth and the back of her head a few times, working quickly in case Beasley or the laborers appeared. He tied her wrists with rope, then her ankles, and threw her in the boot. She revived right away and started kicking the back of the seats, but he was already driving.

"Stop smashing around or I'm going to hurt you," Lin said without raising his voice. He spoke quietly so she would have to calm down in order to hear. "If you start crying and can't breathe through your nose, you'll suffocate. I'm not taking the gag off if you do." The reporter stopped kicking. It was unfortunate to calm her down—as long as she was thrashing about like an animal it meant she wasn't thinking.

The streets were clear on the way to the Flatbush marina where the cuddy was docked. Lin parked a few blocks from the entrance. They were in front of a car-repair shop that still had its gate pulled down, though it was getting close to 9:00 a.m. He held his breath for as long as he was able, one minute and thirteen seconds, and then let it out as slow and evenly as he could. Twenty-two seconds. The next steps to take became obvious. There was a large tool chest on the boat—hard plastic with removable top trays and very strong clasps.

He would keep her out of the way long enough to get the honey shipment forwarded on—two truckloads, at a value of $500,000. It was significantly larger than the previous test shipments had been. Funny that the amount of trouble she could potentially cause was only one car-boot-full but simultaneously half a million dollars. He got out of the car and slammed the door behind him.

CHAPTER 37:

AT SEA

The rocking darkness was spatially confounding—Mims was compressed into a tiny box on a tiny boat, but she may as well have been spinning. When nausea rose up she tapped her fingers along the edges of the walls to orient her body, then the nausea would temporarily recede. She heard a door swing open and slam closed, like a screen door back at her mom's place. There was silence. It was getting very hot in the box; her hair was matted over her eyes and sandwiched with the blanket covering her head, and it was getting hard to breathe. The door opened and slammed again and suddenly time skipped forward a few seconds and the trunk was open. The blanket was pulled off, static crackled in her hair where it wasn't wet, and fresh air assaulted the sweat on her skin, turning it icy.

"You smell terrible," he said. "How can someone smell that bad after such a short amount of time?" He unwrapped the tape from around her mouth and hair.

Mims was indignant. Stress sweat smells. She wanted to spring out like a Jack in the Box but glared instead. She tried to memorize his face.

"Where were you going today?" the man asked.

"I work at the cherry factory," she lied, on the off-chance he didn't really work for Teddy and this was a coincidental encounter with a psycho kidnapper. She shifted her weight so the raw parts of her back weren't pressed up against the side of the trunk. "They'll be worried about me for not showing up." Mims ran her eyes around the boat's interior, forcing her gaze to be slow, not flitting frantically. The space was cramped with stacked baskets, foam, buckets, but the stacks were orderly and there was no dust and no trinkets lying about. It was clean and it smelled like grease. The length of the boat's interior wasn't more than twenty feet, and they were in the kitchen area, next to a sink cut into a metal counter. There was a one-burner hot plate next to the sink. The low ceiling seemed to cause the man to stoop, even though it was a foot above his head, and his wiry biceps tensed and eased at the edge of his T-shirt sleeves.

"Dressed like that, you work at a factory? Little heels and black pearls?" His accent was faint, Mandarin Chinese with undertones of British.

"I . . . work at the front desk," she said.

"Don't tell me any more lies." The "or else" was implied by the way he turned his back on her and stacked a large wrench and a small toolbox on the counter next to the sink.

"Where were you going?" he repeated.

"Well . . . to the cherry factory," she said. "But I don't work there. I was going to pretend that I did and walk in with the other employees."

"That wouldn't have worked," he said. "You look like a druggy Hollywood actress stumbling home from a party where you let men—" He reached down and grabbed a fistful of hair at the crown of her head and, forcing her face up toward him, he spit. He threw her back down into the trunk and returned to the sink, where he started transferring his stack of items to a canvas duffel. Mims squeezed her eyes shut and when she reopened them a strand of spittle formed a droopy bridge from her top to bottom eyelashes and then pulled apart and broke coldly.

"You had a meeting with Teddy. You were going to talk to him about what?"

Mims's eyes burned with tears. She would have told him what he wanted to hear if she knew what that was. "I really was going to sneak in."

"You want me to believe you're that stupid?"

"Desperate people sometimes do stupid things and hope for luck to take over and save them," she said. She no longer believed he worked for Teddy. Probably Teddy worked for him.

He bent and pulled what looked like a pair of bolt cutters out from under the sink and slid them into the bag. "The concept of 'luck' is for idiots, so perhaps you are stupid after all. Every event that happens is a consequence of the actions that preceded it. That's how I can predict the future."

"Put another way, sometimes persistence is rewarded," she said. "It's not luck in a metaphysical sense; sometimes just showing up is half the battle." Her dad would be ashamed to see her hunched in a box crying. He was proud, and she'd learned early to present herself as an equal in spite of power imbalances. Assuming Teddy was distributing the fake honey for this man, it was clear their relationship had soured. She needed to convince him that she and Teddy weren't plotting against him. "If your understanding of the present is flawed, the future won't be what you hoped for. I didn't have a meeting set up with Teddy, I'm investigating him."

The man opened a drawer, pulled out a handful of lighters, threw them in the bag, and then zipped it closed.

"That's a brave thing to say," he said. His anger had disappeared and he chuckled. "We have some similar traits after all? Are you brave?"

Mims decided to risk flattery and hope he didn't see through her attempt to get him to like her enough not to kill her. "I'm sure you're more brave than I am. As much as I'd like to believe I'm tough, I grew up soft. As a kid I wondered 'what part of the animal is meat?' You never wondered that, did you?"

He laughed again. "No, I saw the meat as I butchered the chickens. You're right. You and I are made of different stuff. Both meat of course, but spiritually different."

"Sorry to get your hopes up." Her captor seemed more at ease now, though she regretted the images of human meat impinging at the corners of her mind. Maybe setting a crazy person at ease didn't make him less dangerous.

"What has your investigation yielded?" he asked.

"Teddy might be illegally dumping waste from the cherries. I couldn't figure out how."

"That's as far as you progressed?" She couldn't tell if he believed her.

"I'm not a threat; I don't know anything," she said. "I'm barely a real journalist." They looked at each other as they spoke, he as casual as if he were speaking to someone seated in a chair, Mims unable to stop her high beam eyes taking it all in, even though it seemed safer to be deferential and look at the floor.

"I got that impression from your internet presence. I should have let you go into the factory," he said. "I can admit when I've miscalculated. It would have been easier to clean up everything at once, but it's not worth the risk of bringing you back there now."

The man walked to the end of the cabin and cut the engine, but all she could hear was her fluttering heartbeat. She hadn't realized until then that they had been moving out to sea.

"Where's your phone?" he asked.

"My back pocket."

"Give it to me."

Mims stood, becoming aware of her scraped knee for the first time, and turned her back toward him. Her wrists were tied in front, and she cradled the loose end of the rope in her fingers, trying to breathe as normally as possible and hoping he wouldn't ask her to turn around. The bee sting on her wrist throbbed, but the swelling was going down and there was slack in the rope binding her hands together. The man slipped the phone out of her pocket then turned off the lights as he went out the screen door. It slammed shut after him. Standing in the dark, rocking gently as if on the subway, Mims heard scraping against the side of the boat and a splash large enough to be a dinghy meeting the water. She imagined more than heard the return to peaceful lapping against the side of the boat. She didn't hear him paddling away, though he must have been. She was lifting her bound wrists up in the dim light when the screen door slammed again. Her heart jumped.

"I didn't forget about you." The man placed his palm on the top of her head and pushed down. She resisted for only a second, a reflex, and then obeyed and bent at the knees. The trunk lid banged shut, enveloping her in darkness, and she heard the screen door slam again, muffled this time, and then an oar pushing off the side of the boat.

CHAPTER 38:
ON LAND

Lin threw the canvas duffel onto the pier and then jumped down beside it. He weighed his options—death complicated a situation, and he wanted to avoid it. He had been captain during the deaths of two seamen, two separate incidents, and both had been time-consuming to deal with. He judged the probability of Beasley or any of the factory workers' deaths to be less than ten percent. Beasley's exit from the honey-import business would, however, come with a reminder that Lin was the one in control, the one who *gifted* him his escape, and it would teach a lesson about reneging on agreements. The explosion from the gas leak would partially collapse the offices and garage and create a not-insignificant amount of damage in the main factory. Beasley would take the blame for shoddy gas line work rather than risk an investigation, and that would be the end of their business relationship.

That ten percent chance of death deserved contemplation.

There was going to be a kidnapping investigation, no matter what.

He arrived at the marine terminal whistling. The truck cabs showed up soon after. They pulled empty chassis beds; the shipping containers would be forklifted directly from the ship onto the trucks. His cousin had said once that the empty trailers attached to heavy cabs looked like shaved dogs, scrawny and skeletal except for their fluffy faces. It was an image that never would have originated in Lin's mind; he resented that Weihong wanted to be the kind of person that catered to tiny shaved dogs.

One of the drivers gestured at him and he rolled down his window.

"Are you Chen?" he asked.

Lin got out of his car and approached the window. "Here," he said and handed the driver a security pass for the marine terminal gate. The driver put it on his dashboard. "I'll wait out here and follow you to the factory."

"You got it, boss–man."

Lin repeated the process with the second driver. Neither asked what they were hauling.

The trucks passed through the gate and Lin went back to his car to wait. The day was warming up and sweat pooled in the shelf his belly created below his breastbone.

Marlow looked over at Teddy. He sat against the wall in the basement. One leg was bent and his other leg was crossed over it at the ankle. His foot bobbed up and down nervously, and he was eating a Slim Jim.

"Where did you get that?" she asked.

"Stole it," he said. "From the bodega."

Marlow rolled her eyes. "Stop acting out. Focus."

Most of the workmen were lounging around too, waiting.

The one guy on his feet was fiddling with the machine. He was late forties and had big hair, no gray, and a red shirt. When he pressed against a bulge along the side of the conveyor belt it made a womp sound that faded out into vibration. Then it popped back out again. He looked around the floor, under the machine. "There aren't any more pieces," she told him, even though she knew he didn't speak English. It seemed rude not to say anything. The man pushed the metal flat and hit along the edges with a hammer. It undented a little and then popped out again. "It's because I was jumping on it," Marlow said.

They were also missing some screws, but none of the men had gone out to buy replacements. Marlow couldn't decide whether to go upstairs to the maintenance room and bring them the cherry factory's screws. Did she want to make this process easier or harder? Because no one was speaking or moving, and the secret panel was still open at the top of the stairs, she could hear the doorknob that connected the garage to the main building as it twisted. Marlow sprinted the stairs two at a time, slid the panel closed too hard, so that it bumped the frame and then slid back open a couple of inches, and made it to the door just in time to block the view into the garage with her body.

"Good morning!" she said.

"Good morning, Marlow," Jalen, the front desk guy, said hesitantly.

"There was a spill in here this morning, so we're not going to let people in to use the cubbies today until it's all cleaned up and dry. Can you run and get me a few pieces of paper, a Sharpie, and some tape? I'm going to make signs."

"Sure . . ."

"Thanks, Jalen!"

When Jalen returned Marlow made signs for the door that connected the garage to the factory and for the outside of the garage bay doors. "Garage CLOSED today. Do not enter. Cleaning up a spill." Then she went to the maintenance room and got a little square of wood and the electric drill to screw the door connecting the garage to the factory closed from the garage side. She directed the front desk to cancel all deliveries to the garage for the day. She hoped the closed garage would be beneath the notice of Matt and Jay; the schedule up on the wall said it would have been a light traffic day.

Marlow was careful about sliding the secret panel gently and fully shut before descending back into the labeling room. "Teddy, we aren't doing a good job with this."

He was sitting in the same position as she'd left him, the empty Slim Jim wrapper dangling from his hand. She strode toward him, but as she was passing the youngest of the workmen a light from his cell phone caught her attention. She could see just as she slowed, just as fear came into his eyes and he quit the app, that the text was in English.

"That was TikTok."

He shook his head no, his mouth slightly agape.

"You twat! What is wrong with you working a job like this?" His back, then his whole body, pressed against the wall, as if he could sink into it. She reached for his phone—

HONNNNK

An air horn blasted from outside and above, freezing her arm in midair.

HONNNK

Teddy hadn't moved, but he looked like a baby tasting lemon for the first time.

"Now what?" he asked.

"It's the honey, Teddy. The shipment is here." She clomped up the stairs to open the factory gate. The workmen roused themselves and followed her up.

The motor seemed extra loud as the gate to the street opened. Marlow resisted the temptation to check over her shoulder whether anyone from the factory was looking. As soon as the two trucks could clear the entrance, they rolled through. "Morning!" one of the drivers called cheerfully from the cab.

"Yes," Marlow replied. They backed the shipping containers into the first two garage bays and then disconnected them and drove away. The closing garage doors pinched out the daylight, all of her daring and adventurous spirit stranded on the other side. "Just don't do anything, Marlow," she said to herself, aloud. "For Teddy's sake. It's just a few more hours."

The workmen ran boxes down the stairs. She kept an eye out for the young guy with the suspiciously flatteringly cut pants, but whenever he ran past her he kept his head turned away. NYU–looking motherfucker with his forehead pimples and his edgy haircut had better hope she never ran into him out on the streets when this was over. He'd heard enough to know they were being coerced. The misfortune of others was no way for a kid to make extra money.

Marlow peeked inside one of the boxes to make sure they hadn't escalated to cocaine importers—thankfully no. The box was full of glass jars, and the labels said "golden corn syrup." She hefted the box and joined the procession down the stairs. It all started moving at once—gloved hands ripping cardboard box lids, the machine firing up, the men passing each other up and down the stairs like pistons.

"It's too loud," Teddy shouted from the wall. "It wasn't clanky like this before."

Marlow laughed. "This is like being on acid. It's all one movement, like cellular metabolism, all connected." Actually, it was similar to the cherry assembly line. Funny that she found this one mesmerizing and was immune to the other.

The guy in the red shirt placed the inaugural jar on the conveyor belt.

It approached the air–vent–looking opening, partially entered, and shot out to the side and shattered on the floor. One of the workmen stooped down and picked up the biggest shards. He used a ripped piece of box lid to scrape the corn syrup into a goopy pile and then salad–tonged it into an empty box. Red Shirt pushed up on the mouth of the machine with a twelve–inch metal bracket and then wedged it in tightly by tapping with his hammer. The beam forced the entrance about an inch taller. He stationed one of the other guys at the entrance and then went and turned the machine on again. Other Guy placed a jar on the belt.

Marlow scowled. She followed the jar along the conveyor belt. The machine ripped off the old label, applied tracks of glue, spun the jar in a quick orbit, and affixed a new label. "Vermont Wonderful Honey," it read. The jar landed upright in a cardboard box at the end of a ramp. A few seconds later Red Shirt changed the relabeler to Gatling gun mode and it shot eleven more honey jars into the box. The young guy grabbed the box and walked it up the stairs and out of sight, back into the shipping container.

As Marlow was walking back to the front of the machine, a jar on its way from glue to labeling wobbled over a bump in the conveyor belt, but Other Guy dived for it and set it back up before it could fall. Red Shirt yelled something that sounded exasperated, and they all took up stations along the route.

One box finished, two. Red shirt turned up the speed dial and a banshee wail sprang from the paper tray. He shut it down and one of the guys pulled crinkled paper from the feed. Red Shirt started it up again, slower. After a few minutes they settled into a routine: a guy at the head fed the jars, three along the route darted hands in and out to straighten jars when they got off course, one guy pulled at crinkled labels if they started to jam, a guy at the end made sure none of the jars overshot the boxes, and the last two guys ran the full boxes of "honey" up the stairs.

"It would be faster to do it by hand," Marlow joked. No one responded.

The room filled with the smell of glue and printer ink, but it was faint and pleasant. When Marlow was fairly certain the machine wasn't going to explode, she headed up the stairs to stand guard at the garage bays. She didn't trust that the Sharpie "Keep Out" signs had the gravitas to keep curious cherry employees away. In an hour and a half they had only managed to label ten boxes. Even if the machine were working perfectly it would have taken the crew at least twenty hours to cycle all the jars from the shipping containers through the basement and back. Lin must know a lot more about corn syrup than he did factories; there was a limit to how fast a man could carry a box up the stairs.

Marlow went out through the door at the far end of the garage so she didn't have to open one of the truck bays. She stepped into the sun and closed her eyes, tilting her face upward. Life would get back to normal soon. She should get lunch for the conveyor belt guys. Maybe pizza.

There was a faraway howl and then yelling and then she opened her eyes. She ran back inside and down the stairs.

A man in a green shirt was standing with his hand in an arthritic claw in front of his chest, and there was blood on the floor. Teddy and the others stood around him. As Marlow approached she saw a chunk of meat hanging off the pinkie side of his hand and the bone showed through for a second before blood covered it.

"Teddy, call an ambulance."

"Don't call an ambulance," the youngest man said. He sounded like he was from Queens.

"Teddy, call an—"

"He'll be deported," the young man said. Green Shirt was using his fingers to press the sliver of flesh back onto his hand. There were beads of sweat on his forehead, but he said something and laughed weakly and the others laughed too.

"He wouldn't have gotten sucked into this kind of situation if he had more power," the kid said. "They didn't ask to get mixed up in this whack shit."

"Teddy, go get some paper towels," she said.

"We have a first aid kit," he said. "Hold tight." He ran up the stairs and out. Marlow was glad to see him out of his malaise.

"You're a good kid, Teddy!" she called after him.

CHAPTER 39:
LAKE MICHIGAN

Mims lifted her wrists and pulled down on her left hand. It slipped out of the rope. It had been an hour at least since she'd been tied, and the swelling from the bee sting had gone down. The whole time the man was talking and prepping his bag she had been afraid that he had seen it and was toying with her, waiting to come over and tighten the rope.

She felt along the inner edge of the tool trunk until she found the mounts of two release clasps, one at either edge of the lip, and pulled in. The clasps came undone and she was able to distort the hard plastic enough to pry up one edge of the lid. After that it was easy to jiggle the other clasp free and lift the cover. She popped her torso out and spun her head from side to side, her breath suddenly coming fast. Her eyes had adjusted to the total darkness of the trunk, so she could see well in the dim boat interior. She tilted herself quietly over the edge of the trunk and untied her feet. When she was certain she was alone in the cabin she tiptoed toward a piece of metal pipe, clasped it so tightly her joints ached, and made her way to the helm. The power was off, and she couldn't figure out how to turn it back on. She picked up the radio and pressed the red speak button, but nothing happened, not even static.

She crouched her way back through the cabin, past the trunk, to the door that led to open air. Even squinting she could only look out for a second at a time; she scanned the water but didn't see a dinghy. After her eyes adjusted to the brightness she went outside and walked the periphery of the boat with the pipe still in her hand. When she got to the far side, she saw a tiny speck far out that might have been an inflatable, approaching the shore. The boat she was on rolled slowly from side to side beneath her feet as it tugged listlessly at its anchor in the gentle, gusting breeze.

She was in Gowanus Flats, closer to New York than New Jersey, probably less than a mile from land. This was where the polluted water that escaped the Gowanus Canal met with the Hudson River, two bays removed from the salt water of the Atlantic. Across the way at the closest point of land she could make out a factory building that might be Beasley's, or it might be one of a hundred others. Had the man been watching them? She wasn't sure if she should yell for help or stay quiet. It was unlikely anyone would hear her from land, but the idea that her kidnapper might, and be the only one, clenched at her throat. He couldn't have intended to be gone very long, if he wanted to come back before his boat blew out to sea or into the shipping lane. She had to get to land and to a phone.

Mims took off her low strap heels and fastened them to her belt loop. She almost reprimanded herself for not wearing flats, but an image of herself found dead in dowdy running shoes chased the criticism away. Looking good, feeling good, she told herself. Grasping a rail at the prow of the boat, Mims lowered her body toward the water. Her legs went in and cold waves pushed her toward the hull, which was sharp with barnacles. She tried to pull herself back up, deciding she'd have to jump out and away from the boat, but she didn't have the upper-body strength. After dangling for a moment, she let go and fell into the water, ripping the shins of her pants along the way.

CHAPTER 40

UNINVITED GUESTS

L in walked through the open side door by the front gate without detection and then veered left, into what he'd correctly surmised based on a Google satellite image was the administrative part of the building. He walked past the offices into a long hallway.

He pulled the baseball cap lower over his eyes, hoisted his bag, and reached for the handle of the first door. A mop and bucket. The second held a stack of boxes containing pens and tote bags with "Beasley Cherries" stamped on them. He pulled the third door open. Inside was a wire shelf with boxes of Kleenex, Post-it notes, and other office supplies. He scanned the wall for a circuit breaker or pipes, saw none, and closed the door. He continued down the hall, each room as useless as the last. The final door was locked. Within a few minutes he'd unscrewed the handle. Even without the sign that read "Danger Gas Line," he recognized the neat array of yellow-coated hoses that ran past a regulator switch and into a utility meter. He felt the thrill of approaching victory as he dropped his duffel on the floor and began the work of prying open the meter. Neither his business offices in China nor his home nor his cousin's home nor business paid for gas. This setup didn't have any obvious anti-theft measures; it would be easy for him to split the gas line and bypass the meter. Once he set it up to appear that Beasley Cherries had been siphoning gas, he would damage one of the pipe joints and let the basement fill. A spark would be triggered remotely.

Teddy's gums itched where his tooth had been loose. He was scared to press his tongue against the tooth, afraid it would tilt, afraid that testing it would make it worse. He pressed anyway. The tooth stayed put, and the gums hurt only a little. He ran his thumbnail between the problem tooth and its neighbor and dislodged a bit of Slim Jim casing. "Fucker," he said under his breath, referring to the casing that had caused him pain and to Lin, whom he blamed for both the worker's mangled hand and his uncomfortable mouth situation. For pretty much everything else he'd come around to blaming himself. He closed the silverware drawer and opened the under-sink cabinet and pushed a handful of plastic bags and old Tupperware out of the way.

"Hi, Teddy."

Teddy jumped. He looked up, but Jalen wasn't paying attention to him. He was pouring a cup of coffee. Jalen was the youngest front desk person they'd ever hired, his boyfriend was a bartender, and he was rarely alert before lunch. It occurred to Teddy now, a week too late, that Jalen probably hated him for firing Brittany-Lynne and also for the other part. The two of them were in a book club together and used to hang out sometimes outside of work. *I'll have to try to find some way to make it up to him.* After that thought Teddy was disgusted with himself. What difference did it make if Jalen hated him? Jalen was right to hate him. How was he still such a people pleaser after all that had happened? There was a man with his finger bone exposed in the goddamned secret basement.

"Where's the first aid kit?" Teddy asked. "We should keep it someplace obvious."

"On top of the fridge." The phone at the front desk began a distant, plaintive wail and Jalen hustled out.

Teddy grabbed the first aid kit and pulled the paper towels from the dispenser. Somewhere between a speed walk and a trot he crossed the kitchen and went out into the hallway leading to the garage, though he knew the door was locked and he'd have to detour outside. He slowed as he approached his office. It would only take a second to grab the dental floss from his drawer . . .

There was a wet spot on the floor outside his door. An electric coil rose in his chest. He glanced over his shoulder down the hallway and then ahead toward the garage entrance. There was no one. The light was off in his office. His door was frosted glass. He realized he was clutching the paper towels against his chest and set them on the windowsill. Outside, the front yard was empty. Teddy turned back to the door. He pushed it open.

It was dim, but from the doorway he didn't notice anything amiss. The light switch was awkwardly far from the door, so he stepped forward to flip on his desk lamp. As he reached for it a shadow swept past his peripheral vision; it was trying to sneak out the door. He turned and threw himself at the intruder, his fear turning to anger. "You fucked that guy's hand forever, you fucking fuck!" he yelled.

He realized as his face collided with her collarbone that he was about to crush Mims. She hit the door, he hit the door, and then he landed hard on top of her on the floor. There was a splat sound that at first terrified him, like a watermelon exploding, like her head had cracked open. He pulled himself up, and the front of his shirt was wet, but nothing was red.

"Why are you all floppy and wet?" Teddy asked.

Mims pulled in a loud breath. She'd had the wind knocked out of her.

"Also I'm sorry," he said, "but also what—?"

She managed a ragged "shh." She reached her hand up to cover his mouth, but it was clammy and smelled metallic, so he pulled back. She pushed the office door closed, softly, with her extended leg and then sat up. The office darkened again as the door clicked shut. Teddy climbed off her.

"Who did you think I was?" she asked. Suspicious reptile eyes.

"I've been jumpy," Teddy said. "A homeless guy broke into the factory right before the party, and—"

"Bullshit," she spat back. "There's a man here," she said. "I don't know what he's planning to do, but I have a feeling you're not going to like it. What did he do to someone's hand?"

There were so many ways Lin could hurt him, and he hadn't really thought through any of them in detail. Teddy's fear had been an unexplored dread. Lin could poison a batch of cherries, he could jam the equipment in a way that might hurt someone else, like what had happened to the man in the basement. He could hurt Marlow. He had to go check on her.

Teddy stood and then leaned down and extended his hand to Mims. Her grasp was surprisingly strong as he pulled her up. Teddy considered pretending not to know what she was talking about, but clearly something bad had happened to her, and if she had any clues what Lin had in mind he needed to know. "Are you all right? Did this man say what he—"

"'This man'?" Mims was indignant. Now that his initial shock was wearing off, Teddy noticed that in addition to being wet, she was covered in scrapes and a couple of swollen pink mounds that could only be bee stings. "Don't pretend like you don't know who he is. He dragged me into his car and locked me up on a boat, and he seemed to actually *like* me. I can't even imagine what he has in store for *you*. He came here with some fucked–up–looking tools, saying he was going to 'take care of' a mess."

Lin hadn't come to the basement, so he definitely wasn't there to help with the honey effort.

Mims picked up the receiver of his desk phone. He pressed the switch hook with his finger.

"What are you doing?" he asked.

"I'm calling the police."

Teddy took a pair of scissors out of his pencil canister and cut the phone cord. "Not yet," he said. He wasn't ready to let it all come crashing down after all. He was surprised at his own resurgence of resolve and energy. Mims glared at him, her eyes roving over his pockets as if she were assessing whether she could locate his cell phone and wrest it from him. He stood taller and subtly flexed his biceps, and to his relief she opened the office door and gestured for him to go first. "So what's the plan then?" she asked.

"We have to find him. But I need to drop off this first aid kit first," he said, retrieving it and the paper towels from the windowsill. "Come on." He didn't want to bring her to the garage but also didn't want to leave her alone. There were phones everywhere.

"What's his name?" Mims asked. He knew without her saying so that she wasn't going to budge until he answered.

"Lin."

"Is that his first name or last name?"

"Mims, we have to go, someone is hurt."

At the end of the hall he opened the door to the courtyard.

"We'll be exposed out there—anyone could see us," Mims protested.

"The door connecting the hallway to the garage is locked from the inside."

They rushed, Mims doing a little hop every third step, along the outside of the building, and then slipped into the door to the garage at the far end, past the closed bays.

"Your sneaking needs some work," Teddy said once they were in the cool dark of the cavernous space.

"You would know," she shot back.

Attempting to lighten the mood had been of course insensitive and the wrong choice. "Wait right here," he said gently and slipped toward the sliding panel. Mims's view of the door to the basement would be obscured by the shipping containers, but only if she stayed put. The rolling of the casters rumbled as he slid the panel open, and muffled voices spilled out as he slipped inside and slid the panel closed behind him.

Mims stood at the top of the stairs for a full twenty seconds before she could make sense of the scene below. There was a machine, maybe twenty-five feet long, with a conveyor belt connecting stations along the way. There were cardboard boxes stacked along the stairs and wall, crowding the entrance. They were the same type of box as were in the shipping containers in the garage. Teddy's sister was arguing with a group of East Asian men; none of them were the man from the boat. Teddy was pouring seltzer water onto a red spill on the floor and scrubbing at it with paper towels. He really was the source of the cheap, fake honey the chef had warned her about. He was importing it from China.

"I have EMT training," Marlow said to the youngest man. He was younger than the others by at least two decades and looked like he had a nice haircut poorly styled.

"He doesn't want you to touch it," the young man replied.

Mims searched the crowd for the "he" who didn't want to be touched. One man looked pale, but he was standing toward the back and she couldn't see his body.

One of the other guys looked up at Mims. He bumped his friend's shoulder and gestured with his head for him to look at the stairs. The second guy rolled his eyes and said something in Mandarin that was brief and fed up. Everyone turned to look at her.

Instinctively Mims's hand reached for her phone to take photos; immediately she felt a tumbling disappointment that turned to a flash of anger so hot it stopped her shivering in her wet clothes. Lin had taken her phone. She took a deep breath to send the anger away, forcing time to slow down so she could grab ahold of her thoughts. She wasn't going to let impulsive spurts of rage get in the way anymore. Her life was serious and she was going to act like it.

"Who are these guys?" she called to Teddy.

The men conferred among themselves.

"Who are you?" the youngest guy asked.

"I'm a journalist."

"Yeesh." He translated and the others started grumping and shifting around.

"What are they saying?" She projected her question across the chasm between her and the kid. The basement, the machine, and the red on the floor were bizarre and unsettling, and she didn't want to come down the stairs.

The kid pointed at one of the men: "He says, 'Fuck it.'" He pointed at another: "It's not worth the money." At another: "They didn't even offer us coffee." One of the men walked over to Marlow, who had been staring silently since Mims's arrival, and spoke rapidly and angrily. "He wants to be paid for a half day," the young man told her.

"Did I tell you to come here?" Marlow asked. "Take it up with the guy who told you to come here. I'm not the payer in this situation."

Mims moved to the side as the men started filing up the stairs.

"Wait, don't go," Teddy said. Marlow looked at him and opened her mouth to speak but he waved her away. "Ignore that," he called. "Please leave my loser–cave. I have a compulsive habit of trying to appease people when they are upset and it's getting me nowhere and never has."

Marlow gave him a sharp look.

"Can I talk to you a minute?" Mims asked the men as they walked past, each of them pretending not to hear. She grabbed the young guy's sleeve. "Please tell me what you're doing here." Up close she could see he had acne and was skinny in the way teenage boys are skinny.

"Personally I just wanted to do an undercover story for my high school newspaper about off-the-books construction jobs. This is freaky and I'm getting out of here."

Marlow was heading toward the base of the stairs, so Mims had to focus. She flung away the idea that this kid was a better journalist than she was. She knew the honey was fake. She knew Teddy was changing the labels. The kid didn't know anything. "What's your name, can I contact you?" she whispered.

"I think," Marlow said as she approached, "that it would be best for everyone if we all forget about this 'freaky' situation and move on with our lives." Her tone was unmistakably threatening.

"Mims news 6682 at gmail," Mims whispered as the young man scrambled past her.

Marlow called down to Teddy as she ascended the stairs. "I'm going to go unlock the door by the gate so they can get out. You too, Mims."

"It's unlocked and wide open," Mims said. "That's how I got in."

Marlow sighed and then yelled into the garage, "Hey NYU kid, close the door by the front gate!" She stood eye to eye with Mims from a step below and then took the final step and looked down at her. "Well?"

"I'm pretty sure Lin is somewhere here in the factory. I want to find out why he came here."

"He came in to keep an eye on us," Marlow said, nonplussed.

"And he didn't notice this?" Mims gestured at the unmanned, lopsided machine and the stacks of boxes. "He said he was coming here to 'clean up a mess,' but the tools he was packing weren't cleaning supplies."

"I'm going to escort her out," Marlow said to Teddy.

"Maybe it's better if we keep her with us?"

She looked off into the distance for a moment.

"Maybe you're right. There are plenty of messes that need cleaning to go around today. You guys start looking for him and I'll catch up with you. I just need to grab something. Teddy, look for my text so you can tell me where you are." Marlow ran off before Teddy could answer.

Teddy stood next to the conveyor belt with the roll of paper towels in his hand, looking just like a lost child in a grocery store.

"It makes sense that she wouldn't let me be in charge," he said.

Mims felt sorry for him, as she always did, but also disgusted. She'd been fending for herself since she was eight years old and mothering her mother for almost as long, and here was a man in a beard still expecting to be scooped into the arms of an all-soothing daddy. "Yes," she replied. "It does."

Marlow sprinted to the staircase that led to the roof and then took the stairs two at a time until the last stretch. Her thighs burned. She wanted to know why Mims was all wet, but Mims surely wanted to know why there was a gang of day laborers in their fake basement, so maybe they were even. Marlow caught her breath scanning the roof for intruders. Satisfied that she was alone except for the bees, she walked toward the hive. There was a three-foot plastic bin sitting under it. Previously the bin had sat beside the hive with a brick on the lid to keep the wind from blowing it off, but no one came up to the roof besides her, as far as she knew, and she doubted they'd notice the change anyway. The plastic tub was full of beekeeping supplies, and it was where she had hidden her gun the night before. It had been getting dark then and the bees weren't active, so it was easy to stack the hive boxes on top. Now the bees clung to the front of the hive like a trembling yellow moss. Charlie had explained they did that to escape the heat. Others flew in and out of the entrance carrying pollen and nectar. Marlow took a few deep breaths and hopped up and down like a swimmer about to high-dive into frigid water. "Virgin and unicorn," she said out loud. "Virgin and unicorn. Pure thoughts don't get stung." She strode confidently toward the hive.

Teddy took the lead up the stairs from the basement so he wouldn't have to see Mims taking little bites out of him with her eyes.

"What are we going to do if we find him? Do you have a big net?" Mims asked. She sped up to walk beside him in the dark garage.

He thought for a moment. "No, but I do have some sports equipment in my office!"

They skittered back across the courtyard, sticking close to the wall, and slipped into the hallway. He was excited for a moment picturing himself keeping Lin at arms' length by wielding a baseball bat, how cathartic it would be, but before he even opened his office door he remembered it was actually a bright orange Wiffle ball bat. He also had a Frisbee. Teddy only played laid-back, chill-guy sports. "This isn't going to work," he said.

Jalen came into the hallway from the main factory floor and seemed startled to see them. "Is everything okay?"

"Yes, Jalen," said Teddy.

"Yes, *Jalen*," said Mims.

Jalen looked her up and down.

"Do you want to keep your four-thirty meeting with the Hostess people tomorrow? I tried to buzz you but your extension isn't working."

"Yeah, keep the meeting. Also can you order me a new phone cord? It broke. And I'm going to step out for a minute, so you can just email me any other questions."

"All right," Jalen said. He backed out of the hallway, not taking his eyes off Mims.

"Maybe there's something in one of the maintenance closets we can use as a weapon," Teddy said when Jalen was gone.

"This is a factory—don't you have any acid?"

Teddy closed his eyes and pressed his palm against his forehead and then took a deep breath as he ran his fingers up through his hair. Lin was destroying his company, his family, and his grandfather's legacy, and Teddy's ideal resolution would be to send him away home, never to be heard from again. Disfigurement never entered his mind, and hopefully it hadn't entered Marlow's.

"Yeah, you're right. Forget I said that," Mims said.

"Women are so scary," Teddy said. "The supply closets are in a different hallway, come on."

CHAPTER 41:
CLASH OF THE TITANS

Mims didn't have a good sense of the layout of the factory. She'd been in the courtyard for the party and in the garage just now, and she'd swished from room to room during the raid, but that was all jumbled and quick. She couldn't have drawn a map of how the buildings sat and at what angle and where were the hallways. If she listened to the tight, airless feeling in her joints, the gray hallway where they stood was thousands of miles from civilization and natural light. Teddy held a closet door open. There was a mop. "We can use this," he said.

The handle was made of wood, but Mims was pretty sure it would snap if you hit someone across the back with it. She considered walking out and looking for a phone. Neither she nor Teddy had an understanding of physical violence that went beyond what you might see in a cartoon. She weighed her options. She'd warned Teddy and Marlow that they were potentially in danger, and she had her story now, but she did want to get more details before the police rushed in and limited her access. If she left now, with a bit of bad luck she might run into Lin on her way out, by herself. She decided to stay.

"Let's start in the brining room," Teddy said, securing the mop against his shoulder with the head side up. They took a few steps back the way they had come. This new hallway was also windowless and with low-pile carpeting, but it had the stale cleaning supply smell of the upper floors of a hotel. Very clearly Mims heard a noise like a heavy box being pushed across a floor. It came from the end of the hallway. Mims stopped breathing and looked to Teddy. Pinpricks of sweat appeared on his neck as he stared toward the direction of the sound. It was quiet for a moment; then there was a sound like a mouse chewing, except the mouse was nibbling metal. Teddy turned slowly toward her and they both looked down at the mop handle.

Mims pointed down the hallway and mouthed, "What's that room?"

Teddy shrugged.

They crept forward, neither moving ahead faster than the other. Mims had the urge to grab Teddy's hand but surprisingly not the urge to run away. The tinkling of metal compelled her on; even at the risk of harm she had to know what was making the sound. Both of them crouched lower and slowed their steps as they got closer; Teddy held the mop slightly forward of their advance, like whiskers on a cat.

Just as they reached the door it swung open.

"Whaaa!" Teddy yelled. Lin's lips formed a startled O. He swung his duffel bag in a slow arc and Teddy had to jump back to avoid being hit.

Lin let the bag crash to the ground then kneeled to unzip it. He rose holding a twenty-four-inch wrench and Teddy still hadn't moved.

"Hit him," Mims yelled. "Hit him!"

Lin swung the heavy wrench back and forth and Teddy backed up farther. He tried to meet the swings with the mop handle, still retreating, but it shattered, leaving him with a sharp stump.

Mims backed into the nearest closet and closed the door. Once she heard Teddy and Lin pass, she came back into the hallway. Lin was now surrounded, but they were no better off. She ran to the discarded duffel, hoping to find something she could throw, and as she turned her head, she saw into the room Lin had vacated. Lines of pipes like pneumatic tubes lined the wall, and a blue-and-white warning sign cried out to her from their midst.

"Teddy, gas leak!" she yelled.

Her view of Teddy was suddenly blocked by Lin's snarling face and contorted body hurtling toward her. Instinctively she lifted her arms above her head and shrunk into the corner. The expression on Lin's face changed and the angle of his body was wrong and suddenly he was on the ground. Teddy had tackled him, and Lin was struggling to turn while swatting at his own thigh. Teddy pulled back and dislodged the ragged piece of broom handle from Lin's leg.

Mims reached forward for the wrench Lin had dropped but was too slow; he snatched it up and swung haphazardly toward Teddy. The metal made weak contact with Teddy's lower arm and he dropped the mop handle. They were both on their knees more or less, facing each other, when Lin reared back with the wrench above Teddy's face.

A sound like crashing feet came from the entrance of the hallway and, confusingly, two little black and yellow specks zigzagged toward them. A second later Marlow charged into battle, hair flying behind her. She had a rifle and she had a bee sting on her forehead.

Lin set the wrench down slowly and then stood.

"If you try to walk out of here, I'll shoot you," Marlow said.

"Don't!" Mims said. "He's started a gas leak. The blast might cause an explosion."

"Don't do anything that will cause a spark." Teddy stood shakily, flexing and massaging his arm.

Lin walked calmly past Marlow and around the corner.

Once he was out of sight Mims heard him transition into a loping jog. "You better run faster than that!" she yelled. Marlow smiled at her approvingly.

"You owe it to me to tell me who's trying to blow us up," Mims said.

"Technically he's only trying to blow *us* up," Marlow quipped, gesturing to Teddy and herself. "You crashed this party." She rested a hand on Teddy's shoulder and then stepped around him, her eyes on the open door behind Mims.

"I know you're selling corn syrup as honey," Mims said as Marlow maneuvered around her. She just needed them to confirm it. Marlow looked back at Teddy but then continued on into the room with the "Danger Gas Line" sign. Mims followed her in. "How does Lin fit in?"

"It's his corn syrup," Teddy said from the hallway. "He's angry we wanted to stop distributing it."

"I don't see an obvious way to fix it," Marlow said of the row of pipes.

"Should we turn off this light?" Mims asked. It was hard to focus on their safety, bask in the rightness of her hunch about Teddy, and piece together the last details at the same time.

"No, I think you're not supposed to touch anything electrical with a gas leak," Marlow said. "If he gets away, he's probably gone for good, and who knows what other booby traps he's set up. If he's taking our family business down, he's going down too." She turned and ran off in the direction of Lin's footsteps, the rifle in two-handed ready carry position at her chest. Mims and Teddy ran after her. Mims was scared then not of Lin but for him; she didn't know what the erratic Beasleys were capable of when there was nothing left to lose.

Teddy and Marlow were both thirty feet ahead by the time Mims made it through the labyrinth of hallways to the factory floor. Her leg and back muscles ached from the swim to shore, and damp blisters rubbed against the heels of her shoes. Lin limp–ran ahead of the siblings toward an exit sign, but the distance was closing. Mims's pace slowed further.

Several employees turned in confusion.

"Teddy, there's a malfunction with the—" a man called from above, freezing in midsentence when he saw the commotion sprinting away from him.

Mims stopped. She couldn't breathe fast enough and coughed between wheezes. The man was perched halfway down a ladder that ran up the side of a fifteen-foot white tank.

"There's a gas leak," she gasped. "Evacuate the building."

"Oh shit," the man said. He yelled so that the people nearest him could hear over the machinery: "Gas leak! Go tell two people, tell them to each tell two people, pass it on, and then get out. No cell phones! Don't turn anything on or off. Tell two people and get to the fire safety meet-up point!" He scrambled down the ladder a little ways and then jumped past the last few rungs to the floor. "Our evacuation point is outside the front gates, across the street."

"Okay," Mims said. The man ran off, directing people toward the exit.

She was relieved that everyone was going to be okay. Mims had lost sight of Teddy, Marlow, and Lin. She scanned the room, but everyone was running now.

The equipment came in flashes—silver vat, men in white, a silo-like metal structure. It was smaller than the factory where the corn syrup was made, less modern. Somehow he'd ended up among the cherry processing instead of the row of offices where he'd initially come in that morning, but he was approaching a well-marked exit and would soon be in open air. With each contact between his left foot and the floor a warm flood spread over the back of his thigh and then cooled. The pain was more an idea than a sensation, and he didn't notice it so much as he did the wetness.

"Block the door," the bodyguard's voice rang out from behind him, pleasingly distant.

A burly man, taller than Lin, took a confident step in front of the door. His face remained uncertain beneath his hairnet, and the factory booties covering his shoes gave him the authority of a cartoon clown. In one running motion Lin lifted a metal dipstick from a cart and swung it into the man's face. He collapsed to his knees with his hands up against his shattered eye socket. He'd collapsed right in front of the door and Lin had to choose between scooting around him or trying to jump over. Improbably, the man started to heave himself back up.

"No," Teddy yelled. "No, get out of the way!"

The erstwhile bouncer scooted clear of the doorway on his knees just as a rolling cart eased to a stop a few feet away. Lin didn't turn to look; he knew the woman had pushed it. He stepped through a fine mist of what smelled like vinegar and out into the sunshine.

Three men were striding toward the building. They were not danger-ous–looking per se, but odd, and Lin knew to avoid them. Factory work-ers pushed past him in their rush to evacuate, but before they had cleared the doorframe Lin stepped back inside. He collided with the woman in a vinegar–scented rainbow and she fell to the ground outside. Her grip on the rifle didn't loosen. Inside, he headed for the back wall, where a metal stairway led to a viewing platform and catwalk. There was a door to the left where the catwalk met the wall—presumably heading back in the direc-tion of the garage. His leg stiffened and cramped as he ran. On the stair he hopped with the good leg and swung the other. Phlegm constricted his breathing, so he knew that Beasley and the woman would be too spent to overtake him.

At the top of the steps he pulled out his phone. "Come immediately," he texted the drivers. They had been instructed to park in the neighbor-hood and stay with the vehicles, so they would arrive within minutes. The trucks would then leave with whatever amount of honey had been loaded into the containers—surely most of it by now. He could trigger the explo-sion on the way out.

The steps to the catwalk clanged and he heard Beasley's breathing all the way from the bottom. Bumbling moron. Lin braced his arms against either side of the railing and prepared to kick. A quicker, chirpier set of footsteps joined the first, and Lin peeked over the side of the railing—it was the reporter—and then resumed his cocked posture. If Mims were any smarter than Teddy, she would have policemen with her, though her escape was concerning.

This moment was a test—a matter of willpower, not circumstance—and Lin was confident in his ability to navigate it.

The heavy steps stopped before Teddy's head emerged into Lin's line of vision. The twinkly lighter footsteps stopped a second later.

Teddy paused a few steps from the top of the staircase to catch his breath. He hadn't heard Lin open the doorway on the catwalk, so he knew he was still up there. He'd lost track of where Marlow had gone. They still hadn't worked out what they were supposed to do once they caught Lin. He might still have the dipstick, and Teddy didn't even remember losing the mop.

He realized there was quick, quiet breathing behind him and whirled. Mims. He lifted his finger to his lips in a "Shh" gesture and pointed toward the top of the staircase, as if Mims didn't know they were chasing some-one. He felt dumb immediately. To his right the staircase was flush with the brick wall. To his left and down was an open vat where sixty thousand pounds of cherries soaked in dye. Someone must have left the lid open when they evacuated. The lip of the vat was only a few feet from the edge of the catwalk.

Teddy leaned back down toward Mims and whispered close to her ear, "You rush at him from the stairs, yell, but be careful and be ready to go back down if he swings at you. I'll jump from the side." He pointed to the vat.

Mims shook her head "no" while frowning so deeply her eyebrows almost touched. He couldn't deal with any more women not having faith in him. He had to try to be a hero. Without looking back at Mims, he leapt for the railing of the catwalk. He crashed into it but was able to brace his foot on the outer edge of the vat. As he was hoisting himself over the railing Mims yelled and charged up the last few stairs. It sounded like the war cry of a woman confronting a flying cockroach, more an expression of terrified frustration than an intimidation tactic.

The distraction didn't work—Lin kicked Teddy's hand before he could remove it from the railing. The pain that exploded from his pinky joint seemed to expand past the edges of his body. It took his breath away.

He managed to land his feet on the catwalk, but now he'd never get a chance to throw a punch, and he'd been savoring the masculine knowledge that one makes a fist with the thumb on the outside of the clenched fingers since third grade.

Teddy kicked at Lin's weight–bearing leg and it buckled. He felt almost giddy using his muscles for something real; up close it seemed ridiculous that Lin had been able to hurt him at all. Teddy loomed above him, his thighs twice as thick as Lin's, his chest broader, his arms immense in comparison. The exhilaration faded the next moment, when Mims jumped on top of Lin's chest with her keys between her fingers, her fist above her head. Teddy caught her arm as she swung, horrified at the grisly reality of violence even while in the midst of violence, and as he did so Lin rolled out from under her and punched him in the stomach.

Teddy toppled into a fetal position and Lin kicked him again, in the collarbone, and continued to extend his leg, pushing Teddy half off the cat-walk. Between waves of nausea Teddy launched himself onto the vat below, careful to land with his head away from the opening, where the cherries were bobbing quietly. Teddy stole a glance into the depths. The cherries were undisturbed, sanitary. He reached for the hatch that would seal them away from the fight, but Lin jumped down before he could pull it closed. Flecks of blood spattered around the foot of his wounded leg.

With a sigh that became a grunt that swelled into rage, Teddy hooked his leg around Lin's bloody calf and yanked hard, like he was pulling out a man–sized tooth. Lin lost balance so easily Teddy's fury choked back into fear again. It seemed Lin was playing a trick. But as Lin reached the half-way point of his fall Teddy knew it was real, that this was the time slowing thing he'd heard about when entering "the zone" like an athlete, and that the reality was that Lin was falling toward the vat opening.

Teddy contorted his own body and tried to slide underneath Lin as much as possible to prevent him from falling in.

Lin's shirt must have caught on something—it ripped open and was half off him as he landed with what felt like at least four elbows in Teddy's ribs. Lin's own exposed chest was speckled in sweaty hair. His stomach was slick and glistening with perspiration.

"Goddamn it, get away from my FUCKING! CHERRIES!" Teddy shrieked.

Still lying on his back, he wrapped his arms around Lin's chest and, bracing his leg against the corner of the staircase, cantilevered them away from the exposed fruits. Lin wriggled an arm free and used it to twist Teddy's head over the side of the vat. It was fifteen feet to the floor below.

"Teddy!" Mims yelled. Before he could be fortified by her concern for him, she followed up with, "If you're going to hurt him, hurt him, if you're not, quit going after him!"

Mims clanked back down the stairs, though there wasn't much she'd be able to do but check if he was okay when he inevitably slipped off the side of the tank. Midway, she glanced back and was arrested by Teddy's eyes, which were focused on her own instead of Lin or the floor, as if he'd been waiting for her to turn. There was dog-pure sadness in those eyes.

Teddy unclenched his jaw. "Make sure when you write the story that you emphasize that nothing happened to the cherries! Beasley Cherries is going to keep going without me."

It was laughable for him to be thinking about his legacy at a time like this, but he was so sincere she just nodded in assent.

"Mims?!" someone else yelled, from below and far away, by the doors to the outside. There stood the silhouette of a tall, broad-shouldered man with too-short pants.

"Kai?" Relief drained and softened her body, causing all the raw, sore places to throb harder.

"Yeah!"

"Call the police!"

"We are the police!" a different voice rang out. Kai was with two men. One was lifting his khaki utility shorts, as if he had recently lost weight and had yet to update his wardrobe. The other was wide and low with Popeye arms. All three of them had red, rash-ringed lips. Ghost pepper vodka.

The door at the end of the catwalk, the one that Lin had been heading toward, opened and then closed. "Teddy?" Marlow's voice.

Teddy and Lin were still locked together.

Lin's body went limp, and Teddy's grip softened and released him. The shorter man rolled off Teddy and sat on the side of the vat. He dangled his feet off the edge and then pushed off and over. Mims held her breath. He landed in a squat that collapsed into a neat roll, like an acrobat. He rolled to a stop, but his transition from lying to sitting wasn't smooth at all; he looked dazed. Lin stood up the way an old man would stand, stooped over and without fully extending his knees until after he was already upright.

Marlow came to the railing and extended a hand to Teddy and then pulled him up.

Mims hurried the rest of the way down the stairs.

"I'm glad you've come, officers." Lin projected his voice toward Kai and the other two men as they approached. "I've been conducting an under-cover operation on behalf of the People's Republic of China and with the assistance of the American government's Federal Bureau of Investigation. I was attacked when Beasley realized. I feared for my life."

Kai's friends turned their heads from side to side as they walked, taking in the inside of the factory; Kai looked straight ahead. None of them answered. The equipment had all come to a stop except the vat Teddy and Lin had vacated, and it gave off a quiet churning, humming sound like a washing machine.

Mims looked up to Marlow and Teddy on the catwalk—they didn't seem like they'd heard what Lin said. Marlow held the small rifle obscured between her body and the wall. Mims glanced back at Kai and the police-men—they couldn't see it from their angle. Marlow grabbed Teddy's arm and backed slowly toward the door and then opened it behind her without turning around.

"Hey, stay right there!" the man in khaki yelled up at them.

"We're coming down," Marlow called back, her voice strong and steady. She and Teddy disappeared into the doorway and it slammed behind them.

"Is there really a gas leak?" Kai asked Mims. She felt skittish and kept a cautious distance from all of them.

"Yes," she said. "Con Edison should be here soon."

"No one called yet," Kai said.

"No, I told one of the employees to do it," Mims said.

Kai made a face like he'd stepped in dog shit. "We ran into everyone outside and I told them to hold off. I knew you were desperate to get the police back in here, so . . . I'm so sorry." He hurried back out of the building to make the call where it was safe to use his phone. She reached her arm after him but the unrelenting frustration of it all had sapped the speed from her muscles.

"This guy kidnapped me," Mims said to the men she didn't know and that didn't look like cops but supposedly were. "Don't listen to him." She pointed at Lin.

"Look at me," Lin said, lifting his arms out like Jesus. What was left of his tattered shirt opened, and blood glistened on his lip and temple.

"Look at me!" Mims snapped. They did look at her, and the second their attention was turned, Lin bolted toward the ground–level door that led to the offices and garage beyond. The one in khakis charged him but tackled too soon; they fell to the ground with him grasping Lin's shoes. The muscular one piled on a second after, and it took both of them to hold Lin in place.

"Go get your two friends," the muscle one yelled at Mims. "Tell them to come in here."

"They're not my friends," Mims said, but she headed up the stairs. She stomped her feet so she wouldn't take them by surprise. She didn't want to startle Marlow if she still had the gun.

Marlow took a good look at her brother. He was bleeding. She'd been waiting behind the catwalk door for Lin to bust through and he hadn't. She had waited too long.

"I went back and figured out how to turn off the gas before coming up here," she said. "I don't think it had been going for that long when you ran into him." Teddy didn't speak. She knew his silence was meant to convey strength, but she also knew it really meant he didn't know what to say. They were in trouble and it seemed like the best thing to do was fess up.

"We have to go out there," she said. The police, and the consequences of Teddy's foray into honey laundering, were waiting for them.

"I'm not ready."

"Why do babies like to be thrown in the air?" Marlow asked. Teddy didn't answer. "It's not the thrill of flying, it's the comfort of being caught. They only like the risk in the context of knowing everything is going to turn out okay." Still he was silent. "This situation means we're not babies," she said with an encouraging smile. "You took a big risk for a big gain and it blew up, there's no safety net, but you tried." She punched him on the arm. At least they'd had an adventure together.

"Ow," he said. It's possible he'd never been thrown in the air as a baby.

Someone, presumably Mims, knocked quietly against the door leading to the catwalk.

"I'll go out first," Marlow said. "Here." She handed him the gun. "Go put this on the roof. There's a storage bin by the beehive." He took the gun from her.

Two–year minimum sentence for possessing a loaded firearm in New York City. Plus the "honey" smuggling. What was the charge for what had happened to the day laborer's hand? Reckless endangerment? He startled—how long had he been standing in the stairwell? Teddy resumed the climb with his legs feeling like sacks of wet flour.

As he trudged up and up he remembered a different set of steps. There were six wooden stairs from the beach to the small boardwalk near their former house in the Hamptons. His family used to go for a few weekends every summer when he was a kid, the place where he nearly drowned. They never went during the week, so he hadn't realized his parents owned the house there until they sold it. His mother always made it seem the weekends had been wrested away from someone or something all–consuming and ominous, and once the dates were named, they were inviolable. The summer after sixth grade, the penultimate trip was the same weekend as his best friend's birthday party.

When he reached the door to the roof, he leaned the gun against the wall and used his good hand to turn the handle. He pushed the door open with his shoulder. His injured hand throbbed harder even though he hadn't touched anything with it. He should have listened to the bees and turned the factory into a queenless co-op and then run away.

That childhood summer Teddy had wished he'd get hit by a car and break his arm just so his friend Jason couldn't be mad at him for missing the party. Jason would have to be nice to him instead of being disappointed and furious. Teddy looked down at his hand; his knuckle was smashed, but that wasn't enough; people could still be mad at him with that. Jason was really good at drawing Ninja Turtles, and Teddy had planned out asking him to decorate his cast. There were three lounge chairs on the roof now and several more rows of planters. Bees were thick on the flowers, on the hives. Marlow had made a bee paradise when she was supposed to have driven them away. Marlow was so good at driving people away, how did this happen? Teddy flipped the gun around and aimed it at his head. He wasn't actually going to shoot himself, he just wanted to feel the heft of the possibility, and to see if it made him afraid. "Pshh," he mouthed softly, a quiet version of what a gunshot sounded like. A car hadn't hit him and when Teddy showed up with his Technodrome for their next play date, intending to give the bad-guy fort away as a peace offering and late birthday gift, he'd been greeted with, "Toys are for babies. Maybe Mario wants it." Mario was Jason's six-year-old brother. His request to attend that birthday party had been the last time Teddy had tried to assert his independence, or even his existence as a separate being from his family, and he had lost. A bee landed on his neck, he could tell because it tickled, and then it flew away. His pinky hurt as he bent his wrist to wrap his pointer finger around the trigger, knowing the safety was on. His nose started running before his eyes did. There was no way out so that people wouldn't be mad at him. No amount of pity would outweigh the stark reality that he made terrible decisions and then took underhanded, rationalizing routes to deflect blame.

"It's your turn to take care of the factory, Marlow," he said aloud, but quietly. He was ashamed to be talking to himself, on top of all the other shame. His misdeeds would be all out in the open shortly. "You know you have to take care of the factory. Do it for Grandpa. I tried and I just couldn't. I'll make sure I'm the only one who goes to jail." As Teddy lowered the gunstock, the barrel turning up up away from his face, a bee alighted on his hand, startling him, and his ruined, bloated pinky caught in the trigger and then click and then bang.

CHAPTER 42:

THE ENDING

C harlie closed his eyes and smiled. Marlow took a sip of her iced tea. She was happy to see him look so at peace. She'd added planters here and there on the factory roof until it turned out she'd made a whole garden. It had taken on an unexpected lushness in the heat of summer. The leaves of the succulents were like fat green blisters—shiny and tight with liquid. The vines hanging off the grape arbor were so thick they obscured the wooden latticing, and the switchgrass was almost four feet tall. Then there were the flowers: purple, deep red, white, and yellow with brown centers. Marlow watched the bees.

"What's the temperature right now in Alaska?" Charlie asked. He opened his eyes.

"Probably about sixty-five," Marlow answered. "July is the hottest month." She yelled a little since she wasn't sure how good his hearing was.

"Do you miss it?"

"Yeah, but I don't regret letting it go. It's not even worth thinking about right now. Speaking of which." She looked at her watch. "I'm going to head over to the hospital before visiting hours are over."

The sterility of the hallways was disgusting but also the invisible bacteria that were as much a part of the hallways as the tile were disgusting. It was a contradiction. Marlow lifted each foot gingerly as she walked, not wanting her shoes to be contaminated by sickness. She pressed the elevator button with her knuckle in case she forgot to wash her hands before the next time she touched her face. Although she attributed much of her hardiness to eating dropped food off the floor, not washing out cuts and scrapes, and changing her sheets only sporadically, in hospitals there was an unnatural accumulation of . . . something that couldn't be scrubbed away. Bad energy. Every time she'd ever entered a hospital a family member was dead.

She knocked once at Teddy's room and then opened the door without waiting for an answer. His eyes were closed, his forehead wrinkle–free, and his face had a greasy sheen, as if he were in a deep sleep with no fan running during a heat wave. It wasn't really a deep slumber; he opened his eyes, which were crusted in the corners. His head was wrapped in bandages starting just below where his hairline used to be. Teddy had overextended his arm trying to lower the rifle with his finger still on the trigger, and as he'd pulled down the whole gun had lifted up and fired. His brain was fine, his skull was nearly fine, but he'd blown off a piece of his scalp. She assumed his entire head was shaved under the wrapping, but when he was finally out of this place his formerly luxurious dome would feature a three–inch barren runway flanked by tall weeds. He'd ruined his hair forever.

Teddy would be able to leave the hospital soon, but they were locking him up until the trial. They thought he was a flight risk, if not a continuing danger to himself.

"Hey." She sat on the edge of the bed, cautious of sounding too cheerful. The blinds were drawn and the bouquets of flowers had been cleared away from his nightstand. "Did you hear from the lawyers?"

"Yeah," he said. "The plea bargain is 18 months."

Protective, animal ferocity burbled up from her guts, but before it could spew forth she caught herself. "Maybe we can talk them down a little more," she suggested gently.

Lin had been extradited to China and charged for passing off the high fructose corn syrup as honey. The Chinese government was upset at the damage the constant stream of stories about fake food was doing to that sector of the economy. Plastic milk, poison dog food, plastic rice, and plastic eggs were common, and potentially deadly, and foreign markets were constricting. In order to make an example of him, they had sentenced Lin to decades. The trial had started immediately upon his return to China and had concluded already. His shipping business had been seized. His cousin's corn syrup business had been seized.

The happy side effect of Lin being out of the way was that the American story of what happened was told entirely on the Beasleys' terms. Even so, it was hard to explain away the shipping containers and the two drivers who showed up to claim them. Teddy and Marlow pretended Marlow hadn't known anything about Lin's extortion scheme until the moment they tried to disassemble the equipment. They would have shifted the timeline even further, but it turned out Mims had overheard them talking from inside a dumpster. Teddy had covered for Omar, never mentioning his accomplice.

So far Marlow had escaped charges of any kind, as the United States justice system was lenient toward job creators and someone needed to run the factory. She was confident they could get Teddy's cell time to under a year. He'd been operating under duress.

"Looks like we are both going to be imprisoned for a long time," Teddy said. His voice was hoarse. "You're stuck at the factory you hate. I'm going to actual jail. Of course, once I'm out of sight and the guilt wears off, who knows."

"I told you I don't hate it, Teddy. I've changed my mind. How long do I need to stick around for you to believe me that I'm not going anywhere?"

"More than a couple of months."

She thought to tousle his hair and was glad she stopped herself before she raised her arm. Her eyes lingered too long though and she saw him notice.

"Sales are up," she offered.

"Really?"

"Yeah. Everyone wants organic everything, and we're the first ones to be able to deliver at scale. We're up to 22 percent of retail market share. Hovering at 15 percent for food–service share. We just got a huge hospital and nursing home contract." She'd used the dregs of her trust fund to pay for equipment and get the organic division running.

Teddy's eyes brightened. He almost looked awake.

"Grandpa would have been proud of you," she said. "And I'm proud to be a part of his legacy too, I really am. I'm not trapped, there is no bore-dom. There's just a fear of sitting with myself."

She wasn't sure Teddy believed her. He'd closed his eyes again.

"Can you turn off the lights when you go?" he said. "It gives me a migraine."

"Sure, Teddy."

She turned off the lights as she slipped out the door.

Mims sat in a café in Brooklyn writing on her laptop, and she didn't feel the least inclination to act like she was "over it" or too cool or jaded to be there among the wannabe screenplay writers and novelists. She luxuri-ated in the superiority of not feeling superior, just hardworking and per-sistent. The perfect foam leaf atop her latte sat undisturbed; it was probably cold by now. She took a sip—it was. But she'd spun out the visual enjoy-ment of that leaf for an hour, and it was worth every penny.

The only thing she needed was to come up with a headline for her latest article. It was a follow-up to the one that broke the honey-laundering story, but she still wanted it to be attention grabbing. "Sleazy Beesy Fake Honey Shockers Keep Coming." "Sleazy Bee-zly." She drummed her fingers against the table and looked off into the nothing above the window for a moment. She wasn't writing for tabloids anymore. "More Details Emerge in Beasley Cherries Honey Smuggling Scheme," she wrote.

She blamed Teddy for her kidnapping, and for the motion sickness she'd developed during any vaguely boat-like rocking motion. Elevators, taxis, certain subway lines. But he had suffered too, and honestly she hoped he got better.

She closed her laptop, chugged the room-temperature drink, and stood to go. Forty minutes later she pushed through the subway turnstile into the basement of the Kmart at Astor Place. The store was frequented mostly by NYU freshmen from out of state—kids who weren't yet worldly enough to shun big-box stores and who needed sheets, mirrors that hung on the back of a door, and shower caddies for their dorm rooms. The eighteenth floor of the same building that housed the Kmart hosted the monthly Documentary Club meeting. Young professionals got together to screen their non-fiction shorts and consume unlimited pizza and beer for only seven dollars entrance fee.

James was waiting for her outside the elevator on the eighteenth floor. Mims was impressed by how accurately his image had been imprinted in her brain during their short basement meeting. They had exchanged emails about his accidental infiltration of Beasley's operation, but this was the first time they'd met up in person.

"Am I late?" she asked. "Why didn't you go in?"

"I was nervous. They're going to know I'm not a real video journalist or a documentary director or whatever."

"But you will be!" she said. "Stand up straight." She poked his shoulder and he straightened up, gaining almost two inches. "My friend Bennie's running a few minutes late. Let's go in."

Mims had forgiven James for scooping her in his high school newspaper on the basement portion of her story and had taken him under her wing. She found it a lot easier to be generous with other aspiring writers now that she was getting paid. Plus mentoring James felt kind of like having an intern. This was probably as close to mothering as she was ever going to get.

"Did you decide yet where you're going to go to school next year?"

"I'm thinking about NYU." He laughed. "Apparently I look the part already. Emerson is supposed to have a better journalism program though. My parents want me to live at home in Queens and go to CUNY. I don't know how I'm going to break it to them."

They pushed their way through the crowd to the pizza table.

"They got Two Boots!" Mims exclaimed. "Each bite of that cornmeal crust is like . . . like wet gravel, but I mean that in the way people use 'barnyard,' 'cat pee,' and 'pencil shavings' to describe expensive wine. It's delicious and also delightful and surprising."

Her excitement was slightly tainted by the awareness that she'd been stress-eating since the kidnapping. It was a way of staving off a kind of tingling fear in her stomach by weighting it down and busying all the nerve endings. She told herself she'd deal with it later and grabbed a slice. James reached for a glass of wine and she blocked his arm. "Not so fast there, kiddo."

"Fine." He grabbed a can of soda instead. Mims swirled a plastic cup of the red and sniffed it. "Cat pee?" he asked.

"Vinegar," she said. "Life lesson number sixty-two: free wine always tastes like vinegar." Mims expected it would be at least another five years of successful career building before she encountered decent event wine.

She clinked her plastic cup against James's can and they drank. "I wish I'd known this existed before," Mims said, gesturing around the room. "Always know where the free stuff is when you're on a budget."

"You, on a budget?" James asked incredulously. Mims's jewelry and clothing were as meticulously chosen as ever. She felt arms wrap her from behind and knew it was Bennie.

"Yeah," Mims said. "Especially me." She felt wise admitting it, not embarrassed like she would have just a few months before. "Let's go get seats."

ABOUT THE AUTHOR

Poppy Koval lives in Brooklyn. Her short stories have been published in various literary journals. *Blood Honey* is her debut novel.